"Patti Lacy has deftly knit together the story ....aes, and one growing nation in a tale as relevant as ever— a bold story about the stark realities of race, injustice, hatred, secrets, and pain . . . and the love and healing sovereignty of God. A winning combination of history, gritty reality, and transcendence of spirit that makes for simply great storytelling."

—Tosca Lee, author of *Havah: The Story of Eve* and
Christy Award finalist for *Demon: A Memoir*

"An outstanding novel, *What the Bayou Saw* is as heartrending as it is courageous. Patti Lacy's daring yet beautiful story will astonish and inspire."

—Tina Ann Forkner, author of *Ruby Among Us*

"Patti Lacy has a knack for creating three-dimensional characters, an ear for regional dialect, and an ability to sustain a strong narrative drive that keeps her plots lively. *What the Bayou Saw* is visual, entertaining, and original."

—Dennis E. Hensley, author of *The Gift*

"*What the Bayou Saw* is an engrossing and beautifully written novel about prejudice, healing, and how revealing even the most difficult of truths can transform lives. A captivating story!"

—Melanie Dobson, author of *The Black Cloister* and
Together for Good

"Patti Lacy ha....................... layered novel that gives new meaning t.......................rn molasses, *What the Bayou Saw* is a ri.......................nting, so painfully real, it will follow you.......................ght on the horizon of women's fiction, a.......................

.......................ssion Most Pure* and
.......................*A Passion Redeemed*

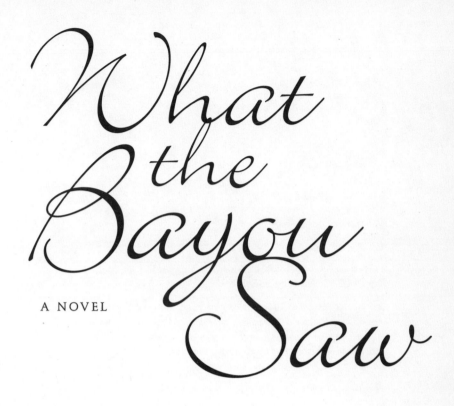

What the Bayou Saw

A NOVEL

PATTI LACY

Kregel
Publications

What the Bayou Saw: A Novel

© 2009 by Patti Lacy

Published by Kregel Publications, a division of Kregel, Inc., P.O. Box 2607, Grand Rapids, MI 49501.

Permissions for lyrics can be found on page 324.

The persons and events portrayed in this work are the creations of the author, and any resemblance to persons living or dead is purely coincidental.

Scripture quotations are from the Holy Bible, New International Version®. Copyright © 1973, 1978, 1984 by International Bible Society. Used by permission of Zondervan. All rights reserved.

Published in association with the literary agency of WordServe Literary Group, Ltd., 10152 S. Knoll Circle, Highlands Ranch, CO 80130.

Library of Congress Cataloging-in-Publication Data
Lacy, Patti.
  What the bayou saw : a novel / Patti Lacy.
      p. cm.
1. Rape victims—Fiction. 2. Louisiana—Race relations—Fiction. I. Title.
PS3612.A3545W47   2009   813'.6—dc22   2009001440

ISBN 978-0-8254-2937-8

Printed in the United States of America
09 10 11 12 13 / 5 4 3 2 1

ACKNOWLEDGMENTS

They say in heaven, Lord, that the first will be last.
But I guess heaven ain't nowhere near New Orleans.
So come thou fount of every blessing,
Come the grace that saved a wretch like me;
And I will let my words be oh, so few.
Save me from my own clipping hypocrisy.
—Daniel Bailey, "Mirrored Glass"

Without the generous help of Louisiana Wildlife & Fisheries personnel, helicopter pilots, nurses, doctors, Air Guardsmen, DNA specialists, two New Orleans newscasters, college professors, school administrators, social workers, counselors, and an eclectic group of Southern women willing to share their stories, *What the Bayou Saw* would lose whatever authenticity I was able to capture on paper.

Indispensible contributors were Christella Ward, Sheila Flanagan, Anita Moore, and Coreatha Chisley, champions of our future through their work with youth. Without Sergeant Rector McCollum of the Dallas Police Department, Lieutenant Dave Warner of the Normal Police Department, and Beverly Stewart, Secretary to the Assistant Chief of the Monroe Police Department, there would've been no Detective Price or Sheriff Hamilton in this story.

Thank you, Pearl Girls Eileen Astels, Lee Franklin, and Becky Melby for your sharp eyes and soft hearts.

Tearful apologies to my brother, Colonel Roy V. Qualls, who was inadvertently left out of the acknowledgments in my debut novel. Roy took the wild ramblings of this wanna-be writer and helped shape them into *An Irishwoman's Tale*. Through the ravages of Katrina, he managed to get edits into my hands and continues to instruct and advise me in my career.

I dedicate this book to Roy; my mother, Ann, a true Southern lady; and my father, Buckley E. Qualls, who loved books more than I do and would have been so proud to see these stories in print.

Special thanks to my incredible husband, Alan; my lovely daughter, Sarah; and my handsome son, Thomas, for the sacrifices they've made so I could write.

PROLOGUE

Hold the Wind, Hold the Wind, Hold the Wind, don't let it blow.
—Negro spiritual, "Hold the Wind"

August 26, 2005, Normal, Illinois

I am meteorologist Kim Boudreaux." Clad in a dark suit, the petite woman smiled big for her television audience. "Katrina's track has changed." She pointed to a mass of ominous-looking clouds that threatened to engulf the screen. "She's no longer headed for Mobile but is on course for the Crescent City."

Sally Stevens checked her cell phone, then paced in front of the television, as if that would make her brother Robert pick up the phone. She needed to talk to him, needed to know that he'd gotten her nieces and her sister-in-law out of the death trap that New Orleans suddenly had become. Needed to have him assure her, with his balmy Southern drawl, that he and his National Guardsmen were going to be okay.

A slender hand pointed to what must be a fortune's worth of satellite and radar imagery. "As you can see, Katrina's moving toward the mouth of the Mississippi, toward the levees . . ." The meteorologist buzzed on, high on news of this climactic wonder.

Every word seeped from the television screen, crept across the Stevens's den, and crawled up Sally's spine. Louisiana had once been her home. Her heritage. What would this hurricane do to the Southern state that she still loved?

A glance at her watch told Sally to get moving. Instead, she once again punched in Robert's number. If she could just hear his voice, she'd know how to pray later as she stood in her classroom pretending to be passionate about her lecture on the history of American music, pretending to act like it was another ordinary afternoon in Normal, Illinois, while this mother of a storm wreaked wrath and vengeance upon her brother. Her home.

". . . the next twenty-four hours are crucial . . ." The camera zoomed in for a close-up, focusing on a perfect oval face that, for just a moment, seemed to stiffen, as if a personal levee was about to be breached. "I'm not supposed to say this." Urgency laced the forecaster's voice. "But I'm telling you. Leave. This is a killer." The pulsating weather image, a mass of scarlet and violet whirling about an ominous-looking eye, seemed to confirm her report. Growing like a cancer. Moving in for the kill . . .

Talk turned to evacuation, log-jammed roads, but Sally barely listened. Years flew away as she studied Ms. Boudreaux's flawless mocha complexion, the tilt of her chin. The determination of this woman to save her city, or at least its people. So like the determination of Ella, that first friend, who'd taken off for New Orleans. It was as if the lockbox of Sally's memories had somehow sprung open. Ella, that friend who'd saved her. Ella. And her brother, Willie, if he'd gotten out of the pen. Were they digging in, evacuating—

A classical song Sally's kids had downloaded onto her phone poured from the tiny speaker as the device vibrated in her palm.

"God, let it be—" She glanced at the readout. 504 area code. New Orleans. Robert. Her fingers suddenly clumsy, she struggled to flip open the phone.

Static greeted her.

"Robert? Bobby?" She was shouting, but she didn't care. "Are you there? Are you—"

"*Ssss*—got them out."

He's out there somewhere, right in the elements, from the sound of it. "Where are you?" Sally cried. "Robert, what's going on?" Sally pressed the phone against her ear until it hurt. All this technology, yet she could barely hear him, could barely—

The whooshing stopped. So did Robert's voice. Sally stared at the readout. Ten seconds she'd had with him. Ten seconds to gauge the climate of a city. A city that might still claim as a resident that once-best friend. Sally whispered a prayer as she grabbed her briefcase and headed to class.

◆

August 29, 2005, New Orleans, Louisiana

"It's no use! The generator's flooded!" A single battery-operated hallway light revealed the faint outline of Dr. Powers, the thin, impeccably groomed physician with whom Ella Ward had worked for a decade. "Ella? Ella?" He groped against the hospital's second floor wall, his hands and arms made ghoulish by the shadowy dark. "Are you there? Ella? We've got to get them out of here! Now."

Screams, howling winds, and debris crashing against boarded-up windows swirled into a hellish cacophony that tore at Ella's heart. What were the three of them, she, Willie, and the doctor—no. Willie didn't count. What were the *two* of them going to do for sixty-three patients writhing in excrement, gasping for breath, thousands of dollars of ventilators and BiPAPs rendered powerless? Dying, minute by minute, second by second?

Just to keep from falling down, Ella dug her fingernails into a wall sweaty with humidity. She opened her mouth to answer, but no words came out. At Dr. Powers's side, she'd watched an aortic artery explode, a patient gurgle in his own blood . . . "The scalpel, Ms. Ward?" he'd said. "Suction, please." With ice-blue cool, Dr. Powers had plucked life out of mangled messes and never even raised his voice. Now his screams pierced Ella's ears, and her hopes. Even with one of New Orleans's best surgeons at her side, the prognosis of surviving this storm was dim. There was nothing for Ella to do but close her eyes and beg. "Oh God. Please Spirit. Please Lord Jesus, please."

Dr. Powers clutched at the sleeve of Ella's cotton scrub. "Where's Willie?"

The doctor's touch and the mention of her brother brought Ella around. Still, she could barely speak for the quivering of her lip. "Where . . . do you think a junkie would be?"

"The . . . pharmacy?"

Even though Dr. Powers most likely couldn't see her nod, Ella went through the motion. Twenty-four hours ago, she'd decided she and Willie would come here together. Yet even in her worst nightmare, she hadn't really believed that they'd die here together.

"Someone, anyone, let me outta here!" It was Mrs. Smith, in Room 215.

"Hold the wind, Lord!" Mr. Lunsford, who'd thought he'd die of cancer.

Ella gritted her teeth. One by one, the patients were seeing the storm's demonic fingers etching out a death sentence, and screaming their response.

"We've got to do something."

Dr. Powers's words sent a shiver through Ella. Had he read her mind? Or had she babbled without even knowing it? She clamped her hands over her ears. *Lord! I'm goin' crazy! Help me, Lord!*

"What's happenin', Lawd? Oh, Lawd Jesus!"

"Sweet Jesus! Where are You?"

What had acted as a twisted tonic to incite the patients to a new level of chaos? Was it the howls of the winds, the thuds and crashes against the windows, the doors, the very roof of this place?

"Jesus, oh Jesus!"

Every moan, every scream, knifed into Ella like a scalpel. Nursing school hadn't trained her for this. Nearly thirty years working at understaffed facilities hadn't trained her for this. Nothing had trained her for this. With taut fingers, she pulled the doctor close, then shoved him to his knees and knelt by him, her hands flush against the wall. "We gotta pray," she said.

Chapter 1

CALL TO ACTION

I see the bad moon arising. I see trouble on the way.
—John Fogerty, "Bad Moon Rising"

October 25, 2005, Normal, Illinois

Need to speak to you before class. Today.* It was just a sheet of paper stuck under the wiper blade of her Suburban. Yet something about the bold black letters sent a chill up Sally Stevens's back. Then she thought of her Sam and thawed a bit. He'd written this, wanting to schedule a coffee date. It was his math professor way of being romantic, yet it seemed odd that he'd disguise his handwriting. Maybe it was a peace offering after that little misunderstanding last night over her headache.

It nagged at Sally as she stuffed the note into her skirt pocket. Maybe it was from a student, since it referenced class. But how had it gotten under her wiper, inside her garage? She fumbled for her keys, then shrugged it off as one of those mysteries, like unmatched socks and empty cookie jars. It was just a note.

A glance at her watch told her she'd better get going if she wanted to spiff up her lesson plans before her eight o'clock class. She started the car, turned on the radio, and managed to back out of the garage without clipping the rearview mirror.

I hear a hurricane's a blowin'. I hear the end is comin' soon . . .

CNN images of post-Katrina New Orleans flooded her mind as Creedence Clearwater's lyrics poured out of her car speakers. By the time Sally had pulled into the nearly empty parking lot at Midwest Community College, her mood was as black as the charcoal-streaked clouds, amassing liquid weaponry as they began to obliterate the blue sky.

Sally grimaced. It was the start of a war—a Midwestern winter. A war requiring her to summon every character trait she'd inherited from the Flowers clan, a genetic jumble of Cherokee, English, and Cajun ancestors, who'd certainly had their share of troubles in this land. A clan she'd left down in Texas. A clan that, with the exception of Mama and her crazy aunt Gayle and uncle Will, hadn't edged a toe over the Mason-Dixon line for a visit. And she'd been up here for nearly ten years—three years in Indiana, over six years in Illinois. The steering wheel became a target for Sally's frustration as she drummed it, squeezed it, forcing one of Daddy's old sayings into her mind: *You can do it—you have no choice. We Flowers not only survive, we thrive.*

The college administration building, a gray concrete monolith, windowless on the long walls, did nothing to dispel the feeling that Sally was in a war zone. As an afterthought, it seemed, someone had planted twiggy saplings and anemic burning bushes around the perimeter of the building. The pitiful things bent in bare-branched surrender to the west wind, the biggest weapon in winter's ample arsenal.

. . . it's bound to take your life. There's a bad moon on the rise.

With a twist of the knob, Sally stopped the music. What possessed some Midwest deejay to play Southern rock and tweak at the chords of her heart like this? She'd accepted being a Midwesterner, and had adjusted darn well. But like any good Southerner, she longed to go back home. And when the sun shortened its daily visits, when the wind hinted at snow and sleet, she almost hated it here.

Hate. Sally shivered, not only from the cold, but also from the emotion involved with even thinking that word. "Hate never solved anything," Mama always told her, waggling her finger and clucking like an old hen. As Sally checked the rearview mirror for orange pulp in her teeth or smudged lipstick, she knew Mama was right.

She leaned closer to inspect her makeup. Menopause's marks made her grimace. A complexion as drab as this campus. Her eyes? Dull as used spark plugs, and ringed with dark smudges from a halfhearted attempt at eyeliner. Even her hair, once a crown of glory, at least according to Mama, had been infiltrated with so much gray, Sally couldn't see any blond in the shaggy mess, even though Sam assured her that he could. But with Suzi in college and Ed having all kind of senior year expenses, a good stylist was out of the question.

Maybe she should succumb to a Clairol kit, but Mama always said those were for trailer trash and fast women.

Just thinking about Mama made Sally raise her head and jut out her chin, considerably tightening up her middle-aged jawline. Mama had taught her to face bad hair days, bad any kind of days, with a smile. *"Don't let them know how you really feel. You can change the world with a smile. Plus, honey, did you know it burns more calories than frowning?"* Sally plastered on a grin that would make even a Southern mother proud.

Maternally fortified, Sally grabbed her briefcase and purse and got out of the truck. She didn't have to shut the door—the wind did it for her. Snippets of the spirituals she planned to play, the pop quiz she planned to give, spun on the turntable of her mind. She had so much to do if she wanted to teach these kids about protest music, so much—

"Well, well. Just who we wanted to see."

Wha—Sally's blood ran cold. It couldn't be, could it? Rufus's hateful voice, Rufus's hateful tone. Risen from the murky waters of that bayou to haunt her. She whirled, and so did the scenery. Like a crazy carnival ride, everything blurred into whites and blacks and grays. She gripped her briefcase, which had become a roller coaster lap bar.

Three of her students slouched against the side of a dingy white pickup truck. Toothpicks dangled from two of the simpering mouths. All three wore black leather jackets and had shaved heads.

"Lovely mornin', ain't it?" The tallest of the three clicked black storm trooper boots and saluted.

The scenery quit spinning, revealing itself not as a bayou and cypress trees but asphalt and, in the distance, Illinois cornfields and a freeway. As if she'd just gotten off the carnival ride, Sally's legs wobbled. Of course it wasn't Rufus. Rufus was dead. Still, when someone or something startled her like this, her mind hit "rewind," and Rufus materialized out of rotting flesh and brittle bones. Sally managed to rub the ache out of her hand and still hold onto her briefcase. These were just students, albeit unsavory ones rumored to have ties to a white supremacy group. Still, Sally perceived them as Matt Hale wannabes, not the vicious man who had . . . with effort, she pushed away the memory of Rufus and plastered on her trademark smile. After all, this was Normal, where a sign at the city limits proclaimed: *Racism: Not in Our Town.*

"I guess you Midwesterners might call it lovely." Sally mentally recited the alphabet, desperate to help her menopausal memory. What were their names?

Alan? B, C—David? Fred—no, not David or Fred. Since that didn't work, she visualized where they sat in her classroom. Back row, clumped together like weeds. Of course. Jay. Rex. Hugh. Because of their clonelike appearance, she had to study them a bit more closely to determine who was Jay, who was Rex, who was Hugh.

"We call anything lovely, as long as it ain't black." Rex and Hugh high-fived like they'd just scored in some sick Aryan sporting event.

If Sally hadn't been so intent on studying every pimple and stray whisker to recollect their names, she might have missed the way they edged toward her. Adrenaline caused her to thunk her briefcase onto the pavement, then clench her fists.

Jay stepped even closer. "You look surprised to see us. Didn't you get the note?" Spittle pooled in the corner of his mouth.

The note. One mystery solved. Sally honed in on eyes the color of arctic ice and shuddered, then clamped down her fear. Something was going on here; to deal with it, she needed to regroup. Fast. "You mean the note that wasn't signed?" It was hard to stall for time and keep her gaze fixed on Jay's dead-fish stare, especially when a million questions flew at her. *Did they give the note to Sam? Ed? Who stuck it on the car? How did they get our address? What do they want?*

"No." Rex talked around what looked to be a wad of tobacco. "What'd ya think we'd send you? A 'Get Well Soon' note?"

Sally pretended to pick lint off her jacket but instead scanned the lot. Her heart pounded the message: empty, except for a cluster of beer bottles around a light pole and some wadded-up fast-food sacks.

"A Sympathy card? Which you might need if you keep teaching this nigger-lover unit." Jay scratched his head, his eyes blank, a nasty grin on his face.

"*Keep your cool no matter what. Be assertive.*" It was Daddy's voice she heard this time, all his years as a college professor counting for something. Sally brightened her smile until her jaw ached. If they thought their threat scared her, they were wrong. After all, she was the teacher here, and she was going to take control of their little game, whatever it was. She straightened her shoulders and stared at Jay, whom she'd pegged as the ringleader, determined not to blink until he did. "You said you needed to talk about class." In a calculated way, she studied her watch. "I've got a meeting scheduled with Ms. Grant. She'll be here any minute." She forced out a chuckle. "In fact, she's late . . . Anyway, what did y'all need to talk about?"

"You mean that ape pretending to teach speech? What a joke." Hugh joined the little tête-à-tête for the first time.

Steam expanded Sally's chest. So they'd noticed her friendship with Daisy Grant, the black colleague who taught in the room next to their humanities class.

"Funny you should mention her." Jay cleared his throat, then spat. A wad of phlegm landed not a foot from Sally's shoe. "That's the class we want to talk about. The class of apes that's overrunning us. The class you keep throwin' at us, pretending you're teachin' culture and music and all that bull—" He cursed, then shoved up his jacket sleeves, as if preparing to fight. Tattooed on his forearm was a mutant spider, four black Nazi legs instead of the usual arachnid eight.

In spite of her resolve to keep cool, Sally's mouth flew open. With effort, she shut it. She remembered with absolute clarity the last time she'd seen a swastika. They'd been in Terre Haute about a month, during which time she'd gaped at the hateful symbols on foam dice that dangled from the rearview mirrors of beat-up pickups in the Wal-Mart lot. But that hadn't been the last time. Oh, no. The last time had been much more subtle. Much more civilized. And much, much worse.

On a sunny morning, Sally had pulled into the parking lot of Suzi's middle school for Parent Volunteer Day. At the same time, a nice-looking woman stepped out of a family-type sedan and walked around the rear of her car, her skirt swishing near a bumper plastered with rebel flag and swastika decals.

The woman had offered Sally a very soft, very white hand. "Hi. I'm Jamie's mother," she said. "You must be Suzi's mother."

Seeming to misinterpret Sally's blank stare, she continued, "You know. Jamie plays flute in Suzi's section? They both take Spanish?" A very nice smile wreathed a very nice face. "I'm so glad they're friends," she added.

For one of the few times in her life, Sally had been speechless. She stayed that way while she and Jamie's mother worked side by side in the library, sliding wonderfully enlightening books onto specially ordered adjustable shelves. Sally never said a word, never asked "the question"—why a seemingly well-educated, well-mannered woman would display such hateful symbols on the back of her car for the entire world to see. Sally half-expected such things out of those pickup drivers, with their beater shirts and blank-eyed stares. But that sunny morning, Sally hadn't said a thing. She'd just returned the nice smile, the inane chatter, her stomach churning and burning all the while.

That night, Sally'd sobbed the story to Sam, and later, she'd sobbed to God.

"Next time," Sam had said.

Next time. The Spirit's whisper had been softer than a sigh.

One look at Jay, who had edged a bit closer, jolted Sally back to the present. She cleared her throat and made sure not to blink as she stared at each boy. That's what they were. Just boys. Thirty years younger than her. But only a few inches taller, a few pounds heavier, if it came to that. *Good thing I'm a big woman, because right now is "next time."*

"You say you want to talk." The Southern niceties that Sally liberally sprinkled in her vernacular were gone—her ears crackled at the harshness of her tone. "Have at it."

Rex and Hugh looked away, but not Jay. "I just got one thing to say to you." He clenched his teeth and aimed a stubby finger at Sally's chest. "Quit teachin' this nigger crap."

Sally took a step toward Jay, her hands shaking, the roots of her hair burning her scalp like she'd dipped her head in scalding water. Being from the South, she had a few reservations about blacks, but she drew the line at the use of the *n* word and she championed the importance of African-American culture to this country. She aimed a bloodred nail at Jay's chest. "I'll teach what they pay me to teach. You don't have any say-so about it."

Jay's eyes narrowed.

Just looking at the hate in the boys' faces kindled an anger that Sally hadn't felt for years. She clenched her teeth until her molars ground together. "Anything else y'all need to 'talk' about?"

They stood there like heavyweights sizing each other up after the gong signaled the final round of a competitive bout. About the time Sally wondered how long she could go without blinking, Jay looked away, then glared at his friends. "You guys just gonna stand there and take this?" he snarled.

A genuine smile played with the corners of Sally's mouth, but her hands still shook.

"You're just chicken . . ." Jay's voice trailed off, as did most of the hostility that had infused his words. He stepped back and slumped against the truck.

"And while y'all are here and we're havin' this nice little chat"—Sally's drawl began its comeback—"may I ask why you got that in the first place?" She pointed to Jay's tattoo.

Jay's face paled, but maybe it was just the reflection of the sun's rays, battling valiantly through the column of gray clouds. "It's . . . it's private. None of your business."

The sag of his shoulders and the way he scuffed his boot on the asphalt sent a twinge through Sally. Here he was trying to be a poster boy for the Aryan Brotherhood, yet he was just a young man, misled by insidious propaganda. Had he been raised in a maelstrom of hate that had twisted his young mind? And how could she reach him, show him the Light that could change everything?

She grinned but folded her arms across her chest, doing her best to be friendly, yet serious. "I'm sorry, but you made it my business when you left me that note, then waited here, didn't you?" Sally smoothed into her everyday voice—the one she used with family, students, friends, the women in her Bible study. "And I do appreciate your concern about my teaching, but it sounds like your problem concerns your own prejudices."

Words flowed now as Sally made sure to look into each boy's eyes. "And according to the school handbook, discrimination by race is illegal." Her gesture toward Jay's arm was quick and could have been taken for a wave. "If I were you, I'd keep that covered up. If it offends me, it's bound to offend others." *Like Shamika.* She thought of Shamika's bright eyes and jumble of dreadlocks or weave or whatever the *Ebony* hairstyle of the week seemed to be. The one who sat front row, middle seat, as hungry for knowledge as a chirping chick for a worm. The one who, after a heated class debate, called these three the slimiest honkies in town. The one with the perfectly sculpted face, so like Ella's. Dear Ella. That first friend who'd gone through things like this with her. That friend who, even after Katrina, Sally still hadn't taken the time to find.

A car drove up. Sally cut a look to her right, managing to keep the students in her peripheral vision. It was Milton Rogers, a colleague who also taught at this uncivilized time of the day.

Sally lowered her voice, her eyes darting from Milton to the boys. "And I know you don't want anyone to be offended. Like the dean or the president."

Before they could respond, Sally grabbed her briefcase and stepped away. "Yoo hoo! Dr. Rogers?" Smiling, she waved, as if Milton had seen her, though he seemed intent on gathering his things and hadn't looked their way. Then she turned to the boys, nodding. "Well, as you can see, my colleague's here. I'd love to sit down with y'all, in a more civilized place." Her hand swept toward the parking lot, which was suddenly filling up with cars whose speakers pulsated the beats of rap and rock and country. "And chat about this, ah, issue. I'm from the South, you know—"

"We know." A hard gleam returned to Jay's eyes. "You've told us about a thousand times."

Sally waved away his comment as if it were a gnat. "And I've got some insight y'all just might not have." Making sure she kept her eyes on the trio, she shouldered her purse and sidled toward Milton's car.

"I thought you were meeting with that—"

"Oops!" Sally shrugged her shoulders. "Did I say Ms. Grant was supposed to meet me? I meant Dr. Rogers." An inane giggle bubbled out of her mouth. She took one more sidestep, then practically galloped away.

Milton, briefcase in tow, shut the door of his gray sedan and turned toward the building. The wind had made a jumble of his coarse brown hair.

Sally clomped toward him as fast as her uncomfortable pumps would take her. She wasn't sure if she wanted to share with him what had happened, but at least they could walk in together and she could chitchat away the image of those black jackets, that black tattoo. That black hate. "How are you?" With both hands Sally gripped her briefcase. Her head flopped back and forth, simulating a wave.

Perhaps Milton nodded, but Sally didn't think so. As if she were invisible, he brushed past her, his gray slacks snapping in the wind.

"What do you think of this cold front?" Sally whirled around and followed him toward the building. In case the students were listening, she chattered on. "I'll swan, it'll blow away our patio umbrella if it gets much worse."

As she strode past the pickup, Sally darted a glance toward the three boys, who were now lined up across the front seat like targets at a shooting gallery. She slowed her step, though her heart continued to thump in her chest. She hadn't been in any danger, really. They were just mixed-up boys.

"Have a nice day," she called to Milton, who had loped ahead. Only her family and best friends would've detected the flint in her voice. And if her eyes could be weapons, Sally would've seared a hole in the back of Milton's tweed jacket. Of course, Milton didn't know what had happened, didn't understand her need for camaraderie. Still, these Midwesterners galled her. People so reserved, they wouldn't change expression if they won the lottery. People who practically wore "No Trespassing" buttons on their lapels. Sally stuck out her tongue at Milton's hunched-over back, then sucked it in. Why was she resorting to such childish behavior?

She knew why. Milton's snub was deflating her effort to rebound from this awful morning. Sally cut across the portico where all the smokers congregated—before, during, and after class. The stale tobacco that clung to what must have been dozens of stomped-upon butts constricted her airways as all of her earlier resentments about the Midwest moved in like the approaching storm. Dragging across the quadrangle, she longed to see something, anything, aesthetic. Where were the cupolas? Statues? Arches? Sidewalks lined with azaleas and dogwoods, petunias and pansies? She closed her eyes and breathed deep, desperate for Southern air thick with the fragrance of magnolias, which melded the scent of vanilla and spice and roses into one mood-changing fragrance. Tears pooled in her eyes, blurring her view of the Fine Arts annex, not that it mattered. More gray. More concrete block. More . . . nothing. She walked inside the building, doing her best to ignore the resentment building even faster than the cloud column.

"Hey, Mrs. Stevens." Jennifer's smile accentuated straight white teeth. She looked like a teen magazine model, except for the plethora of studs in her nose and ears. And probably her navel, now covered by wool pea jacket.

Tension melted from Sally at the sight of a *nice* student. "Hi, Jennifer."

"Could you help me with this?" Jennifer waved a folder at Sally. "It's only a rough draft, but I spent all yesterday and half the night working on it." She bounced as she talked, energizing the cramped hall. "It's funny. I'd never heard of Odetta until your class. Now I'm doing a fifteen-page paper on her."

Joshua fought the battle of Jericho . . . The music came from deep in Sally, pushing away the nasty little scene that, along with the weather, had darkened her morning. She glanced at the clock in the hall, the music growing inside until she began to tap her heel against the linoleum floor . . . *and dem walls came tumblin' down.* Her lecture needed work and she had papers to grade. But teaching boiled down to one-on-one interactions like this; other things could wait.

The warmth from Jennifer's smile spread to Sally's stiff fingers, her pinched toes . . . her heart. "Why, sure. I'd be thrilled to." At times like this, she couldn't believe they paid her to teach; she should pay *them.* Her briefcase plopped onto the floor as she dug around in her purse and found her keys, then unlocked the door and pushed it open. Her eager hand grabbed Jennifer's paper; her impatient foot nudged her briefcase into the room. Buried in Odetta's art, she headed toward her desk.

Words leapt off the page and set off a dozen sparks, which ignited a dozen ideas in Sally's head. She kept reading, barely aware that Jennifer had set her briefcase next to her chair. Jennifer's enthusiasm had shoved the weather, the unpleasant parking lot encounter, into the deep freeze of her mind, where other ugly things had been stored. And with a little help from God, they'd stay there.

Chapter 2

DISTURBING NEWS

Dere's no hard trials, Oh, yes, I want to go home,
Dere's no whips a-crackin', I want to go home.
—Negro spiritual, "I Want to Go Home"

Heads bobbed over the quizzes Sally had handed out exactly five minutes after eight. The only sounds in the classroom were ballpoint pens scratching against paper and the drone of air pouring from the heat register that banked the back wall near Sally's desk.

Sally scrawled an *a* into the grade book next to the names of Jay, Rex, and Hugh. She hated to admit it, but she was glad they were no-shows. It didn't guarantee that she'd get a standing ovation after part two of her lecture linking spirituals and American music, but it'd sure go better without their snide comments, their nasty glares.

Working down the T–Th/8:00 roster, Sally checked a name, then searched for the corresponding face. A sweat-stained baseball cap turned backward—Bob was here. She placed a check mark in the roll book and moved on. Tie-dyed boxer shorts—Debra. Ticking off names, she flipped the page. *Almost done.* Watts, Tucker . . . Williams, Shamika. Sally did a double take. *Shamika's not here.* With those hairstyles, Shamika was hard to miss. The first time Sally had set eyes on her, she thought Shamika had planned to attend the beauty school down the street and had somehow gotten sidetracked. Or perhaps fashion design, judging from the fitted linen dress pants, silk shirts, and high heels. And it wasn't just Shamika's attention to her appearance, but a regal bearing stamped into a nearly six-foot-tall body that made her unique. Plus the fact that she was the only black student in class.

That first session, when they'd filled out "Getting to Know You" cards, Shamika had announced, in bold script, her plans to be an attorney. From that moment, Shamika punched away at stereotypes and a few of Sally's own prejudices toward community college students, especially blacks: They're sloppy. They don't care. They cut class no matter how brilliant the lectures. Again Sally checked the seat on the first row. It wasn't like Shamika to miss.

Even if Shamika hadn't aced the first papers, Sally would've bonded with this student who reminded her of Ella, and not because they both were African-Americans. It was their hunger to learn. Their punctuality. Reliability. Sally flipped back in the grade book. Just as she'd thought. Shamika's first absence.

Gazing out the window, Sally half-expected to see a stately black figure marching across the quadrangle. Yet there was nothing. She craned her neck, looking past the campus and into the fields of the last farm to withstand the development onslaught that had overtaken Northview Road.

Acres of corn, their wilted stalks fluttering like the limbs of old scarecrows, did not scare off three greasy-looking crows. When they swaggered and flapped huge wings, Sally imagined not caws, but the words of that song—*a bad moon on the rise.*

Someone knocked on the door.

Sally dropped her pen, the nib making a squiggly line next to Shamika's name in the grade book. She capped the pen, got up, and grabbed her cell phone. If Hugh and his friends had decided to have a Grand-Wizard-and-his-entourage showdown, it was time to call in the authorities.

The door creaked open. With one hand, Harold, her department chair, beckoned Sally into the hall. His other hand sifted through a grayish mop that dipped over his ears. Faded jeans, with frayed cuffs skimming the tops of scuffed boots, did nothing to dispel the notion that Harold was an aging hippie.

Sally glanced at her students, whose arched eyebrows and audible intakes of breath gave away their curiosity. She was certainly curious herself. Harold would never interrupt class. Unless . . . Nodding and smiling, Sally attempted to dispel any anxiety caused by the interruption, yet iciness crept through her. Leaving the door ajar, she stepped outside.

Harold studied the floor, shifting his weight from one foot to the other. "Ah, Sally," he mumbled. "We've got a little situation here."

Was something wrong with Suzi? Ed? Sam? Sally squeezed her cell phone like it was a panic button, determined to keep a professional demeanor in spite of the shiver spreading through her body. *Oh God. Not Robert. Down there in all that Katrina mess . . .*

Another man—a strawberry blond—stepped in front of Harold. "Good morning, ma'am." Only five ten or so, he nonetheless swallowed up space like a Pac-Man ghost. Even though his dark sport coat constricted broad shoulders and shone at the elbows, the creases in his pants would pass a military inspection.

Something crumbled inside Sally. It wasn't so much the man's dress; it was the flecks of green that fired steely gray eyes, the straight spine, the taut forearms, the stiff handshake that gave him away. He was a cop. And cops didn't bring good news.

Harold touched her arm. "Sorry, Sally. Uh, Mrs. Stevens. This is, uh . . ."

Sally's skin pricked confirmation. Words usually flowed from Harold like lava. Something was wrong with her husband, her kids, her brother. Somehow she kept her smile intact, though her insides quaked. "Hello, officer."

"Good morning, ma'am," the officer repeated. Of course he didn't blink. When he nodded at her, the ruddy face, sprinkled with freckles, dipped to reveal hair too long to be considered a crew cut, too short to be called anything else. "I'm Detective Price."

Goose bumps migrated to Sally's toes, neck, and face. She gulped once or twice. "How can I help you?" she managed. *Oh, dear God, please . . .*

The detective cleared his throat. "There's been an incident with a young woman."

Sally leaned against the door, which thudded shut. *God, no! Not Suzi! Anyone but my daughter.* They'd told her not to jog alone. They'd told her . . . She opened her mouth, but the words that every cell in her body screamed did not emerge. Even her voice had frozen.

"I need a copy of your class roll. And I need to ask you a few questions."

"My . . . class roll?" Sally's heart began to pump blood to all the icy places, allowing her limbs to move, her brain to think. *Thank You, God. It's not . . . Suzi.* Now she could channel her energy to the situation at hand. Her daughter wasn't in trouble, but somebody's daughter was, or this cop wouldn't be standing here. She took a deep breath and resolved to do all she could to help. "Which class?"

"This hour, ma'am."

"Which student?"

The detective tightened his lips. "Ms. Williams."

Sally leaned back, her hip against the doorknob. "Sh—Shamika? What happened?"

"She was assaulted, ma'am."

Sally's knees buckled. "Oh, God, no." Smells and images flooded her, and she stumbled once, twice . . .

With a bracing grip, Detective Price steadied her. "Mrs. Stevens, I know this is a shock," he said, his gaze unwavering, "but we really need your help."

It was his tone, brisk and professional, that reminded Sally that Shamika was her student, and hysteria was the last thing needed here. She darted into the class, flipped through her binder, ripped out a copy of the class roster, and slipped back into the hall. "Where did it happen?" she asked, breathing hard.

Detective Price hesitated but still didn't blink. "The south parking lot."

"When?"

"Last night. After her class."

"Was she . . ."

"Raped. Beaten."

The floor seemed to shift. Sally locked her eyes on the detective to keep from collapsing. Surely God wouldn't allow such a senseless act to snuff out a beautiful life. Surely . . . "Is she—" her voice cracked.

"Serious but stable."

Sally bowed her head, breath rushing out of her. *Thank God. Thank—*

"She should be fine." A half-smile accentuated a mouth lined from viewing one too many crime scenes.

For an instant, Sally wanted to slap him. *Fine?* Shamika would never be fine again, not by any "happily ever after" standards. Sally could tell him a thing or two about it. She clenched and unclenched her fists. Ever since it had happened to her, she'd struggled with . . . personal kinds of things. Like last night. Oh, sure, she'd managed to keep it hidden all these years, using headaches and menopause and the children as excuses, pretending so well, even Sam didn't suspect a thing. But she'd hardly call everything *fine*. Resentment building, Sally eyed the detective. How could he be so calm about this?

Harold shot glances up and down the hall. "This thing could blow up in our face. Ruin our image." He wrung limp hands and shook hair out of his eyes.

Sally's breath caught. He just cared about lawsuits, their precious reputation—everything but Shamika. Only by gritting her teeth could she keep her mouth shut.

"Now, I have some questions, ma'am. Ma'am?"

Her eyes left Harold. She needed to pay attention. This was a cop, after all. She took deep breaths, determined to focus. With effort, she nodded.

"Did anything unusual happen in class last week—you all meet on Tuesdays and Thursdays, right?"

"We do meet on Tuesday/Thursday. Nothing unusual happened last week that I know of."

"Are you aware of any serious differences between Shamika and anyone on campus?"

Though she looked at the detective, Sally's mind was on that swastika. "Uh-huh. You see, Shamika feels . . . some of the boys are racist. They've had words."

"Words? What kind of words?"

"Oh, nothing overt. Sneers. Snide comments made after we'd discuss African-American art." *No, nothing overt. Until about thirty minutes ago.* Thinking of the parking lot incident, Sally glanced toward the hall doors. Were they still out there?

"Ma'am, is something wrong?"

The surety in the detective's voice snapped Sally to attention. Should she tell him about Rex and Jay and Hugh?

"Ma'am, tell me what happened."

Don't lie, Sally. Not to this man. At least not now . . . "Well, sir," she began, "three of my students . . . confronted me in the parking lot this morning. About my . . ."—Sally winced—"nigger-lover teaching." Waving arms and spurting words described the incident.

While the detective jotted something in a notepad, Sally kept yakking but let her mind drift to a place where girls weren't raped and boys didn't hate. It was the only thing that kept her from sobbing.

"Now if you could just describe Shamika's demeanor at the time of the—"

Sally's jaw fell open. What had she been saying? "Haven't you seen her?" she asked, not clear what was going on.

The detective remained nonplussed. "Ma'am, if you'd let me finish my question, I'm looking for her reaction during the incidents in class."

Sally bit her lip. How could a few words describe Shamika's reaction to those boys? Perfectly sculpted cheekbones, sucked in like a spoiled brat who didn't get her way. Miss America beautiful, except for pouty lips and baleful glares. A typical resentful black, just like . . . down South. So many images filled her mind that she rubbed her head. The past. The present. That first day of class.

Shamika had been the only student in the sleepy-eyed group to bite at the lure Sally had dangled—a slide of Michelangelo's Sistine Chapel ceiling. She'd scribbled furiously in a tabbed binder while Sally told of the artist's physical and mental sufferings during the years he'd practically lived on that twenty-meter-high scaffold. The longer Sally pictured that scene, the more she determined to help Shamika through this, in whatever way she could.

"Mrs. Stevens?"

Sally snapped to attention. "Oh, sorry. Let's see. Close to six feet tall. Uh, black—you know, African-style hair, done up in dreadlocks or a weave—Oh, I don't know for sure what you call it. I'd guess she weighs a hundred thirty or so."

A tic worked over the detective's right cheek. "Ma'am, what I've been trying to ask is this. To your knowledge, was there any type of interaction between the three gentlemen involved in this morning's incident and Ms. Williams? Did she curse them? Did they threaten her?"

Sally glanced at Harold, but of course, he didn't meet her gaze. She smoothed down her skirt, wondering just what she was supposed to say. *Yes, Mr. Killer-Eyes Detective, they've had interaction, starting the first day of class. They hate her because she's black; she hates them because they're racist.*

As was usually the case when something stumped Sally, one of her parents whispered in her ear, Daddy this time. *"If you don't know something for sure, Sally, keep your mouth shut."* Feeling the heat from Detective Price's gaze, she knew she'd better trust Daddy. "Not that I know of," she said.

Detective Price clicked his pen and tucked both it and the notepad into his breast pocket. He pulled out a card and handed it to Sally. "If you can think of anything else, give me a call." With a fluidity surprising in such a stocky man, he walked toward the exit.

"Uh, Sally." Harold cleared his throat several times and fiddled with either a set of keys or enough coins to get through the Chicago tollways.

The rattle irritated Sally, but she stood straighter and waited. It was best to keep quiet and listen. Let him get it out.

"Uh, there's a few other things they're keeping, uh, under wraps."

Sally plastered her face with what she hoped was a receptive look.

"Some vandalism. Threatening calls. All race-related. Possibly hate crimes."

Now Sally had to bite back her retort. *So it was only a hate crime if different races were involved? When wasn't crime deplorable, despicable, abominable? Stop, Sally. You've got to keep the lid on or you can't help her.* It hurt to smile, but somehow she managed. Again, she waited.

"We wonder—since you're so good with them . . ." Harold's words trickled out, the empty hall soaking them up.

Sally's nod seemed to bolster Harold. He took his hands out of his pockets and waved them wildly. "We want you to be kind of a . . . a liaison of sorts to, uh, these people." Words slurred during Harold's doublespeak. "Visit them in the hospital. See if you can smooth things over with them."

Them? These people? Why was Harold making Shamika and her family sound like Martians? Sally cleared her throat. "To whom are you referring, Harold?"

"Shamika and her aunt. They moved down from Chicago so she could come here." His smile was bitter. "Get away from gangs, drugs, big-city crime, I imagine." Harold stepped close, his hand cupping his mouth as if he were about to reveal state secrets. "And to be honest, they're worried."

Anytime people said "to be honest," it was a sure signal they were lying. She ought to know . . . Sally swallowed the bad taste in her mouth. If she was going to help Shamika and her aunt, she needed to understand what this limp noodle was talking about. But aggression was the wrong approach. "Harold, help me understand here," she said, making sure her voice was soft and full of concern. "Who is the 'they' you're referring to now? And what are 'they' worried about?"

Harold's smile was sheepish. "Lawyers. The dean. The number crunchers."

Inwardly Sally grimaced, yet she kept smiling, smiling . . .

Harold leaned close, his posture that of coworkers gathering for gossip around the company water fountain. "Well, quite frankly, a lawsuit."

"A lawsuit?" Immediately Sally wished she'd continued her ruse, but she just couldn't help it. How could they even begin to think about money at a time like this? A girl lay broken and torn in some hospital bed, and they were calling in lawyers and huddling with them like a quarterback and his offensive line? Offensive. That's what all the college big dogs were.

"I know. These . . . minorities demand everything. You know . . ."

"No, I don't know." Anger infused Sally's voice. "I mean, a girl just got raped, and those suits upstairs in their big offices—"

"Oh, sure, sure. But we've got to placate risk management." It had taken time, but Harold managed to spread a veneer of empathy over his words. He was all administrator now, smoothing the ruffled feathers of an irate faculty member. "We've got to . . ."

Sally wanted to shake Harold for the way he vacillated to fit the wishes of his superiors. But as he rambled on about red tape and containment, her anger began to seep out, her attention wandering to the roomful of students on the other side of the door, to the girl in a hospital bed. That was what really mattered. That was what all the suits were forgetting. And let them forget. But she wouldn't. She couldn't. Her hand on the doorknob, she gave Harold her brightest smile. "Sorry to interrupt, Harold, but I really need to get back to—"

"Oh, sure, sure." Smiling, he wiped his brow. "So you'll visit them?"

"Of course. Right after class."

"There's something else." Harold crooked his finger at her, as if he were letting her in on a dirty little secret.

Sally pursed her lips, emotions building again. But she chirped, "Sure, Harold. Whatever you need."

"Maybe you could offer—oh, we haven't figured it all out, but if someone could tutor her in her own home, at least in something like Humanities. She can do the math, the science, the economics, online." He practically purred now. "It would save Sha—how do you say that name?"

"Sha-mi-ka," Sally spit out, then wiped off her mouth. Harold was pushing her to a hard candy boil.

"Yes, Shamika." Something like a gargle came from his mouth. "Anyway, it would save her the embarrassment of having to come back to campus. And I think it would make them feel catered to. Make them—"

"Forget about a lawsuit?" Sally made sure to smile, only she didn't see anything pleasant about the fact that their concern wasn't really for Shamika. It was about their precious budget having another zero or two on some bottom line. On the other hand, to tutor Shamika, with her intellect, one-on-one? Sally's head spun at the possibilities.

"I mean, it did happen in our parking lot, and—"

Sally touched Harold's sleeve. "I can help her." She took a deep breath. "If they'll let me."

Harold's laugh had a circus clown ring. "If they'll let you? They'll jump at it."

Gripping the doorknob, Sally swallowed hard. *If he doesn't shut up . . .* "And I'd better jump to my students before they jump out the windows."

As quickly as it had come, Harold's jolly demeanor faded. "Of course we can't pay you." His eyebrows became mountain peaks. "You know . . ."

Sally nodded, even though she didn't know and, quite frankly, didn't care about the money, which was probably tied into the union and their precious bargaining agreement. She never had been into political maneuverings—she just wanted to teach. "She's at Regional, right?" Mentally Sally was already adding to the errands she'd jotted on the back of a used envelope and stuffed into her purse. *Groceries. Cleaners. Hospital . . .*

"Yep." Harold glanced at his watch, then touched Sally on the shoulder, the most intimate gesture he'd made in two years. "And thanks, Sally."

As Harold pattered away, Sally stared at the gleaming linoleum, steeling herself to go back into the classroom. It was so polished, so antiseptic, in stark contrast to the filthy cycle of abuse, which had now soiled the life of one of her students. And as Sally well knew, nothing would ever be quite so clean for Shamika again.

Chapter 3

SHAMIKA

Troubled, troubled, troubled in mind.
If Jesus don't help me, I surely will die.
—Negro spiritual, "Troubled in Mind"

It had already been a long day, and it was about to get longer. Sally heaved her briefcase into the back seat. Even though she gladly provided meals for church members recovering from surgery, gladly visited shut-ins, she avoided hospitals like she had an autoimmune disease. Hoping music would settle her, she turned on the radio as she pulled out of the parking lot.

The heartrending lyrics of Tracy Chapman blared out of the one speaker that still worked in the old truck. Disturbing lyrics. Distracting lyrics. Sally had to grip the steering wheel, check the rearview mirror, just to keep in her own lane. Ever since the Katrina debacle, racism had again taken over the driver's seat in America. She tried to turn down the volume but instead set the windshield wipers to swishing. *Whish, whish,* they scraped against glass, desperately trying to do their job. But all the cracked and worn rubber blades managed to do was smear around a layer of sludge.

Her eyes still on the road, Sally flipped them off. Nothing had changed in this country. Slavery still muddied up things between the races, even way up here. And it wasn't just *her* people's fault. Blacks contributed to the quagmire, the way they viewed everything as racist, shutting out whites in the same manner they'd once been shut out.

Smoothing into Chapman's lyrics, Sally drove down Main Street. When were they all going to let bygones be bygones and treat each other like equals, the way God intended? She'd do her part, show Shamika and her aunt that she wasn't prejudiced. Since they'd moved up North, she'd grown so much. Hadn't she added the unit on spirituals? Now she'd readily agreed to Harold's little scheme, not even knowing if they'd accept her help. As Sam was so fond of saying, had she again bitten off more than she could chew? Every good Southern girl knew this racial thing was complex. Like Mama always said, a good Southern girl has to be careful when dealing with the blacks.

When two girls, arm in arm, stepped off the curb and into the street, Sally waved them on, then endured the sustained honk of the driver behind her. They were so cute, those two, their heads thrown back in laughter, their eyes bright, as if they hadn't a care. Just like her and Ella, down by the bayou.

And it suddenly came to Sally. She'd go through that old box of letters. Find Ella's address. She'd meant to do it after Katrina brought New Orleans to the forefront of national news, yet she'd kept putting it off. If Katrina had forced Ella to move, maybe Robert's military connections could help find her. They'd get in touch, chat like the old days. Maybe Ella could help her deal with Shamika. After all, Ella knew . . . Revitalized, Sally sped forward, switching lanes. If this incident could reunite Ella and her, with God's help, several broken things might be fixed.

The song disappeared into a hiss of static. Sally fiddled with the knob and tuned into a news station.

"This is Dawn Kennedy, with award-winning WJCC news. Katrina refugees continue to swamp Houston, straining the city's resources and angering local citizens."

Sally turned up the volume, as she did every time Katrina was mentioned. "The population of New Orleans has dwindled to a twenty-year low as former residents grapple with the aftermath of North America's largest natural disaster."

Even though Robert had safely evacuated his family, he remained in New Orleans, working double and triple shifts, thanks to The Big One. Sure, he called when he could, but not enough to suit Sally. And with all the cellular disruptions, she'd learned more from CNN than she had from her brother.

"In local news, police have just released information about the recent attack on a college student at the main campus of Midwest Community. Anyone with information is asked to contact the Normal Police at . . ."

Shaking her head, Sally turned off the radio so she could maneuver into a parallel parking space close to the hospital entrance. This news bulletin wasn't about some anonymous person but rather her student, her community college, her town of Normal. Sally grimaced. She had a feeling things weren't going to be normal for a long time.

When she opened the car door, her purse tumbled to the floorboard, vomiting wadded-up candy wrappers, lipstick tubes, a baggie of Oreos, coupons whose expiration dates had long passed, the grocery list, and a pocket-sized Bible.

Sally scooped up her things, smoothed down the ripped lining of her purse, and stuffed everything back in . . . except the cookies. She popped one in her mouth, barely chewing it before she stuck in another, another, and another, hoping to do something, anything, to help her get through the hospital lobby, past the maternity floor, and up to Shamika's room. Now this whole thing seemed like a bad idea, but she'd promised Harold. And at her age, she'd better get over this dread of hospitals. No telling when another body part would quit working and *she'd* be admitted. Using the rearview mirror, she licked off crumbs, freshened her lipstick, and tried to do the same with her spirits.

With a whoosh of revolving doors, Sally stepped into the foyer, a prayer on her lips. *Lord, please. Cover this situation. Both for me and my student.*

Scrubs-clad doctors bustled about with clipboards. Nurses pushed patients in wheelchairs to what looked like a handicapped holding tank. Bright-eyed aides carried vases of carnations and, for a few fortunate patients, long-stemmed roses. Their unmistakable scent managed to overpower ammonia and Lysol just long enough for Sally to envision all the agonies and ecstasies being played out right this minute. She'd been part of one—what had it been?—twenty-five years ago.

As Sally turned the corner, the Coke machine near the coffee shop beckoned her to visit. It was so easy to rationalize, especially with the chocolate crumbs and gooey filling sticking to her molars. And the baby blue balloons waving to her from the gift shop. Since the cookies hadn't done the job, she'd try a Diet Coke. Sally put in her money, waited for the *plunk* and *thud*, popped the tab, and drank. But the fizzy sound, the feel of the icy metallic can, usually sure bets, failed to soothe her. She chugged it in record time and chucked it into the trash. With mincing steps, she made her way back to the welcome station.

An elderly lady sat behind a mahogany desk, her gray head bent over a book.

Sally cleared her throat. "Good afternoon. I need the room number for Shamika Williams."

With a yawn, the woman set down a Danielle Steel novel and glanced at a list. "Room two twenty-four." Without once looking at Sally, she hurried back to her romance.

"Thank you very much." Sally smiled even though she didn't feel like it. She walked past the Watercolor Society's display on the lobby walls and pushed the button on the elevator.

Doors slid open. A man tried to maneuver a woman in a wheelchair out of the elevator as it began to close. But Sally barely looked at either of them. A tiny blue bundle in the woman's lap captured Sally's heart, her soul, and sent a stab into her gut. She dodged the bewildered-looking couple, shoved open a stairwell door, and managed to take the steps two at a time. It was no use. She'd tried all her usual distractions—food, a soda, a prayer—but they'd failed miserably.

Hate moved in just like that storm had, and Sally hated feeling all this hate. But she really couldn't help it, not at all. She hated the antiseptic cleaners masking the grim reality of sickness and death. The stark white walls. The fluorescent lights. The cold indifference of the staff. The blue blanket, which reminded her of the blue baby lips, the blue baby fingers. Baby Blue was her pet name for him, even though she'd never shared that with anyone but Sam. Baby Blue, the one who had never come home from a place like this. Baby Blue, her one and only natural-born child.

Her sides heaving, Sally paused at the top of the stairs. She wouldn't set foot on Shamika's floor until she'd transformed herself into Sunny Sally. Buttercups and bright skies, sugar and spice and everything nice. The last thing Shamika needed was a gloomy face.

"Are you all right, ma'am?" A janitor, one hand holding the door ajar, the other on his mop cart, gazed at her, his eyes soft even under metal halide lighting.

Sliding past him, Sally nodded. She had to move on, do what she came here to do. Her stomach a knot, she hurried down the hall to Room 224 and rapped lightly on the door. When there was no answer, she stepped into the room, around a partition, and to the bed. "Hi," she managed to squeak out.

"Hi, Mrs. Stevens." Shamika pulled several pillows from behind her back, then grimaced as she tossed them aside. Her skin was clear except for two angry bruises under her right eye. In spite of the fact that some of her hair appeared to have been shaved off, she managed to retain her regal bearing. Yet there was a vulnerability in the way the hospital gown hung off her, in the fact that her tall, proud body was sandwiched between mattress and sheet.

"Just call me Sally."

When Shamika scooted over and gestured for Sally to sit on her bed, Sally set down her purse but kept standing, patting Shamika's sheet-covered feet. "We missed you today."

"That school of piranhas? I doubt it."

Sally whipped around, the motion knocking her purse to the floor. Who in the world was talking like this? Her hospital-visit smile died on her lips.

A generous-sized woman ambled to the bed. Her double-breasted suit didn't conceal the starched lace ruffle of a high-necked blouse. Coffee-colored eyes were set deep into a plump, wrinkle-free face, making it hard to determine her age. Sixty? Probably more, Sally figured, noting silver glints in tight curls, which were perfect complements for steel in the voice and spine. *At least sixty, maybe even seventy.*

Southern etiquette came in handy, as it usually did. Sally pictured herself in a receiving line and offered her hand. "Good afternoon." She made sure to talk slowly, the drawl in full force. "I'm Sally Stevens, Shamika's instructor at MCC."

A smile battled an otherwise grim countenance. "Good morning, Mrs. Stevens. I'm Ruby Brown, Shamika's aunt." The alto voice had the same rich texture as her skin, her eyes. "Sit down." She pointed to one of two chairs that crowded the tiny space.

Sally obeyed.

"Shamika's told me about you. And your class." Ruby's smile disappeared, her face becoming masklike.

A twinge went through Sally. Had Shamika regaled her aunt with dinner-time discussions of poor teaching? Or was Ruby making reference to the back-row racist mutterings? As if sent by the Holy Spirit, lyrics popped into Sally's head. *God put a rainbow in the sky, a rainbow in the sky . . .* Her smile returned. "Please. It's Sally."

There was a hint of sun through Ruby's gloom. "I appreciate all you done for her. She told me how you like her writing."

"Well, who wouldn't? It's amazing. I mean, I could've sent that Ellis Wilson paper to a refereed journal. The *AA Review* or . . ." Words spewed from Sally like oil from a derrick. "And we'll get her back to writing as soon as we can. In fact, that's why I'm here. Of course, I wanted to see how she's doing, tell her how much all of us at MCC regret what happened."

When Ruby put her hand on her hip, her bosom jiggled. "I'll just bet they do."

"Well, *I* certainly do." Sally's mouth ached from so much grinning. "She looks great, and with all our prayers and the Lord's help, she'll be outta here in no time."

"That's what *I'm* talkin' 'bout. Gotta get *them* talking release date." Ruby's eyes turned velvet soft, then hard as she looked out the window. "Gotta get her outta here. Today or tomorrow at the latest."

Sally craned her neck to follow Ruby's gaze, then grimaced. Patients on this floor were regaled with a view of a windowless concrete hospital wing. Even if the sun did dare to shine, Shamika wouldn't see it. "Oh, I agree." Sally's head bobbed as she talked. "There's nothing like home. And I'll pray for her and—"

Ruby's growl almost lifted Sally out of her seat. "That's the second time you mentioned prayer." Her eyes blazed to match her voice. "You think I ain't done that nonstop? You think we need a white woman to come in here and petition the Lamb for us?" Ruby punctuated each word with a tap of a beige leather pump. "And as for our home, we done left the South long ago. Ain't gonna have another home till He sends for us."

"Really, I know just what you mean." Sally began, eager to prove she was a different type of white. "When we moved up here—"

"You no more know what I mean than a dog knows 'bout a cat."

Shamika's giggle filled the room.

Sally beamed the way she often did when civilized situations went tense. There was no reason to put on armor and unsheathe her sword. Inside, though, every part of her scowled at Shamika's rude giggle, Ruby's uncivilized comment. Here she was, endeavoring to keep the subject light and happy. Things were awkward enough without picking at the racial scabs that covered all of them.

Someone knocked on the door.

Ruby ignored it. "And I'll bet—"

A second knock did what Sally's silent smiles had not managed to accomplish—hushed the room. In the quiet, Sally heard the *beep, beep, beep* and the *whoosh, hiss, whoosh, hiss* of thousands of dollars worth of equipment designed to calibrate and then report on human life.

Ruby jutted out her chin. "Come in."

The same ruddy-faced officer Sally had met earlier stood before them. "Good morning. I'm Detective Price." He offered a hand to Ruby. "Your name, ma'am?"

"I'm Ruby Brown. Shamika's aunt."

Sally tugged at her sleeve, then used her hand as a fan. Should she try to excuse herself, or would that make things even worse?

"Ma'am." The detective nodded in an ambiguous way at Sally.

Ruby thrust out her hip and her upper lip. "'Bout time somebody more than a rookie show up."

"Well, ma'am, Officer Warren—"

"Still got baby powder on his bottom."

Detective Price's neck and forearms reddened to match his face. "I'll try to make this as easy as possible."

Sally stared at her shoes. *Good luck.*

"And if you'd prefer talking to a female officer—"

The tapping of that blasted shoe continued. "Surprised you good ole boys ain't run 'em all off."

The detective pulled out his notepad, a behavior Sally could have predicted. "Well, truth told, we have run most of 'em off, but there's a few stubborn ones still hangin' around."

It was said with such courtesy, such dignity, that Sally's jaw dropped. And so did Ruby's.

"Meantime, if you'd like to talk to one, I have one available."

Ruby's mouth twisted as if she had eaten nails.

"I'll take that as a no." The detective cleared his throat and stepped toward the bed.

Sally took a deep breath, got out of the creaky chair as quietly as she could, then sidled toward the door. This was the cue she'd been waiting for. They could chat education later. Or never. "I'll just run out for a bit, let y'all have some privacy, and—"

"No! I'd like you to stay, Mrs. Stevens."

Sally turned just enough to lock on eyes blazing out from that bruised face. The face of her student. The void of human sound allowed the machines to take over again, with their ticking.

Sally nodded, then sat down on the bed, scooting closer to Shamika, placing herself squarely between shooting lasers from both green-gray eyes and brown eyes. Time would tell which shots would be the most deadly.

◆ ◆ ◆

Thanks to what happened to Daddy, Shamika had never liked five-o's. And with a pounding headache, stabbing pains in her groin, those vile images in her mind, she pretty much hated them right now. Especially this smug-looking, know-it-all cop.

"Ms. Williams, you live with your aunt, Ms. Ruby Brown; is that correct?"

"If you know that, why you wasting our time?"

"And you've lived here for how long now?"

"'Bout four months, give or take."

"You previously resided in Chicago?"

Shamika managed a nod, though it about split open her head.

"And what prompted the move here to Normal?"

Bile rose within Shamika, adding an upset stomach to the other ways her body was assaulting her. She clenched her jaw and swallowed hard. It was none of this cop's business about Charles and her momma. She hadn't even told Auntie 'bout him tryin' to cop a feel. Just said she needed to get outta the 'hood. And Auntie assumed what they all assumed—the drugs, the pimps, the despair. And welcomed her, with down-home cookin' and clean towels, in this podunk place called Normal.

Ruby flew out of her chair, waving her arms like a preacher caught by the Spirit. "It ain't none of yo' business why she stayin' up here."

Great minds think alike. Shamika smiled sweetly at her aunt. But Ruby seemed too busy fixing her paddle-yo'-bottom look on the cop to notice her niece's nonverbal touché.

"Do I need to call a lawyer?" Ruby continued.

Detective Price rubbed his eyes, red and bleary. Probably from stayin' too late at some redneck bar. "As I'm sure both of you know, you're free to call one at any time during this . . . interview." He extended a thick hand toward Mrs. Stevens. "But we've got your instructor here, and you're here."

Steam rose in Shamika at Price's innuendo that this white teacher could stand in for a trained lawyer. Oh, sure, she'd appreciated Mrs. Stevens's enthusiasm, even if she was spacey as some of them street vendors back on Michigan Avenue. Besides, she'd been the one to insist that the woman stay . . . and why had she done that? She wasn't sure. Something about those big eyes, that wide grin, warmed this cold room.

"So I think we could just proceed without . . ." In his placating tone, the cop rambled on, every word so grating, so irritating, Shamika rubbed her aching temples. It was best just to shut up and get on with things. Auntie's secretarial salary couldn't stretch to pay for an attorney. And she sure as heck didn't want no-court-appointed fool. One day, if she could just get through all this, *she'd* be the one with the JD after her name.

"So just do it!" Shamika yelled.

Mrs. Stevens shuddered.

This white woman might'a bit off more than she can chew, if things go like they usually do with cops and us folks. Yet the thought didn't give Shamika quite the satisfaction she'd hoped. She readjusted her pillows, folded her hands, and leaned back. "Sooner you get started, sooner you'll get done."

"Now, Ms. Williams, you say this incident happened—"

"I *say?*" Shamika screeched. "It *did* happen."

"If that college was doin' what it s'pose to, they'd have surveillance. Could'a caught that creep with his pants down." Auntie had taken over again, her voice booming loud enough to include the whole hospital wing in this thing.

The detective seemed unperturbed. "It happened in the south lot?"

"Only one where they let students park. Guess that north lot, with street visibility and easy access and all, ain't good enough for ho's." Shamika folded thin arms across her chest, the motion causing her gown to slip farther off her shoulder. As she covered herself, she thought of the things that man had called her, then fought off tears. Charles had called her that, and worse, when she'd shoved him away and threatened to tell Momma.

"Well, ma'am, you'll have to take up matters of parking and security with the college."

Shamika waved her arms, more trying to get rid of Charles's nasty grin, the raving maniac's toothless smile, than the cop's snide comment. "Don't you know we plan to? Soon as I get outta this . . ." Shamika cursed under her breath, as if street talk would shut out the men who came a' huntin' in her pain-riddled mind. Flinging back the sheets, she thrashed about. Mrs. Stevens scooted off the bed, but not before Shamika grazed her side with an accidental kick.

"You get ahold of yo'self." Ruby lumbered toward her, but Shamika was too busy staring at her legs to pay much attention to her aunt. Nasty bruises made them look like they'd been tie-dyed brown and blue. She touched one, surprised that she hadn't felt the pain before now, then winced. It hurt, all right, along with everything else. She supposed pain overload kept her from passing out. That or a speck of heavenly mercy.

"Uh, look, uh, Miss." Detective Price seemed to have a catch in his throat. "We need—"

Ruby grabbed a sheet corner and jerked. The thin cotton billowed then settled over Shamika with a sigh. "Y'all can't even recollect her name. To you she's just another nigger."

Mrs. Stevens let out a little snort, and Shamika half-expected her to run whimpering from the room. Instead, she clicked right over till she was in the cop's face and gave him one of those fake Southern smiles.

"Detective Price, so nice to see you again." Maple syrup couldn't have dripped more sugar than Mrs. Stevens.

The detective seemed unimpressed.

"You probably don't remember me—I know you meet hundreds of people in your line of work. Of course, it was just this morning."

"Yes, ma'am, and thank you for your help when I spoke to you on campus."

Shamika did a double take. Was the man being sarcastic or polite to her teacher? And why hadn't he said nothing about the earlier meeting? Looked like all kind of games were being played in this room.

"After class, I just had to get up here." If possible, the lipsticked mouth smiled wider. "You see, I'm a friend of the family. That's why I was so upset when you told me the news this morning."

The way the cop's eyes narrowed, Shamika bet he didn't believe a word Mrs. Stevens was saying. And why should he? Nothing but lies were spilling out of that drawly Southern mouth. Shamika didn't know what kinda trip her teacher was on, but she'd bet it had to do with the college trying to weasel out of responsibility for this. *White man's money, same as always, talkin' loud.*

"Well, nice to see you again, ma'am," the cop finally managed.

"I know y'all want to get to the bottom of this, and—"

"Y'all? You're from down South too?"

So now they're gonna have a nice lil' rap session, like we're not even here. Shamika debated letting out a bloodcurdling scream, just to see what they'd do. One of the reasons she planned to go into criminal law was to rid the system of this "good ole whitey" network. Again she folded her arms over her chest, wincing when the IV insert pulled on the skin of her hand. Mrs. Stevens was just like those self-righteous teachers at the magnet school, so desperate to show they weren't prejudiced that they put her on display like a prize hog at the county fair. And then when she didn't grunt just right, or weigh in like they thought she would, they sent her to the slaughterhouse.

"Now, Detective Price," Mrs. Stevens continued, in that annoying drawl that stretched every word like taffy, "we don't want to have to contact the FBI—I mean, I've heard those Feds can get so territorial and all, but this does seem to be a hate crime, and if y'all aren't able to do something—I mean, I totally can understand your workload here in Normal, lost cows and missing bicycles and all." She shrugged her shoulders and, if possible, widened her moony blues.

What's she doin'? Shamika glanced at her aunt just in time to catch her roll her eyes. Mrs. Stevens was lying, just like . . .

"Feds'll only get involved if this proves out to be a hate crime, ma'am." Green lasers fired at Mrs. Stevens. "But if you can convince them to get involved, I'll be glad to work with them. And until then . . ." The detective's back bent as he pulled a chair close to the bed. He sat down, flipped open his notes, and turned all his attention to Shamika. "Let me first express our condolences." His voice gleamed and glittered, not counterfeit, but not genuine, either. "Second, I want to assure you that we'll do our best to lock up whoever did this."

She might as well get this over with and get him outta here. With a nod and a harrumph, she settled back on the pillows and released her lips from the pout she'd held steady ever since the cop came in the room.

A file folder emerged from somewhere within Detective Price's sports coat. He appeared to scan a typewritten page. "Officer Warren got a copy of the doctor's report, so we don't need to go over that again."

"I should surely hope not."

"Ms. Williams." As if to stop Auntie from interrupting, the detective sped forward. "Do you know the person who did this to you?"

It hurt to sit up straight, but Shamika managed. No matter what he said, this was an interrogation, and she'd better be careful if she was going through with this. "You mean scumbags?"

The detective fished in his pocket, pulled out a crisp handkerchief, and wiped his brow. "I'm sorry—we all are—that you had to be subjected to that."

Shamika gave a slight nod. He was a jerk, but he could be worse.

"Now, back to the suspect." He leaned so close to the bed that his hand grazed the sheet. "What can you tell me?"

"They . . . were . . . white . . . men." With blazing eyes, Shamika started reading the detective, then her teacher, daring them to argue with her.

Detective Price's eyebrows became question marks. He scribbled into his notepad for quite a while. "That's the first I've heard of this."

"Well, that's 'cause you ain't been listenin'." She thought of how they'd tried to tell the cops Daddy hadn't owned a gun. But they'd never listened. Instead, some fat white pig all decked out in blue had stamped "Closed" on the inquest folder. And Daddy'd been buried as just another loser black man stirring up trouble in the wrong neighborhood.

Those weird-colored eyes locked on and intercepted her anger, and Shamika had to work to keep from looking away. "You said 'they,'" he finally managed. "How many were there?"

"Three."

"Three, you say?" The cop took the gravel out of his voice and replaced it with disbelief. "Anything unusual about them?"

As if the number three were freaky or something. Shamika shrugged her shoulders and stuck out her lip. "How should I know? Y'all all look alike."

Mrs. Stevens sighed so long, so loud, that her bosom jiggled, and for a moment, Shamika regretted her teacher seeing this side of her. Then she thought of all those other teachers, setting her up as the "Great Black Hope," and what had happened when she hadn't aced the SAT, like they'd all planned. Of course, they hadn't known what happened with Charles the night before. She pressed her lips together. No one would ever know, not Momma, not Aunt Ruby. It would hurt them too much.

Detective Price clicked his pen but didn't seem to react in any other way. "Short hair? Long hair? Facial hair?"

Shamika froze, then blinked, but it didn't help rid her mind of the awful image that had nothing to do with facial hair.

The detective pressed on. "If you didn't see facial hair because of the poor lighting conditions, did you feel it?" He seemed to study Shamika's face for rashes. "Any abrasions? Tickling?"

Questions hung in the air like smoke over a pool table.

"A large man? Small? Big hands? Little—"

"Tall. Skinny." With a huff, she sat up straight and glared resolve into her system. If she couldn't convince this man, she'd never convince a jury. "After he slapped me, then pounded me with his fists, all the while sayin' he gonna kill me, I kinda shut down. And when he tore my hair out"—she ducked her head but kept her eyes on him, trying to decide if he was buying any of it—"and I screamed, he said he'd carve me like a turkey if I made another sound." Her arms clapped together when she folded them across her chest. "Then I kinda blacked out . . . kinda. Still heard all them words from the back seat. Called me everything and anything. Mother—" Obscenities streamed yet again from Shamika, but they were just words. She couldn't summon the hate they demanded.

Whoosh, whoosh, psst, whoosh. The machines had their way with the room. Shamika lay back in the covers, unsure if she could sit up again. This man threatened to drain the very fluids those machines were desperately trying to pump into her.

Click, click. Even with her eyes closed, Shamika knew Auntie was going to the door.

The clicking stopped. "I think she been through enough for now," came from around the partition.

"Well, ma'am, I would like to get some additional photos."

"You got yo'self a nice little collection?" Auntie hollered as she huffed back into the room.

Shamika's eyes fluttered open just in time to see the detective nod at Mrs. Stevens and amble over to her aunt. The pen and notebook disappeared into his coat. "Tell you what, ma'am. I'll get my equipment, get the female uniform to come up here—"

"Black or white?"

"It's colored now. And digital." Detective Price turned and winked at Mrs. Stevens. "We haven't used black-and-white film for years." Out came business cards, which the man dealt like it was poker night. With a nod, he left the room.

He couldn't have gotten to the elevator when Ruby turned to Sally, her hands on wide hips. "Why'd you tell him that?"

Mrs. Stevens, who'd been messing with her fingernails during the last exchange, raised her eyebrows and looked at Auntie. "Tell him what?"

Ruby pointed at Sally, then at Shamika. "That we're friends."

Good question, Auntie. Shamika fought dull aches and sharp pains and groaned her way to a more upright position. What *was* this crazy woman up to?

The way Mrs. Stevens closed her eyes, she seemed to be praying. She pressed her hands together, then got that wide-eyed look again. "Well, Ruby, we're all Southerners, right?" Even with that drawl, words flew out of her mouth. "And Shamika and I adore Ellis Wilson and Gayl Jones and . . ." She wiggled about as if she had on a too-tight girdle. "Did you know your niece is a cubist?"

It started as a growl, from deep inside Auntie, then bubbled up like a batch of cooking fudge, rich and sweet and full of promise. "Lord, Lord. I don't know what a cubist is and don't think I want to. But sounds like you sho' nuff gotten to know my girl." In that seesaw way she had of favoring her bad knee, Auntie moved forward until she stood an arm's length from Mrs. Stevens. "I believe I owe you an apology, ma'am. But you still ain't got a clue of what it's like to be a black woman, marked like Cain the day the doc slaps you on the hiney." Her eyes narrowing, she thrust out her hip at a right angle. "Where yo' people from, anyway?"

"Texas. Louisiana." Mrs. Stevens's eyes got misty, like she'd just read a favorite old children's book.

"Louisiana?" Auntie's voice cut through the mist. "Get outta here."

"Us too," Shamika added, even though she remembered nothing about Louisiana but a gator farm and a back yard crammed full of smiling cousins.

"Monroe for me."

"We got her godmother down in N'Awlins." Pointing at Shamika, Auntie beamed.

"My brother's down there now. And maybe . . ." That moony look returned to the woman's blue eyes. ". . . an old friend."

"Did yo' brother get through all right?"

"Yeah. They live across the bridge. Their neighborhood didn't get hit too bad, just some water damage. A couple of roof repairs, and they were good to go."

"Across what bridge? The 'Keep Out Blacks' bridge?" Auntie finally asked, wrinkles creasing her forehead.

Oh, no. Shamika braced herself for more ugly talk. Surely this woman had more sense than to bring up The Bridge. But then it was always a bridge, where their folk and whites were concerned.

Mrs. Stevens nodded. "I know what you mean." To compound her stupid comment, she giggled like a little girl. "It's so—"

"And what you think you know about it?"

The words flew out of Shamika and her aunt at the same time, slammed into Mrs. Stevens, and seemed to push her toward the wall. But her teacher didn't whimper a mushy good-bye and scuttle out of the room, as Shamika expected. Instead, she stared toward the window, then bowed her head, mumbling like she was speaking in tongues. Finally her head snapped up, and she practically marched to one of the chairs near the bed and sat down.

"Okay, I'm white," she said, her voice smooth as Auntie's banana pudding. "I can't change that. But I can tell you a thing or two. She gestured for Ruby to sit next to her, and to Shamika's surprise, her aunt obeyed.

"Maybe it'll help y'all trust me," Mrs. Stevens continued. "And if you've got time, I'd like to tell you about them now."

Shamika stretched, trying to feign disinterest. "Well, sure, I've got time. I'm not goin' anywhere."

"Not right now you aren't." Mrs. Stevens crossed her legs, as if she were settling in for quite a spell. "But after you're out of here, I hope we can move on to something really important. Like your education." She paused, and Shamika could feel those blue eyes on her, demanding a response. Stiffly, as if her neck hurt, Shamika turned and allowed what seemed like genuine kindness and warmth to wash over her. She waited until those eyes softened her like butter. Then she nodded.

◆ ◆ ◆

Sally couldn't tear her eyes away from the bruised girl on the bed, yet she really wasn't seeing Shamika. Dust mote memories floated about, threatening to take over. A rooftop conversation, Colored Town, Ella's face, bone-jarring pain, a bloody rock, scribbled secret notes.

Tell them what you're remembering.

When Sally tried to take hold of each memory, it vanished, and so did her desire to speak.

Tell, Sally. Now.

A still, small voice moved in, even though she clasped her hands over her knees, bowed her head, and argued with the Presence that shone over the little gray particles, revealing them in a different light. *I can't tell them all this, just out of the blue. And where would I start? It's too much. Too little. Too long ago. Too soon. And how could it help this angry black girl? I do want to help her, Lord. Isn't that why You sent me here?*

The memories clumped together, in a way that made sense. But Sally continued to resist them. She hadn't even told Sam. How could she tell these women she barely knew?

Brilliant light seared the particles, magnifying dust and grime, then purifying them as only His presence could. Sally sat still and let the Spirit speak.

I am what I am . . . the God of all comfort, who comforts us in our troubles so that we can comfort those in any trouble . . .

The words spread a glow throughout Sally, and she bowed her head to His greatness. *Lord, I don't want to,* she prayed. *I'm afraid of where it might end.*

Do not let your heart be troubled. And do not be afraid.

A final prayer seemed to rein in the last of the fragments; Sally was ready now. She breathed deep, then smiled. "Okay, I'm white," she said, shrugging. "I can't change that. But I can tell you a few things I know, starting with my first memory . . ."

Chapter 4

FIRST MEMORIES

Talk together, children, don't you get weary . . .
—Negro spiritual, "Talk Together, Children"

Summer 1959, Martin Hall, Baylor University, Waco, Texas

The first floor of the athletic dorm had gotten quiet. But that didn't mean things weren't happening behind swinging hall doors. This time of day, after college classes and before sports practice, Sally's brothers did magic tricks and played cards, even went to the moon. And if Sally got her way, she was going with them. She begged her legs to slow down as she edged closer to the plate-glass window that gave a view of the switchboard and the dorm director's office. Her daddy's office. According to some of her brothers, the SOB's office, whatever that meant. She peeked into the window, then broke out into a smile. Her daddy's chair, the one the brothers called the throne, was empty. "Yippee!" Sally's insides fueled up. It was time to get on her spaceship and fly to the moon.

Sure that Mother was lost in her new painting, Sally skipped past their apartment and tugged at the heavy stairwell door. She couldn't afford to wait for the elevator, not with Daddy liable to appear any minute. Finally she got it open. She clattered up two sets of stairs, flew past what seemed like a hundred dorm rooms, and in no time stood before the exit sign, its eerie green glow sending a shiver through her. Would Tommy be on the moon too? Would he and the other brothers show her how to light a firecracker, teach her to play that card game whose name she never could remember? She put her ear against the metal door and, hearing nothing, gave the secret knock—three raps, then a slap of her palm against the entrance to the moon, which really wasn't the moon at all but the dorm roof. But Sally loved to pretend, and when she stood near the concrete ledge and peered down onto tree-lined sidewalks and scurrying students, she felt like God must feel when He looked down on earth. And the fact that she wasn't supposed to be up on the boys' floors, much less the roof, made it even more exciting.

Sally leaned against the door, straining to hear voices. There was a faint rustle, like leaves on an oak. Except there were no trees on the roof. It was the brothers! Jumping up and down, Sally tried the secret knock again.

The door creaked open. Water hissed from the cooling tower that air-conditioned the dorm. The door opened wider. A brown eye stared at Sally. A mouth flew open. "What's she doin' here?"

"This ain't good."

"It's okay. She won't tell."

Voices streamed toward Sally, one trumping all the others. It was Tommy, the star pitcher, her favorite brother. A smile started deep in Sally and grew until she laughed. She pushed against the door so hard that sweat beaded her forehead. When it flew open, she half-stumbled, half-fell, onto the moon.

"Whaddya doin', Dimples?" Tommy bent over and pulled Sally off the sticky hot asphalt. Pea-sized gravel stuck to her knees.

Sally dusted off her legs, a grimace on her face. It always smelled like tar and burned rubber up here, but today there was something different. Like burning leaves and pepper and cotton candy, all mixed together. "What's that smell?" she asked Tommy, then stepped toward hunched backs.

A group of brothers sat cross-legged around an old fruit crate. The brother who was a quarterback, a cigar clamped between his teeth, dealt cards to the others. Eyes rolled, shoulders shrugged. Heads ducked behind fanned-out cards.

"Hey." Tommy put a calloused hand over hers and tugged her away from the table. "Let's check out the earthlings down there."

Coughing, Sally shook her head. Last time she'd almost figured this game out. She'd stood real still and didn't interrupt.

"I tell you, it's not a good idea."

"If the SOB finds out, we're dead meat."

Tommy patted Sally on the head. "She ain't hurting anything. Besides, she'll never tell. He'd tan her hide if he found out."

The card-playing brothers groaned and shrugged but didn't say she had to leave. Careful not to move, Sally studied the hearts and spades and diamonds and puppy-feet suit. Sure enough, the brothers seemed to forget she was there and began chattering about mean coaches and cute girls. A blond brother groaned when he got the queen of spades. Another brother wrote scores on a piece of paper. Yet another brother scooped up the cards and shuffled them.

"That's the second time I got that ugly mother," came from the blond brother.

"Speakin' of spades, that spade ain't bein' recruited after all." The quarterback brother puffed on his cigar, then set it on the edge of the table.

The boys pulled their cards close to their chest and stared. "Whaddya mean?"

"Some bigwig alum says it ain't biblical. Don't mix with foreigners and all that. And Coach says we ain't ready for it."

"Well, we'd better get ready for it. Them bunnies are movin' into everything. It's just a matter of time till they'll be here too."

Sally only half-listened. What did "being recruited" mean, anyway?

"The stupid jigs. They—" The blond brother stared at Sally, suddenly quiet.

"Hey. If they can play ball, I say bring 'em on."

"And *you're* gonna room with a jungle bunny?"

The brother winning the card game leaned across the box and jabbed the blond brother in the chest. "No! You are."

Even though Sally knew this was a time when she should keep quiet, she just couldn't, not with the questions swirling. "Hey, y'all," she blurted out, hopping around the table, "what's a jungle bunny?"

"Well, now . . ." For some reason, the quarterback stammered like something was stuck in his throat. "It's your play, Hank," he said, glaring at no one in particular.

Sally stuck out her lip, then let the images of fluffy, cuddly rabbits take over. Her shoes crunched against the gravelly surface as she hop, hop, hopped about. She was the first rabbit on the moon. She was Little Bunny FuFu, hiding in the—

The roof door arced open, then slammed against the brick wall.

"I'll be . . ."

"It's Doc!"

Cards floated over the table, then fluttered down. Gravel flew. Brothers scrambled to their feet. Like he was heaving a last-second pass, the quarterback hurled his cigar over the side of the moon.

"Freeze!" Shrill as a whistle, Daddy's voice cut through the sound of shoes skidding across gravel.

Her hop long gone, Sally scurried to Tommy, clung to his legs, and tried to hide behind his back. She'd gotten a spanking for riding her bike down the hall, much less this. Even though she wanted to be brave in front of the brothers, she couldn't. Little sniffles found a way out of her, and her body shook.

"It's okay," Tommy whispered, taking hold of her arm and pulling her close. "I'll tell him it was my idea."

Condensation from the water cooler seemed to have formed a mist about the door, which was now propped open with a metal chair. With his shoulders hunched up, Daddy looked more boulderlike than ever. Sweat glistened his jet black crew cut and poured down his tanned face. In one hand, he held a baseball bat. His other hand, fingers spread, gripped the waistband of his green sweatpants.

Brothers sucked in their breath, pulling more air from the steamy rooftop. *They* were scared of him and didn't know half of what she knew.

Sweat mixed with tears and stung Sally's eyes, the sobs becoming hiccups, which she desperately tried to suck in. Crying would only make Daddy madder and would guarantee a spanking.

Daddy pounded across the gravel, clearing a path as he swung the bat. "Where is she?" he thundered.

The brothers parted like the waters of the Red Sea, all except Tommy, who clamped his hand on Sally's shoulder.

As Daddy got closer, Tommy shrank back, back, back until Sally's universe was reduced to her red-faced, heavy-breathing father. And her trembling self.

Boys scuttled for the door.

"Freeze!" Again Daddy's voice echoed across the rooftop.

Shoes scuffed against gravel; then all was quiet.

Daddy grabbed Sally's slick arm, his fingers biting into her skin. "I'll be back for you gentlemen," he said, without taking his eyes off Sally. After he spoke, his lips pressed so tight, they almost disappeared.

Sally winced. Would she get a spanking? Or just a talking-to? She wanted to become a bunny again and somehow hop out of Daddy's grasp, but that was impossible, especially now that he'd picked her up. With a jerk and a grunt, the bat still in his hand, he led her past wide-eyed brothers.

Tommy waved and gave Sally a sad smile, as if he too feared a spanking.

The whimper started deep in Sally as Daddy thudded down the stairs. All the signs were there for a spanking. Tight lips, boiling eyes, and, worst of all, silence.

Sally buried her head into Daddy's thick chest. It wasn't comfortable, not with the bat occasionally conking her in the head, but she didn't dare move. And she didn't dare cry either. Just more whimpers.

The front door of their dorm apartment responded to a shove from Daddy's shoulder. Two, three, four steps, and they were in the kitchen.

A frown creased Mama's brow. She put down a can of paint, then cleared her sketch pad and drawings off the bar that served both as their table and her art studio. Her doughnutlike bun threatened to tumble loose, the way she was shaking her head, and the same red and blue paint that had spattered her faded dungarees streaked her cheeks. She glanced toward Sally's room, then back at Sally. "Where've you been? I thought you were taking a nap." Mama's eyebrows arched, her chin dropped, until her whole face became a question mark. "Why are you so sweaty?"

Sally tried to bury her face in Daddy's chest. Usually Mama took up for her when Daddy was mad, but today, Sally didn't think that would happen.

Daddy plopped her down on a stool. He strode into the kitchen, grabbed a towel, and used it to mop off Sally's face. "She was on the roof."

Mother's mouth flew open, so wide, Sally could see the silver fillings on her back teeth. "On the roof?" Her voice came out like the caw of a crow.

The whine resumed in Sally's belly and rumbled out. She knew what was coming next, and even though she was worried about the spanking, she was almost as worried about the next thing—no more playing with the brothers.

Daddy jerked her off the stool, then popped her on the bottom with the towel. "Get in your room," he said, his voice tight, "or I'll give you something to cry about."

Even though her bottom stung, Sally didn't make a sound as she streaked toward her room. If that was all Daddy was going to do, she'd gotten off easy.

"You said she was on the roof. What, exactly, happened?" Mother asked.

A stool scraped across the kitchen floor.

Sally stopped short. She had to listen to this. Her life might depend on it.

A cabinet creaked open, then something tinny slammed against the countertop.

Daddy sighed, so loud, it sounded more like a snort. "One of the janitors found some cigar butts, some empty bottles of booze. I guess they've been playing cards up there. So I went up to check. And there was . . . Sally."

Sally leaned closer, careful not to make a sound.

"Cards? Cigars?" Something thunked onto the counter. "That switchboard stunt was one thing. But she could've killed herself up there, could've—"

A twinge went through Sally. Last week, when Tommy had been night operator, he'd let her say, "Martin Hall, can I help you," then stick colored cords in the right holes. How could they have known the college president would call the athletic dorm so late?

"You don't have to overreact. Tommy was up there and—"

Mother snorted. "Tommy? The one who let her man the switchboard? The one who taught her the words to 'Tom Dooley'?" Somehow Mother had drained off the anger from Daddy's voice and taken it into her own.

"Look. She'll be in school soon and won't have time for all this." Suddenly Daddy was pleading with Mother, almost as if he was the one trying to get out of trouble.

"We'll still be living here."

"Now, Ann, we agreed to this. You know how long it takes to get one degree, much less two. Especially while supporting a family."

Sally cringed. Were they going to rehash Daddy's degree plan? She dragged into the old closet that they called her bedroom and plopped backward onto her bed, partly relieved that she hadn't gotten a real spanking, partly sad at the way Mother talked about their home. Why didn't Mother love the dorm like she and Daddy did? She folded her arms across her chest and stared at the ceiling.

Dumbo trumpeted a wake-up call to the Seven Dwarfs, who marched off to the mines, picks and shovels on their shoulders. And Rapunzel's golden locks curled around the tiny space, vines for chimpanzees and toucans to hang on. As she let Mother's poster board paintings take her to another place, the stiffness left Sally's shoulders, the smile returned to her face. Mama had done so much to make this closet a real little girl's bedroom. And if Mama just didn't understand about the brothers, Sally would have to grin and bear it. In fact, that's what Mama always said when things didn't go right. *"Just grin and bear it, Sally."* Then Mama'd plaster a red-lipstick smile across her face and plow into cooking or cleaning as if the smile had set her on fire. Mama. Sally jumped from the bed. She just wanted to hug both of them now, which would let them know that she was sorry about the trip to the moon. She ran toward the kitchen, then stopped short at the heat in Mama's voice.

"I just don't know how much longer it can go on."

"It has to go on."

Daddy spoke so quietly, he was hard to hear over the gurgle of percolating coffee. To catch each word, Sally tiptoed around the fridge, then peeked at Daddy. Lines still cut into his jaws and his eyes.

"But the rooftop?" Mama's voice rose to a shriek. "Honestly!" Mother kept pulling on Daddy, stretching him like a rubber band. And if Sally knew her father, any minute now, he was going to snap.

"It's just boys, horsing around after class." A growl had entered Daddy's voice.

"That's the problem. She's not a boy. And as far as her being up there—"

"Whose fault is that?"

Mama, her face as red as the glowing burner, stepped to the stove, grabbed the pot, and sloshed coffee into two cups.

Sally pressed against the wall. The room was so small, Mama had to see her, unless the argument was grabbing hold of Mama's eyes and blocking everything else. She glanced at Mama, then let her breath out. They weren't that mad . . . yet.

"I'm here all day in six hundred square feet, and—"

"Be glad we have it."

Sally hunched her shoulders. Now Mama and Daddy *were* at war, their voices battling for control.

"You don't have a clue what I'm going through."

Daddy downed coffee with long, slow slurps, then sighed. "We've been up and down and around this. She starts school next week."

"And why didn't it start up when the college did?"

Daddy threw his hands into the air. "What does her school have to do with this?"

"It's all rolled together, and it's got to stop. Her hopping around like—"

"Like what?" There was a rumble in Daddy's voice that sent a cringe through Sally. This was her chance, and if she didn't take it now, the war would get worse, she was sure of it. Her heart plopping, she flew to the bar. "Mama, Daddy, what's a jungle bunny?"

Her parents got so still, the only motion in the room was steam curling from their coffee cups.

"And where did you hear that, young lady?" Mama finally asked, the lines about her mouth so tight, it looked like her face might crack.

"On the roof," Sally said, her eyes on the floor.

Mama blotted her lips with a napkin, then threw it down. "See what hanging out with them does? Up there talking about Negroes? No tellin' what else she heard."

Sally climbed onto a stool, most of her concern about the fight vanishing in light of this new fact. So jungle bunnies were Negroes. And Negroes were coloreds. And Sally already knew coloreds were so dangerous, they had to be herded up and corralled into their own part of town. Yet the quarterback said they might come to college. Was that the real reason behind this fight? That she might have a jungle bunny brother?

Daddy banged his cup onto the bar, rattling the sugar bowl and some spoons.

Sally leaned closer, eager to help them get through the war but more eager to hear about jungle bunnies. She'd never seen a colored person, had always wondered about Colored Town. And now that coloreds might live here in the dorm, she had to find out more. "It's okay," she said, waving her arms. "I could be the jungle bunny's sister, like I am the other . . ." One glance at her mother shut Sally's mouth. She couldn't be a sister to a jungle bunny. What had she been thinking?

Mama hugged her arms to her chest. "It most certainly isn't okay, young lady. And these dorm boys aren't your brothers."

"Tommy said they were."

"Well, now, they are." Daddy leaned back on his stool until it groaned. "Annie, they're kinda like brothers."

Licking her lips, Sally nodded. "Yeah—I mean, yes, sir. Sorta brother pals."

Mama used both hands to straighten her bun, which had tilted and made her head look lopsided. "But they're not family. Family lives in the same house, uses the same bathroom—"

"I've been in their bathroom." As soon as the words came out, Sally wanted to suck them back in. But of course she couldn't.

Mama jerked her head so sharply that her bun slid off its perch and seemed to be suspended from the side of her head.

Sally covered her mouth with her hand. If she laughed, she positively would get spanked. But if she hurried, just about now . . . Sally slid off the stool, plopped her feet onto the floor, and tugged on her father's shirt, her mind full of strange-looking black creatures that went hop, hop, hop. "Can I ride my bike?"

Her face stern, Mama fussed with her hair. "If you think for one minute—"

"Not down the hall, Mama. Outside."

When Mama nodded, the bun jumped up and down. Then she set her scowl on Daddy like she'd never stopped. "You didn't answer my question."

"What *was* your question?"

"My question is, what are you going to do about this?"

Sally tiptoed to her room, grabbed a nickel and the rag dolls that she pretended were her family when the brothers weren't around, then checked the clock before she darted out the door. They were so busy fighting each other, Sally was sure they'd forgotten about the spanking. Daddy would follow up with those poor brothers on the moon and Mama would get captured by her painting and dinner wasn't for another hour and a half. Suddenly Sally was hopping and skipping, a bunny and a spaceman all rolled into one, flying across the quadrangle just like the students did when they were late for class. She was going to Colored Town.

◆

If even half of this is true, no wonder she's so crazy. Shamika raked fingernails across her arms, wondering if she was allergic to that cream they spread thick or that IV tape pulling on her skin. Her brain cells itched too. What was her first memory of Whitey? Probably that day The Man came collecting the rent. She rustled about the bed, itchy with questions. "How old you say you were?"

"Six. Nearly seven."

"And you hadn't seen a black person yet?"

Mrs. Stevens shook her head. "I know it seems crazy, but—"

Auntie's forehead became rutted like a South Side street. "You expect me to believe that in the South, you ain't never set eyes on a black person?"

Sweat and a red flush popped out on Mrs. Stevens's face. She mopped her brow, rubbed her chest, wiggled about like she was having a conniption fit. Yet that goofy smile didn't budge. "Not until I disobeyed Mama and Daddy. All of them, really. I just had to see for myself. I had to venture into Colored Town."

Shamika nodded, though Mrs. Stevens couldn't have a clue what she was thinking. In her own way, this lady was allowing her a ramble into White Town. Whether she liked it or not, whether the stories were true or not, they'd grabbed ahold of those more recent painful memories and had stuffed them into a musty old closet. And if Mrs. Stevens kept talking, maybe they'd stay there.

Chapter 5

COLORED TOWN

Oh, way over Jordan, view the land, view the land.
—Negro spiritual, "View the Land"

C ome on, y'all! We gotta hurry." Propelled by imagination and squeaky wagon wheels, Sally pulled the dolls she'd named after the Boxcar Children on sidewalks that curled through oaks and magnolias. Past the Student Union, she broke into a run, her cheeks puffing as the wagon clattered along behind. When they sped past redbrick buildings and veered at a corner bench, Benny and Henry flopped out.

A couple, holding hands like her parents often did, giggled and waved. Some days Sally stopped to talk. Sometimes dorm boys would piggyback her to the statue of Patt Neff, the founder of the university, and with a grunt and a foothold, boost her onto a big bronze lap. But today Sally had no time for things like that.

"Now, you gotta stay put." She clucked her tongue as she put her dolls back in the wagon. "And don't even be askin' about Colored Town. 'Cause you're not goin'." The campus became a kaleidoscope of greens and browns as Sally clattered on. When coeds squealed and jumped out of her way, everything but their beehive hairdos jiggled. Boys in belted trousers and collared shirts waved their arms and whistled. "Go faster, little one! Faster!" Even oaks and pecans rustled their own cheer.

Sally sprinted to the corner, then leaned against the light pole at the intersection of University and Fifth. Her chest heaving, she stared past the Forsgaards' store and into Colored Town. Dare she do it? A shiver ran through her as she slipped her sweaty hand into her pocket and fingered her nickel. Surely old man Forsgaard would've left by now. And the students who worked this shift wouldn't know Sally. Better yet, they wouldn't know Daddy. Sally licked her lips, all the running making her thirsty. She'd get a soda, then sneak into Colored Town. Soon she'd understand the mystery about those creatures.

Sally turned her head and scanned the quad, deserted this time of day. And thank goodness. Daddy had spies everywhere. Satisfied, she looked back at the store, picturing the red cooler that kept the ice-cold drinks. It was the last encouragement she needed. She parked the wagon near the base of the streetlight and streaked across the crosswalk, her heart racing. Daddy's words followed: *"It's not safe even in broad daylight, not for white folks."*

She tiptoed over trampled grass and peeked around the storefront. The same oaks and pecans that shaded the campus were on this side of Fifth. But yonder in Colored Town, the trees waved spooky limbs, just like in storybook forests. Sally tried to ignore the painful thuds of her heart against her chest, warning her about this strange breed of people with dark skin. That's how they got colored, wasn't it, with some kind of paint? But clowns painted their faces, and they weren't scary, they were funny. Sally swallowed down her fear and stepped toward Forsgaard's. She just didn't understand. Soon she would, but that drink was gonna come first. Her mouth watered, just thinking about the fizzy, sugary taste.

The front door, plastered with signs announcing daily specials, creaked open. She'd get a grape Nehi, then get an eyeful of those half-human, half-devil creatures. It was a shame the kids couldn't come along, but she wouldn't risk their lives. Plus, with that clackety-clack wagon, that yackety-yak Violet, it'd be hard to get in and out. That Violet. She was—

"Well, if it isn't Sally Flowers!"

He'd worked late. Sally's heart flew into her throat. When she tried to speak, nothing came out.

Mr. Forsgaard set down a crate of bananas, tilted a straw hat back from a tousle of snowy hair, and bored blue eyes into Sally. "Whatever are you doin', this side of the street? And all alone, at that."

A thousand stories ran through Sally's head; one by one, she let them go. He knew her parents. He was going to tell. She had to think of something to stop him.

Mr. Forsgaard stepped close. He wiped his hands on a grimy apron, then touched her shoulder.

It was the unexpected gentleness after the sharp words that made her go limp. "I'm sorry," she said. "I didn't mean to." She held up the nickel, lies about to pour out. But good lies, not bad lies. Story lies. "We found this on the quad, me and my dolls." She pointed out the front window, hoping the old eyes could see her dolls, her wagon, across the street. "And I was hot and I wanted a drink." With her eyes, Sally tried to plead her case, but she had to rub out tears first. "You won't tell, will you?"

Mr. Forsgaard chuckled.

Sally cringed. Did he think this was funny? She'd be paddled like never before, and all he could do was laugh?

"Come on." He led Sally past crates of produce and shelves of funny-smelling spices. A cloud of cold air gushed out of the red cooler when he opened it. He rolled up his shirtsleeve, then pulled out a purple bottle beaded with condensation. His brow furrowed as he used the bottle opener on the side of the cooler to pop off a shiny metal cap. Turning to Sally, he patted her on the head, then handed her the fizzing Nehi. "Your secret's safe, little one," he said. "And keep yer nickel for next time."

He understands! Sally threw her arms around his waist and buried her head in an apron smelling like the musty storeroom in the dorm. It was just the way her grandpa would've handled it. She wiped the last trace of tears. Almost like Grandpa, anyway.

With the same gentle movement as when he'd touched her shoulder, Mr. Forsgaard knelt by Sally. "But you need to promise me something."

Sally nodded. He was like Grandpa, after all. With Grandpa, there was always a trade. Mr. Forsgaard worked the same way, trading the bottle for a promise. Sally knew before he said a word what the promise would be about. And Sally planned to forget her dangerous plans and keep her promise.

Mr. Forsgaard handed her the bottle, a tight jaw telling her to listen good. "Don't disobey your parents, child. They know what's best." Then he tottered down an aisle and began shelving canned peaches.

Her heart light, Sally skipped out of the store. Cars zipped along University, giving her a chance to chug down the syrupy grape drink before she crossed the street and went back home. She had planned to go to Colored Town, but the promise she'd made to Mr. Forsgaard changed everything. With a gulp, she finished the drink and wiped purple off her mouth and onto her arm. She'd just cross the street, play with her dolls, perhaps go—

"*Psst.*"

Sally ignored the sound. It was just a leaky tire, a motor scooter putt-putting. *"Psst.* You."

Sally clenched her right hand into a fist. Somebody behind her—from Colored Town—was making that noise. Whirling around, Sally raised her left arm, bending it into a stiff angle, her fingers grasping for a better hold on the bottleneck.

A boy about Sally's height stood under an oak tree just behind the store, his face hidden by spooky shadows. Skinny legs poked out of ragged blue jeans. When he stepped toward Sally, she jumped back.

"Come here." He crooked a finger toward Sally. Sunlight beamed across his face, now that he was out from under the canopy of branches and leaves. His eyes were the same chocolate color of his skin, which was so smooth, Sally knew it wasn't painted on. And she knew something else now and wanted to kick herself for being so dumb. Colored people looked like the Africans in *National Geographic*. Why hadn't she realized that?

"You a scaredy cat?" he asked.

Sally shook her head. Even though it was true, she wouldn't admit it. Aching to be brave, she stepped closer, closer.

"Why you over here?" he asked.

Something about the way he held his head high, like he owned the place, lit a fire in Sally. She stuck out her hip—and her lip. "'Cause I wanna be."

The boy bored eyes into Sally, as if to show her who was boss, but they had the opposite effect he intended. Those eyes were hazel, just like Daddy's. In fact, he looked like Daddy, with his high cheekbones and strong jaw. Something opened up in Sally as she wiped clammy hands on her shorts. She wasn't afraid of this boy. And she was going to show him how she felt. Ask people questions to warm them up, Mama always said. And Mama sure knew how to be nice to folks. "Does your mama have brown eyes?" she asked, fighting a wavery voice. "Or blue? See, my daddy's—"

"Trade ya a fishhook for that." He stepped yet closer, pointing to the Nehi, his hand grazing hers.

The touch electrified Sally, and she nearly dropped the empty bottle. But the boy got holding-your-breath still, calming her a bit. Questions welled up, like her mind was a soda that had been shaken up. Did he get darker if he sunbathed? Was it really dangerous over here? But she didn't ask those. "Why? What do you want it for?" she finally managed to squeak out.

"Ole man over dere, he trade us greens and turnips for 'em."

He talked funny, letters rolling out soft and lazy like they were doing flips in the air. And Sally wanted to hear more. "Why does he want empty old bottles?"

"For his corn likker. May-o-nnaise jars better, but I ain't found none."

A nervous feeling returned when things got quiet except for an occasional whoosh of traffic. Eager to fill the silence, Sally wiped off the bottle lip with the front of her shirt. She'd show him Tommy's trick. Then maybe he'd talk some more. She blew on the bottle until it whistled. "Can you do that?"

The boy threw back his head, laughter bubbling from him like the creek waters after a heavy rain.

It made Sally want to sound like him, look like him. And she wanted him to like her too. She smiled her best smile, then handed him the bottle.

A car honked.

The boy ducked his head, revealing close-cut, fuzzy hair. Sally'd never seen anything like it, except for clothes-dryer lint. Yet it didn't scare her. Not at all.

Dong-dong—

Sally stiffened. Why were the campus chimes going off? It hadn't been an hour, had it? She was going to be in big trouble now.

Dong-dong—

Without saying a word, Sally turned and ran across the street like a dog was chasing her.

"Hey. You ain't got your fishhook. Hey!"

Sally grabbed the handle of her wagon and kept running, barely glancing at the rag dolls.

A few students slumped across the quadrangle. Her heart pounding, sweat pouring off her face, Sally slowed her pace too. Every so often, she studied the pink, white, and tan faces of the students she passed. When they smiled at her, for some reason she couldn't explain, she didn't want to smile back. She made herself, because that's what Mama had taught her, but her heart wasn't behind it. They were so pale, so dull . . .

It seemed to take forever, but Sally finally got home. She shoved her wagon against the flower bed where she sometimes played, grabbed the dolls by their hair, and dragged up the steps.

"Hey, li'l sister." Tommy picked her up and twirled her around.

When he set her down, she bent over and got Violet, whom she'd dropped, gave Tommy a small smile, then went inside. Tommy wasn't really her brother, after all. Her dolls weren't real family either.

In their apartment, Mama hummed as she stirred a pot. Her back to

Sally, she spooned something out of another pot, and took the lid off the deep fat fryer.

The sizzles hinted at what one strong sniff confirmed—fried chicken. It was an overwhelming aroma—most days. But today Sally wasn't hungry.

"Hey, shut that door, Sally!" Mama called. "The air's on."

When Sally obeyed, the click of the lock seemed final and cold.

"Where have you been?" Tendrils of hair escaped Mama's bun and bobbed about the nape of her neck as she bent over and opened the oven. The yeasty, buttery aroma of biscuits drifted Sally's way. So did a vinegary leafy smell.

Sally rested a sweaty hand on the cool Formica bar. If she told the truth, she was somehow letting that colored boy down, that boy who wasn't scary, but nice. She wanted, needed, to lie for both of them. It would be easy to lie, with Mama's eyes on her biscuits. And why shouldn't she lie? She couldn't explain what she was feeling, anyway.

"Did you hear me?" Mama whipped around.

Sally gulped, the decision made. "Digging in the flower bed," she said, then wished she could take it back. Her hands weren't dirty. Neither were her knees.

"Hmm. I didn't see you."

Even though Sally made sure not to look, she felt Mama's gaze on her and prayed she wasn't inspecting clean hands and knees. Another lie popped into her head, this one involving the college mascots. "I went to the bear pit too." Words tumbled out now. "Me and the kids pretended a bear escaped and—"

"Good." Mama grabbed a pot holder and pulled out the tray of biscuits, the curious tone erased from her voice. "Good, sweetheart. Now go wash up. Dinner's ready. Your favorite."

Sally flashed a smile at Mama, then slumped toward her room. Even the promise of fried chicken, biscuits, and collard greens couldn't lighten the heaviness from her chest. And why? She should be glad Mama didn't catch her lying, but she wasn't glad, she was sad. Sometimes getting caught and punished cleaned everything up, and she could start fresh. Instead the lie clung to her and weighed her down.

On her way to the bathroom, Sally knelt down by her bed. Mr. Forsgaard had told her to mind her parents, and though she hadn't, she did remember something they always told her: *When you're confused, talk to God. He'll help you.* But they'd also told her how bad Colored Town was and how dangerous colored people were, and that wasn't true. So was the talking-to-God part true? Sally bowed her head, but no words came out. Instead, colors swirled around inside, some orange and yellow and red, but mostly black and white. She clenched her eyes tighter and waited for words. Waited. Waited.

God is love.

Who had said that? "God is love," Sally repeated, over and over until the words ran together. Then she thought of the boy's bubbling laugh, how it ran together too. She jumped up, washed her hands, and hurried into the kitchen. Mama had made her favorite meal.

◆

This ain't easy for her.

When Mrs. Stevens stopped talking, the only sound in the room was beeping monitors and a clicking noise as Shamika picked at her fingernail. The sight of that bent round head, the scraggly, streaky blond hair, opened up a part of her heart that had been barricaded to white people since that high school counselor had started talking beauty school instead of brainy school.

"You were one crazy little white girl." Shamika laughed, though she hadn't planned to.

Her teacher let out a jiggling guffaw that would make a sista proud. It even looked like tears put stars in her eyes.

"Huh." Her hands folded across her chest, Auntie didn't seem convinced. "Sounds like you was runnin' wild on that campus." That was Auntie. Always shooin' folks into place.

"I pretty much did. Back then, they just assumed a college campus was safe."

Except in Colored Town. The thought robbed Shamika of another laugh and planted back talk in her mouth. "'Course it wasn't safe. Not with 'jigs' just across the street."

Mrs. Stevens scratched her head. "Like I tried to say, that wasn't true." For the millionth time, she smiled sweetly and sugared her words.

Shamika threw up her hands and tilted her head. If she ever wanted to be a lawyer, she needed to stick to the facts. Refuse to be swayed by emotion and pretty words. "You think that pretty little tale helps you understand what it's like to be black?" She made sure to snort loud. "You have no idea where I come from."

A smile remained on Mrs. Stevens's lips but a hardness darkened her eyes, like when she'd cut off those bigots right in the middle of their rant about folk songs. "That 'pretty little tale' is my life. And if you expect me to understand what you've been through, you have to look at where I've come from."

In a flash, Ruby was out of her chair, pacing the small space between the bed and the chairs. "I got a tale too. 'Ceptin' it ain't too pretty."

Cringing at what was coming next, Shamika bowed her head, hoping to ward off the blows hitting a bit too close. Like last-night close.

"I was seven when it happened to me. Jes' like you." She pointed at Sally.

Shamika had this one memorized.

Auntie interlaced fingers that Shamika knew had picked cotton, kneaded bread; most recently had input data into a Dell. "Lord, Lord, I was skippin' down the road, nuthin' but that fishin' hole on my mind. Mama'd done tole me to keep away from it, but naw, I didn't listen. Not to her, Daddy, nor my brothas." Even though her tone was harsh, the memories softened her face and set it aglow.

"That cracker come out of nowhere—probably hidin' in one of them cotton fields. I'll never forget those mean eyes, that spittle runnin' down a chin stubbled with whiskers. And words mo' hateful even than his looks. He gave me a real good Southern education—the kind I ain't learnt yet in school. 'Gonna catch me a little nigger,' he said, grabbing my pole and hookin' me right in da back." She pointed to the place between her shoulder blades. "I twisted and pulled like dem fish do. But it jes' made him laugh. So I just fell down on da dusty road till he had his fun wit' me."

"Did he—" Mrs. Stevens seemed stuck on the *r* word, but Shamika's brain didn't have a bit of trouble with it; in fact, wouldn't say anything else. *Rape. Rape. Rape.*

Ruby shook her head. "Uh-uh, thank da Lord. He jes' left me grovelin' and gaggin' in that dust, wit that hook stabbin' me in the back."

Shamika choked down the worst kind of taste. How long were her people going to have to take this kind of crap?

The teacher slid out of her chair, twisting and untwisting her hands as she moved near to Auntie. "I'm . . . so sorry," she said. "It's all so . . . wrong."

Her aunt nodded. "That's when I knew somethin' sicker than sin gwine on with white folks. And jes' in case I didn't learn it good, Momma beat it into me when I got home."

Mrs. Stevens's gasp made it past all the humming and ticking of the machines. "She beat you? After what you'd been through?"

Some of the hardness returned to Auntie's face. "She had to learn me and learn me good. It was the only way I gwine survive."

The way her teacher was rubbing her hands together, shaking her head, it seemed she was getting a clue about what it was like to deal with things like those bigots in her class. Shamika had to give her credit for bringing spirituals into the curriculum. Both them bigot and white liberal intellectual types surely flapped their lips over the mention of the "G" word within the rooms of their ivory towers. As if God hadn't been a part of music since day one.

"I've . . . I've been here long enough." Mrs. Stevens wobbled to her feet, looking a bit out of it, like a wino about to be hauled off a corner. She picked up her boat of a purse and tottered toward the door, taking that warmth and compassion . . . and those crazy white woman stories with her.

"Don't go!" Her eyes electric, Shamika shoved back the covers that Ruby had draped about her legs. "Tell me more. Both of you."

"Say what?" Auntie's mouth flew open.

"*I said* tell me more. Now." Shamika wagged her finger at her aunt, feeling her eyes dance as if last night hadn't happened.

The teacher spun about, looking like a different person. A white chameleon. Shamika chuckled at her private joke. *That's what she be. A white chameleon.*

"Well, now, I'd love to, but you need to rest. I've got groceries to get, papers to grade." She cut a glance at Auntie. "But I could run by—when you're up to it, of course—with your assignments, answer any questions, and then we could talk about the old days."

Shamika nodded, nodded, till her aching head ordered her to stop.

"It would just be for a while, of course. Until you're ready to come back—"

"I ain't never goin' back to that racist school," Shamika spat out. After what had been done to her, she'd never give those creeps the satisfaction of seeing the bruises on her face, of gloating over the bruises that they couldn't see.

"Well, I don't know about that." Auntie uncrossed her legs and rubbed her forehead. "But this tutorin' thing's movin' pretty fast, and I ain't used to hoppin' on no train and speedin' off when I don't know where I'm going."

"Now, Auntie . . ." A gray area emerged between the black-and-white regions of Shamika's mind, an area where all of them might be able to hang out. Especially Auntie, who seemed to want those BS and JD degrees as much as Shamika did. "If she tutors me, I won't have to set foot on that campus." She sat up and edged one foot toward the floor. "But I can still get my hands around an education."

"Girl, what you doin'?" Auntie huffed out of her chair and settled the sheets back over Shamika. "You get back in that bed."

"All right. But only if you agree."

Mrs. Stevens smiled as if she was familiar with this game. Of course she had kids, so she probably was.

Auntie seemed to chew on the situation, then shrugged her shoulders. "Mrs. Stevens, if you willing to take her on, I guess this tutoring thing'll be all right with me."

Mrs. Stevens reached for and found Auntie's hand. "Please. Call me Sally."

This time, Auntie nodded. And acted like she really meant it. Keeping Auntie happy sure would make havin' this white woman over a whole lot easier. *'Cause if Auntie ain't happy, ain't nobody happy.*

◆

Price's finger was poised to push the elevator button. Then he jerked it back and headed for the stairwell, determined to work off his frustration from interrogating another foul-mouthed minority victim, not to mention the paunch developed as a result of too many hours behind a desk. Ole Aunt Ruby had been no picnic, either; scowling at him as if he alone were to blame for slavery.

He took the stairs two at a time, trying to catch up with his thoughts, then slowed when his heart hammered him with an irregular beat. That Shamika didn't quite fit the ghetto cookie cutter, with her angel face but the mouth of a no-account punk. A mouth that had already given conflicting testimony. Yet the preliminary look into her life hadn't quite been what he'd expected. Straight-A student. Pre-law, no less. The perfect little church girl. Of course, it was all blacks who were saying that, circling the wagons around one of their own. But the records were black-and-white. The records didn't lie. Price sighed as he banged into the lobby and whisked past a nurse, who looked darned good even in loose-fitting, neon-rainbow scrubs. He'd get to the bottom of this, one way or another. And if things fell like they usually did, this black girl would have a kink or two in something besides what was left of that strange-looking hair.

Chapter 6

PLANS

Where shall I go for to ease my troubled mind? Where shall I go?
—Negro spiritual, "Where Shall I Go?"

Another hot flash. Sally resisted the urge to pull over to the side of the road, rip off her sweater, and sop up sweat surely brought on not just by menopause, but the hospital visit, the mad tear through the grocery store, and the stalled traffic at the railroad crossing. Instead, she jabbed at the accelerator, intent on moving forward. As she sped past the familiar landmarks of Normal, she had to figure out what they were having for dinner, decide what to do about Thursday's lecture. With a swerve into her driveway, she was home.

Except for a rusted-out basketball goal, a fall wreath, a few clumps of asters, 4205 North Lee was just one of a dozen mass-produced houses on the horse-shoe-shaped street. But it was close to Sam's school, Sally's school, Ed's school. And as long as it held the three of them—four when Suzi was around—it was home.

So she could wedge the Suburban into what the realtor claimed was a two-car garage without clipping the rearview mirror, Sally braked until tires screeched. To help, Sam had hung a tennis ball from a string, tacked it to the garage ceiling, and outlined the parking space with chalk. When Sally eased forward, the truck bumped into the fuzzy yellow ball and set it to swinging like a pendulum. Daily, Sally stifled an urge to yank the ball down, but she trumped spunk with the knowledge that Sam knew best.

You could tell a lot about a man by studying his garage. Sam's was lined with shelves that held paint cans, the mix date written in permanent marker, and color-coded boxes of tools. Hooks from the ceiling held holiday decorations. And then, of course, the parking contraption. Organized, efficient, practical. That was her Sam. And Sally thanked God for him, every day.

She grabbed her briefcase and somehow balanced a sack of groceries on the shelf that was her midsection. With her knee, she shut the car door and headed inside. *Sam . . . What would I do without him?* He'd kept things in order for years, even that box of old letters, sealed with masking tape and secreted away somewhere—probably in the basement. The one Sally was going to ask him about, when she had time. The one that might have Ella's last address. Of course, in this mobile society, what were the odds Ella would still be in New Orleans? Still, it was a starting point. And with Google and those search engines Ed and Suzi raved about, surely she could find her old friend.

Sally heaved the groceries onto a counter, then checked the blinking answering machine.

"Mom, I won't be home for dinner. Nick and I are studying after tennis."

Sally rolled her eyes at the stupid machine, as if it were its fault her family never seemed to manage to eat together. Nonplussed, the machine beeped again.

"It's Linda. The study's Thursday night. 6:30, right? Hey, I'm not giving orders, but how about those espresso brownies?" A few giggles, then a dial tone.

Sally's mouth watered just thinking about chocolate. Of course she'd make them—a triple batch. For Linda and the Bible study girls, for her boys, for Shamika. But did she have any cocoa? Any eggs? Now she remembered those last items on the list that she'd lost somewhere between the hospital and the grocery store. She hit "pause," then sashayed across the kitchen.

The cabinet banged open as she shoved back jars of allspice and cardamom and curry. *Aha!* A can of powdered egg substitute. Now for the important thing, the chocolate. Then she'd get to her lesson plans, get to dinner, and maybe, if she had time, she'd pray.

Standing on her tiptoes, she could just reach that top shelf, where she'd hidden a bag of semisweet chips during her last dieting debacle. *Just a few won't hurt. Just a few.* She'd open them later, anyway, when she made the brownies. With her teeth, she tore the cellophane and funneled them right into her mouth, something she'd smack Ed for doing. Grabbing another handful, she hurried back to the phone and pressed the button.

"Hey, Mom."

When she heard Suzi's voice, Sally's heart melted. She missed those lazy bedtime talks, the occasional shopping trips, the little notes Suzi would some-times prop up on her dresser. She missed having a girl in the house. She missed her daughter.

"Mom, I need to talk to you. Oh, it's nothing important." Sally had to strain to hear over laughter so raucous, it sounded as if half the dorm was in Suzi's room. "Later, Mom."

Sally replayed the message, her eyes squeezed tight so she could concentrate on every word. Was Suzi's cheeriness forced? And why hadn't she e-mailed this week? The worrywart side that Sally supposed every mother possessed sup-planted her more rational side. Last month, just a block from the campus of Suzi's small Christian college, a jogger had been raped. And now Shamika . . .

One of Sam's favorite sayings slipped past the ugly images: *"There's no guar-antee, Sally. Only God."*

The machine beeped again.

"Sally, this is Harold."

A frown creased Sally's face. Since when did her department chair call her at home?

"Uh, something's come up. Can you come by? First thing in the morning."

Sally replayed that message, just like she had Suzi's. Something was up, all right. Her department chair didn't like unscheduled meetings—for that mat-ter, he didn't like scheduled ones. Hurrying to the cabinet, she fished out more chips. *Someone's behind this besides Harold. It's those boys . . . I'm sure of it.*

The bag half empty, Sally slumped down the hall, feeling no better, just bloated. What she should do was lace up her shoes and jog to the park. She could talk to God there, and often did. But she was so, so tired. That idea dis-carded, she climbed the stairs.

The western sun streamed into Suzi's old bedroom, which Sally had usurped for her office when Suzi left for college. Thanks to Sam's skill with a paintbrush, three coats of "Buttercup Yellow" managed to erase all vestiges of Suzi's navy blue and the residual glue from her glow-in-the-dark stars. An airplane plant, a fern, and a cluster of cacti near the window labored to improve air quality in the room, and Sally did breathe easier, here in her sanctuary. Over the computer table hung a still life of magnolias that was so realistic, Sally half-expected the familiar heady fragrance to engulf the space. Kicking off her shoes, she settled into an overstuffed chair and propped her feet on an ottoman.

Comfortable for the first time all day, Sally raised her hand in praise. "Father God, You are the sovereign Lord. My Maker, Creator, Redeemer, and Friend."

It was then she sensed the Spirit's presence, and His glow lit Sally's heart and soul and mind. She groaned as her troubles were washed away, nothing left except Sally and the Lord. "Holy One," she whispered, the phrase starting an avalanche of prayer and praise.

When Sally opened her eyes, she checked her watch, then jerked books out of her briefcase, dog-eared a few pages, jotted down some quotes from Martin Luther King and Alice Walker, made a note to photocopy a couple of Ellis Wilson paintings, then put down her pen. The setting sun lased through the window and infused the luscious blooms of the magnolia painting with an otherworldly glow, like the surreal light of Byzantine pietas. Light illuminated everything—the dusty computer desk, every serrated frond on the fern she'd nursed through Midwest winters for years—so why shouldn't it clarify this latest dilemma? Still she waffled. Should she really alter her lesson plans like this? Trap her students in their uncomfortable chairs and use art as a vehicle to discuss racism?

Her head bowed, Sally waited, a hard thing for a woman who needed to fix dinner and had no idea what was going to be on the menu.

When God didn't answer after two minutes, Sally stuffed her books back into the briefcase and, her feet echoing against hardwood steps, started down the stairs. She was going to do it. God hadn't said no, had He?

Tap. Tap. Tap.

Sally gripped the banister. With nobody else home, the house became a Venus flytrap for every little noise—squeaks, rattles, groans—then amplified them and released them, one by one, in a way that chilled Sally's bones.

Clunk.

Something's wrong! All the little noises became big noises, rushing at Sally, unlocking the images she kept in the secret place—the snarling sneer, the stained teeth, the nauseating stink of sweat and blood.

With tiny steps, then bolder ones, she made her way to the first floor. She was letting what happened with Shamika bloom into a hideous stink flower of memories that was affecting her imagination. It was just a silly little noise. The nearly antique refrigerator or the on-its-last-legs furnace. She needed a distraction. And soon.

It was only a few steps into their family room and to the entertainment center, but it seemed like a mile. With a flip of a switch, music poured out of the speakers, music that Sally hoped would shove back the ugly things that kept crawling out. Images forty years old and stronger than ever.

The fun-loving lyrics of Hank Williams Jr.'s *Jambalaya* seemed to set the family room to two-stepping and yee-hawing. The music, and the mention of Cajun-style food, pulled Sally back from the dark places. Her mouth watering, she visualized catfish, fried shrimp, crab cakes—and tried to take captive another negative thought about the Midwest. What was it, fifteen hundred miles to the nearest coast? Not counting the Great Lakes, of course. She might as well crave Mexican mole as fresh seafood—*That's it! Mexican!* Sally snapped her fingers and wiggled all the way to the kitchen. So easy, and Sam would think she'd roasted and chopped and pureed all afternoon.

With a thrust of her hip and a pointed toe, Sally continued to let the music do its magic. She opened the fridge and pulled out some leftovers, a wilted stalk of celery, an onion that had lost its tear-jerking capabilities last week, and some peppers. A fry pan was Sally's next target, and she whisked one onto the burner, squirted in some oil, and turned up the heat.

Frustrations dissipated with each *thwack* as Sally chopped vegetables and funneled them into the sizzling pan. Next came chicken, after she'd rolled it in cumin and salt and the spice she added to almost everything, lemon pepper. Sally swabbed a finger into the concoction and gave it a taste. It needed . . . some Jack, some Colby. Sally dug through the grocery sack, still on the counter, but the cheese wasn't there.

Sally slapped her forehead. Of course. It was in the other bags, the ones still in the car. She set down a wooden spoon, twisted off her wedding ring, which was gooey with the filling, and rinsed it off before sticking it back on her finger. "Do one thing at a time," Sam always told her. Well, if she did that, nothing would ever get done. Her mind raced ahead. Had she forgotten the cheese? Would she have to go back to the store and get some?

Still licking her lips, Sally made her way to the garage. The cheese and the ice cream and the butter would be fine, thanks to the frigid temperatures that transformed the old 'Burban into an icebox on wheels. Sally could comb the town for bargains, cram all the sacks into the back seat, and forget about them. And what a system for a Diet Coke addict! Just keep a six-pack on the floorboard and yank a can from the plastic rings whenever the urge struck. They'd be take-your-breath-away slushy cold. The only problem was sometimes they froze, expanded, and exploded. Like her diets seemed to do. And she had to be careful with produce, having once ruined a whole bag of lettuce and tomatoes and cabbage and okra and—

"What in the—" Sally's foot hit something round and mushy, and she bobbled and nearly fell. A quick glance at the concrete floor told her it was the tennis ball. But how did it get down there? Had she knocked it loose? It was supposed to hang right—

Sally looked up. Something hung from the garage. And it wasn't the parking device. Her scream reverberated across the enclosed space, bounced off the metal doors, and flew back at her. She screamed again.

An old scarecrow swung from a noose looped through the hook where Sam's parking contraption had been. Straw stuffing spilled out of the right-angle joint between the head and neck. A grisly red smile had been smeared across a face darkened by what looked like brown spray paint. The torso swayed back and forth in response to a breeze that came through the open garage window.

Sally's knees buckled. *Who did this? Why?* She leaned against one of Sam's shelves, a spasm gripping her stomach. She couldn't look at it. She couldn't— she looked. This time when she opened her mouth to scream, nothing came out. She'd had this happen one other time. Her mouth, usually so active, failing her. But not her eyes.

With what looked like permanent marker, spiders had been tattooed onto the once-beige Suburban hood, vulgarities scrawled onto the windshield. Someone had been in here. Those noises earlier hadn't been figments of her imagination but someone carrying out a rotten, nasty prank.

Sally groped for the door but slipped on something slimy. Her palms slapped, her knees thudded against cold concrete. Whimpering, she pushed up into a squat. There was another of those awful spiders, drawn with what looked like tar on their garage floor. Tar or . . . Retching, Sally crawled away from the stomach-wrenching smell of excrement, wishing she had four legs, like that . . . *four* legs. Not a spider. A swastika. Just like the one tattooed on Jay's arm. Jay. Still on all fours, she paused. Those boys had done this.

Southern trees bear strange fruit . . . The lyrics she'd heard over forty years ago, the ones she'd just jotted down in her lesson plan, captured her mind. *Black bodies swinging in the Southern breeze. Strange fruit hanging from the poplar trees . . .*

This time when Sally retched, she gave way to its urgings and vomited onto newspapers Sam had bundled and made ready for the recycling bin. It seemed to help, as if she'd purged the vile images from her mind. Without a backward glance, she staggered into the house and called the police. Then she called Sam.

◆

"Good evening. I'm Officer Scott." His words seemed garbled, perhaps because of a bulge in his right cheek. The brass on his uniform and service cap caught the sun's final light as it streamed through the front windows and glinted coldly at Sally.

Sally offered her hand, but Officer Scott was so busy inspecting the accoutrements of the entryway that he didn't seem to notice. With brisk strides, he beelined through their house.

At the threshold between the kitchen and garage, Sally caught him and managed to introduce herself.

The officer tugged on the waistband of his blue trousers, then plodded down the garage step. "This is the . . . Oh, I see."

For the third time that day, Sally watched a police officer scribble facts into a notebook. This one seemed to be writing a novel. Was he noting Sam's well-organized garage? Or recording the awful words written on their windshield, as though their truck was a float in a white supremacist parade?

Sally shifted her weight from one foot to the other. "Officer, one of my students was attacked last night."

A toothpick darted out of the pouchlike cheek. "At Midwest."

Sally nodded. "And I had an incident this morning—I teach there. Three students accosted me outside the—"

The toothpick disappeared. Officer Scott rolled his eyes and gave Sally an annoyed look. "What do you mean by 'accost'?"

"Well, I—"

"Did they make physical contact with your person?"

"Well, no."

"Hmm." Now the officer fiddled with a walkie-talkie. "Did you report it?"

A dispatcher's squawking voice and radio static filled the garage.

Sally resisted an urge to cover her ears. "Well, no. Well, kind of." She hadn't called Detective Price, but she had talked to him.

"Kind of?" Officer Scott plucked the toothpick from his mouth and used it to scratch his cheek. "Any witnesses?"

"No, sir." For a moment Sally was paralyzed. Was that his all-purpose pick? For teeth and pimples and itchy places? The bad taste in her mouth returning, Sally swallowed once or twice. "You see, the class starts at eight. I'd gotten there early to prepare my lesson—you know, set up the video presenter and all, get the CDs ready—"

"Ma'am, you've answered the question. Twenty words ago." Squeezing a bulging abdomen past trash cans and recycling containers, he pushed the garage door opener. With a rumble and a groan, the metal doors unveiled the effigy for the whole neighborhood to see.

Sally longed to tell this man off, longed to spew out the bile that had pooled down deep. And she might have, except for the fact that her Sam was pedaling up the drive, his hair windblown, his pants legs rolled up, then clipped to keep them out of the bicycle's chain and sprocket. Sally closed her eyes, then opened them, wanting to memorize the strength in his shoulders, his jaw—wanting, needing for the image of her handsome man to shut out all the others she'd seen today. She half-staggered, half-ran toward him.

Without taking his eyes off her, Sam removed his helmet and hung it, like he always did, on padded handlebars. Then he uncharacteristically let the bike crash to concrete and enveloped Sally with a crushing hug.

"It started with that note you stuck on the truck." Words poured out of Sally, who was desperate to tell her husband all that the day had brought. "Oh, I guess you didn't do it, did you? Then these students—the ones who did this—accosted me. And Shamika's been . . . raped." Words mingled with sniffles and sobs. "What are we going to do? And what if they hurt Ed?" Tears soaked the bristly tweed of Sam's jacket.

Sam's eyebrows shot toward his temples. "What note? And who's Shamika?" Sam cleared his throat, then patted Sally on the back. "It's okay. One thing at a time, now." Still holding his wife, he managed to turn toward the policeman, who was studying the scarecrow. "Sam Stevens. Sally's husband."

"Hello, sir." The toothpick disappeared again, this time into the left cheek. "I'm Officer Scott." When the walkie-talkie came alive once again, he studied it for a moment, then clicked it off. "Your wife's a little upset."

All of the angst of the day boiled up in Sally, and she longed to hurl it at this joke of a policeman. Yet the pressure of Sam's hand on her shoulder, and his slight nod, kept her civil. Polite. The way a teacher should be.

Sam studied the scarecrow figure, his face stoic as usual, but his fingers trembling as he massaged Sally's shoulders. "I can certainly see why." The gaze that intimidated some folks locked onto the policeman. "And what do you plan to do about this?"

The officer fiddled with his holster. "Well, sir, from what I can tell, it's a simple case of vandalism. Unless . . ." With narrowed eyes, he surveyed the rows of boxes and tool kits and bikes. "Does it appear that anything was taken?" The edge had left his voice.

"Not that I can tell."

It might seem to the policeman that Sam barely looked at all his stuff before he answered. Sally knew differently.

"For now, we'll just file a report. I will ask you to keep an eye on things."

"Speaking of eyes . . ." Sam cleared his throat, then pointed to the end of the drive. A group of neighbors clustered around their mailbox.

It sent a twinge through Sally to be stared at like they were animals in a zoo. She recognized Tina and Edith, but the other two were just "the driver of the BMW," "the mother of the cute little toddler." Six years here, and that was all she knew about folks who lived not twenty-five yards away. Now in the South, things would be different. Tears fell again, and Sally didn't bother to wipe them off.

Sam winked twice and raised his brow.

The policeman probably didn't notice Sam's signal, but Sally did. It was Sam-Sal, the secret language they'd developed after more than twenty-five years of marriage. And Sam had said, *Go handle it, Sally.*

It was the jolt Sally needed to wipe her eyes, force a lilt into her step. And smile.

The garage door descended as soon as Sally walked out. "Thank you, Sam," she whispered, glad that he'd shut down their personal neighborhood freak show. What would she do without him?

"What happened?" Tina, the spinster who seemed to run a hostel for cats in her dilapidated ranch across the street, flopped her hands in a vain effort to keep a dirndl skirt from whipping about birdlike legs.

"Was there an . . . accident?" Edith Perkins, their next-door neighbor, a squatty woman whose jowls and nose bore an uncanny resemblance to those of Tutu, her pet Pekinese, somehow managed to be heard over Tutu's yips.

"Huh-uh. Just a little incident." Sally's voice stayed cheery, but inside a storm brewed. The Perkinses kept their windows shuttered year-round, emerging so rarely from their home, Sally wondered if that fluff of a dog used a litter box. For six years, they'd barely deigned to speak. Now they showed up, drawn to the "incident" like filings to a magnet.

"On *our* street?" Edith's eyes grew big as saucers.

"Right here on Lee." Sally didn't even try to keep the sarcasm from her voice. In fact, she halfway hoped someone would notice the irony of it all. From the time they'd moved in, Sally had tried her best to make North Lee Street a community. In a rather bizarre reverse welcome wagon, she'd taken homemade cookies to all of her neighbors, including the Perkinses, the day after their stuff had been unloaded from a U-Haul trailer and a moving van. Mrs. Perkins had nodded politely from her foyer, using the front door to shield a view of what must be a meth lab, the way she protected it. Or was she really just that horrendous a housekeeper?

After the perfunctory handoff of goodies at the front door, Sally, her hopes dissolving with a slam and a click, had gone home. The next morning, when Ed set the trash and recycling by the curb, he'd seen the tin that Sally had so carefully stenciled with daisies in the Perkins's trash pile. He'd pried off the lid to find Sally's specialty, those Neiman Marcus nut-and-chocolate-chip cookies that the Internet had made famous. When he brought them home, tin and all, Sally hadn't even tried to match Ed's guffaw, which he managed to get out in spite of a mouthful of cookies. Instead she'd grabbed some of her treats and tried to sugarcoat her frustration with gooey chocolate, meaty walnuts.

"Shush, Tutu!" Edith set the wriggly dog in Sally's yard. "Now, be a good boy for Mommie! Do your business." She hunched closer, inches from Tutu's "business." "Well, are you okay?" she asked Sally.

Sally withstood the temptation to kick two glistening tootsie rolls onto Edith's property. Now wasn't the time to be catty. "We've been better," Sally said, her voice absent its usual syrup but at least not tinged with the frost that was coating their grass nearly every morning now. Maybe, just maybe, it was going to take something like this to bring Lee Street together.

Edith's eyes widened to the size of blue jawbreakers. With a jut of her chin toward the garage, she asked, "Why? What's in there?"

"Just a little prank." Sally managed to keep her voice steady. "Probably one of my students. You know how they are."

A brown-haired woman, known to Sally only as the driver of the BMW, put a hand on a thin hip. The shoulder pads of a tailored suit and shiny leather pumps with heels just the right height couldn't overcome a rather mousy appearance. "Then why call the police?" the mouse asked.

"*When all else fails, tell the truth.*" Once again, Sally turned to a Mama-ism, which had helped her hurdle many a tough situation. In actuality, Sally would've preferred to lie. It seemed to spread over things better, like softened butter. But women, with their knife-sharp instincts, could often cut through even the best of lies. "*And your game face just isn't on.*"

Sally held out her hand. "I'm Sally, and—" she pointed toward the closed garage—"that's Sam. Sorry we had to meet like this."

A nod was the only reward for following the rules of Southern etiquette to a T.

"And what did you say your name was?" Sally persisted.

"Jean Smith, attorney." Her eyes gleaming, Jean smoothed down a wool skirt. "Now what's going on in there?"

None of your business. Did Jean expect them to hire her as their lawyer, on the spot? The woman acted like she was at the courthouse, filing a case. Of course, they just might need an attorney, if this sort of thing continued. Sally managed half a smile. "Someone painted an old scarecrow, made it look like a . . . a dead man, and hung it from a hook in our garage."

The women huddled closer, like eager birds around a refilled feeder. "But why?" Jean asked.

"That's what the cop's trying to determine." Did she have another smile in her? Sally hoped so but wasn't sure. "Now, if y'all will excuse me, I've got to get dinner."

"I'll get pizza for you all." Jean nodded, as if she'd already called for delivery.

Sally's mouth flew open. "Oh, no. We couldn't impose like that. Besides, I've already started."

"Then unstart." Smiling, Jean straightened the collar of her jacket. "This is no time to be around the stove."

It was funny how that half-smile warmed Sally even though she totally disagreed with what Jean had said. This was *exactly* the time to be around a stove or a table or anything that had to do with food. All good Southerners knew that food smoothed over the worst problems. Wasn't that why you whipped up casseroles for sick people and shut-ins? When Sally shook Jean's hand, she could feel every sinew, every bone.

"I'll bake a chicken for tomorrow." Finally the mother of the cute kid spoke up. Sally had about decided the only language she knew was baby talk.

"A cake would be nice."

"And a roast. Maybe some mashed potatoes?"

Edith and Tina chimed in, a magpie and a crow.

"Oh, well, ah—" Syllables sputtered out of Sally. It was all happening so fast here on Lee Street. And while she was grateful, she could envision those cats slinking over Tina's countertops, dipping sandpapery tongues into the mixing bowl, licking half-thawed meat . . . Still, after six years of living in a Midwestern demilitarized zone, it was a start. "You're too kind," Sally said, her eyes narrowing. "But there is something you can do." She lowered her voice, the four of them coconspirators now. "Keep a watch on the house. You know, Block Watch USA."

Tina laughed out loud.

Edith snorted like a contented pig.

"I work till five, but I could stroll by after dinner. You know, before it gets dark."

Sally smiled to imagine the new item on Jean's to-do list. Nonetheless, some of the tension seemed to slide off. God had just proved, for another time, how He'd worked for good in spite of a very bad thing. Waving and grinning, she headed to the front door, not slumping until she walked into her house.

Chapter 7

MORE REVELATIONS

You say you're aiming for the skies,
You must be lovin' at God's command.
Why don't you quit your telling lies?
—Negro spiritual, "God's Command"

Τhe officer doesn't seem to think there's a connection between this and Shamika's rape." Sam set down a piece of the pizza Jean had just brought over. "Speaking of Shamika, she's gonna be okay, isn't she?"

It was a struggle for Sally to swallow her last bite. Shamika would never be "okay." She tried to stem the flood of tastes and smells and sounds and—*no, Lord. Not the touches.* Greasy fingers. Half-moon gouges on her thighs. She closed her eyes, but the images remained. *God, I've kept it in for so long. Help me. Help . . .*

"What's the matter?" Sam asked, his voice suddenly quiet.

Sally did her best to swallow the pizza and the past, which was fast becoming the present. "N-Nothing," she managed to say. "It just got to me, seeing her in that hospital, all bandaged and bruised."

"No wonder." Sam took their dirty plates to the sink. "Did you call the prayer chain?"

"Not yet. But I will." *Keep busy. Keep moving. Think about Shamika.* Sally's eyes darted toward Sam, then back at her plate. *Dare she bring up that other thing? The timing seemed perfect.* "Harold's asked me to tutor her."

A sponge in his hand, Sam did an about-face. "When?"

"Just until she's ready to come back." Sally smoothed her voice past the lump in her throat and smiled, knowing Sam was watching her. She should have waited to talk to him before she told Harold yes. But she didn't. Now she had to deal with it.

"That's not what I meant. When do you think you have time for it?"

"Now, Sam, I'm sure it won't take but a couple of weeks." Sally swept crumbs off the table and into her palm, determined to make Sam understand. "They're paying me extra, so it'll help with the bills." Sally tried to widen her lying eyes.

"But I thought we agreed—"

In an instant, Sally was at the sink. She disposed of the crumbs, then threw her arms around him. " I *have* to do it, don't you see?"

Sam pulled away. Sharp eyes dug into Sally. "You could've talked to me first, not last."

"Harold had to know. Right then and there." When she stretched, she could just reach Sam's jawline. She gave him a peck, hoping the tic in his cheek would disappear. "Report to the dean. The union. You know how it is."

The tic didn't stop.

Deception rose up in Sally and threatened to choke her. She really didn't mean to lie so much, but lies kept things going on the highway of life. Yet there was a price. She'd varoom along, picking up nails and glass, weakening her tires with each new lie. Finally a tire would blow, either from a really bad nail or from sheer accumulation, exposing the unprotected rim to the road. The car would spin out of control and crash through a guardrail. Fortunately, most people, including Sam, didn't file an accident report to learn what caused the crash in the first place. But was he going to file one now? Get to the bottom of this?

Sally continued to use her eyes, her hands, to convince Sam. "She's one of those rare ones. Special." Sam had students. He'd understand.

Nothing. Not even a nod.

Sally smiled. When lies failed, she had to pull out of the car trunk one of the most effective tools—the dumb blond routine. Dimpled cheeks, pursed lips, a helpless shrug. Of course it helped that she cared about Shamika. After all, she was doing this for her.

Sam's jaw tightened, but the tic disappeared. He handed Sally a dish towel. "You're special too. Come on. I'll wash, you dry."

◆ ◆ ◆

From: SuziQ
To: Sally Stevens
Subject: Hi, Mom
Date: Tues., Oct. 25, 2005 21:25:24

Hi, Mom! We keep playing phone tag—you must be busy as me! LOL! I met a new guy named Joseph. He's got hazel eyes, like Ed's. And he's almost as tall as Dad! He likes cappuccino. Mom, don't get any ideas! We're just friends! Later, Suzi

Sally's fingertips grazed the keys, then pulled back as if they'd stabbed her. Why burst Suzi's college bubble with the razor-edged reality of rape? Vandalism? Let Suzi enjoy college. With all she'd done to earn a scholarship, she deserved it. Besides, rape wasn't the kind of thing to discuss by e-mail. She pushed back her chair until it rolled to the edge of the static pad, and swiveling, found her cell phone under a pile of to-be-graded papers. She'd call Mary. The phone opened with a snap, and she scrolled down her directory to Freeman, Mary, then hit Talk.

The phone rang, rang, Mary's usual blunt message failing to kick in. As Sally slammed the phone shut, she glanced at her wall calendar of Wildflowers of the Irish Burren and felt her irritation melt. *No wonder Mary shut off the machine.* If things had gone according to schedule—and knowing Mary, they had—the Freemans were over in Ireland, basking in the bosoms of Aunt Jo and Uncle Joe. The thought of all that red hair—and memories of her own Southern folk— put a smile on Sally's face. She'd call her mama, soon as she got through these papers.

◆ ◆ ◆

"I don't want him to know." Sally paced in front of their bedroom window, the events of the day moving in like the curtain of night. Darkening her spirit.

With a *plunk*, Sam's magazine landed on the nightstand. "We've got to tell him."

Sally twisted the rod that closed the miniblinds, wishing she could so easily shut out the image of that swinging scarecrow. It upset her to be like this, but it upset her more that her Sam and Ed, maybe even Suzi, would be affected.

"Hey, y'all! Mom? Dad?" Ed, as always, took the stairs two at a time. "Hey!"

Sally hurried to the edge of the bed and sat down just as Ed stuck his head into the room. In spite of all that had happened, it was impossible for Sally not to smile at the dimpled face of her youngest. "What's new, baby?"

"Not much." Standing in front of the dresser mirror, Ed studied his profile, tilting his head first one way, then the other.

Pride swelled in Sally as she feasted on wheat-colored hair, hazel eyes. Clear eyes that didn't need to be clouded by what had happened.

"Hey, did y'all hear what happened over at Midwest?"

Sally nodded.

"They said on the news that it might be race-related," Ed continued.

"Did they mention any suspects?" Sam asked.

Ed shook his head. "I guess stuff's been sent to the crime lab."

Sam shrugged, a classic Sam-Sal signal for Sally to dive in. She didn't want to, but it was better she do it now, soften things up a bit. If not, Sam would give every gruesome detail. "I had—have—she's in one of my classes."

Perfume bottles shook as Ed bumped into the dresser, then whirled to face his parents. "No way!"

Sally bit her lip. Sam had been right. Ed had to learn that even in Normal, things like this did happen. "Yes, way. They beat her up pretty bad."

"You saw her?"

"Yeah. At Regional."

"Is she gonna be okay?" His arms and legs restless, Ed plopped onto their bed.

Sally nodded, then cut a look at Sam. She'd let him take over now.

"Uh, Ed, there's something else."

"What, Dad?" Ed quit drumming the beat of an unknown song on his knees and sat Indian-style, his back against the footboard.

"Someone, uh, vandalized our garage. And our car."

"You mean, like, they egged it?" The drumming resumed, at a frenetic pace.

"More like graffitied it. Not to mention the scarecrow."

"A scarecrow in the car?"

"In our garage."

The beats silenced when Ed clenched his fists. "They came in our house?"

"Just the garage." Sam spoke deliberately. Calmly. As always. "It's okay, son. They don't think it's related to the attack."

Ed unfolded his legs, rose, and stalked back to the mirror. Restlessness had invaded his eyes, and his face paled.

Sam slid off the bed and made his way to the dresser, putting his hand on Ed's shoulder. "Son, we're not going to let these hoodlums—"

"Dad." Ed blanched, his howl tinged with sarcasm. "Nobody's used that word since the Dark Ages."

"I am from the Dark Ages, son." A tinge of heat entered Sam's voice. "In any event, we're going to give this to God."

"That's what you always say." In spite of Ed's harsh tone, his father's comment seemed to soothe him. He plopped back onto the bed and leaned his head against Sally's shoulder.

With experienced touches, Sally massaged Ed's neck, then drummed at the perennially sore spot between his shoulder blades. This was what she did best, soothing and smoothing. Sam was good at the hard things, the wrap-up.

"Hey, guys." Sam scooped his Bible off the nightstand and flipped through the pages. "'He who dwells in the shelter of the Most High . . .'"

Sam read the words they'd relied on so many times, starting with the death of Baby Blue. Somehow God would work through the "fowler's snares" and the "deadly pestilence" referenced in Psalm 91, and Sally could rest in that.

They joined hands, bowed heads. Sally's heart lightened as she prayed for Shamika and their friend with cancer. Ed remembered the girl on the volleyball team who'd been in a car wreck. With a subdued voice, Sam prayed for whoever had vandalized their home. Then Ed kissed his parents and throttled the stairs, probably eager to drum those fingers against the keys of the basement computer.

"I love you," Sally called to her son.

"I love you more," Ed intoned, completing the ritual begun when he was three.

Sally put on her pajamas and went into the bathroom. She stared at the mirror, sucked in her stomach, then stretched the waistband until she could see the tag. Size 16? She had to start walking soon, or her weight could get out of hand. Soon. Like tomorrow. She hurried to bed, burrowed under a quilt, and curled into a fetal position, yet her mind replayed all the day's images. Shamika. Those boys. Ella. She crooked a finger out into the cold and touched Sam on the shoulder. "There's something I want to ask you."

With one swoop, Sam pulled her to a chest and abdomen hardened by years of biking, jogging, and noon basketball.

"Hey, I can't breathe!" Sally protested.

Sam kissed Sally on the ear, on the neck, on the shoulders. His breathing became erratic as he moved down her body, caressing her, his warm fingers probing—

"Sam, stop it! This is important." Sally pretended not to hear his sigh, which feathered out a lock of her hair. "Where did you put my old keepsake box?"

"I'm not sure. Probably in our study closet. Or maybe in the basement, with your old lesson plans, my old rock collection."

Sally planted a kiss on his forehead. "I knew you'd know."

"What are you looking for?"

"Oh, just some old letters."

"Not an old boyfriend's, I hope." He gathered her hair in hands big enough to palm a basketball.

Sally pushed him away and rolled back into the fetal position. At times she recoiled when he so much as touched her arm, and at other times her entire body tingled, wanting more of him. Of course she knew why, but he didn't.

Sam sighed again; Sally matched it with one of her own. How often had she wanted to explain it, been so close to spitting it out that she could feel the words against the roof of her mouth? For over twenty-five years, they'd had a relationship most of her friends were envious—no, downright jealous of. How could she tell him now about something that happened so long ago? What kind of statement would that be making about trust and companionship and honesty?

Her legs drawn close, she waited. She knew her Sam. And his habits.

Soon she was rewarded; Sam breathed slowly and steadily. Asleep.

Sally eased her body out of its cramped position. What a blessing it was, that men just let things roll off like that—maybe not all men, but her man. She prayed until peace nestled over her, an emotional quilt warmer than her covers, and her eyes closed . . .

Something scratched at the window.

Bolting upright, Sally glanced at the clock, which glowed the unsettling evidence that it was 2:59 AM. A whistle split the night air. Branches slammed against the window.

Trembling, Sally curled back into a ball and tried to concentrate on specific sounds, the most obvious being Sam's raspy intake, which usually soothed her. But not tonight. The other sounds . . . had those boys returned for an encore? Or was she just hearing the wind rattle tree leaves?

As a girl, Sally had loved the southern breeze, which whispered through cape jasmine bushes and perfumed the air with their scent. That southern breeze, which had witnessed her secrets down by the bayou, then roiled them into a funnel and buried them in a watery grave. But this Midwestern wind was different; if it kept blowing against her, she might collapse under the pressure.

Sally flipped over and tried to go back to sleep, but faces kept floating through her mind. That horrid man . . . then Ella. Dear Ella, her cocoa-creamy skin, straight teeth, loyal eyes. Gone. Gone. Gone. Like that southern wind.

◆ ◆ ◆

Sam made sure to keep his breathing even, lying there like a stone beside his wife of twenty-seven years. The one whom he'd met in softball class. Eighteen years old, and she'd made his blood run hot, with all that blond hair, those big blue eyes. The same girl who proceeded to steal his heart, then his mind. The one who had grown to be a loving woman. The one who, with increasing frequency, seemed to be a total stranger.

A branch clawed at the double-paned window.

Sally whimpered and curled into a ball.

Not Sam. His brain had trained his body to withhold reactions until it could identify the stimuli and provide a logical response. He did blink once or twice, but his breathing stayed the same until the answer came. *Of course. Just the wind. Just as weather.com had earlier reported, using satellite-generated charts and graphs.*

But Sally . . . a handpicked team of the world's greatest logicians couldn't fathom the mysteries buried beneath that ditsy-looking exterior. So why should he do any better?

He rolled on his side, affecting a natural shift just in case Sally was listening—a perfectly logical soporific response to an uncomfortable back, a strange dream. His precious wife scooted away and huddled on the edge of her side of the bed.

Sam did his best to push away decades of memories, to no avail. How long had she been like this? Had it begun after their little son was born . . . after he'd died? Some kind of postpartum/postmortem reaction? Then they'd adopted Suzi, and Sam had selfishly hoped that that little pink bundle would serve to rekindle Sally's sex drive. So when she'd crawled into bed after midnight feedings, he'd reached for her. "Please, Sam. Not now. We might wake the baby," she'd said, her big eyes only serving to ramp up his burner. He'd had a mind to turn off the blasted baby monitor that Sally tuned so high; when little Suzi rustled the crib sheets, it sounded like the scrub cycle of a dishwasher.

Years tumbled now—soccer matches, sleepovers . . . When had perimeno-pause started? He felt a frown crease his forehead. A mathematician should do better. Somewhere along the way, it had ballooned into menopause. His own mother, a Rock of Gibraltar in the emotions department, had been torpedoed by it, according to Sam's dad. So why shouldn't it shake his own wife?

Sam watched the clock change—3:15, 3:16. He shoved back the covers and sat up. How often had he told himself it would get better? He was tired of this physical chasm between them and wanted it torn down, no matter what the cost.

When Sally sighed in her sleep, remorse flooded him. He adored her even more than that first day he'd seen her, in softball class, her cap turned back-ward, slapping her teammates' palms long before it was "cool." And then their wedding night—in that demure way he'd found so sexy, she'd given herself to him. And the blessed release . . .

Sally moaned, making Sam remember something else. Something he didn't really want to remember. An image he hadn't let cross his mind in twenty-seven years. Sally, sobbing on their wedding night at the San Antonio hotel . . . long after they'd been informed that their reservation had been lost . . . long after they'd been told that the hotel was overbooked . . . long after Sally's convoluted story about her nephew the ring bearer tossing the pillow into the choir loft set the manager into such convulsive laughter, he moved them into the honeymoon suite. Long after room service delivered complimentary champagne and filet mignon. *But not long after I made love to her.*

That honeymoon night, Sally's cries had jolted him from a half-awake state. He'd crushed her in his arms and smothered her with what they had dubbed "angel breaths" ever since the first time they'd kissed. All the excitement, she'd claimed. All the emotion. Her wide-eyed look, toothy smile, absorbing the moonlight that poured into the lavish room, had given her face a golden glow and melted Sam's doubts . . . until now.

Like a man who thought by numbers, painted by numbers, lived by numbers, Sam tried to be rational. *So what? Nobody's perfect, not even Sally.* She'd filled his life with love and laughter and scores of people he never would've met other-wise, adventures he never would've embarked on without her. They'd adopted Suzi, who in many ways was just like him, then Ed, who claimed to be like him but was more like Sally.

When Sally turned toward him, her faded pajamas gaped open.

Every fiber in his body twitched to alert. *She's as desirable as that first time, in spite of a few bulges here and there. And she doesn't have a clue what she's doing to me.*

With a nod, Sam added one item to his mental Day-Timer. He'd make an appointment with Pastor Todd. See him tomorrow, if it were possible. *Isn't this what pastors are for?* But he wouldn't tell Sally. Not now. Probably not ever.

Chapter 8

A COMPLEX MATTER

And our hearts are made to bleed for a thoughtless word or deed . . .
—Negro spiritual, "We'll Understand It"

Sally made a beeline for the kitchen, hurrying away from CNN's coverage of more New Orleans bad news.

". . . continued delays with the delivery of FEMA trailers . . ."

Thanks to Katrina—and this looming meeting with Harold—she needed chocolate. And a long chat with Mama. But Mama probably still had her sleep mask on, her hearing aid off. She fished a bag of Oreos from the cabinet and carried it back into the den. As grim statistics poured from the newscaster's mouth, Sally ate cookies until only crumbs remained. Why hadn't Robert called her lately? Of course she knew the answer. Like all the king's men, he was trying to put together half a million American dreams shattered by that she-devil of a hurricane. Even though Sally was eight hundred miles from New Orleans, she felt the clouds gathering, the winds picking up. *A bad moon on the rise.*

She checked her watch, hurried into the bathroom to brush her teeth, and prayed that the sugar fix would fire up her sluggish spirit. Yet as exhausted as she was, her mind continued its double overtime shift. All night she'd tossed and turned, unanswered questions keeping her awake. Was Ella stuck in FEMA purgatory? Or had she long ago bailed out of New Orleans, carrying their secret with her? What would Ella think if Sally told Shamika that secret now, betraying their blood oath? What on earth had Harold called a meeting about? Sally bowed her head, determined to call on God before she took another step.

◆ ◆ ◆

Arlene, the Fine Arts secretary, had worked hard to soften the starkness of the office even though not much could be done with state-issue furniture. African violets lined modular shelves. A well-stocked candy dish offered sugar addicts a free fix.

Her nostrils pinched, her eyebrows arched, Arlene managed to tear her attention from an e-mail. "They're waiting," she told Sally, ice hanging off her words.

Sally grabbed a chocolate drop from the dish, unwrapped it, and crammed it in her mouth.

"And they have been, a good four minutes."

Harold hadn't said anything about "they." And was she really late? She glanced at her watch, the second hand seeming to rotate faster and faster, echoing her heartbeat. "Okay," she managed, grabbing several more chocolates after Arlene returned her attention to her keyboard. So her premonitions had been right after all. Her heart hammered as she hurried down the hall.

There was Harold, holding open the glass door of the department's all-purpose room—lunchroom, conference room, storage room, adjuncts' office, just to name a few of its uses.

"Come on in, Sally." His smile tight, his tone pseudo-friendly, Harold motioned for Sally to enter. "Have a seat. Please. Over there." His pointer finger indicated a place near a familiar-looking woman.

Perspiration dampened Sally's forehead and chest. Something was brewing; it was obvious after a glance at the table, which had lost its usual pile of junk. Dated copies of *The Vidette*? A clogged hole-puncher? Four staplers, emptied of staples and laid out like gutted deer? All gone, the table so polished that Sally could see her reflection. Even the stench of butter substitute, burned popcorn, and stale pizza had been zapped away with Arlene's citrus air freshener.

Chairs scraped against the floor, and a gaggle of people stood as if ready to recite the Pledge of Allegiance. For some reason, Sally couldn't focus on anything except that spotless table, couldn't move, couldn't—

"Mrs. Stevens."

What's the dean doing here? Sally stumbled forward, the stiffness in the dean's voice shocking her into action. Hurriedly, she whispered her own pledge—to the Holy Spirit.

"Mrs. Stevens," the dean repeated.

Sally waited, just long enough for the dean's face to come into focus. Then she gulped once or twice and managed a smile. "It's Mrs., Dean Sorenson."

The dean, his bald head reflecting fluorescent lighting, nodded at two people who stood like bookends on each side of him. "Yes. Well, Mrs. Stevens, this is Mr. . . . and Ms. . . . ."

In spite of not catching their names, Sally nodded. The dean and his bookends nodded. Harold nodded. But not those three with the turned-backward baseball caps, the ever-present leather jackets, who slumped in their chairs, seemingly mesmerized by the window view of whirling storm clouds. And not the stern-looking black man who towered over Jay, Rex, and Hugh like a transmitting tower, sending signals that chilled Sally's bones.

"Good morning, Mrs. Stevens. I'm Mr. Pierce, the attorney hired by the American Civil Liberties Union on behalf of Messrs. Staugh and Turnbull and Davis." The black man offered Sally a cool hand, which was dominated by a rather ostentatious class ring.

Sally mustered every precept of civility that had been carefully distilled into her by Mama. "Nice to meet you." She shook Mr. Pierce's hand, hoping he didn't notice how slick hers was. If she kept focusing on how his mahogany eyes complemented his walnut skin, maybe, just maybe, she wouldn't lash out at the insanity of some black lawyer from the ACLU representing these neo-Nazis or whatever they were.

"I'm Danita Daniels." Closely cropped nails, a Timex watch, preceded an electric handshake. Gray streaks coursed through brown hair, which was pulled tightly into a no-nonsense ponytail. "As the union representative, I'm here to represent you." Ms. Daniels's tailored silk suit blended perfectly with a roomful of gray and brown wool. But not the boys' black leather biker jackets, which stood out like Hell's Angels in a wine tasting room.

Of course. She'd seen Ms. Daniels at the in-service meeting. It hit Sally, as she shook Danita's hand, how wrong she'd been for thinking she'd never need the union.

"Go ahead and sit down." Ms. Daniels didn't suggest, she commanded.

Sally slid into her seat, wondering what she'd done to warrant a meeting of five stuffed shirts—six, counting the boys' attorney. She hadn't a clue, and that was as scary as anything else.

Like an empathetic nurse right before the cotton swab, astringent smell, needle jab, Ms. Daniels patted Sally's arm. Sally winced, knowing pain was coming.

"Good morning." Dean Sorenson's voice echoed off the walls as they all sat down. All except for the three boys, who'd never stood up in the first place.

"I think we all know why we're here," the dean continued.

Ms. Daniels pushed back from the table, giving her room to cross her legs. "Actually, we don't." Again she touched Sally's arm. "And we'd like to know why you've called this woman from her classes, her prep time." Her glare iced first the lawyer, then the three boys.

With tapered fingers, Mr. Pierce smoothed the lapel of what looked like an Armani suit, rising as he did so. "There's a fundamental reason I'm here, Ms. Daniels. So fundamental it holds together the very fabric of this nation." His words evoked memories of Lincoln, of King, but not his eyes, drooping in spite of their deep set in a chiseled face. "On behalf of the ACLU, we feel Mrs. Stevens has violated our clients' rights to free speech as guaranteed under the First Amendment."

Ms. Daniels picked up a gold pen and tapped it on the table. "And how do you perceive Mrs. Stevens did that?"

Still standing, Mr. Pierce pointed to Hugh's forearm. "She forbade my clients' freedom of expression."

In a casual way, Jay rolled up black leather and wrinkled cotton. Not one but two swastikas shouted their ugly message. The newer one had been tattooed in bloodred.

Harold gasped.

The dean's aides twiddled their fingers, yet the dean didn't so much as flinch.

Hugh and Rex pushed up their shirtsleeves. It was no surprise to Sally that they'd tattooed their arms in the same way.

A sneer flattened Ms. Daniels's face. "You've called us here for *that?*"

"In addition—"

"This is outrageous."

"In addition"—Mr. Pierce managed to be heard over Ms. Daniels's booming voice—"she's subjecting my clients to material outside the scope of the humanities curriculum that they find offensive."

"Such as?"

The dean and aides and Sally seemed to balance on the edge of their chairs, waiting for the fatal blow.

Mr. Pierce adjusted wire-rimmed bifocals, then opened a folder and withdrew a single sheet with such flourish, it might have been the Magna Carta. "She's made numerous references—both in song lyrics and lecture material—to

Jesus Christ. She's insisted on linking slave narratives and protest chants to what she calls 'age-old hymns,' then suggests these Christian principles are the 'cornerstone of American culture.' I have some notes here from a lecture purportedly on . . ." A gold watch and a slim wedding band gleamed as Mr. Pierce enumerated the ways Sally had violated his clients' rights.

Sally squirmed about in her seat. If she thought she was uncomfortable, how about this man, eloquent in speech and dress, who, by virtue of his profession, was forced to represent thugs who resented his very existence?

". . . harassed them, humiliated them in front of their peers . . ."

Ms. Daniels and the dean's aides scribbled wildly on their legal pads.

The dean's nose twitched as if he were stifling a sneeze.

In a bizarre sleep cycle, Harold nodded off, then jolted awake to stare out the same window that had hypnotized the boys. Sally felt her blood pressure shoot toward the ceiling. Her job was on the line, and it was just a nap time for Harold.

". . . I have no choice but to ask that Mrs. Stevens be placed on leave until this matter can be fully investigated."

Hugh tossed back his head. His lips curled to reveal greenish teeth.

Sally couldn't take her eyes away, though she wanted to. She remembered another tormenting face looming over her, eyes bulging, tongue lolling. For a minute, hate roiled inside, and she longed to match Hugh's sneer with one of her own. Then she remembered that he was just a boy, she was his teacher—but they were trying to take that away from her. With effort, she looked away from all three boys. She had to do something fast. She wanted, she needed her job.

"That's ridiculous. She hasn't even had a chance to obtain counsel." Ms. Daniels was on her feet now, her notepad a fan. "There's been no formal notice—this is a kangaroo court."

"Our materials were presented to the department and . . ."

Cupping her hand against her mouth, Ms. Daniels sat back down, then leaned toward Sally. "You don't want to go on leave, do you? It may affect your benefits, your retirement—"

In a flash, Sally was on her feet. "Of course not."

"*Psst!* Sal—Mrs. Stevens, what are you doing?" When Ms. Daniels tugged on the lapel of Sally's jacket, her folder slid down her lap and landed at Sally's feet.

Sally let her gaze linger on the faces of the aides, Harold, and the dean as if she were memorizing them. She wasn't leaving this room until she'd said her piece. After all, she had rights too, didn't she?

"Mr. Pierce spoke of a fabric," she began, silently praying as she spoke. "Humanities works like a fabric too. What we think, what we say, what we hate, what we love, all woven into songs and dances and paintings, even buildings. Frozen music, they call them. A giant tapestry out there, all of it." Sally strode to the window and pointed past cornfields to the distant freeway. Cars streamed north, their taillights visible against a darkening sky. *Hurrying away from the rising storm. Just like me.* "We can't pick and choose which part of our past to include. Religious forefathers. Oppressed slaves. If they lived it, we have to show it. On canvas, marble—"

Mr. Pierce jumped to his feet. "I hardly think this is the time for a soliloquy."

"Thank you, Mrs. Stevens. Mr. Pierce," the dean said as Sally returned to her seat.

Ms. Daniels leaned close, the smell of cologne and breath mints coming with her. "Well done." Her eyes shining, she appraised Sally as if seeing her for the first time. "I couldn't have said it better myself."

Sally forced a smile on her face, shoving away the suspicion that Ms. Daniels considered her a dumb blond.

The dean rubbed his hands and nodded to his aides. The three stood in unison, a trio about to perform.

"I'm scheduling a formal hearing." The dean nodded toward Mr. Pierce. "You'll get notice of the date." Next Sally was subjected to "the look" that supposedly sent shivers down the spine of many a faculty member. Including her. Thankfully, crinkles about the dean's eyes hinted at a smile. "Until then, I have no grounds to place Mrs. Stevens on probation. She'll continue in her current position unless notified otherwise."

A bit of the tension eased off Sally. For now, anyway, things were okay.

Mr. Pierce nudged Jay and Rex and Hugh, who bobbed their heads as if he'd awakened them. Hugh rose. With that devilish grin still plastered on his face, he pretended to slash his throat with his index finger.

Sally met his gaze. Would he be so bold if he knew that she'd killed a man?

The three boys grinned now, cats that had swallowed a cageful of canaries.

Sally might have grabbed those boys by the collars of their ill-fitting jackets if Ms. Daniels hadn't purposefully led her to the door. Was this whole charade really over song lyrics? Or were their motives as murky as the waters of a Louisiana bayou?

On her way out of the office, Sally pulled memos from her cubbyhole mailbox. With the same lightning speed in which rumors zapped the campus, Sally sorted the messages. There were encouragements from colleagues and students. A couple that might be classified as hate mail. Some chatty tell-me-more notes. She stuck some in her bag. Some she crushed into wads and tossed in the trash. But not the one from Shamika, who wanted to start their sessions "ASAP." Her step lighter, Sally left the building

◆ ◆ ◆

Here Sam stood, at the threshold of the associate pastor's inner sanctum. A place for hysterical women, grieving widows. But not men like him. Until now.

With a nod, Pastor Todd motioned for Sam to enter.

Beams from a brass floor lamp cast halos across rows and rows of impressive books. Sam paused at a wall of bookshelves and ran a finger over spines protecting the words of Lewis and MacDonald and Piper and Chambers and Murray, even a worn copy of Calvin's *Institutes*. As usual, he thought of his wife, who'd love to get her hands on these. For the first time since Sam had scheduled the appointment, he felt confused, like when he'd tried to grasp the theological tenets laid out in *Institutes*. Was this going to help or just pull things off a marriage shelf that was well-stocked, just dusty?

Pastor Todd sat behind a desk stacked with periodicals and newspapers. A sweep of silver hair lay stiff against a boxy head. He looked like—he *was*—someone Sam could trust.

Even the pastor's clothes—a work shirt tucked into blue jeans—comforted Sam. He'd been right to come to this rock, both the church and the man. After a long career as pastor of a big-city church, Todd had returned to the black soil of his boyhood home. Then God used heart problems to yank him off a tractor and steer him back into ministry. For three years now, Todd had rolled up his sleeves and dug into whatever the head pastor had asked of him, including youth mission trips. Strange assignments for a man with irregular heartbeats. *But God can take care of that.* A tremor went through Sam. *And He can take care of this.*

A rawboned hand enveloped Sam's shaky one. "How's ISU treating you?"

"Can't complain." Sam tried to settle into a chair better suited for a parlor, and prepared to talk around the subject, like men did. "How was that conference at Moody?"

"Pretty good. I stayed with an old friend who moved up there when his wife died." A smile crinkled lines about his face. "And Chicago's nice in the fall."

"Very nice."

"But you're not here to talk about the window displays on Michigan Avenue."
Sam's laugh was brittle.

"So tell me what's going on." Todd crossed his legs, then leaned back.

Now it was Sam's turn to shift about in his seat. Why was this so hard? Pastors were sworn to confidence. Besides, who'd be interested in their little sex problem? He took a deep breath. "I'm here because Sally and I, we're having . . . oh, a bit of trouble."

Todd's eyebrows shot toward the ceiling. "You and Sally?"

One glance at Todd's slack jaw told Sam all he needed to know. Any time he tried something spontaneous, emotional, something so *Sally*, this was what happened.

From their places on the shelves, all the books pushed in on Sam, their voices a rumble, then a single accusatory shout: *Traitor!*

Sam gripped the armrests and stifled a snarl at Sally's allies, who seemed ready to jump down from their lofty spots and choke him. He fought the urge to jump out of his chair and bolt, but what good would *that* do, now that he'd committed? Speaking of commitment, it wasn't like he'd divorce Sally. They were in it for life. He had to search his memory's hard drive to recall their last fight, not counting the bedtime "issues." Oh, yeah. Sally wanted to slip a little extra into Suzi's checking account and he didn't. Something important like that. And now he was here, in this froufrou chair. He shifted about, his back aching, his heart doing the same. He shouldn't have come.

Todd stepped around the desk and clapped a grizzled hand on Sam's shoulder. "I should've done this first. It's just . . . well, you took me by surprise."

Both men bowed their heads.

"Dear Lord, You direct our discussion," Todd began, his hand still on Sam's shoulder. "Show us how we can love our wives as You love the church. In Jesus' name." With sure steps, he returned to his chair, picked it up, then moved it close to Sam's. "Just start at the beginning," he said, his gaze steady.

Sam propped his right leg on his left knee and stared at the sole of his shoe. With puffs of shaving cream on his face, he'd recited his speech to the mirror, and the mirror had understood. Why was it so hard now? And how far back was he supposed to go? To their wedding night?

"Sally just—" Words died in his throat. Wasn't he betraying Sally by revealing details of their sex life to this preacher who knew Sally as the woman whose drawl soothed infants in the nursery, old folks in the nursing homes? The woman who led that group of renegade women through the Bible?

Silence enveloped all the sound waves in the room and blotted out everything but years and years of memories.

"Not now, Sam. Please. I know you understand. Nothing, Sam. It's just . . . I'm tired. I have a headache." Then that phony smile. *"Sleep well, love. I just . . . can't. You understand, don't you? Don't you? Don't you? Don't you!"*

Sam squirmed about in the blasted chair. How could he explain this tactfully and not sound like a sex maniac? "She's just . . . not interested in, ah, intimate things," he finally managed, avoiding Todd's face.

"And that bothers you."

"Well, yeah. I mean, I love her." Waving arms punctuated Sam's words. "Always have. Always will. But yet . . . I want to have . . . that kind of relationship."

Todd leaned over and put his hand on Sam's shoulder. "Have you talked to her about it?"

"Well . . . not really." The words wrapped about Sam like a noose. "No. No. I haven't. At least not in a long time."

"You don't need me to tell you that's your first step."

"But I'm . . ."

"You're what, Sam? What?"

"I'm afraid. I don't want to hurt her. She's a wonderful mother. Wonderful person." The lump in his throat made it hard to continue. "I love her." He thought of how she threw out her arms and rewarded him and stray dogs and children and students and old ladies with hugs warm enough to ward off a winter chill. Maybe that was the problem. Maybe there was nothing extra for him at the end of the day when they lay side by side in bed.

There it was again, the overwhelming billow that masqueraded as silence. More disquieting than the sound of a thousand probing questions. Sam wanted to yell, wanted to lash out, anything to stop the stealthy attack of silence. And why was Todd just sitting there? Wasn't he supposed to get to work, tell him how to fix this?

"Go on." His eyebrows half-moons over unblinking eyes, the pastor waited.

"But I'm still a man." A torrent of emotions spilled from Sam like water over a causeway. "I'd like to—I'm just not ready for that part of my life to be over."

"Has she gone through menopause?"

"Well, yes. I mean, she's doing it now." Sam wiped sweat from his brow, wanting to laugh at the irony of this. Sally'd drenched their sheets off and on for the past year. Was he having sympathy sweats now? Or was this subject just too much to handle?

"You need to talk to your doctor, Sam, but as a woman ages, things change. You may have to change your, ah, techniques."

"Things haven't changed, Todd. They've been like this for years."

"Now, Sam . . . I mean, you have two beautiful children."

"Adopted."

"Well, yes. But—"

"Todd, I could count on one hand . . ." Sam bit back the rest of the sentence but didn't stop the words streaming through his mind . . . *the times she's enjoyed sex. And don't ask how I know. I just do.* No. He couldn't let his friends—the numbers—do this. Unlike books, numbers weren't restricted to the English language Sally spoke and wrote and read so fluently. His friends—integral, infinite companions—spoke in a universal way. They called out from the alarm clock. They wrapped up the intricacies of sports in the box scores he pored over every morning. They quantified and qualified his checkbook, his lectures, his life. And he was going to reduce his relationship with his beloved to a series of tally marks on a metaphorical bedroom wall?

All the memories of raising children and nurturing Sunday schoolers—and there were dozens of them—rushed up to stop the assault. No. He wasn't going to betray Sally this way. Not with the numbers. It wasn't right. He studied his ring finger, the one that bore the eighth-of-an-inch-thick fourteen-karat gold band Sally had placed there twenty-six years, nine months, and five days ago. She'd promised to love, honor, and cherish him, and she'd done her best to keep it. If she could do it, he could too.

The chair groaned when Sam stood up. "If you'd just pray for us, Todd. I'm sure it'll work out."

"Of course I will."

Sam moved toward the door.

"Sam . . ."

Sunlight poured in the window, its sudden brightness making Sam's eyes water. Unable to speak, he nodded at the older man.

"Is there any history of physical or sexual abuse in Sally's past?"

"Heavens, no." Sam grimaced at both the titter of his voice and the absurdity of the question. "Her father was a college professor, her mother, an artist type. Pillars of the church. That was one of the things that drew me to her, was—"

"Sexual abuse creeps into shacks and mansions alike, through ripped screens and the most elaborate security systems money can buy."

Sam shook his head. There was just no way.

As they stepped into the hall, Sam cast a look toward the secretary's desk and then the other way, to the senior pastor's office. *Good! No one in sight.* He dug a handkerchief out of his pocket and mopped his face. Did men go through *men*-opause?

Todd leaned against the office door frame, his eyes cloudy.

Queasiness enveloped Sam's gut. This had been a huge mistake.

"Here's the game plan, Sam." Todd straightened abruptly, as if a decision had been reached. "Talk to Sally. Ask her to schedule a doctor's appointment. You do the same." He dusted off his jeans and motioned Sam toward the office exit. "We'll pray. Both of us. And call me in a couple of weeks."

Without looking back, Sam scurried outside. Gray and black and white clouds shifted in a power struggle that cast shadows over the handful of cars parked in the lot. Sam pulled out his keys and got in his clunky old Ford. Had this done any good? Any harm? He felt as wishy-washy as the weather.

The engine rumbled, then died. Sam pounded the dash, sick of trying to jump-start everything. This session had served no purpose except to further exasperate him. And what if Sally found out and it flooded the good parts of their marriage? Good except for no sex life. Unless you counted an occasional roll-on-your-back, eyes-shut, jaw-clenched compliance. And he didn't.

Finally the car started. Sam lurched and bumped his way toward the campus. He really didn't want to talk to Sally about this. He really didn't want to keep living this way. And he really didn't know what he was going to do.

Chapter 9

MOVING

Ole Satan he a busy man. He roll stones my way.
Mass' Jesus is my bosom friend. Roll 'em out o' my way.
—Negro spiritual, "Come Go with Me"

Get your mind off yourself"—and that stupid meeting. "Help someone else." As Sally drove through a part of town real estate agents would call "transitional," she sure hoped Mama was right. She glanced at her directions, then pulled into a brick driveway.

A shuttered colonial stood proud and shadowed a well-preserved carriage house. Long ago, horse-drawn carriages had probably delivered satin-gowned women and tuxedoed men to this very address. White women. White men. And black servants had bowed low, their calloused hands making sure hems stitched by house slaves' nimble fingers wouldn't graze silty Illinois loam. But things had changed, thanks to the efforts, the struggles, of so many. Or so Sally hoped.

The yard abutting the north side of Ruby's property bespoke a different struggle. Beer cans and dandelions partnered to choke out gasps of winter grass. A Pi Kappa Alpha flag flew at half-mast from a broomstick affixed to a classical column that had once probably supported the Union Jack. Order seemed to be just barely hanging on, a dilemma Sally, after her meeting, could relate to.

Briefcase and bag in hand, she pushed the bell, then jumped back. It was one of those old-fashioned types with an electrifying buzz. She couldn't help but wonder, with that kind of welcome, if she was doing the right thing.

There was a rustle at the window. Then the door opened, just wide enough for Ruby to peek out. Her smile cut through the chill that had had Sally shivering all morning. *So cold up here, always so cold . . .*

"Come in, Mrs. Stevens."

Now it was Sally's turn to smile. The resentments Ruby had displayed at the first meeting seemed to have been left at the hospital.

"Please, call me Sally." She stomped frost onto a woven welcome mat, then hurried inside. "How is she?"

"Good times, bad times." A frown creased Ruby's face. "Mainly bad. But here, let me take your things. Come on in." She disappeared down a hall, Sally's black crushed velvet coat and hat carried in her outstretched hands as if they were royal robes.

Sally stared at her feet, wondering if she should take off her boots in the home of black folks. *"Act like you're with royalty,"* Mama whispered, *"if you don't know what to do, and it'll work out jes' fine."*

"Should I slip these off? This is such a gorgeous floor, and . . ."

"Oh, no need to, Mrs.—Sally," Ruby's voice wafted down the hall. "Jes' come on back here and sit a spell."

Sally stepped inside, breathing deep of home cooking, floor wax, and a hint of gardenias. To her right was a parlor; to the left, a dining room. Wool rugs gave pattern and color to burnished oak plank floors. Sally squinted, her eyes adjusting to the darkness, for in both rooms, damask draperies shrouded floor-to-ceiling windows. Sally wanted to grab the lustrous material, fling it back, and let light work its miracles. If she found darkness depressing, what would it do to this girl who had just been raped? Her jaw tightened as she determined to bring sunshine into this house.

"We got her home this mornin'. She's been workin' on them things you gave her." Ruby motioned Sally forward. "Now if you wanna slip off those boots and warm your toesies, won't bother us a bit."

"Oh, that's okay." Whispering prayers, Sally followed the path Ruby had trodden, down a picture-lined hall.

Those few steps took Sally into a room bursting with light and life. A rose-colored davenport stretched along a plate-glass window whose sill was crowded with blooming African violets. Occasional tables added depth and interest. Tiny collectibles—a Baccarat paperweight, a Lladro figurine, a simple wooden cross—testified of treasured moments. Yet it was the two cane-backed rockers fronting a stone hearth that grabbed Sally and pulled her in. A person could find refuge here, in front of the fire. A person could let the flames warm cold hands, cold hearts, could let the sparks coax out the world's problems, then melt them away. A person—Sally stifled a gasp. The rail-thin collection of arms and legs mounded into one of the chairs *was* a person: Shamika. Thinner, if that were possible. More vulnerable-looking. Sally longed to throw her arms around Shamika and cry. Instead, she managed a smile.

"I'll leave you two alone." Humming to herself, Ruby shuffled out of sight.

The fireplace's crackles and pops punctuated the silence. A few embers glowed, allying with sunlight to warm the room. Sally clutched her briefcase, eager to seize this opportunity, yet willing herself to go slow. Careful not to bump into Shamika's rocker, she smoothed into its twin, a cross-stitched pillow cushioning her bottom. She leaned across the armrest and patted Shamika's hand. "I'm so glad to see you."

Shamika shifted her body so that she faced Sally. Her eyes were wet with tears, yet her jaw jutted out with an attitude. "Are you?" With a bruised hand, she played with the fold of a velour robe.

"Of course I am." Sweat beaded on Sally's forehead. Her heart clamored for her to tell her story now, but her mind again warned her to go slow. "And have been since that first day in class." This memory made her smile. She pulled Shamika's hands into her own, kneading out the girl's clenched fingers. "Have you been a teacher? I mean, like vacation Bible school or Sunday school?"

"Just to my dolls. And if bossin' my friends counts, I'm practically tenured."

They both laughed, tension-breaking laughs. The chairs creaked, as if they wanted to laugh too.

Sally released Shamika's hands and moved her briefcase off her lap. "As a teacher, that first day in class is the roughest. The brittle faces, eyes narrowed to nothingness, studying every move you make. Just daring you to misspeak so they can pounce on you and devour you."

Shamika uncurled and pulled her chair closer to the fire. "You got that right."

"I'd gone through the spiel about the class being like a marathon and had charged into the 'let me tell you about myself' routine." Words flowed as Sally warmed up a bit. "When I said I was a Christian, some stared as if a button had popped off my shirt. Some fiddled with their pen. A couple of them had such hate in their eyes, I thought they might jump me."

"I sure know who they are." Shamika was alive now, and so was the fire. Oranges and reds danced about the logs, desperate to engulf them.

"Do you remember what you said to them?"

Shamika spread her palms toward the flames as if begging for some of their warmth. From the set of her jaw, Sally wasn't sure if she would answer.

Strains of jazz filtered in from another room, seeming to take command over the last little bit of tension in Shamika's spindly fingers. It was Wynton Marsalis, coaxing salve from his trumpet.

Doubt melted off Sally until all that was left was a warm glow. She sighed deeply, and hummed along with the infectious notes. She'd done the right thing by agreeing to this tutoring. By getting up close and personal. And perhaps Shamika wouldn't need to hear her whole story, but only the "lite" version.

"Marsalis does that to you too, huh?" The high notes in Shamika's voice lowered half an octave. "Smoothes out the wrinkles."

"You don't have any wrinkles, dear girl."

A smile played with the corners of Shamika's mouth. Was it the music? The memory of that first class session? Both, Sally hoped. "Of course I remember," Shamika finally said.

Sally puffed out her chest, imitating Shamika's gesture that day. "'Bout time we got some believers in this place.'" She narrowed her eyes, once again like Shamika had. "'If they stuff much more agnosticism down me, I might just throw up.'"

Laughter like a bubbling brook filled the room.

"So don't ask me if you're special," Sally said, and joined in the laughter.

They chatted a bit, then Sally dug her teacher's guide out of her tote. It was time to get into the academics. "About that chapter . . ."

Shamika held up her arm like a traffic cop. "I've started. And finished. Read ahead five chapters. Done the summary. Got a rough draft ready for you to annihilate."

"You've been busy."

"Tryin' to get my mind off that—those men."

"I can understand that." *And it's gonna be a struggle, sweetheart.*

Shamika popped open the rings on a binder, pulled out papers, and gave them to Sally. "I done my part of the deal," she told Sally, her arms folded over her chest almost defiantly. "Now it's your turn."

A draft swept through the room and chilled Sally down to her boot-clad toes. Why did God keep pushing this thing at her? The first little story had been okay. And there were a few more childhood reminiscences tinged with just enough color that might be helpful without digging too deep. But the rest— could Shamika handle it? Could Sally handle it? Sweat beaded her forehead, thanks to a hot flash or the fire or both. She had no choice; she'd promised. God would have to steer these words—He was behind this wheel.

◆ ◆ ◆

The dissertation's about done, and so is our time in Texas. Even though Mama had prepared chicken-fried steak and mashed potatoes, Sally dawdled with her food. For years, her parents had prepared her for this. Sally had prayed that God would stop it, especially since fall would've marked her sixth and final year at Meadowbrook, the best elementary school in Waco. But a hall lined with taped and labeled boxes informed her that her prayers had failed.

"I'll be defending in the morning, when the movers come. Y'all can—" Daddy set down his fork and glared at Sally. "What's the matter now?"

"I don't want to move."

"It's a little late for that. We'll be there next week."

Mama sugared her voice, like the tea she poured into Daddy's glass. "Now, Sally, it'll be fun. We've talked about your new school, your new friends—"

"I don't want a new school. I like mine."

The baby registered his vote, banging "No!" on the high chair tray.

"Robert, quit it!" Daddy's eyes clouded, warning of a storm. "You too, Sally."

"Donald, it's hard on her. She's just eleven. Why, at that age, I—"

Daddy slammed his fist on the bar; forks and spoons rattled back. "It's ridiculous. I finally get a job, and all y'all can do is harp about it."

Mama stuck out her lip. "Have I complained?"

"You don't have to. That pout says it all." He shoved back his stool and tossed his napkin onto the bar. "When we lost the homestead, Pa dragged us outta bed at midnight, told us to pack up. We didn't open our mouth till we got to Texas, or we would've been slapped off the wagon." Daddy snapped his fingers. "An Okie to a Texan, just like that. Made me what I am."

Sally squirmed in her seat. Daddy'd had to leave in the middle of the night? Without saying good-bye? She'd already told the dorm boys good-bye, carted Robert to their favorite campus places. Poor Daddy hadn't gotten to do any of that in Oklahoma. With a jump, Sally was at his side. "I'm sorry, Daddy."

Daddy pulled her close. "It's all right, baby."

Sally patted his cheeks, wanting Daddy happy, wanting them all happy. "I'll bet we . . . like Louisiana." It made her sniff to say the words, but she didn't cry.

In a gentle way, Daddy grasped her hands. "I've got an idea." Hazel eyes danced. "Why don't you write a report about it?"

"Louisiana?"

He nodded.

"Kinda like your dissertation?" With a plop, Sally was back in her chair. She hurried a few bites into her mouth, chewing as fast as she could. She'd go to the library—without Robert. It would give her something to do besides worry.

◆

Sally Flowers
August 10, 1963

Louisiana

Louisiana was the eighteenth state to join the Union. It was named after a French king. The state bird is the pelican. They have bodies of water called bayous. Snakes and alligators live in them. They are also called swamps. I don't think they sound very pretty.

The capital of Louisiana is Baton Rouge, which in French language means red stick. Most people in Louisiana farm and fish to make money. There probably are some stores too.

Monroe is a town in the north and middle part of Louisiana. It has the Ouachita River and many other oxbow lakes, bayous, and streams.

I don't think we are going to like living in Louisiana very much, but at least Daddy says we'll get our own house.

◆

Someone knocked on the front door.

"Hey, get that, Sally!" Mama yelled.

Two men, their shirts soaked with sweat, stood in the hall. Another man, his shoulders hunched, his head bent, stood behind them.

100

"We're with Allied," the bigger one said. Sally guessed his name was Frank since that name was sewn on his shirt pocket. Freckles dotted sunburned arms. Frank stretched his neck like it had a crick.

Sally nodded and held out her hand. It wouldn't be nice to let these men know how she really felt about the move.

The smaller man, whose shirt said he was Ron, stepped back. "Little miss, got diesel fuel and no-tellin'-what on us. Right nice of you, though."

Both men came inside, leaving the third man outside. A colored man.

Sally spluttered, then tried to act like it was a cough. The colored man wore the same uniform as the others, except his shirt didn't have a name on the pocket. He fidgeted like something itched but kept his eyes to the floor. It was hard to take small steps backward when Sally really wanted to turn and run. But that wasn't good manners, even if the man was colored. "I'll get my mom," she said, still walking backward. When she got to the hall, she turned and ran into the bathroom. "There's men out there," she told Mama.

"Well, let them in." Mama had laid Robert on a towel and was changing his diaper. She didn't even look up at Sally.

"They *are* in—well, two of them. And one's outside. He's . . ."

"What?" After the diaper plopped into the water, Mama swished several times. "He's what, Sally?"

"He's colored."

"So?" Mama washed her hands and dried them on her skirt. "You finish up," she ordered. "That too." She pointed to the toilet, then hurried out the door.

Sally dressed Robert, balled up the wet diaper and put it in a bag, then lugged her brother into the front room. Negroes worked in the college Laundromat, but that was different from trusting one of them to move their things. And how could Mama let a Negro in their apartment? She stood behind Mama, watching the men, wanting to question Mama, knowing she couldn't.

"Of course I don't mind if he comes in." Mama was using her soothing voice as she spoke to Frank and Ron.

Frank cleared his throat. "Well, some folks do, ma'am."

The colored man still stood outside the door, studying his hands.

"And if it's not too much trouble . . ." Ron's voice trailed off.

Frank jostled Ron's arm and shook his head, as if Ron had gone too far.

Ron brushed off his pants, went outside, and spoke to the colored man. They both came back into the apartment.

The colored man bent his knees nearly to the ground and wrapped his arms around several boxes. Perspiration beaded his face. Every now and then, he made a straining sound, kind of like a quiet groan.

Mama walked around some boxes until she was right by Ron. "You didn't finish what you were saying. What did you need?" When he didn't answer, she touched his arm and gave him her company smile. "Please. It's okay."

Ron licked his lips, his eyes leaping from Frank to Mama, then back to Frank. "Amos here, he ain't been to the john—pardon me, ma'am, the bathroom—since we left the Florida panhandle."

"When was that?"

The colored man froze, his legs buckling under the weight of the boxes. "Before dawn."

Mama's hands flew to her face. "Why, of course he can use it." Her giggle sounded like a hiccup. "Give me a second, Amos." She hurried out of the room.

"Yes'm." Amos kept stacking boxes on the cart, his face twisted in a grimace. Sally tried not to stare at him, but couldn't help it. How did he keep from elbowing them all out of the way and charging to the toilet?

"Sally." Mother snapped Sally out of her shock. "Come here."

Still carrying Robert, Sally hurried into the bathroom.

"I was afraid of this. You didn't flush good." Plopping onto her hands and knees, Mama scrubbed the toilet bowl with toilet paper and the last sliver of a soap bar until the water foamed. She wiped her brow and pointed at a packed box, then at Sally. "Dig through there and get some towels."

"I can't," Sally whined. "It's already taped up."

"Then untape it, for heaven's sake." A curl had fallen into Mama's eyes. "He's our guest."

An image of Amos's pained face flashed through Sally's mind. "How far is Florida?"

"Too far." Mama's bun bounced as she used more paper to wipe off the toilet seat. "It's inhumane." She stalked out before Sally could ask more questions.

With a rattle of the handle, Sally flushed. Water and soap funneled down the toilet, but not Sally's shock. She never would've thought Mama would let a Negro in their house, much less in their bathroom. She understood why Amos shouldn't have to hold it all that way, but who was making him hold it so long, he had to use *their* bathroom?

After she laid out some towels, Sally peeked around the door, watching Amos at work. Except for having dark skin, he looked like the other two men. His muscles rippled when he picked up the boxes. Great splotches of sweat stained his shirt. Every so often, he stopped to wipe off his brow with a white handkerchief.

Light pierced through the dark muddle in Sally's mind. Maybe it was okay if colored people worked in white people's houses. Maybe that kind of thing was okay. But whites would never work for colored people. A smile broke out on her face, and she skipped into the kitchen and stole a cookie out of the picnic basket.

"Hey, get out of there!" Mama teased, her laugh letting Sally know it was really okay. *"A good snack's like a good hug,"* Mama taught her. And of course she was right.

While Sally ate, Amos went to the bathroom and came back. Mama kept staring at the workers as she finished up in the kitchen. Then she pulled cookies, fruit, and sandwiches from their picnic basket and stuffed them into a paper bag. "Here," she said, crooking a finger at Sally. "Give this to them." Mama rolled the top of the bag down so nothing would spill. "Amos too."

Chapter 10

AN ALIEN PLACE

If some of ya'll never been down South too much,
I'm gonna tell you a little bit about this so that you'll understand what
I'm talking about. Way down yonder, down in Louisiana . . .

—Tony Joe White, "Poke Salad Annie"

Would you look at all this?" Daddy asked, pointing into darkness. Sally rubbed her eyes. Every time she tried to focus, headlights of an approaching car blinded her. She sat up, wondering why Daddy's voice sounded strange. And why wasn't the car moving?

"Lock the doors." Mama reached across the seat and jostled Sally's arm. "Now."

"Wha—what's the matter?" They'd stopped at a filling station in a place called Shreveport, then driven to some ugly bayou Daddy had wanted to show them. Shreveport had only been a couple of hours from Monroe, their new home. Was this Monroe? Was this—

"Just do what she says." Daddy's voice boomed from the front seat. "Now."

Sally locked the door with shaky fingers, then pressed her face to the window. Part of her wanted to see what was scaring her parents; the other part wanted to tumble over the seat and bury her head in Mama's lap. She squinted but couldn't see much past the blackness.

Cries started low in Robert's belly. He waved his arms, his eyes bright with tears. Sally never understood how a baby could know something was wrong, but Robert always did. She leaned over Mama's seat and rubbed his curly head. *He must smell it.* "It's okay," she told him, trying to keep the quaver out of her own voice. "I'm right here."

With a lurch, Daddy drove through an intersection and pulled into what looked like a parking lot. Through the opposite passenger window, Sally spotted an old shopping cart, maybe a stack of crates. She shifted in her seat, trying to see better.

"You can't stop here!" Mama cried.

"And what do you want me to do? We've been driving around for an hour."

"Find something . . . somebody!"

Daddy's snort cut off Mama's words. "Nothing but apes over here."

The words stuck in Sally's mind, and she tried to digest them. Apes, like in the jungle? What was going on?

Mama whipped her head around but seemed to stare right past Sally. "We've got to get out of here."

"Don't you think I know that? That's why I pulled over. If you're just going to fan your face with it, give me that map."

"But I'm hot!"

"Well, then, crack your window!" Both of them muttered and fidgeted and rolled down their windows about an inch.

Sally'd seen Mama scared before, but not Daddy, who'd supposedly played a football game with a broken nose and two cracked ribs. What was out there? Curiosity edged in and conquered Sally's fear. She scrambled over the back of Mama's seat and peered out the windshield, but smashed guts and twisted bug legs clouded the view. She slid close to Mama and looked out her window.

Street lamps towered over the asphalt lot, but only one beamed enough light to reveal shattered glass, thick as dew. Shadowy figures seemed to flow about the strange scene. When Sally's eyes finally adjusted to the dimness, she understood everything. Daddy had driven them into Colored Town.

With a catch in her heart, Sally tried to take it all in. Dark people huddled around what looked like campfires, but why would they light fires in a grocery store parking lot? Yet tongues of fire curled skyward, adding orange and red to a black night. A woman, her hair bound tight in a kerchief, held a baby in her arms and moved from one fire to the next as if she were swimming a slow, sure side stroke.

Sally blinked. These colored people swayed in a way that the Baptist church back in Waco wouldn't have approved of. It had to be a sin, moving like nothing else mattered. Yet it stirred something in Sally. She longed to roll the window down farther and see if the movement stirred the air too.

Cackles and shouts and fragments of song seeped into the car. A mournful wail split through the other noises. Sally scooted over, clutching Mama but making sure she could see. "Wha—what's going on?" she asked.

"Over there." Daddy pointed toward the storefront. "Can't you hear it?"

It was hard to hear anything, with Daddy's mutters, Mama's clucking noises, Robert's cries. Sally craned her neck forward, looking past the woman and baby, past the fires.

Something rumbled, then hummed. Sally leaned close to Mama's window, willing her ears, her eyes, to do a better job.

A man stood on an upside-down crate, as if he were a preacher. Dark fingers caressed the buttons of a funny-shaped gold instrument, coaxing out notes that were both sad and happy. The music sent a shiver through Sally, and she didn't know whether to be afraid or glad. "What is it?" she asked.

"Some fool's playin' a saxophone. Stupid jigs think they can have a party, right here in public." Flames cast shadows across Daddy's face, making him look scary.

When the music stopped, the lot erupted in cheering and clapping, as if a parade were passing by.

The man bowed, then held a finger to his lips. But the crowd roared louder, and Sally wanted to join in and thank the musician for such a wonderful, beautiful song. She could be part of it. She could—

Daddy slammed his fist on the dash. "Dumb niggers. Think this hullabaloo will change things."

"Now, Don . . ."

"Don't 'Now, Don,' me. They're causing such a ruckus with their darned music, a man can't even drive."

Blackness again moved over Sally, strangely coinciding with the snuffing out of some of the campfires. All the questions she'd had since the day, four years ago, when she'd visited Waco's Colored Town, pushed in. She clenched her mouth, clenched her fists, even clenched her gut. What was wrong with colored people? Why did Daddy call them "niggers" one day, then the next day, say it was a bad word? Was it just a fact of life that you avoided dark-skinned people like you avoided busy streets, or people with colds?

Daddy's angry face forced another question to the surface. Why hadn't Daddy minded that Mama had given Amos their lunch? Sally's stomach rumbled through all the confusing thoughts. Why *had* Mama done that? They needed food too. Robert was the only one who'd eaten since breakfast. And that had just been a jar of mushed-up bananas. Sally tapped Mama's arm. "I'm hungry."

Mama fiddled with Robert. Daddy fiddled with the map.

All the fiddling made Sally's rumbling worse. "I'm *really* hungry." She put a whine into her voice. "I haven't eaten—"

Daddy rolled up the map and swatted Sally with it. "We'll eat later. Just sit there and be quiet."

As if in response to Sally's bleak mood, the musician folded up long limbs and sat, hunched over, on the box. He hugged the saxophone like music was the last thing he had left. And it might have been, because the crowd began making its way onto nearby streets, heads bowed, shoulders droopy. Slowly, slowly, they shuffled by, as if they didn't really want to leave, but something made them. Sally had felt that way when she had to go back inside a stuffy classroom after recess. She'd take baby steps, hoping a miracle would occur so she could stay outside all day.

When the crowd had cleared, the musician lifted his head and stared toward their car. As far as Sally could tell, it was the first time any of the colored people had acknowledged their presence. His eyes still on them, he set down his saxophone and walked closer, closer . . .

"Don!" Mama clutched Robert to her chest, but it didn't comfort him. In fact, he yelled as if he'd been spanked.

Daddy put down the map and gripped the steering wheel. "What in the—"

Sally curled into a little ball, right next to Mama. If Daddy was that scared, something bad was going to happen.

Rap. Rap. Rap. The man leaned over and peered into Daddy's window, teeth gleaming, his skin almost as black as the night. Sally buried her head in Mama's side, unable to stand any more blackness. Daddy had to get them out of here.

"What are we going to do?" Mama clutched Sally's arm and pulled a blanket over Robert, as if to shield him from the darkness menacing them all. It only served to make him screech like a crow.

"Get out of here, that's what." Daddy grappled for the keys, curse words slipping out.

Rap. Rap. Rap. The sound seemed closer. Louder.

Sally jerked her head up and stared. The glass reflected a flat nose, those white teeth, and . . . friendly eyes. Eyes like the ones she'd seen years ago, in Waco's Colored Town. Eyes that continued to dance, though the music had stopped. Or had it? Had the people just quit listening? Was the music still playing, even now?

While Mama heaved like she was sick, Sally stretched across Mama's lap and rolled her window all the way down. Eyes like that man's couldn't be dangerous.

"What are you doing?" Mama hissed, grabbing Sally's hand, trying to wrench it off the handle. "You roll that—Don, stop her."

A shadow hurried to Mama's side of the car. It was the black man.

"Hi. I'm Sally Flowers." Sally's voice shook even more than her hands, but she leaned close to the window and kept talking. She had to let them see that the man was okay.

"Well . . . Sally Flowers." The man's laugh rumbled from deep inside. It was the shopping center Santa's laugh, the one who did such a good job that Sally wanted to sit in his lap even though she knew the truth about him.

The man's back bent as he craned his neck even closer to the open window. Dark hands rested on dark pants. "I'm Jesse George, at your service."

"Jesse, we're from Texas, and—"

Mama made a sound like the air coming out of a tire.

"—we're lost. We're staying in a motel until we find a house."

"Sally!"

Jesse's laugh smoothed the last shakes from Sally. "You done found the right person. Ole Jesse live in Monroe his whole life." When he stepped back and straightened up, Sally saw that he was a small man, not much taller than Mama. "I reckon the driver need the directions." With a shuffling step, Jesse moved back to Daddy's side of the car.

Daddy jerked his head, as if his life depended on following Jesse's every movement. His lips had nearly disappeared into the tight set of his jaw.

"Don . . . Don." Mama clutched at his arm, but he pushed away and opened the door. With two lumbering steps, he approached Jesse, then paused, his shoulders hunched up so far, his neck disappeared.

Mama tapped Sally's arm. "Roll that up."

Sally cranked the handle of Mama's window slowly, keeping her ears pricked to catch the men's words.

Jesse leaned close to Daddy and pointed out something on the map. Daddy nodded and nodded.

When Mama's tap turned into a prod, Sally rolled the window tight, then climbed into the back seat to get away from Mama's smothering fear. She pressed her face against her window. What was Jesse saying to Daddy?

Robert's sniffles, Mama's sighs, blocked out any chance of hearing. Then the lone streetlight went out, and Sally's vision was reduced to shadows, Daddy's engulfing Jesse's. Two heads, both black now, nodded, as if dancing to the same song. Two hands moved close, then clasped and shook. It was enough to set Sally to bouncing, now that Daddy seemed to hear Jesse's music.

The door opened. Daddy plopped onto the seat, like he was exhausted.

Sally patted him on the shoulder. Of course he was. He'd driven all this way while they slept, and now it looked like he'd get them through Colored Town.

The keys jingled and jangled when Daddy stuck them in the ignition. While the engine idled, Daddy craned his massive neck around until Sally saw cloudy eyes, tight lips. "Don't ever do that again," he told her, "or I'll *blister* you."

Sally's face crumpled. Hadn't she just been trying to help? She looked to Mama, who always softened the blow of Daddy's words.

"Don't look at me, miss." The way Mama's brow furrowed, she seemed madder than Daddy.

Sally folded her arms, her fists tight knots. She'd helped them find the way out of Colored Town, hadn't she? Why were they afraid of those brightly dressed, swaying bodies? She thought of the wild animals splashed across the walls of her old bedroom. Was that it? Were Negroes wild from their days in the African jungles, chasing after lions and tigers and zebras?

"And don't tell anyone"—Mama practically spat now—"we've been on the wrong side of the tracks." She drooped over, her head resting against Robert's, as if all the energy had been sucked out of her.

Without a word, Daddy drove away. He clutched the map in his hand, occasionally cupping it close to his face.

The parking lot had seemed bright compared to the blackness that engulfed them now. Occasionally their headlights shone on tin and plywood shacks. Sally squinted, just making out shadowy figures on porches. Like darting fireflies, cigarettes haloed their hands with light.

The car rattled when they crossed railroad tracks, and Mama and Daddy cheered, considerably lightening the mood in the car. Yet Sally couldn't let go of the resentment that had stiffened her body. What had been wrong with talking to Jesse? He'd done nothing but help them, no matter what color he was. Through the clunk of their tires over rough pavement, Sally could still hear the sounds Jesse had mined from that gold saxophone. And the memory of his smile, brilliant against dark skin, lit up the dark side of Sally's thoughts yet confused her at the same time. Why did her parents think black people were so bad when they seemed so good?

Chapter 11

THE OTHER SIDE OF THE FENCE

Come gather 'round people wherever you roam and admit that the
waters around you have grown . . . for the times, they are a-changin'.
—Bernard Allison, "Times They Are Changing"

Her parents didn't seem to hear the knock, but Sally did. A real estate agent was expected; not a moment too soon. Spending seven days with a two-year-old in a cramped, windowless motel room had reduced Sally's life to boxes, sacks, suitcases, and smelly diapers. Even though they'd gotten to swim in the hotel pool, she wanted her books. Her dolls. Her old room. Her old school. She wanted Texas.

"Yoo-hoo." The knock got louder, yet Daddy kept reading the paper.

Mama fiddled with the hem of Sally's dress. "Remember, dear." Her voice became shrill and bossy. "First impressions . . ."

Sally scrambled away from her mother and flung open the door.

A woman, blond hair stiff as a mannequin's, straightened sleeves of a powder blue suit. "You must be Sally." She offered a ring-laden hand. "I'm Mrs. Tucker. You can call me Nancy Leigh."

Mama tottered to the door on wobbly heels. "So nice to meet you," she said, in her Sunday morning church voice. "Come right on in." Mama looked like a choir director, the way she waved and crowed. "Sorry it's such a mess."

"Even Heloise couldn't gussy up somethin' this small." Nancy Leigh rubbed her hands together. "That's what I'm for. Get y'all into y'all's own place."

"This is Donald, my husband." Mama's hand-waving and fluttering continued.

A grunt came from behind the sports page.

"And that's Robert."

"Well, isn't he jes' darlin'!"

Robert grimaced when the agent pinched his cheek but thankfully didn't holler.

Nancy Leigh gushed on about Robert's dimples and how smart Sally looked.

Sally itched to blurt out something sassy. *How can you tell I'm smart? Smart's givin' a good answer or talkin' like a grown-up. What she really means is I'm ugly.*

"Jes' the nicest family." Nancy Leigh brushed at her suit, slanting the rhinestone roof of a house-shaped lapel pin. "Well, we'd better get to business," she said, grabbing a neatly folded newspaper off the TV. "Three bedroom . . . big yard . . ." She tapped the longest fingernails Sally'd ever seen against the want ads her parents had pored over and marked up. "A wee bit out of our range." She seemed to be talking to herself more than Mama and Daddy. "That one's on the south side . . . Not that pile of matchsticks."

Sally rolled her eyes. She could imagine that phony voice playing "This Little Piggie Went to Market."

"Time to go, isn't it?" With one heave, Daddy hauled Robert off the bed and huffed out of the room.

Now it was Mama's turn to roll her eyes. "He's so irritable." She seemed to have acquired Nancy Leigh's syrup as she drawled on. "All these changes, you know."

Nancy Leigh fanned herself with the paper, a flowery scent spilling from the top of her blouse. "Honey, don't worry your pretty head. Heat does that to men." She swished toward the door, which Daddy hadn't bothered to shut. "He'll purr like a big ole tomcat, soon as we get him his own place."

Sally and Robert followed the giggling women as they made their way single-file out of the motel and into a sun so blinding, it set stars in Sally's eyes. The heat was liable to melt them before they even reached the parking lot. She wiped sweaty palms on her legs. Nothing about Monroe had been like she'd hoped. But now that they were looking for a house, surely things would get better.

"Here you go!" Nancy Leigh caught up to Daddy, then motioned them all toward the biggest car Sally had ever seen. Sleek white fins caught the rays of the sun and gleamed a message to Sally: Nancy Leigh was rich.

Daddy's whistle pierced through hazy air. "This sure is a nice Caddy. A new model?"

"A '62." Nancy Leigh rubbed at a smear on the sparkling fender. "Got a great deal. Up here, honey." She ordered Daddy to sit in the front seat, Sally and Mama and Robert in the back.

They drove past used car lots and old buildings, Nancy Leigh's bouffant hairdo brushing against the felt car ceiling. One hand gripped the wheel; the other waved at Daddy. "Those ads you marked are a wee bit out of y'all's range— you know, until you get a raise or two. Then I'll help y'all buy up."

Daddy leaned closer to Nancy Leigh. The two of them seemed to absorb all the cool air that was blowing through the little vents, leaving the rest of them to bake. Robert kicked against the seat, then pinched Sally with sweaty fingers when she grabbed his leg.

"But here's the good news," Nancy Leigh purred. "There's a great little neighborhood, just getting goin', called Town and Country. New construction. Big yards."

"Quit it!" Sally yelled at Robert, then wished she hadn't. Before they could scoot out of reach, Daddy managed to slap both Sally's arms and Robert's legs with one swoop.

Robert let out a squawk that would make a parrot proud.

"It'll be perfect for y'all's little family." Nancy Leigh yakked louder, as if she could gush over the aftermath of Daddy's slap.

Sally bit her lip but a quiver continued. Why did Daddy have to embarrass her in front of a stranger? She made a face at Daddy's back, then leaned close to Robert. "Shut up," she whispered. "Now. Or he'll whip us."

They stopped for a light. Sally pressed her face to the window, dazzled by the blinding white glare that followed them wherever they went. Finally her eyes focused long enough to read the green sign. *Bayou DeSiard.* "D— DeS—" Sally gave up trying to pronounce the name and feasted on the scene. Ski boats whirred about, slicing through diamond-studded water. Swimmers bobbed up and down like tops. A funny-looking bird with a long gold snout and a squatty white body perched on a rotten log. Something about its gleaming eye pulled a giggle from Sally. Unlike that Shreveport bayou, this one sparkled with life. Sally longed to splash into the water, get close to that bird . . .

"Like it, honey?" Nancy Leigh, her eyes shiny as pebbles, caught Sally's glance in the rearview mirror. "There's a bayou practically out your back door."

"Aren't they dangerous?" Mama asked.

Nancy Leigh shifted so Sally couldn't see her face anymore. "Well, no, not really. And it's not that close." Her voice shifted gears too. "More like down the street." Her waving hand found a folder and shoved it at Daddy. "Three bed-rooms. Two baths. A great room. New shag carpet."

Daddy's head ducked over the papers. "Is it all-white?"

Nancy Leigh fanned at Daddy like he, and his question, were irritating gnats. "Heavenly days! Y'all don't have to worry about that." She leaned so close to Daddy, their shoulders almost touched. "It's not like down in New Orleans." Red nails tap-danced on the steering wheel. "Around here, it never comes up."

"In Mobile, they're pushing on in." Daddy talked low, as if sharing a secret with Nancy Leigh. "When I interviewed there, that King fella had stirred things up good."

Sally leaned against the back of the seat, the air conditioner vent ruffling her hair, Daddy's talk ruffling her feelings. Where was Mobile? Daddy had applied for a job there? She thought those two trips he'd taken were for research. Would Mobile have been better than here? And why hadn't anyone told her about it?

Nancy Leigh maneuvered around a sharp curve, one hand on the wheel, the other waving at Daddy. "We don't have to steer our nigras. They know their place." Her voice became whispery. "King got met at the airport right here in Ouachita Parish. *His own kind* told him they didn't need his help. That things were fine." She touched at her hair, her voice loud and brittle again. "And they are fine. In fact, they couldn't be better."

Talk about Negroes. Again. Sally rubbed sweat off her neck. Would she ever understand whether colored folks were good or bad?

In the time it took them to span the intersection, the bayou had changed, and not for the better. Rotted stumps and clumps of plants dotted murky green water. Gray moss dripped from trees whose branches were knotted and gnarled like witches' fingers. Everything seemed dead, or headed that way. Sally half-expected to spot an alligator lurking beneath the water, hidden, like the secrets in her own family. Hidden, like the mysteries of Colored Town. She cut a look at Mama, hoping for a reassuring nod. But the tears on Mama's cheeks delivered an unsettling message: Mama missed Texas too.

They rounded another bend. A sign, *Welcome to Town and Country*, rose above a grove of pine trees. Peeling billboard smiles with four upturned noses greeted Sally. They looked like the characters on *Father Knows Best*, except this family had blond hair.

Nancy Leigh reduced their speed to a crawl, then reached over and flicked open the folder. "Third, fourth . . . here we go. Idell." She put on her blinker and turned onto Idell Street. "Looky! Can't y'all jes' picture it now?" Her giggle split into Sally's skull.

Brick houses lined both sides of the street. Sprinklers slung water across grassy yards. A girl about Sally's size pedaled a bike into a driveway. Sally thought of the cramped dorm apartment, then shot a look at Mama, whose tears had dried up. Sally could picture it, all right. And Mama could picture it too.

"Here it is." Nancy Leigh parallel parked in front of a neat little house, the yard canopied with pecan trees. Drapes lined a wide picture window. Flower beds just about burst with thick green bushes and long-stemmed flowers with violet beards.

In spite of Mama's shushes, Sally whooped as she jumped out of the car. If they could live here, maybe Louisiana wouldn't be so bad. Pulling Robert from Mama's lap, she set him on the grass then chased him about the yard. So this is what regular kids did, kids like the ones on that billboard. Kids who had a house. A yard.

Nancy Leigh glanced at the folder, which she'd somehow gotten back from Daddy, then nodded toward the house. "3812 Idell."

Mama, her face glowing like a Christmas angel's, clasped her hands together. "It's darling. And just look at the irises!"

Daddy was the only one of them who didn't seem convinced. He stood near the mailbox, his arms folded across his chest, a scowl on his face.

Sally chased Robert until sweat dripped from her brow. She wiped it away, but the air was so thick, so humid, it did no good. She thought of that sparkling water, longing to be in it. "Where's the bayou?" she asked Nancy Leigh.

The adults seemed to freeze on the front steps.

Nancy Leigh studied Daddy's face, then Mama's. "A ways out back."

Sally waited, expecting her to ramble on about how scenic it was, but she didn't. It left Sally wondering if a bayou was a good or a bad thing.

Nancy Leigh pulled out the keys, unlocked the door, and they all went inside. "Would y'all just look at this?" It was a spacious den, made cozy by a brick fireplace and a bank of windows. "Plenty of room for four." Nancy Leigh winked at Mama. "Maybe five." She clickety-clacked into a breakfast room, a hand on one hip, the other hand against a sliding glass door. "And looky out there!"

Sally dragged Robert to Nancy Leigh's side. "But where's the bayou?"

"Just look at that patio!"

Sally, looked, but not at the patio. Huge trees let branches droop over a yard that seemed to stretch for miles, all the way to a chain-link fence. A sandbox fronted a shed, which blocked the view of the house behind them. Sally locked her knees to keep from dancing. It was a paradise for kids who'd been cooped up in an apartment all their life! Forget the bayou; this was a yard!

"Ooh. Mama." Robert babbled and patted the glass with his hands.

Sally longed to do the same thing. They could play tag, get a swing set, build a castle in that sandbox . . .

Nancy Leigh winced, pulled a tissue from her purse, and dabbed at the greasy spots where Robert's hands had been.

Sally gathered up a squirming Robert, then turned to Nancy Leigh, who was still cleaning off the glass. "Can we go out there?" Her heart raced as if she and Robert were already playing tag.

"Why, sure." Nancy Leigh glanced toward Daddy, who was on his hands and knees, peering into a cabinet and tapping sink pipes. "That is, if your folks don't mind."

Daddy didn't even look up. "Fine with me," he said.

Nancy Leigh slid the door open, then pointed to the shed. "You could play dolls out there if y'all buy it." She shot Sally a red lipstick smile, as if they were keeping a secret from Daddy.

Mama followed them outdoors. "Oh, look. A magnolia." Her voice wafted away on a breeze that rebounded with a fruity scent, stronger even than the scent of the roses Daddy had brought Mama after their last fight. Sally's nose crinkled, and she sneezed. Then she picked up a magnolia bloom, buried her nose in ivory petals tinged with brown, and breathed deep. This time a rotton odor mixed with the powerful fruit smell. Sally flung the flower on the ground, then smashed one of the petals with her toe. In this place, good and bad mixed together so strangely, it made her head swim.

"Come, Fally!" Robert tugged at her shirt, then beelined for the sandbox. Sally jogged, then sped up, until pecan and magnolia and pine and oak trees became a blur of blue green and forest green and grass green. Sally's breath came in gasps, and not just from the running. This place had surprised her again.

A cinder block cottage, not a shed, as Sally had first thought, bordered the property line, its back wall only a few feet from the chain-link fence. Smashed pecan shells littered its roof. A tar paper base peeked through torn shingles.

Sally looked over her shoulder. Mother had disappeared. Robert had climbed into the sandbox and was flinging sand up in the air. She bounced up and down, then hopped at the sheer joy of so many possibilities. "It's our place," she cried, her imagination leaping to join the rest of her. The Boxcar Children could call it home, plus there'd be room for Nancy Drew to set up shop. Even as she skipped, she knew she was too old to play like this, but pretend friends were the only ones she had right now, except for Robert, and he didn't really count. When her breathing slowed, she made her way to the playhouse. She peeked in a window, but a thick layer of dust kept her from seeing.

Thoughts continued to whirl, quicker than she could organize and file them. A secret hiding place. Midnight court sessions.

Squeals from Robert made her check the sandbox, then the patio. Assured that her brother was all right, and that her parents weren't watching, she rattled *their* playhouse door—the want in Mama's eyes, the hope in her own heart, encouraged her to think this way. It was locked. Of course they'd hide the key. She raised the dusty welcome mat, then grimaced. Nothing but cottony spiderwebs, dead roly-polies. She scurried around the house, searching for something, anything. Triumph surged through Sally as she lifted a clay pot. But there was nothing but more bugs and dirt.

Leaves rustled. Sally jumped, then whirled around.

In the yard behind theirs, a sandbox interrupted a carpet of smooth grass. A dark head and a blur of white seemed to rise from beige and green.

Sally crouched onto her haunches, peering through the open spaces in the chain-link fence. Did their neighbors have children? She squinted and looked again.

There stood a girl, about Sally's size. Fuzzy eyebrows arched as she met Sally's gaze. Her face was full of angles, like a queen on one of the foreign coins in Daddy's collection. She wore a dress so white, so pure, it boasted of a hundred bleachings and starchings.

Sally rested hands on her knees, trying to stop trembling legs. The girl was colored. And Nancy Leigh had said colored people didn't live in Town and Country. Nancy Leigh wouldn't be happy. Neither would Daddy and Mother.

The girl moved closer to the fence and rested a hand the color of chocolate pudding on the barrier between them. "It's under that eave there."

This girl had been watching her look for the key? And should she believe a colored girl? Her back tense, Sally managed to crane her neck just far enough to keep her eyes on both the girl and the playhouse. Right under the downspout was a small plastic bowl she hadn't even noticed on her walk-around. Her head swiveled, all attention again on the girl. "How do you know?"

"I seen them get it." When the girl smiled, her dress became dingy, a pitiful gray-white compared to her glistening teeth. Her eyes widened and softened, and she smiled again. "By the way, I'm Ella. Ella Ward. It's nice to meet you."

At first Sally could only stare. She was beautiful. Polite. But still colored. The thought made Sally gulp once or twice. What would the adults do if they knew?

Another brilliant smile shoved away Sally's concerns about Nancy Leigh, her parents—her concerns about everything. "I'm Sally," she said. "We may move here." Words bubbled out. "I'll be in the sixth grade."

"Me too." Smile lines creased nearly flawless skin. "Where you from?"

"Texas."

"You a cowboy?"

Ella's chuckle made Sally laugh too. "Well, ma'am, I reckon I am."

"Ella!"

A cloud dimmed dark eyes, but Ella didn't change expression.

Sally stepped back, then darted a glance past the girl, past the sandbox.

A shadow darkened the screen door of the neighbor's house.

"Christella Grace Ward, you get in here." The door creaked open, a dark shoe and a dark arm now visible. "Right now."

Her hand arced in a wave, Ella twisted away. Ebony braids flopped across lace. Petticoats swished, as if to say good-bye.

Sally captured every step until Ella became a flash of white. When the door again creaked and then slammed, Sally stepped back like she'd been slapped in the face. So a colored family lived here, in spite of what Nancy Leigh had said. Her fists became knots. This would never be their house if Daddy found out. She bowed her head, eyes squeezed shut. *Oh, God, don't let them find out. Oh, God, let us . . . live here.*

Her prayer still in her heart, Sally shuffled through cushiony pine needles to the playhouse, then lifted the bowl. There was a key, just like Ella said. Wanting to keep it secret, like her knowledge of the colored girl, she covered it with dirt.

"It'd be perfect for your tools, Don," Nancy Leigh was saying when Sally joined her family on the patio. "Or how about a little art studio?"

Desire swept across Mama's face and lit up her eyes. She pulled Sally close, as if desperate to share what she felt inside.

Sally pulled away, scared of the desire she already had, scared to take on more. She wanted to say something, anything—no, not anything. The right thing. The thing that would make them buy this house.

Chirping birds cut through Nancy Leigh's talk about lease to buy, no down payment. The wind joined in, ruffling Sally's hair and urging her to speak. She tugged at Daddy's shirtsleeve as they all walked to inspect the playhouse. *Her* playhouse. "Can we get it, Daddy? Please!"

Daddy and Mama smiled at each other, but Nancy Leigh smiled more.

◆ ◆ ◆

"I had a cousin named Ella." For the last half hour, Shamika had barely moved. "She wasn't anything like that, though. Kinda nasty and rude." She stretched out, amazed at how down-home she felt with this white woman. "Did y'all become friends?"

"Not friends. Best friends." Mrs. Stevens set the rocker whining as she moved back and forth. "In my life, I've had several of them. A red-haired woman in Terre Haute, Indiana. A studious college roommate who turned out to be not so studious after all." Firelight mottled her pale face. "But Ella was that first friend." She wiped her eyes, which seemed all watery, probably due to an allergy.

As if it were the most natural thing in the world, Shamika reached across the armrest and touched a cocoa-butter-soft white arm. "And how did that happen down there? Are y'all still close? Did y'all—"

"Whoa, girl!" Sally exclaimed. "I never heard you talk so fast."

"I never talked to a white woman 'bout nothin' like this. Gotta get it out before I change my mind."

Mrs. Stevens giggled so long, so hard, that she started hiccupping. Then she reached down and pulled off her well-worn boots, some crazy zigzagged socks, then wiggled fat pink toes like they'd been set out of the deep freeze to thaw. "Blood sisters, we were, Ella and me. Until . . ."

The doorbell rang.

Shamika's breath caught. Yesterday and this morning, Auntie had shooed away her church friends, who'd streamed in and out, crying and laughing, carrying on like it was a wake. And she hadn't been downstate long enough to hook up with anyone yet. Not that there was anyone worth hangin' with here in Normal. So who was setting off that buzzer? Surely it wasn't that creepy . . . She rose, the rocker's creak sending a cringe down her spine.

Auntie's pattering came down the hall. Prob'ly been prayin' in her bedroom. Then Shamika heard a fluttering, like those drapes were pulled back, click, click click of the dead bolts slidin' open, and the squeak of the front door. She let out a chest full o' fear. Auntie wouldn't let no freak in here.

"Hello, ma'am."

Shamika muttered under her breath. It was that fool detective. Or maybe not such a fool. She could just picture Auntie's jutted-out hip, her jutted-out lip. "How can we help you?" Auntie sounded polite, but Shamika knew better.

"I'd like to go over a couple of things with your niece."

In spite of the near inferno in the fireplace, Shamika huddled under a throw. What kinda ideas this man be havin'?

"We finally got her restin'. I don't think this is a good time."

"It's okay, Auntie." Sooner she got rid of this man, the better.

With Auntie at his heels like a junkyard dog, the man tromped in as if he owned the place. He played at that blank-face game.

"I really need to be going. A friend's stopping by, and . . ." Her teacher kept running at the mouth as she stuffed her socks in her briefcase, then pulled on her boots. She was one strange woman.

"See you tomorrow?" Auntie asked, hopefulness in her voice. *Old Auntie's warmin' up to this woman too.*

Auntie hurried out of the room with Mrs. Stevens.

"Good morning, Ms. Williams," the detective said, after they heard the front door click shut. With jerky motions, like he was on uppers, he got out a notebook and pen. "I just wanted to follow up on a couple of things."

It sounded like Auntie was slamming dead bolts into place. Keeping danger outta here. But not this dude.

Shamika grimaced and turned her head so she wouldn't have to look at him. "We got a witness?"

"We've received a call on the hotline about a man in the parking lot around the time of the assault. A sergeant's interviewing someone as we speak—he'll probably take them in, see if we can't sketch something up. Before we do that, I wondered, does this in any way refresh your recollection about the number of men who accosted you?"

Shamika shot up from the chair. "How many times I gotta tell you, there were *three* of them pimply white faces in on it."

The detective didn't look up from his writing pad. "Let's back up. You say you saw three. Which one did you see first?"

Shamika clapped her hand against her forehead. "How should I know that?"

The chair and the officer's knees creaked when he sat, uninvited, in one of the rockers. "Let your mind go blank. When you stepped across the grass and onto the pavement—"

"Far as you's concerned, my mind is blank." She folded her arms across her chest. "I ain't got nuthin' else to say."

The pen and the pad disappeared into Detective Price's sports coat. He stood and turned for the door. "When you're ready to quit wasting your time, and mine, just let me know. You've got my card."

Chapter 12

DEEPER WATERS

Been wadin' through deep waters tryin' to get home
But the waves of sin, they dash so high.
—Negro spiritual, "Deep Waters"

Sally hurried in from shopping, set down some sacks, and shut out a dozen strange noises as she jabbed the answering machine button. Even a recorded voice could ease the fear that gripped her every time she set foot in their empty house. Thanks to those boys, just pulling into the garage sent a stab into her chest.

"Sweetie pie, it's me. Someone canceled on that tour I was tellin' you about, so I'm off to see the Vermont leaves. Oh, and that silly cell phone y'all gave me isn't working, so just call the church if there's a problem. They'll know how to get ahold of me." Sally envisioned puckered red lips and the omnipresent tilted bun. She missed Mama badly.

Another jab. Another beep.

"Hey. I'll be late. Challenge matches today. Oh, and Mom, could the guys come over afterwards? Just pizza or something?"

Sally smiled at the phone. Her son had good timing. Maureen would be over any minute for their monthly "shake and bake." They had decided not to compromise family nutrition by giving in to the fast-food fever that gripped the nation. No respectable Southern woman would. But Maureen was Irish. And like Mary, her other wonderful Irish friend, cooking topped Maureen's list of passions. Only God could have arranged for her to make two Irish friendships in the Midwest. But two Irish food-lovers? It was a miracle!

Just thinking about food set Sally's mouth to watering. She battled her way past the countertop, where the brownies she'd whipped up called to her from under a thin layer of foil, but she couldn't get past the goody drawer. Humming an Irish jig, she grabbed some Hershey's Kisses, unwrapped and inhaled them on the way back to the phone, then pushed the button again.

"Sally? Harold. There's an issue we need to discuss. Call me when you get this."

What issue could've come up since this morning? Sally rolled the foil wrappers into tight little balls, then shoved them in her pocket. Her heart pounded as she picked up the phone and dialed one of the few numbers she'd memorized. It wasn't Harold's.

"Sam Stevens."

"Sam?" Sally stared out the window, wondering how to word this. "I'm glad I caught you."

"Me too, hon. What's going on?"

"Ed wants to have some friends over for dinner."

"Okay . . ."

Sally could hear Sam's gears grinding. They always had kids over; what was the big deal? How could she verbalize the fear that gripped her at the sound of Harold's voice? Did Harold's "issue" have to do with the tutoring? She had to be careful on that topic, since Sam didn't know the whole story. Intuition told her the message concerned something darker. Something to do with those boys, or something even worse.

"Tell you what." Sam's voice got soft, Sam-Sal effective even across phone lines. "I'll get home early if I can. We'll sit on the porch if it's nice. Have a Coke. Talk."

Sally stared at a gust that threatened to blow away their maple tree. *Fat chance of it being nice in this climate.*

The doorbell rang.

"Sam, I've got to go. It's Maureen."

"Tell her top o' the mornin' for me. And I want some of her stew."

Sally opened the door and smiled. Curly hair, freckles, and grocery bags never looked so good. "Hey, girl." She hugged her friend and grabbed a bag.

"Hey, yourself. And where would ye be puttin' my grits?"

Sally giggled and let the thick brogue pull her in. "No grits today. Just brownies."

"And I've got shortbread."

Squealing, Sally grabbed another sack and lugged them inside.

Even before Sally had finished unpacking their moving boxes, God had put Maureen into her life, and they'd complemented each other like red beans and rice. Maureen homeschooled, Sally taught at the community college. Maureen talked brogue and cooked Irish, Sally drawled and cooked Southern. Yet they both loved the Lord and their families. Besides, Maureen made Sally laugh. And she needed a bit of laughing right now, so she nixed talking about her student. Anyway, that would violate some privacy act. What she needed from Maureen, other than yummy food, was female advice.

Words flew as they headed to the kitchen. There was no time to mess around, not if they were going to make jambalaya, kitchen sink pizzas, and enough Irish stew to stock the freezer. While Maureen unloaded the sacks, Sally put on her favorite CDs.

. . . we're gonna do it easy. But then we're gonna do the finish rough. Tina Turner's growling voice poured through the speaker Sam had hooked up in the breakfast nook.

"Real rough." Maureen echoed Tina, strutted to the stove, and set water to boil.

"I didn't know jambalaya could be rough." Sally pulled out a cutting board and chopped onions and garlic and peppers to the beat of "Proud Mary."

Rollin', rollin'. They danced about as they diced and mixed and kneaded pizza dough. Flour and cornmeal soon coated the floor.

Sally laid a moist towel over the dough, then grabbed a Diet Coke and a bottled water from the fridge. She'd put it off long enough. It was time to talk.

A French love song flowed from the speaker as Sally took a seat.

"This kind of music will slow things down, won't it?" Maureen asked, a dusting of flour on her cheeks.

"Yeah, and that's kinda what I wanted to talk to you about."

Maureen's eyes opened wide as she pulled a chair close to Sally's. "France?"

"Huh-uh. Me and Sam."

"You and Sam?" Maureen leaned back in her chair, uncapped her water, and drank deep. The sparkle had disappeared from her eyes. "What's up?"

It had seemed like such a good idea. Now it seemed stupid. Sally'd planned it so well, but she'd forgotten how to start it. How far back should she go? To the bayou? No. Not now, anyway. Maureen would think she was a weirdo.

A hand weathered from gardening and cleaning gripped Sally's. "It's okay. You can tell me." One look into Maureen's eyes told Sally that she could.

"It's no big deal, really." Sally raised her voice to be heard over a particularly ardent chorus. "It's just I . . . I don't seem to enjoy sex."

Maureen's mouth fell open. "That's it?"

Sally nodded, unable to speak. So Maureen didn't think she was a weirdo, didn't think this was inappropriate . . .

"You're going through the change, right?"

Sally nodded again.

"You need hormones." It was as if Maureen had eaten an energy bar rather than hunks of cheese and snippets of veggies. "It'll change *everything*." She lowered her voice as if they were talking during a sermon. "Brian couldn't *believe* the difference."

Sally opened her mouth, then shut it and just listened. Almost in sync with the smooth-voiced *homme francaise*, Maureen was singing the high notes, was holding the whole notes, was at the climax of her hormone success story. How could Sally butt in and dredge up that dark, nasty thing buried under the waters of a Louisiana bayou?

"Don't wait another day. I tell you, it'll change everything." The blush in Maureen's cheeks supported her premise.

Sally nodded, eager to validate her friend's efforts. Yet she seriously doubted some little pill was going to magically solve something that had been simmering on low for nearly thirty years.

◆

"Honey? I'm home."

Sally set some of Maureen's shortbread on a plate, then slid into a chair. As if she didn't know it was her husband from the clunk of his shoes when he took them off, then stuck them on that silly shoe rack by the back door. The clink of the hanger as he hung his jacket in the closet. Her Sam. Orderly and predictable. Just what she needed.

Sniffing and grinning, Sam walked into the kitchen. "Did you tell Maureen I love her?"

"Better watch out," Sally laughed. "I'll get jealous."

"Her cookin's got nothing on yours."

"Tell me that after you eat one of these."

Sam stepped to the fridge and opened it. "I promised you a Coke, but hot chocolate might be more like it."

"I need my caffeine," Sally said. "It's your fault, you know."

Sam popped the tab on Sally's Coke, not knowing, of course, that it was her third of the day. He tore a paper towel from the dispenser and wrapped it around the can.

"Voilà." With a swoop and a bow, he presented it to Sally as if it were a flute of champagne. "How could I have known you'd drink them for breakfast, lunch, and dinner?" He pulled his chair close to Sally's, then massaged her shoulders. "Besides, it wasn't Diet Coke. It was Dr. Pepper."

In the spring of 1971, Sally, a college freshman, had signed up for softball. Before long, she'd fallen hard for the fiery-eyed instructor who shared his passion for Jesus along with his passion for base hits and bunts and the other nuances of the silly sport. Once or twice, she thought his gaze lingered on what she hoped were wide eyes and a sunny smile. It wasn't until the last week of class, their culminating tournament game, that she was sure . . .

It was the last inning, the score tied. With a pitiful blooper that seemed to have eyes, she'd managed to get on base. The next batter slashed a grounder through the hole. Sally rounded second and huffed toward third, glimpsing a white blur. Under a puff of dust, Sally aimed for the base, instead jamming her foot into a crouching boulder of a boy. Her ankle twisted, and she lay writhing in powdery red dirt.

Through tears, Sally watched Sam streak to the nearby intramural field and grab a can of Dr. Pepper out of the hands of a startled spectator. Huffing, he flew back, bent over, and used the can to ice Sally's puffy leg, all the while barking orders to stunned students.

Sally'd known then that she was going to marry Sam. Of course she hadn't worked out the logistics, but God showed her that he was the one. Someone calm, in control, who wouldn't let anything ever happen to her again. And it certainly didn't hurt that a smile from Sam sent shivers down her back.

Sally took a slug of Coke and plunked the can on the table. "Where's yours?"

Sam made a bridge out of his hands. "I'm cutting back. Greg and I talked about it."

Without telling me? Sally swiveled toward Sam. This was very uncharacteristic. Very un-Sam. "You went to the doctor?"

"Last week."

"You never go. And I didn't see it on the calendar."

Sam chuckled in what Sally thought was a nervous way. "Something can happen without being on your precious calendar."

"Not if I can help it." Sally wadded up the paper towel until it was a tight little ball. "Nothing's wrong, is it?"

"On the contrary. Just a checkup. Everything's fine." He patted Sally on her knee. "And I recommend you have one."

Sally groaned. She was overdue for her annual mammogram, which involved a fair amount of pinching, prodding. But that wasn't the worst part. Nor was it when the technician reached into her gaping gown and positioned first one breast and then the other between Plexiglas plates, all the while saying in a monotone, "Don't move." The worst part was waiting for a generic postcard to tell her everything was okay. Or a phone call saying it wasn't.

Sam seemed to read her mind. "I really want you to go. For me. For the kids."

"But I don't have time, with that tutoring I've agreed to. And my classes."

"Make time." Sam-Sal vibes disappeared, thanks to the way Sam's eyes got cold and hard.

The door banged open.

"Hey."

"Hey, Mrs. Stevens, Mr. Stevens."

What sounded like a herd of cattle clomped into the house. Boys clattered to the basement.

All the noise pounded into Sally's head, which was answering with a painful throb. She waited until the noise abated, then tried to smile and make her voice light. "What's this really about, Sam?"

Sam cradled her hands in one of his. With the other hand, he tucked a strand of hair behind her ear. "Menopause has zapped you with the hot flashes and, uh, mood swings. Maybe you should cut out a few things. Talk to the doc."

Sally opened her mouth, ready to retort that she knew best about her health, and then remembered the other night. Perhaps this had nothing to do with mood swings, sweaty sheets—her mouth clamped shut. This had *everything* to do with sheets and what *wasn't* happening underneath them. She'd been right to talk to Maureen. Maybe she *did* need hormones. "I'll think about it, sweetie," she intoned. "I'm sure you're right."

◆

Sally used her briefcase to shove through the glass doors and, as usual, blustered, along with a wind gust, into the building. Once again, winter pushed hard on her, and she struggled to hold the front line. Of course, it didn't help that they'd stayed up late, playing Ping-Pong with Ed and his friends. And then she couldn't get to sleep, thanks to the jitters, for the second night in a row. She was definitely calling the doctor, getting those pills. When she had time.

There was Harold, leaning against her classroom door, bad news plastered all over his pasty face.

"Well, good morning." When Sally plunked down her things, a muffler slipped off. She picked it up and wrapped it around her neck until she felt like a well-dressed snowman. She needed some defense; she was sure of it. But something told her the muffler wasn't going to help in the slightest.

Harold took Sally by the arm and motioned her to a foyer sitting area. "Why didn't you call me back last night?" he asked.

"Well, my son had some friends over, and then we got to playing Ping-Pong—"

"I really needed you to call." As words hissed from Harold, a pert-looking woman, shiny black hair smoothed into a side ponytail, smiled brightly at both of them.

Harold's face and neck turned as red as Sally's scarf. "Sally, I'd like you to meet Yvonne. She'll be covering your classes until we get this thing cleared up."

What thing? Sally longed to lash out at Harold, but how embarrassing would that be for this twenty-year-old or whatever she was? She nodded and mumbled a greeting, then watched as Yvonne entered *her* classroom. If she wasn't such a young thing, Sally might sit her down in one of these lounge chairs and give her a good talking-to.

Anger enabled her to match strides with Harold as he hurried down the hall, but she didn't look at him for fear that first, she'd burst into tears, and second, bust his jaw. "What's this about, Harold?" It was difficult, but Sally managed to keep her poise by focusing on the building's gray-blue walls, which had been enlivened by the artwork of faculty and students. An abstract rendition of warehouse clutter, stark charcoals of human figures. Walls she wouldn't be looking at for a while, it seemed.

Students and their noisy chatter filled the halls, a sure signal that class was about to start. The class she wouldn't be teaching.

"Mrs. Stevens?" Two girls, both art majors, both in her ten o'clock class, bounced toward Sally.

Sally smiled, hoping they didn't notice she'd wiped away tears to see them.

Harold cleared his throat. "I'll be in my office. Waiting," he managed, then hurried down the hall.

"How you doin'?" asked Joyce, the taller of the two girls.

"Oh, fine." Sally hoped her voice sounded chirpy.

Joyce pulled out a notebook and flipped it to the class syllabus. "Can we see a foreign film instead of a drama?"

"Well, girls, that depends on which film you're talking about."

"Sorry, girls." Danita Daniels moved in like a one-person SWAT team, grabbing Sally by the elbow and steering her toward the women's room. She kept whispering to Sally, who couldn't hear a thing over the chatter of students.

"E-mail me, okay?" Sally yelled over her shoulder. *Even though I may not be teaching you, go ahead and e-mail.*

When they reached the women's room, Ms. Daniels pulled her inside. She bent over and peeked under the stalls, then turned on the faucet, as if whatever she had to say necessitated a hand-cleaning. "First, I want to tell you how sorry I am—we all are." She yanked a paper towel from the dispenser and carefully dried her hands.

"How . . . how did you know?"

"They had to notify the union." Ms. Daniels licked chapped lips. "Plus things like this spread like greased lightning."

Sally glanced in the mirror, amazed at how composed she looked when her world was about to crumble into tiny little pieces.

"When the suits upstairs reviewed your records, thanks to dear Mr. Pierce, they found some discrepancies. Apparently someone forgot to confirm a few things." The union representative dug into her tote bag and came up with a sheet of paper. "Section IV, Part A: 'Falsification of an application' . . . blah, blah, blah, 'grounds for immediate discharge.'"

Sally's muffler slipped to the floor again, and she let it lie right by a ribbon of toilet paper. "You mean they're firing me?"

"Oh, no. They don't have the nerve to do that. Not with the litigious climate out there. Plus, we'd throw a fit. And they're in hot water already over that age discrimination suit."

"I'll be right back." Sally entered a stall and latched the door. She needed to be alone. To think. It was the application, she was sure of it. When they'd moved, she'd only had a couple of courses and the thesis left to finish up her master's. Since she planned to complete her work over at Illinois State during the summer, she'd filled out the application as if the diploma was signed, framed, and hanging in her study. Except it was not hanging anywhere, because in some ridiculous state rivalry, akin to the annual football showdown, Illinois State refused to transfer Indiana State credits.

So she didn't technically have a master's. But she'd been teaching, off and on, for nearly twenty years. She had plenty of experience without a silly piece of paper. Apparently Harold was so desperate to fill that last-minute opening, he—or some clerk—hadn't really checked up on her credentials. And things had been so busy, with the kids, that she hadn't felt she could commute from Normal to Terre Haute, just to get a diploma.

"Hey, are you all right?"

"Uh-huh." Sally flushed the toilet, exited the stall, then washed and dried her hands while surreptitiously studying Danita Daniels. Could she trust this poster girl for women's rights, with her no-nonsense black suit, her pinched face devoid of even a hint of makeup? Not yet she couldn't. "Well, I don't know what they're talking about," she began, hoping evasion could provide a quick, if temporary fix. "False application?"

Ms. Daniels pierced her with such a penetrating gaze, Sally looked away. "They called Indiana State. The registrar's records clearly show you didn't finish your master's."

Sally shoved open the bathroom door, gulping air. Students' titters and the shuffle of boots, flip-flops, and tennis shoes created a surreal atmosphere in light of Danita's proclamation. But at least she could breathe.

"And Sally?"

Sally didn't move, just leaned against the half-open door.

"One more thing. Your students have filed a lawsuit against the college."

"Which ones?"

"Those scumbags have filed a discrimination suit. And your precious student Shamika has filed a suit over lack of security, lack of lighting, lack of about a dozen other things. But at least that one's not about you."

As Danita Daniels railed on, bad news piled upon bad news, creating an overload in Sally's brain so that she had to struggle to think. How had lawsuits been filed in three days? And just how did Danita know that Shamika was "her precious student"? Of course she knew the answer to that question, at least: At MCC, gossip traveled faster than the speed of light.

Chapter 13

A DAY TO FORGET

Someone cryin', Lord, Kum Ba Yah.
—Negro spiritual, "Kum Ba Yah"

Sally stepped to the door, one hand poised to press the buzzer, the other clinging to her briefcase as if her sanity depended on it. Was there a way she could broach the subject of the lawsuit and not fall off the tenuous bridge she'd constructed to reach Shamika and Ruby? She knew the answer without any more thought. *No. No. No.* These women's dealings with the college were none of her business.

The door flew open. There stood Ruby, hands on her hips. "Get on in—what happened to you? Look like you seen a ghost!"

With all the grace she could muster, Sally smiled. "It's just been one of those days." She worked hard to remember these women had reasons for their actions that she, with her white skin, could never understand. And as the union rep had so aptly pointed out, they hadn't personally named her in the complaint.

Ruby continued to scrutinize Sally. "Hmm. When you called awhile ago, you sure sounded down in the dumps to me."

"Yes, well . . ." Sally squirmed. This was so embarrassing, so humiliating. She tried, but failed, to shut out the memory of Harold's smug face as he'd confirmed in his office what Ms. Daniels had shared in the bathroom.

"Here, let me have that."

Sally handed Ruby her coat, determined to mentally hand over images of Harold so she could focus on Shamika. That was what mattered. "I'm glad you let me come over." The rich, smooth trumpeting of a jazz tune—probably Miles

Davis—wrapped around her and warmed her more than the coat ever had. She loved this music, this house, these women . . .

"Let you?" Ruby set Sally's coat down, then offered a strong brown hand and pulled Sally down the hall. "After all you've done for her?" Ruby lowered her voice. "She been in there studying on that book, keepin' her mind off it all. Then she conked out."

"So she's better?"

Ruby nodded. "Now that them *po*-lice done tromped outta here."

"They've been here again?"

"She like to blow a gasket when they told her she gotta go in and look at some pictures."

Sally stiffened. "Pictures? You mean in a lineup?" In the background, the trumpet got louder, urgent now . . .

"Yep. Nailin' this thing down." Ruby stepped close; so did her spicy perfume.

"Is she sure about all this?" Sally made her voice a whisper, suddenly aware that a strange emotion, akin to fear, had intruded upon their cozy little gathering.

Ruby's eyes got glassy. "She say she is, but I don't know. I jes' don't know."

As Sally made her way down the hall, something niggled at her, something she couldn't grasp. It was something Shamika had said the other day . . .

"What am I doin'?" Ruby snapped to attention. "Mama May'd have a cat, me actin' like I got no home trainin'. Sit on down, now. I'll get you a little sumthin'."

Sally took a deep breath and forced a spring into her step.

A sudden darkening of the already gloomy day cast a shadow on the room, dulling the sheen of the brass lamps, the collectibles. But it didn't seem to matter to the figure curled up in the rocker. Shamika had either been studying or throwing things around, judging from the papers strewn all over the floor.

When a spark flew out of the fireplace with a pop and a hiss, Sally tiptoed forward and shut the metal screen. This girl needed her rest. She'd just sit here, by this nice fire—

Shamika groaned and stretched both arms over her head. "How you doin', Sally?"

"I've had better days. But what about you?"

"That architecture chapter put me to sleep."

"Frozen music." Sally reached into her briefcase for the glossy photos that just might wake up this girl, might wake up both of them. She stuck on reading glasses, and with a flick of a folder, she'd flown away from Normal and all her little problems. Fallingwater. Sagrada Familia . . . She was in Barcelona now, strolling along ancient cobblestones, peering down dusty alleys . . .

Shamika's giggle and a crackle of the fire pulled Sally from a dream state. She collected the pictures, one of which had slid onto the floor, then dug in her briefcase for her notes. After flipping around a bit, she found the "For Critical Thinking" questions. "How'd you do on these?" she asked, peering over the top of her glasses.

Shamika stepped to the hearth, thumbed through her notebook, and pulled out a blue file folder. She handed it to Sally. "It's all in there." Even though her tone remained flat, the spark had returned to her eyes. "Now get on with your story." She cocked her head. "Please."

◆ ◆ ◆

"You can't learn on an empty stomach." Mama unwrapped yet another coffee cake, cut a chunk, put it next to a mess of scrambled eggs, then set the plate and orange juice in front of Sally. "And it'll help make a good first impression."

Sally glanced at the food, wondering if the colored girl would be at school, wondering if she'd make some friends. All her questions jumbled so, she didn't dare take a bite lest everything spew back out. "Another cake?" she managed, weakly.

"Sally Flowers!" Mama's hands flew to her hips. "They've welcomed us with open arms, and all you do is complain? Why, I've hardly had to cook for weeks."

The thought of cheesy casseroles and smothered steaks made Sally's stomach cramp like it had when she'd gobbled up handfuls of raw cookie dough. But it really wasn't due to neighbors' cooking. It had started last night, when Mama reminded her that this was the first day of school.

Mama retied the bow of Sally's pinafore, then sat down. "You've got to eat. It's a big day." She put a cool palm on Sally's forehead. "What's wrong?"

Unable to talk, Sally shook her head. How could she explain how last week's visit had affected her? The school, old and musty, had loomed prisonlike from a parched strip of land. And the woman in the office was the perfect warden—spitting out questions about accreditation and transfers. Mama smoothed over everything, promising to get records sent, forms filled out, but it hadn't helped. For the first time, Sally understood why the Boxcar Children hated school.

Mama's soft hand tried to smooth away Sally's frown. "It'll be okay. Think of it as an adventure. You get to walk, all by yourself. You're a big girl now."

Sally nodded, though resentment shot through her. She'd been a big girl for a long time, babysitting Robert, doing dishes, putting up with this stupid move . . .

"Hey, give me a hand with this."

A wave of Old Spice hit Sally, turning frowns to giggles. With that silly tie, was Daddy working on good impressions too? Did his stomach hurt like hers?

"How's my girl?" Big arms encircled Sally and gave her a squeeze.

"Hey, hold still!" Mama ordered as she fixed Daddy's tie.

Sally picked up her fork and mashed the eggs until they looked like baby food, hoping to keep from bursting into tears.

"Remember where you cross over?" Daddy asked.

In spite of six rainy days in a row, they'd managed practice walks, Mama ticking off landmarks. "Go to the yellow house. Turn left at the picket fence." As Sally nodded at Daddy, she flashed a look out back but couldn't see through all the trees. Maybe that colored girl—what was her name?—would be walking too.

"It's only a half-mile." Still standing by the table, Daddy rifled through the newspaper. "Nothing to it."

Sally hoped Daddy wouldn't go into his predawn paper route, his five-mile trek to school through a blinding storm, homework, the cows, the garden . . .

Daddy kissed her and Mama, then went out the garage door.

Dishes and pots clanged and banged into the sink. "Come on"—Mama hollered over the stream of water—"and get your supplies. They're in that sack over on the counter. So is your lunch money."

They made their way to the mailbox, Sally lagging behind Mama, who managed to balance Robert on her hip and smooth down pedal pushers. Her bun smelling of Dippity-Do, Mama planted a final smack on Sally's part line. "It'll be okay, sweetie," Mama said, more to herself, it seemed, than Sally.

Sally headed down the street. Every time she looked back, Mama was waving and blowing kisses, making Sally feel like a scout being sent out West. When children rushed by, Sally pretended they were Injuns, except for one girl, dressed as smart as a mannequin in a fancy store, with a pink skirt, short-sleeved sweater, and lacy socks. *She's the settler's daughter, and those Injuns took her captive. I'll trail them, rescue her . . .*

As long as Sally stayed in make-believe, the tightness that had crawled from her stomach to her throat wasn't so bad. Before she wondered too much about why the children didn't speak to her, they darted around the corner and out of sight, leaving Sally alone.

With each step, the stomach cramps got worse, so Sally pretended harder. She was a hobo, hopping on a train to Texas. When she reached the first intersection, she curled the toes of her shiny Mary Janes around the curb and glanced right, then left. No cars, no children. Nothing. Worst of all, no yellow house or picket fence. Her face crumpled, and she avoided the urge to plop onto the curb for a good cry. As she pivoted about, she remembered to stop and pray. Head bowed, she whispered, "Dear God, help me find the school. Help me not to be scared."

A mockingbird taunted her from the scraggly branches of a scrub oak. *This way, this way, silly! Don't you know? Don't you know?*

Hesitation in her step, Sally turned right.

A sudden gust rustled yellowed newspapers, which skittered across weedy grass, the sound so creepy, Sally's hands flew to her chest. Her bag plopped to the sidewalk, supplies tumbling everywhere. Sally bent over and scooped them up, her legs trembling all the while. She was lost. And she'd be late if she didn't find the right road.

She walked faster, then broke into a run, occasionally stopping to look back. Sideways. She kept going, past shabby houses, on a path running along a drainage ditch. An occasional horn honk, a distant whoosh, gave her just enough hope that she was going the right way to keep her from collapsing into tears.

When she came to another corner, she set down her bag. Her shoulder ached, and so did her heart. Any chance for making a good first impression was over. Mama would be so mad. And Daddy . . . Sally didn't even want to think about his tight lips and red face.

A truck, its engine idling, pulled in front of Sally. She glanced at it, then picked up her bag. Her eyes on the uneven pavement, she waited for the truck to move on so she could cross the street. *Step on a crack, you'll break your mother's back.* "Step on a crack . . ." Desperate to drown out the rumbling engine noise, the knowledge of being lost, she sang the silly rhyme out loud.

Creak, creak . . .

The noise made Sally raise her head.

A leathery-faced man grinned at Sally as the driver's window rolled down.

Creak, creak, creak.

Sally darted a glance to the right. *Nothing.* To the left. She swallowed several times, but the lump in her throat didn't move.

"Well, ain't you a pretty thing." Crooked, mossy teeth appeared when he smiled wider. Like the seam on a football, a scar ran across his cheek.

The hair on Sally's arms stood at attention. Not even Mama and Daddy said she was pretty. Cute? Maybe. Pretty? No.

"You're late, ain't ya?"

Though Sally shook her head, shock waves traveled through her. How did he know?

"And if you don't let ole Rufus give ya a lift, ya gonna be in big trouble."

A gold tooth winked at Sally. Eyes the color of ice gave her a squinty stare.

Sally took small steps backward, careful not to topple over, not daring to take her eyes off the man. Something was wrong; she'd read it in those eyes. She tried to think of what Mama would do. *Easy does it, Sally, even if you're scared. Don't let them know how you really feel.* She gave the stranger her polite smile. "Thank you, sir, but I'm almost there." The next part flowed out without Sally even thinking. "You know, it's just over that way." Her whole body tensed as she pointed toward the rushing sound of traffic, which surely was getting louder. There was a store over there, if not the school.

The smile vanished. The man's nostrils puffed out and then got small. Leaning a tattooed forearm on the partly rolled-down window, he crooked his finger toward Sally. "Come here. I've got a nice surprise for ya."

The door creaked open, as if it didn't want to cooperate. The whiny sound hurt Sally's ears. She froze, her teeth grinding together. Should *she* cooperate?

"Here." Rufus crooked a grimy finger. "You'll like it."

Even though Sally wanted to run, she took a baby step forward, her eyes on his face. He was an adult; she was supposed to mind adults. Yet even as she moved, something again told Sally not to mind this adult.

The man's eyes narrowed into slits of meanness.

Sally took a step back, then froze.

A bony hand shoved the door open. All arms and legs, the man stepped out. With that same bony hand, the man reached into his trousers.

Gagging, Sally's hand flew to her mouth. Why was the man showing her . . . it was his private parts! *Why . . . what*—blood pounded into her skull, mixing all her thoughts. It wasn't a surprise, she had to get out of here, he'd lied. *Mama. Daddy.*

Sally streaked down, then up the face of the ditch. The wind screamed for her to go faster as it whipped up her skirt. Saliva streamed from her mouth; she ignored it. She had to get away. Nothing. Else. Mattered. She pushed at the air, desperate to recruit it to her side. She slipped in mud, yet fought for her balance. She had to run, run, run.

Gravel crunched close, sending a shiver through her. "A big surprise, isn't it? And all for you, little girl." Again gravel crunched.

His voice, at her back now, sent chills down her spine. The louder the crunch, the faster Sally ran, her world reduced to pants and grunts and heaving steps. Closer. Louder.

"You better stop, or I'll tell 'em you're skipping school. Tell 'em that you wanted to see . . ." The words, slimy dirty nasty things, crawled closer, closer . . .

Wetness trickled out of Sally's panties and onto her thighs, but she kept running. She didn't understand the ugly words, but her heart told her they were the blasphemy the Bible talked about. And that he would hurt her. If only he could catch her.

Faster Sally ran, until her vision blurred. Faster, faster, desperate to separate herself from all the ugliness. The gravelly surface was a thing of the past—now the path was smooth. When Sally didn't hear an echoing crunch, she slowed down until her eyes focused. Her sides heaving, she clutched at her belly and darted a backward glance. The truck remained parked where she'd first seen it, but the man had vanished. She whirled back around, wondering if it was some kind of trick. But he was not in front of her, either.

She staggered to her right, a faded red stop sign coming into focus. A long-legged bird perched atop the rusty octagon, its head tilted, its eyes blank, like it had lost something. When Sally stumbled toward it, grateful for the company of anything besides that man, with a flap of powerful wings, it disappeared.

Sally looked back once again, still afraid that the man might be lurking nearby. But there was no man. And now the truck was gone. Her breath came out in gasps and no longer stabbed at her chest.

A horn blared once. Twice.

Fingers trembling, Sally grabbed the stop sign pole and clung to it, not daring to look. Where had *this* car come from? And what would happen now?

The horn honked again.

Sally peeked. It was a truck. A white truck. A different truck. Engine rumbling, it moved very slowly toward her. Rays of sun cast a glare over the windshield. Sally stepped backward, keeping her eyes on the vehicle.

The truck inched closer.

Sally gripped warm steel, her fingers aching, her lips racing in prayer. Somebody, something, had to help her.

With a lurch and a grumble, the truck stopped. The idling engine growled at Sally like a motorized wildcat.

Dear God, help me. Continuing to pray, Sally crouched, making her body as small as she could.

"Miss, you need help?"

Sally peeked at the driver's window of this white truck. It was not Rufus. But it was a colored man. She gripped the sign so tightly that her fingers ached. Would this man be a bad man too?

Velvety music poured from the vehicle, music that made Sally hope that the man would be soft, like the music was. But he was colored. Once again, her emotions warred. She didn't know what to do.

"*Psst!* Miss! It's okay."

He had fuzzy hair, like black dandelions. Something about him looked familiar, but that wasn't possible, was it? The man's smile loosed Sally's grip on the sign. He couldn't be bad, could he, and smile like that? She remembered helpful Jesse from Colored Town, and then that neighbor girl . . . Stored-up fear came out in dry heaves, slow at first, then faster and faster. Tears flooded Sally's eyes and streamed down her face.

"It's okay, little miss. It's okay," he called from the truck.

Sally wiped away tears, yet they kept coming. He'd called her "little miss" like he respected her. Like he'd never hurt her, whether he was colored or not.

Long legs stretched out of the truck. The man straightened, then leaned back and let the vehicle hold him up. He held his hands out, showing Sally palms that were much lighter colored than his face. A frown rippled his forehead and eyebrows. "Someone hurt you?"

Sally nodded, shook her head, then burst into tears. "He . . . didn't," she managed, "but he tried to."

When the man nodded like he too had seen that ugly face, Sally's sobs and heaves evaporated. He had taken on a bit of her fear. She studied his high cheekbones. Flat nose. Eyes like muddy water. Sad eyes.

"Where you live, miss?" The fear seemed to have settled down enough for him to find his voice.

Music thick and rich as honey continued to pour out of the truck and spread over the man. He leaned his head back, his eyes half shut.

Sally inched toward the truck, toward the music, toward the man. "In Town and Country. We just moved here from Texas."

The man's whistle hurt her ears, yet she stepped still closer, drawn to the music, drawn to the sad, sad eyes.

"*Mama may have, Papa may have . . .*"

The music gurgled like boiling water, seeming to soften the man—Sally peered at his face. Why, he wasn't a man! He was a teenager! And as the music kept playing, his eyes got so heavy, he looked like he might fall asleep.

"God bless the child that's got his own, that's got his own."

"We're bringin' y'all Billie Holliday, an oldie that—"

The boy turned from Sally and climbed back into the truck. With a click, the radio stopped. As if he was itchy, he rubbed his head with his knuckles, twisted and turned and looked every which way, then motioned Sally closer. "Where you need to go?" Even though his words hissed out between his lips, Sally wasn't scared.

"To school. I'm already late. You see—"

A car whizzed by.

The boy whipped his head around and stared, as if the passing car had been important, then refocused those familiar-looking eyes on Sally. "Little miss, I ain't tryin' to be rude, but I don't want to know nothin' 'bout it. They gonna skin my hide as it is." He darted another look over his shoulder. "Now run over there and get in." He pointed to the passenger side of his truck.

Sally obeyed.

"Duck down."

There was authority in the voice, authority that calmed Sally even more. She hugged her head to her chest and closed her eyes. Beads of sweat popped out on her forehead like a fever had broken and she knew she'd be well soon.

The truck jerked. Sally heard the *click, click* of a turn signal. Air rushed through the open window, dried all the sweat and tears, and did its best to suck the image of the bad man right out of Sally's mind.

The boy drummed his fingers against the steering wheel and hummed to the memory of that sweet, sweet song. Her eyes heavy, Sally sank into her seat. He could have driven her back to Texas, and she'd just lay back like this. Especially if he'd put that radio on . . .

"I gotta let you off here, little miss."

Sally opened her eyes. The boy leaned forward, his chest against the steering wheel, his eyes roving about.

Sally straightened, curious to see what was wrong.

They'd stopped down the street from the school's circular driveway. The American flag and what Sally guessed was the Louisiana flag rippled in a stiff breeze. Other than the harsh cry of a blue jay, the school grounds were eerily silent. Prisonlike. Not a place where Sally wanted to be. But better than being with that ugly man. What would he have done to her? What would—

A tan sedan pulled past them and veered into the drive. The boy ducked. "Go!" His voice was a bark now. "Git!" Fingers spread, he waved his right hand.

Sally's breath caught. Her supplies! She ran a hand along the seat, bent over and looked on the floorboard, trying to remember when she'd last had them. But all she could think of was the man's ugly face, his ugly words. "I don't have my supplies!" she wailed.

There was a sigh. "You got to go or they'll kill me." The boy spoke with such urgency, Sally knew she had to forget about the new notebooks and bright crayons and sharpened pencils. "And don't you tell nobody, you hear?"

Sally studied his face. Why would he mind people knowing he'd helped her?

"Please, miss. Please," he said, his voice husky now.

She stared at him. The urgency in his eyes made her nod. Still nodding, she pulled up the handle, pushed against the door, and slid off the seat.

The truck roared away, fumes pouring out of its tailpipe. The image of the dark-skinned boy with the kind eyes also vanished—another image crawled into the void. The evil smile, the bad teeth . . .

Sally ran through heavy doors, looking for somebody, anybody to take on some of the fear that had reappeared now that the boy was gone. Straight ahead was the glassed-in office of the snippy secretary. She stepped closer, wincing at the tapping sound her shoes made. Alone, every step seemed to tap. Alone.

His shoes clicking louder than Sally's, a man approached from down the hall.

Events of the morning squeezed until Sally had trouble breathing, just like before. Her thoughts fired in quick bursts. If she told about the bad man, she might get in trouble. If she admitted riding with a colored boy, she *would* be in trouble. There'd been a paddle in her old principal's office. Surely the principal of this school had one too. And probably wouldn't hesitate to use it.

"Can I help you?" The man smoothed a tie over his shirt and adjusted his glasses. His gaze started at Sally's head and worked its way downward. She longed to get away, but her legs wouldn't move. She couldn't talk either. "What happened?" He stared at Sally's legs.

She was almost afraid to look, but she did. Smears of mud stretched from her knees to her ankles. Her legs were scratched. Another tally appeared in the imaginary slate in Sally's mind. Bad impression.

The man's eyes narrowed. "Thought you'd play hooky, didn't you?"

Suddenly the walls of that dark, quiet hall closed in, pushing Sally back out to that drainage ditch. She saw the nasty scar, smelled the sour sweat.

"Went down to the bayou, eh?" Now the man's eyes were slits. Like Rufus's.

He wanted her to agree, so she did. She nodded, slowly, then faster. "I'm Sally, a new girl from Texas." She stuck out her hand, then grimaced to see blood on her finger. "I got lost on the way. And I did . . . play in the ditch." The words flowed now, so desperate was she to get things right. She was pretending, like the Boxcar Children. Like Nancy Drew. "You know, the one down there?"

When the man didn't answer, didn't even nod, Sally worked harder. "It's all muddy, I guess from the rain. And I lost my supplies and my lunch money."

The man shrugged, as if he'd either lost interest or believed her. "You've got to get to class. And soon."

Sally went limp. So this was what she'd tell them, even her parents. It would keep her from having to explain about Rufus and the colored boy. It even took care of the supplies, ruined by the mud; the lunch money, dropped and lost. If she could wash up, dry off . . . "May I use the bathroom first?" she asked, pointing to her legs.

The man seemed relieved too. "Of course. Down that hall." He nodded toward the glassed-in area. "Then just go in there. That's the office. They'll get you to the right room." He pointed to Sally's cut finger. "And they can get you a Band-Aid. Fix you up good as new."

The words brought tears to Sally's eyes. A dumb ole Band-Aid would not fix this problem. For the second time today, what an adult had said was not true.

Chapter 14

WELCOME TO SIXTH GRADE

School days, school days, dear old Golden Rule days.
—William D. Cobb, "School Days, School Days"

The doors lining the hall bore lettered banners. *Welcome to Second Grade. New Beginnings.* One was decorated with balloons, like the first day of school was something to be celebrated. Only Sally had shown up dirty. Late. Not just a bad first impression, a *really* bad first impression.

"Fourth door on the right," the lady in the office had said.

"100, 102, 104 . . ." Sally ticked off the room numbers, her heart pounding along with every footstep. *106, Mrs. Reynolds.* A second glance told her she'd found it, but the pounding in her heart didn't stop.

The door to 106 was bare except for sticky remains of old tape. No cute cut-outs of animals. No stars or apples. Nothing. Sally grimaced. If the teacher didn't even pretend to be excited about the first day, how bad would it be?

She knocked on the door, quietly at first, then loud enough to rattle it. She was poised to knock again when the door jerked open. There stood a blond woman with thick glasses. A scowl telegraphed how she felt about the interruption.

"Hello. Mrs. Reynolds?" Her brightest smile didn't draw even a nod. "I'm Sally Flowers. Sorry I'm late," Sally managed to eke out.

"You certainly are." Eyes flashed. Cheeks flushed. She might have been pretty, except for that scowl.

Sally focused on the eyes, then determined to try again. It was Mrs. Reynolds's first impression of her. "You see, we moved here from Texas, and Mama had me take practice walks, but somehow I took a wrong turn and fell in a ditch."

The room rippled with giggles. Sally bit her lip to keep it from quivering. Why hadn't she asked the colored boy to drive her home? She could have avoided this.

Mrs. Reynolds pushed owly glasses against her nose. "All right. At any rate, we'll get you marked in and accounted for." She pointed to the back of the room.

As Sally sidled past rows of desks, dozens of eyes stared her down, like she was a three-legged dog. She smoothed her skirt, then slid into the seat of a right-handed desk, wondering if she was the only left-handed, late student in the world. She squinted, trying to see the chalkboard. Left-handed. Late. Nearsighted.

Mrs. Reynolds. September 3, 1963, she finally made out. Math problems and a writing assignment covered the two other boards.

All the eyes goggled at Sally. Then bodies rustled about. Hands picked up pencils. Finally, for the first time since she'd left the house, Sally felt like she could breathe in a normal way.

A pencil rapped against wood. "Miss Flowers? Where are your supplies?"

The students, the wall clock, everything except a raspy mockingbird, perched on a branch right outside the window, held their breath. So did Sally. Again.

"I—I forgot them." Something about the students, the teacher, dammed up the lie about playing in the ditch, so she told another lie. An easier lie.

"She's so stupid." The students whispered it. Mrs. Reynolds stared it. The bird chattered it, over and over. Sally wanted to lash out at them, tell them what had really happened. But the words stuck in her throat, and she just sat there, the target of more stares and giggles and glares.

"Here." Mrs. Reynolds rustled around in a drawer, then held out some paper. A pencil. "Use these. If you don't have them tomorrow, I'll send you to the office."

The office. Sally slumped down in her seat, wanting to make herself invisible. Even that office would be better than this.

◆

The morning had been a disaster, and it was about to get worse. It was lunch time at a brand-new school.

The room came alive as children jostled toward the cloakroom. Bumps and stumbles brought the other students close, but stares and pointed fingers isolated Sally more than ever.

Mrs. Reynolds rapped on the desk. "Row by row, please."

Broken ranks gave way to an organized army marching single-file into the cloakroom, then back into the classroom, where they stood at attention. Only a curly haired girl with freckles sprinkled on her nose seemed unimpressed. She unrolled her bag and slipped out a cookie.

"Line up, over here."

Metal lunch boxes clinked. Bags rattled.

"If you're buying, over here."

Sally's stomach growled, just thinking of food. She was supposed to be buying; Daddy insisted. Bologna sandwiches and a wrinkled apple were poor folk's food. But how could she buy with her quarter out by the ditch somewhere? She had no choice; she got at the end of the "to-buy" line.

Thirty sets of eyes glared at Sally like they knew she had no money. In a million ways, she was different than them.

Mrs. Reynolds wheeled and took off, her arms swinging like a majorette's. They paraded, still single-file, down a hall.

A girl with thick brown hair and blue pointy glasses nodded at Sally and whispered to Miss Freckles.

Sally gave them her best smile, born out of a desperate yearning to have a friend, to sit by somebody. Anybody.

"Not only that, but she's ugly."

With the words, Sally's smile crumpled, and so did her hopes for a friend.

The comments multiplied, now that Miss Freckles had ruled on the newcomer. Every snort, every smirk, crashed into Sally like colliding cymbals. She hated this place.

"Shush, right now, or you'll stay in for recess." Apparently Mrs. Reynolds followed through on threats—soon the only sound was shuffling feet. She led them into the lunchroom, then disappeared down another hall.

The group with sack lunches clattered to bench-style tables and set to trading food like the dorm boys used to. The buyers got in a line and handed quarters to a stern-faced woman whose hair was covered with a blue hairnet.

Sally looked for the least crowded table and sat down. When a headache pounded at her temples and the back of her skull, she cradled her head in her hands and slumped over, trying to forget the stares and cackles. Her growling stomach reminded her of another part of her body rebelling against this disaster of a day.

Someone touched Sally on the shoulder.

She snapped up like she'd been shot.

A colored woman, her faded checkered apron acting like a girdle to hold back an enormous bosom and belly, bent close. Even though she hadn't said a word, her eyes were so soft, Sally wanted to bury her face in the apron. But a last hope for a good impression with someone, even a colored woman, stifled that desire.

"You all right, chile?" The woman laid a weathered hand across Sally's brow, just like Mama had that very morning. "Why ain't you eating?"

The warm hand felt so good, so right, Sally longed to be sick and have this woman take care of her. "I got lost on the way here," she blurted out.

It started as a hum, then became a coo, sounding like a lullaby Mama used to sing, but with no words. The woman took her hand off Sally's brow and used a dishrag to push crumbs from the table into her hand. She worked and hummed, keeping her eyes on Sally. Drawing out the truth. Or a tiny part of it.

"And I fell in a ditch, and I think I caught me a fever." Somehow the words freed Sally from all that had happened. She sat up straight, her hands waving about her head.

"Ooh, chile! You ain't foolin' me, is you?" The woman's mouth formed a perfect O and showed a mouthful of gold fillings.

"And I lost my stuff." She bit back the next part, about the bad white man, the good colored man. She couldn't take a chance on telling that part. Not to this woman. Maybe not to anyone.

"Heavens to Betsy! You don't mean yo' lunch, does you?"

"Lunch money. And my supplies."

"You done had you some mighty big aggravation." She slung her head about and rolled her eyes, looking like a wild stallion, right out of one of Daddy's Westerns. "Old Lavania can't let one of her'n miss out now, can she?"

"Hurt my hand too."

"Lord, Lord. You done got wronged in the worst way. What's your name?"

"Sally."

"That's what we call my cousin. You new?"

Sally nodded.

"Lord gracious." She wiped her brow, as if she'd caught Sally's fever. "What a day."

"We're from Texas."

"Well, I'll be!" Lavania's belly rolled like thunder. "My brother's out that-away. Uncle Sam got him stayin' in Houston."

"Yes, ma'am."

"Hold on. I'll fix you up in no time."

After a final flourish of the rag across the table, Lavania scuffed off, then returned carrying a tray heaped with corn bread, hominy, greens, and some kind of meat, covered with sauce.

Sally rubbed her eyes, not believing what she was seeing, then broke into her first real grin of the day. "This sure beats the food at my old school."

A howl escaped Lavania. "Ain't no cafeteria food. That's Lavania's food."

The food took over then. Sally's right hand curved around the plate and she leaned forward, already tasting the tangy pepper sauce, the tart onions, the buttery corn bread. She shoveled forkfuls into her mouth.

A giggle, then a guffaw, made Sally look up.

Lavania winked at Sally and then swayed back to the kitchen.

Onion and pepper-smothered steak disappeared first. Sally was sopping up pot liquor from the greens when Mrs. Reynolds's scowl darkened the lunchroom. With a crook of her finger, chairs scraped. Students stood. Sally watched one or two march their trays to a window; then she did the same.

A pudgy dark arm materialized from a stack of dishes and patted Sally's wrist. "Lavania's gwine be prayin' for ya. It gwine be okay."

With a lighter step and a full belly, Sally hurried to the line of students and returned to class.

◆ ◆ ◆

"I been the new girl a time or two." Shamika rubbed at a sore place on her elbow. "The only black girl once or twice. Been in magnet schools, revamped schools, down-and-dirty schools. But I never had to move." *Until now.* "Guess I had that goin' for me."

Mrs. Stevens stretched out her hands, working on cuticles ragged as quilt scraps. "I blamed the whole state for the actions of a few silly kids and a sourpuss teacher. I kept thinkin' of their syrupy drawls, putting a sugarcoat over rotten cores."

"You never did tell your folks about that man, did you?" *Just like I never told Momma, nor Auntie, 'bout Charles. Momma got enough troubles, jes' tryin' to get by. And it ain't like he got nowhere with me.*

The teacher's big blue eyes got real wide, like she was fixin' to nod, but then she looked toward the fire and shook her head.

Shamika fidgeted about in her seat, then leaned close enough to smell that flowery perfume that was a bit much for her tastes. "Why?" she asked, thinking as much about Charles as that nasty old white man who had tried to mess with her teacher. "Why didn't you?"

Now her teacher was the fidgety one. She ripped on those cuticles, rattled around in that briefcase, did everything but answer. If Shamika didn't know better, she'd assume old Mrs. Stevens wasn't telling the truth, the whole truth, and nothing but the truth. So help her God.

Chapter 15

A LIFE ON HOLD

Let's talk it over, baby, 'fore we start.
I heard about the way you overdo your part.
—Brownie McGhee, "Don't You Lie to Me"

It's what the Scripture says, y'all." Sally let her eyes rove the room without really focusing on any of the women in her Bible study. Sometimes—like now—she wondered why she'd let the pastor talk her into this.

"Well, I just can't agree with that."

"The Bible says one thing here, one thing there—"

"Things have changed, you know, since the Dark Ages."

Maybe compliments will work. "Great discussion, y'all." Sally tried to be heard over the buzz coming from the seven women seated in her den. Small but cozy, as she'd planned. Cedar-scented candles added fragrance, if little heat. The fire Sam had built in their fireplace took care of that. Planked floors, built-in bookcases, provided aesthetic warmth. There was plenty of color, thanks to framed Native American portraits and bayou scenes on the wall, sienna and turquoise trade rugs on the floor. And these women seemed comfortable enough to say whatever they wanted. And it made Sally uncomfortable. "Any final comments before we move on?"

One woman snorted. "We could camp here all night and never hash this out."

"Yeah! Will you make us brunch?"

Smiling nervously, Sally leaned back on the couch. Again, her strategy had worked—too well. The crab dip, cheese biscuits, and Mama's virgin milk punch recipe, topped with her famous brownies, had given them a boisterous high, like she'd spiked the punch with Red Bull. Maybe she should've snuffed out the candles, doused the fire, and cut hors d'oeuvres to crackers and cheese.

"He won't love me no matter what."

"What's love got to do with it? I'd settle for being liked."

Female voices crescendoed to a feverish pitch, and Sally let them go. As a teacher, she could reel them in if she needed to, but maybe they needed to get things off their chest, literally and figuratively. As she studied their faces, she couldn't help but feel a bit smug about her marriage. Sure, she and Sam had their little disagreements, but they knew how to compromise. Her eyes fell on the oak entertainment center, a perfect example of how a good marriage worked. Sam insisted they have a television here in the den, but he agreed to keep it shuttered, armoire-style, when his sports programs weren't on.

The ladies got louder.

Sally smoothed down a page of her teacher's guide. It was time to take control. Shamika had scheduled their third tutoring session bright and early tomorrow, and she needed to wind this thing up and get to bed. "I'll just read question three for—"

Thirty-five-year-old Becky slung glossy black hair about her shoulders. "I still find it impossible to give respect to a man who doesn't deserve it."

The paneled walls somehow sucked in Becky's words, then amplified them. In the uncomfortable aftermath, someone yawned. A book slammed shut.

Sally glued her eyes to the page heading, "How to Keep God's Fire in Your Marriage." Just because Becky's husband divorced her, why did she have to use this as a forum to blast him? Of course, if Sally'd been married to that bum instead of Sam . . .

"I'm not gonna change, and he's sure not gonna change, so let's just agree to disagree." With a harrumph, Becky folded her hands and stared toward the fire.

Another woman made clucking sounds, nodding as she filed her nails. "Someone has to start it, don't they? Give respect when it's not earned? Kind of like grace?"

"Amen."

A couple of women, including Becky, groaned.

When the pastor had asked Sally to mentor this group of women some would call eclectic, others, misfits, she'd agreed in her head-nodding, fingers-crossed way. She'd had doubts about how two married professional women— one currently separated—a single teacher, two homeschooler moms, a divorcee, and a recently widowed grandmother would get along. There had certainly been disagreements, like this one on the exhortations in Ephesians five. Luckily, love and that very thing they'd been discussing, grace, had acted as a salve for the raw nerves and open wounds the lessons exposed, then irritated. And Sally planned to goop up grace and spread it on Becky right this minute.

"I respect what you're saying. And I know you've done your very best—still are, in fact." Sally's smile lingered on Becky, then migrated to the other woman who was separated and fighting to keep her marriage alive.

It took awhile for Becky to smile, to settle back in her chair, but Sally was willing to wait. Her girls needed to feel God's grace; that was the main thing.

"Any other questions?" Again Sally waited. Several women flipped to the next page; Sally followed their cue and did the same. The guide highlighted some verses, posed a question or two. Sally skimmed them silently, glad she understood sexual submission, glad Sam and she didn't have this problem. But even if they did, she'd never discuss it in a group like this. "Ta da!" she announced, trying to lighten things up a bit after Becky's outburst. "Y'all have been holding your breath for this part, so let's get to it."

The den practically vibrated with giggles and harrumphs.

"It's just like her to cut to the chase."

"But she uses a bread knife, so it doesn't hurt too bad!"

As the women chattered, the one widow in the group, Eileen, shifted about in her seat as if itching to add to the discussion. Yet she didn't say a word.

Now that they were moving on, Sally settled into the couch cushions, cozy between the two homeschooling moms, who looked like clones with their straight backs, severe brunette buns peeking out from lacy hair coverings, and home-sewn skirts tickling the tops of sturdy tie-up shoes. All they needed were balls of yarn and half-crocheted scarves to complete the stereotype. It was enough to make Sally gag—yet she wouldn't dare. One had brought homemade chicken noodle soup when the Stevenses had come down with the flu last winter. The other somehow found time, between teaching and sewing and farm chores, to volunteer at the Crisis Pregnancy Center.

"First Corinthians seven—we'll focus on verses three through seven. Eileen, could you read them for us?"

"'The husband should fulfill his marital duty to his wife, and likewise . . .'" The light from a floor lamp transformed gray hair into a crown of silvery wonder. Except for etchings about Eileen's forehead and mouth that spoke of burying a beloved husband last summer, she looked a decade younger than her seventy-five years.

"'. . . do not deprive each other except by mutual consent and for a time, so that you may devote yourselves to prayer . . .'"

"Thanks, Eileen."

Blazing embers seemed to come to life, shooting sparks of reds and blues up the chimney. Before Sally could throw out the suggested discussion question, one of the homeschooler moms waved her hand like a student desperate to get a hall pass.

Sally nodded at her.

"Is that last part referring to . . . sex?"

Sally reread the teacher's notes. Suddenly she felt uncomfortable, though she didn't know why. She certainly responded to Sam's . . . advances. With her fingernail, she underscored the answer, grateful for a legal cheat sheet. "In this passage, Paul's discussing the total commitment, mind, body, and soul, of a marriage vow." After a verbatim recitation from the guide, Sally looked up. The eyes on a cypress stump in the bayou painting on the wall seemed to be staring at her. Pushing in . . . "Ah, yeah. Sex and everything else. Yeah."

The woman separated from her husband dug through onionskin pages like she was competing in a Bible drill, then looked at Sally, a question burning in brown eyes. "What about Paul's admonition for men to love their wives like Christ loved the church?"

"Yeah. If someone really loved you, would they make you . . . perform?" One of the homeschooler moms seemed to deflate right before them. "We're not on call, are we?"

Becky's laugh was bitter. "It sounds like we're call girls to me."

"Wasn't Paul single?" When one of the professional women plunked down her purse, a bottle of nail polish rolled out, the sound echoing across a suddenly quiet den.

Sally felt every woman staring at her. In times like this, Daddy's teaching tips came in handy: *"When you don't know the answer or don't want to answer, pass the question like a hot potato to a smart student. Nod. Smile. Say 'aha' and nothing else."* With more confidence, Sally chose the first option. "Eileen, what do you think Paul meant by this?"

Eileen seemed to find great interest in the fireplace. A tear slid down her cheek, leaving a shiny line in pancake makeup. She blinked in rapid succession, then shook her head. "I don't know. I just miss him. The way he held me all through the night, so close, I felt every one of his love handles. And *loved* them." She dug a tissue out of her bag. "I'm . . . sorry. It's just that all this other stuff doesn't matter to me." The workbook and her purse crashed to the floor.

Her heart opening wide, Sally flew to the huddled-over, shaking woman. It was awkward, trying to hug Eileen through the louvers of a chair, but Sally found a way.

Eileen buried her face in her hands. "We were . . . intimate until the day he dropped dead."

Sally's breath caught, yet she kept stroking Eileen's back. Had the others heard? Surely the poor woman was delusional. How could Eileen and Bill have sustained . . . that kind of relationship into their seventies? Sally was only fifty-something, yet she hadn't felt that way for—she didn't even know how long. Doubt crept back in, doubt about her ability to teach this, doubt about whether she took care of Sam in . . . that way.

When Eileen's sobs continued, Sally massaged shaking shoulders. "I'm sorry," she whispered. "I never should have asked you to read that."

Between sniffles, Eileen shook her head. "I should have . . . stayed home, but . . ."

"Of course not." The other women chimed in their support.

"You're part of the group."

". . . it gets so lonely." Sally's ministrations seemed to help Eileen regain her composure, at least so she could speak more coherently. "It's the little things. The way he whistled when he burst into the house at five thirty sharp. The way he splashed aftershave on each fresh-shaven cheek, every day of his life."

"I'm so sorry." Tears blurred Sally's vision, but she kept massaging the stiff old shoulders. This part, she understood. Bill had had kind eyes, a nice smile. She imagined he'd been organized. Punctual. Like Sam.

For a few minutes, the room was reduced to Sally's coos and pats, Eileen's sniffles and sobs. Then Eileen picked up her purse, dug out a silver tube, and applied coral lipstick. "I'm ready," she said. She talked a bit more about Bill.

Still listening, Sally flipped ahead in the study guide and her plans. Maybe she'd been remiss in this part of her marriage. And later tonight, she'd do something about it.

◆

Sally hurried upstairs, listening for Sam, who'd come up from the basement now that the women had finally left. Thanks to that draining get-together, she longed to sling her clothes on the floor, throw on her flannel pj's, and bury herself under her quilt. Instead, she got on her hands and knees and rummaged through her bottom dresser drawer. Like a dog searching for a bone, she dug past dingy Cuddl Duds, run-plagued knee-highs, balled-up socks. Where was that gown Sam bought her back—gosh, had she been thirty then? She kept digging, past the slip she wore to her cousin's wedding, past—there it was. Midnight blue. Slinky. Just what she needed. Rising on creaky knees, Sally held it over her work shirt, snuck a peek in the mirror, then frowned at the frumpy woman staring back at her. She looked like a peasant trying on a colorful scarf.

Sally pulled off her clothes, sucked in her stomach, and squeezed her buttocks together. She'd make this work. She stepped into the negligee and pulled. And pulled. The stupid thing wouldn't budge past her thighs. Maybe it had shrunk or it was Suzi's or . . . she'd really gained this much weight. She jerked it down around her feet, then kicked it off. It slapped against the wall and plopped atop a floor lamp, transforming a hundred watts into something better suited for a madam's parlor.

Sam plodded up the stairs, slow but sure.

Sally whisked the wisp of shimmering blue off the lamp and shoved it under the bed, then grabbed her pj's and hurried into the bathroom.

For the first time in years, she didn't use cotton balls to take off her eye makeup and left the cold cream in the middle drawer, next to a dried-up jar of Dead Sea masque. It took a bit of rummaging, but she found that bottle of musk oil Sam had found so stimulating a few years back. She dabbed brownish-gold oil on her pulse points, a secret she'd learned from her old college roommate. Her nose itched, and she stifled a sneeze.

"What's that smell?" Sam stood in the doorway, sniffing, his eyebrows lopsided.

Sally bit her lip. "Nothing, really."

Still sniffing, Sam began his nightly rituals. Brisk combing of dark hair. Thorough toothbrushing. A minty floss. "They sure stayed late."

"Not really." Sally looked into the mirror while conjuring up an image of Elizabeth Taylor in *Cleopatra*. She puffed out her lips, tossed back shaggy hair, and narrowed her eyes. "It's early."

"It's tomorrow that'll come early. Your classes, that is."

"My classes?" Too late, Sally tried to take the shock out of her voice.

Luckily Sam was absorbed with flossing and didn't see how her face turned pale. Of course she noticed, from her perch by the mirror. She didn't dare tell him there was no class tomorrow for a teacher on leave. Then she'd have to explain that whole résumé thing, and it was too late to talk about it tonight. She had other things to do.

Sam, his flossing over, stared at her reflection. "How are your classes, anyway? Haven't heard much about 'em lately."

"Let's not talk about work." Sally hoped her wink, her giggle, would be effective. Sexy.

Sam nodded, but kept the slit-eyed stare. "So how was the Bible study?"

"Great." Feeling like the mouse that escaped the cat, she tiptoed down the hall and into Ed's empty room. After she flipped on the lava lamp that served as Ed's night-light, she allowed herself a smile. *He's still at the game.* She pattered back to her room and climbed into bed. Her own little game was coming along nicely.

When Sam reached for Sally, his touch electrified her body. Sheets rustled as she rolled over, her breasts cradled against his chest, her belly against his loins. He radiated heat and smelled of the Ivory soap that she supposed he'd used his entire life. Plus a hint of something musty, yet comforting, like steamy pavements after a rain.

Every nerve ending in her husband seemed to come alive. His kisses grazed her hair, her eyes, the lobes of her ears. His hands began to caress her body . . .

Rufus's nasty smile appeared, those greasy hands. The smells. The noises.

Sally clenched her teeth and tried not to stiffen, but it was too late. How had those memories squeezed their way in when she'd done everything within her power to prevent them? She ordered her body to relax and think about this man who had never demanded anything except that she love their children as much as he did and love him as well as she could. But her body disobeyed.

As Sam pressed himself into her with slow, grinding motions, Sally disappeared to a place deep inside and played what she hoped was the eager, turned-on wife. She moaned when he moaned, threw her arms and legs about him, and planted kisses on his sweaty chest.

The sheets were a soggy tangle and smelled of sex when Sam got up and slipped into the bathroom. Soon he returned, and pulled Sally into his arms. "I love you, Sal." With gentle strokes, he swept snatches of hair away from her face and kissed her forehead.

It was only then that Sally felt like she could act normal again.

Minutes later, Sam relaxed too—his deep breaths making the whole thing almost worth it. But not quite. In her agitated state, Sally bit her lip. *What about me? What's wrong with me?* She wrestled with the sheets, then flipped over and tried to settle in, but it was no use. When tears came, she started to wipe her face on the sheet, then remembered that her eye makeup was still on and curled into a ball on the edge of the bed. Her eyes clenched shut, Sally thought and thought, hoping a plan would come to mind. *I'll clear this up. Somehow. Some way.* At half past one, it came to her, and she smiled to realize both Sam and Maureen had suggested it. Tomorrow she was calling Dr. Morris.

◆

It was a morning for a Southerner to give thanks over. Sun poured into the window and through the French doors, giving light and warmth to the breakfast room table. The aroma of fresh ground coffee beans and chicory, with a hint of cinnamon, wafted across the room, thanks to her sweet husband brewing her favorite kind of coffee. She had lots to be thankful for, now that she had a plan to get things back on track for herself and Sam.

Sam. At least she'd been a wife to him last night. She smiled, just thinking of the pleasure that had softened his face. Still smiling, she poured a cup of coffee, held it close enough to let the steam warm her face, then drank deep. Maybe tonight she'd broach the subject of her job. It was time to be a wife communication-wise as well.

A ringing cut through Sally's peace. Who would call this early? Didn't everyone follow Mama's rule—don't even pick up the phone after midnight and before eight unless someone's dead or critically injured? She raked her hair with her fingers. What if something was wrong? Another bad moon on the rise? She walked to the desk and answered it.

"I'd make other plans this semester if I were you." Danita Daniels's nasally voice made Sally grimace. So East Coast. In-your-face. Danita should've been a lawyer.

"Wh-why?" Sally managed.

"They've been granted a continuance to gather more information for their complaint." Danita talked a bit longer, then hung up.

Questions pushed in on Sally, so persistent, so troubling, her hands shook, and she slopped coffee onto her shirt. Would the hearing be public? Should she get an attorney? When, and how, could she tell Sam? She could barely breathe;

she had to do something. Again she picked up the phone. She'd stay busy, take care of that other problem so she wouldn't think about her classes.

Minutes later, she hung up the phone, the appointment made. Yet it hadn't answered a single question, hadn't really done a single thing but add an item to her Day-Timer, which was pretty empty these days.

It wasn't far to the pantry and the rolled-up sack of doughnuts. Dunking them in the last bit of coffee brought out the powdery sweetness—kind of like cheap beignets. Her mama would tsk-tsk her right out of the room. *"Breakfast is the most important meal of the day, Sally." "You are what you eat, Sally."*

Without a doubt, Mama was right. Sally wadded the empty sack into a tiny little ball. Powdery and sweet on the outside, confectioner's sugar fooling everyone with a white pastry welcome. Inside, nothing but a bunch of additives and fat and things that weren't good for you. With the palm of her hand, Sally wiped her face. Really, these doughnuts were just like her. That phony outside coated over lies and secrets and all kind of things that looked good, tasted good, but really weren't good. Not good at all.

Chapter 16

TANGLED WEB

Sometimes I's up, sometimes I's down.
Keep me from sinking down.
—Negro spiritual, "Sinking Down"

Like any good physician, Dr. Morris tried to make his patients feel comfortable in his waiting room. Recessed lighting cast a burnished glow, softening the features of the dozen or so women who sat stiffly in matched leather chairs and sofas. Original Impressionist landscapes bursting with light and life and color broke up the monotony of pale walls. Still, Sally longed to run through the etched glass doors, taking her uncomfortable problem with her.

She checked in, then sat down and pretended to read *Ladies' Homes Journal*. The glossy photos, the autumn comfort food recipes, did nothing to ease the tightness in her stomach. And the "Can This Marriage Be Saved?" article rankled her. Who would send personal issues for a magazine editor to sort through as if they were yesterday's mail?

An interior door opened. It was Elaine, a former nurse at the college.

The last thing Sally wanted was to see someone she knew, especially one who might have heard about the other little problem regarding the school. Still, she managed a smile.

"Sally. How the heck are you?" Elaine asked.

"Great. And you?"

"Can't complain. But I miss playing mommy to all those students."

As the former MCC nurse, Elaine was reputed to have saved more than a few babies from suction catheters by soulfully sharing her own abortion experience

156

with young women. Yet she was all business at her new job, whirling to the counter and grabbing a clipboard. A little too "all-business" for Sally, who felt distanced by Elaine's efficiency. Elaine's thinness. Elaine's control.

"Let's check your weight . . . height."

Sighing, Sally prepared for the first of many ordeals. Why couldn't they just stick something in her ear and have it digitally flash the weighty truth? There was bound to be a less humiliating way. And why did they need to verify that she'd ballooned since last year's visit?

"How's Sam? The kids?" Without waiting for Sally to answer, Elaine pointed straight ahead to the hateful calibrated contraption and motioned for Sally to step up on it.

A refusal floated on the tip of Sally's tongue, but she bit it back, like she was doing with so many things these days. Why put Elaine on the spot? She was just doing her job. Plus it would be awkward if Elaine had to insist.

Stalling, Sally slowly unlaced boots, inched down thick wool socks. She needed every ounce, the way she'd been cramming in chocolates, slurping down lattes.

"On you go, Sally," Elaine demanded.

Sally stepped gingerly onto the springy base of the scales.

When Elaine slid across not one weight, but two, Sally cringed. Next would come the lecture, always in a spirit of concern, yet blunt as a crowbar. And she wasn't up to it.

The scales achieved equilibrium, but what felt like a lead weight sank into the pit of Sally's stomach. Ten more pounds, and she'd match her pregnancy weight.

To Sally's relief, Elaine didn't say a word, just took Sally's height, then scrawled the miserable figures in the folder.

Sally picked up her boots and socks and followed Elaine down the hall. *One hassle down, a dozen more to go.*

With a flip of a light switch and a nod, Elaine motioned Sally to a chair.

While Elaine updated the chart, Sally focused on Elaine's brown eyes, white scrubs, and lime green Nikes, which hinted at that feisty personality Sally'd glimpsed occasionally at MCC. She read Dr. Morris's diplomas, studied a poster of the developing fetus, focusing on anything but the stirruped contraption that belonged in a medieval torture chamber instead of being a fixture in the office of every ob-gyn in America.

With deft but thorough motions, Elaine checked pulse, temperature, and blood pressure. "It's a bit elevated." Lines creased her forehead as she removed the cuff from Sally's arm.

Just like my irritation, Sally thought as she watched Elaine scrawl another statistic into the chart.

"Any meds?" Elaine dabbed her finger to her tongue, then flipped through the chart.

"Just a One A Day."

"So what's going on?"

No, Elaine. It's what isn't *going on.* She visualized Sam, and that made it easier. "I'm . . . really not enjoying sex anymore," she stammered. "And my friend—you probably know Maureen—mentioned hormones. Bio—" Sally slapped her thigh. "Oh, what are they called?"

"Bioidenticals?"

"Yeah. Anyway, I thought they might help. So . . ." Sally again studied the diplomas, the fetus chart, anything but Elaine. ". . . that's why I'm here." There. She'd done it. Two hassles down.

Elaine noted Sally's answers and stuck the folder in a rack on the door. Her thin body a dervish, she opened a cabinet and pulled out one of those paper gowns that, after all these years, Sally still couldn't figure out how to get on.

"I . . . I just need the meds," Sally protested, wanting to curl up into a ball.

The gown was in Sally's lap now. "He still may want to do a look-see."

Sally's lips curled. Since when was probing private parts a "look-see"? She had half a mind to put her boots on and get out of here. This had been a mistake.

The gown swished to the floor and tangled with her feet. It was enough to make Sally wring her hands and cry from the humiliation of it all.

Elaine found a tissue and handed it to Sally. "Tell him what's going on. Call me tonight, if you need to."

The door shut very gently.

Sally ducked her head. Why had she gotten Elaine involved in this? She sniffed up her tears and fumbled with the stupid gown, not really caring if she had it on backward or forward. Every year, the examining table seemed harder to mount. In a couple of years, she'd have to bring her own stool.

The steel table neither absorbed her warmth nor offered any of its own. And the gray-white stippled ceiling that she was staring at conjured up grotesque images—the limp body of her baby boy. That other memory too. Sally flipped over, drawing her legs to her chest. The gown ripped, but that was the last thing on Sally's mind. She was fifty-three years old, and a doctor visit still dredged up memories that she prayed every day would dry up, like seed pods, and blow away. But God hadn't seen fit to answer her prayer. At least not yet.

◆ ◆ ◆

As he examined her, Dr. Morris trumpeted the benefits of long-distance running, a good ploy to distract her. It didn't work.

Gritting her teeth, Sally focused on the silver that glazed the close-cut hair at his temples. Not once did she whimper, even though the images remained.

"All right. You can sit up now. Thank you, Mrs. Stevens." Dr. Morris offered a cool, firm hand, dappled by age spots.

Holding on tight to Dr. Morris, her other hand clutching the gown, which at this stage resembled a large, soggy paper towel, Sally struggled to a sitting position. She'd always liked Dr. Morris's pleasant yet formal style. None of this "Well, hey, Sally," and some obtuse joke to try to lighten the indignity of the thing. And she could tell that he'd tried to be gentle. But the chatter, the light touch, didn't help much, not with that ugly sneer, that smell, finding a way even into this sterile room.

With a roll and a spin, the doctor rose, pushed the stool to the side of the examining table, and pulled off disposable gloves as he strode to the sink, then washed and dried his hands. "You may get dressed now," he informed Sally. "Just crack the door when you're ready."

It didn't take Sally long to get her clothes back on, not with the temperature in the room set to preserve meat. Shivering, she sat down and tried to take comfort in the fact that the ordeal was nearly over.

Moments later, Dr. Morris came back in, a slight shuffle the only hint that he was over sixty. He pulled the stool close to Sally's chair and sat down.

Sally tried to imagine his job, his burdens. What would it be like to face, day in and day out, bundles of overwrought hormones, yeast infections, dry vaginas? Further, how did his wife handle it?

"Mrs. Stevens." His voice was gentle, patient, in spite of the fact that he probably had someone in the ER, three dilated mothers-to-be in holding patterns, and whatever dramas lay in each of his examining rooms. "Why don't you tell me what's going on."

It should've been easy, since she'd already told Elaine, but it wasn't. Still, if she could just get the prescription, maybe get some samples to jump-start things, then get out of here, she'd be okay. "I've been struggling a bit with my sex drive," she finally managed.

Dr. Morris sat with perfect posture, the chart on his lap. He seemed content to wait this out for as long as it took.

Sally rarely liked silence—in its own white-noise way, it crushed everything else. She fiddled with her hair, crossed and uncrossed her legs. *No! Anything's better than this deadness.* With intentionality, she cleared her throat. "And I think I need hormones."

The doctor nodded like they were discussing a common cold. "I see."

"I mean, I don't think I'm a weirdo or anything. I'm a normal woman and all . . ." Sally bit her tongue. What was she saying? It didn't even make sense.

"When did you first notice this, Mrs. Stevens?"

Sally's face sagged. How in the world would she know the answer to that? She didn't keep a sex diary in her bedside table drawer.

Now it was the doctor's turn to clear his throat. "Perhaps a better question would be, has this problem gotten progressively worse since your last visit?"

Images filled Sally's mind, then took over her voice. Rufus crashing their wedding night party, Rufus slithering between the sheets and spreading a slimy layer of filth between her and Sam. What kind of sicko would she be if she admitted all these things to this very nice, very Christian doctor? She wouldn't, couldn't answer.

The chart came into play again, the doctor flipping back several pages. "Last year, you reported menopausal symptoms. We ordered lab work, which revealed estrogen and progestin levels below normal." He set the chart aside, his eyes on Sally. "How are those symptoms now?"

Sally burst into tears. "I'm a mess." She buried her face in her hands. Of course he didn't need all his diplomas to see that.

His voice soothing, he handed Sally another tissue. In the same gentle way he'd examined her, he questioned her. She tried to share just enough without opening up the dark place inside her that seemed to be growing like a cancerous tumor. He talked of dryness, anxiety; a whole laundry list of middle-aged women's issues. Of course she had all of them. He recommended hormone level tests, thyroid tests; enough tests to keep three insurance clerks busy. He was so professional, so soothing, that tension flowed off Sally. Perhaps this was a form of therapy, albeit a bit strange. And once she got on the hormones, things would get better, she was sure of it.

Dr. Morris shifted about on the stool. "Mrs. Stevens," he said, with a firmer voice, "has anybody ever hurt you?"

"What do you mean?" Sally blew her nose, then tried to use the tissue as a shield from his knowing eyes. What made him suspect the truth? And why should she tell now?

He didn't move a muscle. "Forced you to do something with your body that you didn't want to. Entered you in a painful way. Maybe it was a relative. A—"

With stiff fingers, Sally crushed the tissue. "Doctor, I've been married over twenty-five years. My husband is a sensitive man who wouldn't hurt anyone."

The doctor removed his spectacles and rubbed his eyes, suddenly looking like he'd delivered four babies and made hospital rounds before he came to his office. "Well, that's good to hear," he said, "but it doesn't answer my question."

Sally swallowed hard. What if she did answer his question? What would he do? Send her to counseling? She didn't need some shrink telling her about repression. Christians didn't need half-baked psycho theories. In His timing, God would help her. But it certainly wasn't going to be here. "No," Sally said. "Of course not."

The doctor opened his mouth, then stopped.

Envisioning, then modeling, a statue with a plastered-on smile, Sally sat firm. *He'll give in. They always do, when you smile long enough.*

As if he suddenly realized that he had a waiting room full of women, the doctor snapped into action, letting Sally know her secret was safe. He yanked a prescription pad off the desk and scribbled madly. "Let's retest the hormones." He tore off that sheet and started another one. "This'll help with lubrication," he added. He stuck the folder on the rack, turned, and shook Sally's hand. "When you're ready to talk, Mrs. Stevens, give me a call."

◆ ◆ ◆

Two nasty appointments in one day, first that intern ripping out stitches like he was redoing a hem, now another five-o interview, here on the cops' home turf. Shamika eased her still-sore body onto a couch as lumpy and ratty as the one on that crack house's front porch, down the street from Momma's. Two cheap table lamps and tattered issues of *Field and Stream* and *Reader's Digest* made it look like this interrogation room was a getaway cabin for beer-guzzling, deer-hunting white men. And it took her back, ten years, to that other stuffy, stinky room, when they'd laid into Momma like it was her fault Daddy had driven into the wrong part of town.

The door burst open. "Good morning, ladies." It was that same blocky old detective with the same reptile eyes. Same notebook. Same pen. Same smirk.

Looking just like the one that'd said Daddy had been going for a gun. Shamika sniffed away drippy sinus at the thought of that dark stiff hand still holding onto that worn black Bible as the cops shot him dead. *Guess the Word some kinda weapon. But not a gun.*

"How are you today?"

Shamika snorted. *Like you really care.*

"As well as can be expected," came from Auntie.

"I appreciate you coming down."

Same old tune, same old words they said to Momma, made Shamika fold her arms and fix him with a stare. "Like we had a choice."

The detective turned sweaty red and moved in on them like a street punk guarding his corner. "Ms. Williams, I want to make one thing perfectly clear. I want to catch this guy as bad as you do. If you continually butt in with your personal vendettas against me and the other white men in this building, it's going to be difficult for us to get to the bottom of this and punish the man who raped you."

Shamika stuck out her lip. "Men."

A shadow passed over the detective's face. "Yeah. Now . . ." He pulled a chair near the couch and set his notebook on one of the end tables. "Let's start at the beginning."

"I, Shamika Williams, was born on December 22, 1985, in New Orleans, Louisiana. I—"

"I see that I need to be a bit more specific." The pen became a switchblade as he jabbed it at the already pocked end table. "On the night of October 24 at approximately 9 PM, you exited the west doors of Midwest Community College and headed to the parking lot, correct?"

Shamika nodded, eyeing him like he was a cobra. Course he was, coiled up and ready to strike at any move she made. She'd have to be careful. Lay low.

The detective grabbed his notebook and flipped it open. "What happened next?"

"Like I told the dude in the ER . . ." Shamika felt her brain get all squashy from the effort of remembering what she'd said after being brutalized, then poked and prodded. "I called my friend to see if she wanted to come over." Her words sounded hazy, so she put starch in her back, hoping to do the same with her voice. "When she didn't answer, I hung up, walked to the lot, set down my backpack, unlocked my car. Next thing I knew, one of those creeps shoved my head against the door."

The detective arched his eyebrows. "And then?"

Ruby jumped up. "How do you expect her to remember all this?"

The smell of mouthwash hit Shamika in the face as the detective pounced toward them. "She'll have to remember it backward, forward, and upside down if it goes to trial. Plus her testimony isn't exactly matching that of our eyewitness."

"That's what they said 'bout my daddy."

"Oh?" The eyebrows jumped up to smack against the edge of the man's awful hairstyle. *Whaddy'a know*. She'd finally surprised him.

"Baby girl, we ain't gwine there," Auntie growled.

Shamika slouched over, her lip pooching out so far, *she* could see it. There wasn't no way outta *this* bad mood.

"Your father's had run-ins with the law?"

"Just one big one," Shamika said, not able to hold it in. "When they shot him dead."

"And what year did that allegedly occur?"

The couch sagged when Ruby got up and edged forward till she was a foot from the detective's nose. "We ain't gwine go there, like I said."

Like rival gangstas on neutral turf, they glared and stared. It was no surprise to Shamika, who'd had dealings with Auntie since she'd been in her crib, that the detective backed down first.

"I guess it really isn't relevant." Suddenly his voice sounded lawyerish instead of hickish. "What *is* relevant is that her testimony ain't addin' up."

Shamika rolled her eyes. Now he gonna try to street talk?

"But I'm sure it's because we . . . misunderstood it. That's why we're going over it again." He seemed to recover momentum, pointing a finger at Auntie and slicking back pitiful wisps of hair. "So let's button up the attitude and tuck it in."

Ruby sat down. So did the detective, who sighed and wiped his brow. "Mrs. Brown . . ." His tone flip-flopped between a whine and a beg. ". . . I could order you to leave, but I don't really want to do that."

Ruby opened her mouth, then clamped it shut.

"What I want to do is catch this creep."

"Creeps." Shamika winced as she pulled at a scab on her arm. Why did he keep digging at that sore spot?

"Yes, Ms. Williams. Of course." Detective Price fixed an unblinking stare on her, making her dig at her arm like she had psoriasis. He had some kinda mind game going on, and she didn't know whether to play it or pack up her toys and go home.

Detective Price leaned so close, he might as well have plopped down on the couch between them. "What I also want is to get you all out of here as soon as I can." His cheap minty breath smell washed the stale air. "So please. Let's do this."

It was the word *please* that settled Shamika back onto the lumpy, itchy fabric. She did want out of here. Mrs. Stevens was coming over. She folded her arms across her chest and nodded.

"Now, what happened after you were shoved against your door?"

"When I shoved back, tryin' to get away, I saw the tattoo. That's when I screamed. Then he slapped me, yanked my hair, pushed me down on the seat."

"So you were facedown?"

"Yes." Shamika flinched, feeling the weight of all that sweaty flab coming down on her . . .

"So the man who grabbed you, shoved you, slapped you, and pushed you into the car was the one with the swastika?"

Shamika nodded.

"What color was the swastika?"

"Black."

"He was the only one with a swastika?"

Shamika gouged at her right arm. "They all had them. I think."

The cop's square shoulders slumped just low enough, the thin lips pressed together just long enough, for Shamika to read his Instant Message. She'd blown it. Over what? She tried to visualize those three beater shirts, covering up not near enough of those pasty white arms. Which one of the creeps had had tattoos? It was some stupid racist riddle. Indecision paralyzed Shamika, like she was caught in the crossfire of a gang war. Like she'd notice arm tattoos with all the other gross things she'd had to see. But this cop didn't care about any of that, she thought as she stuck out her lip. "I just don't know," she finally said, planting herself in a neutral place.

Detective Price's jaw tightened. "Okay. Did you get a good look at the face of the one who raped you?"

"Not a great look, but enough to see those pale fish eyes."

"Again, what was his name?"

"One of those three jerks in Mrs. Stevens's class. I don't know their names." She glanced at a stupid magazine cover with a man and his bigmouth bass, hoping to keep out of the range of those searchlight eyes. Of course she knew their names. Who could forget them?

"Okay."

She glanced back at him. If he was mistrustin' her, he kept it off his face.

"You said there were others."

Shamika nodded.

"How many?"

"Two."

"Did you recognize them as well?"

Shamika shrugged her shoulders. "I didn't have as good of a look, but I saw enough to recognize the no-good scum."

"Hmm."

The coffee table shook when Shamika stomped her foot. "Why are we goin' through this again?"

"And again. And again," Ruby chimed in.

Detective Price slammed his folder against the table. "Like I said, it doesn't jive with what the witness said. Your ER interview doesn't match the one you're giving me now. And if this goes to trial, they'd better look like identical twins."

The thought of sitting through trial paralyzed Shamika, and Auntie didn't move, either. Lord Jesus, there had to be another way. She imagined long, black robes behind the bench, long white faces in the jury box. No. There was no way.

Their nonreaction seemed to calm down the detective. He fiddled with his collar, then leaned back in his chair. "So he shoved you facedown into your car. What happened next?"

"He got out a knife and cut off some of my hair."

"Did you see him do it or just feel it?"

"Both."

"This is the same man?"

"Yes."

"Where were the others during this time? Do you know?"

"They'd climbed into the back seat." Shamika shivered and hugged her arms to her chest. "One of them spit on me, cussed at me. It was, 'Nigger, we gonna teach you your place. Nigger this, nigger that.'" In spite of squeezing her eyes shut, tears rolled down her face. She had to keep talking. Get this out and get out. "They slapped me around good," she continued, feeling Auntie shifting around on the nasty couch. "There was a ripping sound. And all that time, their mouths dissing me."

The room was quiet except for Detective Price's scribbling on his notepad.

"And then . . ." Shamika only wavered for an instant. "There was an awful pain down there, and I knew . . . that my insides were ripped up. Then everything went black, and I don't remember anything else till them ambulance men arrived."

Sobs shook Shamika in earnest now. Auntie smothered her in that big bosom of hers, rubbing her back, cooing, but the pain didn't budge from her gut, her heart . . . her other parts too. Just thinking about what he'd taken away from her when he'd raped her knifed into everything from her chest to her ankles.

"It's gwine be okay, baby girl," Auntie kept saying. But it wasn't okay.

Shamika finally came up for air to watch the detective flip through his notepad. Then he shook his head, grimaced, and thumped his pen against his knee. "Ms. Williams?"

"Yeah." Shamika's voice was whispery, weak.

"Do you think you could look at some photos?"

"She has already, hasn't she?" Ruby's growl came alive.

Shamika squeezed her eyes shut, but opened them when she pictured that snotty white face, looming over her. She fell back into the safety of Auntie. This nightmare would never end.

"Yes. But we just want to nail it down, ma'am." Detective Price laid glossy sheets on the end table near her. "If you could examine these mug shots, please. Each page contains the pictures of six theoretical perpetrators, but only one on each page is the actual suspect." If the man's expression had been impassive before, now it was a blank page. "Please, take your time." Detective Price slid back into his chair and waited . . . waited . . .

In stages, Shamika uncoiled from Auntie. First her feet hit the carpet. Then she stretched her arms to her knees. She leaned across the table, and with barely a second glance, pointed to the top left photograph.

The detective didn't blink. All he needed to complete his sunning reptile look was a slithery forked tongue.

"Him. Him." She closed her eyes again, unable to take in another white face.

Detective Price clicked open his ballpoint pen and handed it to Shamika. "If you'll just put your initials and the date next to each of those, we'll be done."

Through half-lidded eyes, she managed to sign on the dotted line of those creeps' freedom. Jay. Hugh. Rex. Of course she knew their names. It was official now. One of Mrs. Stevens's students was charging three other students with rape. And if that didn't make headline news here in Normal, Shamika didn't know what would.

◆ ◆ ◆

Without ever looking back, the women marched, heads held high, like dig-nitaries across the atrium. Past the planter box, its plastic flora glowing a lime green not biologically possible. Past the too-chatty receptionist, the too-large "Welcome" sign. Past all the accoutrements vainly trying to make people feel comfortable in this place where they got bad news, gave out bad news—*Face it. We cops are bad news.*

Then the old aunt groaned as she pulled open the ziplock-tight door, and the black women left, carrying their grudges and their allegations about police brutality with them.

Price stared at the bright cloth wrapped around what was left of Shamika's dreadlocks or whatever they were. How could he get into her mind? More im-portantly, get her to see that he loathed the scumbag who did this to her as much as she did? *Scumbag, not scumbags. I'm surer of it now than ever.*

"Hey, Dicey Pricey!"

It was hard not to lash back at the receptionist who always had a cutesy nick-name, a stupid joke—her way of coping with stress, he supposed. With a curt nod, he strode past, wondering how *he* could continue to cope with this job. Fif-teen long years it had been, his rookie euphoria vanishing like the kidnap victim he'd never found, the one whose schoolboy face mocked him as he begged for it to go away and let him sleep. And now Shamika's face had joined that 2 AM haunting. He ought to be grateful Normal had only a few crimes that kept him awake. But that fact didn't console him a bit.

"Pricey, Chief'll be in your office in ten."

A decade ago, that message would have shot adrenaline through him, would've caused him to streak to his office and flip through all his reports to make sure he'd followed protocol to a T. Right now, he felt nothing but irritation.

The disorganized state of his office exacerbated Price's mood as he sat in his chair, then slapped down his papers. Folders were stacked everywhere—on the floor, on top of his desk, in his chair, like he'd been playing a Jenga game with official reports. The thought pulled a sardonic chuckle from him. At least that would be more productive than what had consumed the hours on his re-cent shifts—sitting in this ratty chair, his mind a broken video, playing scenes from the Williams case over and over. Her hard attitude, yet stellar record. The testimony that didn't add up. For the tenth time this morning, he grabbed file number 200419.

167

He leaned back, his chair groaning with the strain of his unexercised butt, and flipped through the first interview in the ER. Words blurred. He fought heavy eyes. And that knocking sound. What was it?

"Price? Are you in there? Price!"

When Price tried to lift up his head, it seemed impossibly heavy. The voice bombarded him, again and again.

I'm coming! Hang on! Price willed himself to speak, but nothing came out. He fought harder to hear the muffled voices. Everything was a battle, a battle . . .

"Detective. Detective!"

With a start and a gasp, Price sat up, the motion knocking Shamika's file onto the floor. He wiped saliva from his mouth, then leaned over to pick up papers that had come loose from a clip. "Yes, Chief."

"Just read a study about catnaps. Good for productivity."

The way he burned, Price was sure his face, ears, his scalp, were bright red.

"Now, about the Williams case . . ."

A groan escaped the detective's lips.

"NAACP's calling, ACLU, Reverend Watson, the mayor . . . all of those nearest and dearest to us men in blue."

The frustrations of Price's life—his failed marriages, his ridiculous case-load—pressed in. "And what do you want me to do about it?" Price cringed, surprised at what he'd said and the tone with which he'd said it.

The chief, a former all-state linebacker, slammed his fist on the desk, rattling some pencils and knocking some more files onto the floor. He put his hand on the detective's armrest and leaned closer, closer, until they were eye to eye. "For starters, drop the attitude."

It was impossible to meet the chief's fiery gaze. Price bowed his head and tried to formulate an apology. Officers didn't mess with this man, not if they wanted to keep the best shifts, the best beats. "I . . . I'm sorry," he managed.

"Tell me something I don't know." The smile that worked with the media and the politicians was back in place, setting off perfect teeth.

In a flash, Price had Shamika's file open, his notebook open, his mind . . . open.

The chief took a seat, then stretched back. "Now that we've dispensed with the formalities, what do you have that can get the aforementioned off my back?"

Even though Price glanced at the file, he could recite it all from memory. "2130, received a call from MCC parking lot. They'd already called the ambulance. Reported victim beaten, unconscious. Unit arrived at 2135 and shut down scene. Caller did not witness the crime. Estimated time of attack, 2100."

"Why no witnesses? They have night classes, right?"

"Till 2030. I guess they rushed outta there. Apparently the vic stayed after class. Librarian says she checked out a book at 2045."

"Time stamps?"

Price shook his head.

"Okay. Continue."

"Officer on patrol—"

"Warren, right?"

"—had gotten a brief description at the ER—white male, pale-complected—'like all of you,' to quote the vic." When he didn't even get a change of expression from the chief, the detective continued. "General impression, blond-haired, blue-eyed."

"Sounds pretty typical for a from-behind assault."

"Except there's a couple of problems."

"Go on." The chief got up, stretched, then walked to the window.

"When I interviewed the vic—on three occasions, I might add—suddenly there were three of them, all with swastikas. I could've sketched them blindfolded, from her description."

"So our victim becomes clairvoyant."

"Yep, IDs them to a T." Price uncrossed his legs and leaned closer to the chief. "And they're carbon copies of three skinhead types in her eight o'clock class."

"Ah. The suspects in that teacher's vandalism complaint."

"Three and the same." Sarcasm tinged Price's voice. "I think our gal's got a race card up her sleeve and a chip on her shoulder that she's unloaded in a big way."

"She's already suing the college, Detective. Keep talkin' like that, and you'll be slapped with a complaint yourself. Maybe by me." The chief had never needed to raise his voice to be heard, and even though he had his back to Price, this time proved to be no exception. "And wouldn't our new black senator just love to ride to the White House on comments like that?" He whirled backward, a Southern hemisphere tornado, until he was in Price's face. "You get this straight, Price. Pull off whoever you need from patrol and get this thing done. And if a few sleazy Nazis go down, you think I give a rip?" Things became X-Acto-knife sharp when the chief shoved his finger into Price's chest. "Give our black citizens what they want. Have I made myself clear?"

Price was tempted to stick out his tongue and salute from the phoniness of it all but feared he'd end up flat on the floor. He couldn't mess with the chief. Not if he wanted to keep his job. And his health. "You have, sir."

The chief smoothed what little hair he had, probably prepping for that afternoon's photo op with some Japanese visitors who were touring a wind turbine project just outside the city limits. "One last thing. Get those women surveillance."

"But—"

"24–7."

"But—"

"TGIF, Price. You got nothin' better to do."

Chapter 17

GROWING FRIENDSHIPS

Blow it right, calm an' easy Fare you well, fare you well
Do not alarm my people Fare you well, fare you well.
—James W. Johnson, J. Rosamund Johnson,
"In Dat Great Gittin' Up Morning"

As they had for a week, they sat in the rocking chairs in front of the fire, yet today a chasm had sprung up between them. Sally kept striking educational matches, trying to draw Shamika into the new unit, but after a brief flare, things kept fizzling out.

"Do you see evidence of postmodernism in Gaudi's Sagrada Familia?" Sally asked, for once eager to get home and get to cooking dinner.

Shamika buried her nose in her notes. "While some view Gaudi's work as art nouveau gone mad, his cathedral incorporates organic elements that shatter the definition of architecture as a closed-in space. He blends sculpture and architecture to create a new genre, studded with his own political agenda—independence for Catalonia."

Sally blinked. Shamika had nailed the cathedral aesthetically, yet her tone had no passion; she might have been talking about a trailer park instead of one of the architectural wonders of the world. Then again, at least she'd started talking.

"And it doesn't hurt my argument that Sagrada Familia still exists in that fluid state—in fact, they're working on it right this very second."

Glad to have a reason to laugh, Sally glanced at her watch. "Since it's midnight in Barcelona, I doubt it. But you're right about the rest. Did you feel his passion, feel his—"

"Have you ever felt closed in?" The reds and oranges of the fire flickering on her face, Shamika leaned toward Sally.

Like right now? No job, and my husband not knowing yet? Sally very slowly set the teacher's guide in her briefcase. "What do you mean?"

"Like you've built a wall around yourself." Shamika jerked forward, then arched back, her chair creaking in response. "Oh, I don't know how to say it. The wall's already there, but you keep adding another layer of mortar. Another and another and . . ."

Shamika's words took Sally back, way back. "I know about fences." She stared at the fire, seeing the faces of two little girls, one dark-skinned, the other light-skinned.

◆

There was Mama, on her hands and knees, digging into what folks called Louisiana gumbo. Sally was both glad and afraid to see her. What if Mama asked what happened? She could say she fell at recess. She could say—

Mama brushed off her pants and stood up when she saw Sally. "How was it?" Hope colored her cheeks with the same rosy tint as her favorite azalea blooms.

"Terrible." The word came out before Sally meant it to.

A frown shadowed Mama's face and her eyes narrowed. "What happened?"

It didn't take but a second for Sally's face to crumple, for tears to fall. She was in Mama's arms, the smell of earthworms and dirt enveloping her. She let Mama hold her, not having to say anything, not having to do anything, at least for now.

"It'll get better." Mama hugged and talked until the last sob came out. "There, there," she kept saying. "It's always hard the first day."

Sally opened her eyes and studied the curve of Mama's eyelashes, her bright cheeks. Could Mother understand about the bad man, the colored boy, the lost supplies? Her voice whispery, Sally took a baby step toward truth. "Were you ever the new girl?"

Mama, who always had something to say, instead studied a clod of dirt.

"Were you, Mama?" Sally persisted.

"I'd lived in Tyler my whole life," she finally said. "Never had left the city limits. But when I was thirteen, Daddy dropped dead on our living room rug." Mama tugged at her bun, her voice whispery now. "He and I were the only ones home. And suddenly I became the 'new kid.' People pointing, staring, like

I'd somehow killed my daddy. For years, I thought it was my fault." Her face crumpled, then she smoothed back a stray curl and plastered on a smile. "Sure, I know what it's like," she said brightly, caressing Sally's shoulders. "It'll get better. I promise."

Sally knew what was coming next, even before Mama bowed her head. "Dear God, we thank You for Your loving hands. We thank You . . ."

As Mama prayed, a restlessness took hold of Sally. Why did God let her get lost? And why didn't He keep the man away?

"In Jesus' name, amen." With quick slaps, Mama brushed dirt from her hands as if she was done with all the talk about being lonely, feeling different. She got up, then pulled Sally to her feet. "Come on. I've made you a snack. That always helps things get better."

Even though Sally nodded and tried to smile, she didn't feel done with her feelings at all. Instead, she had a funny feeling that they'd just begun.

◆ ◆ ◆

The phone, which was mounted above the kitchen countertop, rang. Mama got up from the table where they both were sitting.

"Flowers' residence. Oh, hello, Mrs. Reynolds." Mama's head swiveled to find Sally. "Please, call me Ann."

Sally froze in the middle of taking a bite. She was in trouble now.

The phone cord became a tangle around Mama's finger. "She did? Hmm. She *did*? This is the first I've heard of it."

Sally swallowed, but the cookie had lodged in her throat. She'd have to tell parts of the story, but which parts? Sally pictured the muddy ditch, the beat-up truck, the sneering face. Nobody had seen her, of that she was sure, except for the black boy, and he didn't really count. After all, who would *he* tell? Certainly not Mrs. Reynolds! She sat up straight in her chair, hoping she could keep her story straight as well. Getting lost, losing the supplies; that was all she'd tell.

"I'm so sorry. Yes, ma'am. Well, I appreciate you doing that. She'll have them tomorrow. The lunch money too."

Before Mama hung up, Sally was at the sink, washing her plate and glass very carefully, determined to be just as careful with her story.

Everything about Mama changed, thanks to the call. Her brows knit together, she marched into the kitchen, took Sally by the arm, and led her back to the table. She stared at Sally's shoes, the front of her dress, the Band-Aid as if seeing them for the first time. "Why were you late to school?" she demanded, her knuckles white where she gripped Sally's arms. "And what happened to those supplies?"

Sally sat down, folded her hands in her lap and studied them. "I'm sorry," was all that came out.

"Look at me."

It was hard, but Sally managed to make eye contact with Mama and not cry.

"Sally Day Flowers, tell me. What happened to your things?"

When Mama used her whole name, trouble followed close behind. And she'd had quite enough trouble, so she had to tell the same story she'd told the teacher and the man in the hall. Rufus's twisted sneer, his vicious threat, closed off any other choice. Plus she'd promised that nice boy she wouldn't tell. Mama would never understand her taking a ride with a colored, anyway. And Daddy—sobs mounted inside just thinking what Daddy would do about that. She rubbed a sore place on her wrist, as if to confirm what she needed to say. "I got lost and started running. Then I fell down, and I got . . . scared." Saying the words reminded Sally of all that had happened, and tears rained again. She'd told the truth, at least part of it. And she prayed that it would be enough for Mama.

"Oh, dear." Mama planted a kiss on Sally's forehead. "It's all right. I'll get a cold rag for that scrape." Clucking her tongue, Mama hustled away.

The rag felt good, as did Mama's coos and assurances that they'd get new supplies, that school would get better. And Sally did all she could to make herself *feel* better, boxing up the memory of Rufus and shoving it into a tiny corner of her mind. But in spite of her best effort, Rufus didn't go away. And neither did the fact that she'd lied again.

"Can I go outside?" Sally asked, when Mama finished her doctoring.

As soon as Mama nodded, Sally was out the back door.

For the first time since lunch, Sally breathed deep. The yard, littered with crisp leaves and pecans that squirrels hadn't buried in some hole, gave off a musty smell. Occasionally a wind gust gifted her with a whiff of magnolia— vanilla and gardenia and something else, something exotic. It helped to push away the smell of Rufus.

A blur of white caught Sally's eye. She glanced back, then broke into a run, headed for the property line. It was that colored girl! What was her name?

On the other side of the fence, the girl squatted in her sandbox and dumped a bucketful of sand onto what looked like a castle. Sand dusted her face, her arms, her kneecaps so that she looked like a sand princess, her white dress free from wrinkles, her back straight, her neck arched like it was proud to hold such a well-shaped head. When the building crumbled into nothingness, she scolded the pile of sand. "Stupid serfs! How dare y'all disobey me? I'll have y'all's heads."

Sally darted a glance to the left, to the right, then leaned closer, wanting to understand what she was doing. It sounded like a pretend story! Sally stretched out and put her hand on the fence, careful to avoid the sharp barbs.

The colored girl startled, dropping her bucket. She stared hard and then smiled.

"Hi," Sally said. "I heard you talking."

The girl's eyes narrowed.

"What were you doing?" Sally asked, in a louder voice.

Her jaw set, the girl seemed to study the ground. "Nothin'." A breeze ruffled her skirt, and, brushing sand from her hands, she smoothed it down.

Everything about her drew Sally closer. She longed to leap over the fence that separated them. Instead, she just stood there, wondering how to make friends with a colored girl. She'd never had trouble making white friends, even though she sure hadn't made any at school today. But how would she make a colored friend? Mama's sayings about friends came to mind. *Ask them about themselves. Compliment them.* Sally didn't often admit it, but Mama had taught her lots of things. "That game looks fun." Sally hoped her smile looked fun too.

The girl barely moved, except for a shrug of her shoulders.

"Is it make-believe?" It wasn't clear to Sally whether the girl nodded or not, so she pressed on. "That's what I do, all the time."

The way the girl looked at her, Sally felt she was being tested, so she kept smiling until at last something opened up in that coffee-colored face, those full, pink lips. "I'm the queen, and I'm tellin' my servants to build a castle so strong, ain't nobody gwine tear it down."

"I pretend like I'm the Boxcar Children, these orphan kids," Sally blurted out. "I pretend I'm Nancy Drew too. She's a girl detective about our age. She—"

"I know who she is. I read that book about the twisted candles."

"You can read?"

It was like someone had thrown water in the girl's face, the way she jerked her head up. Yet her expression didn't change, except for a pooch in her lip.

Sally could tell she'd said something wrong, but she didn't know what. Wasn't it a common fact that coloreds couldn't read?

With a toss of thick braids, the girl glanced behind her. Then to Sally's surprise, she seemed to flow forward, like a river, her skirt fluttering with every step. Soon she stood so close to Sally that, even with the fence between them, if they each took one step forward, their noses would touch. "Been readin' since I was five," the girl said.

"Me too!" Sally wiped a sweaty brow. It was hard work, making a colored friend.

"Mrs. Brown let me borrow her daughter's old books. I can keep 'em as long as I want."

When Sally cocked her head, the girl did too. Sally thought of two sparrows, getting ready for some bird talk. "Who's Mrs. Brown?"

"That's who stay at this place. Mr. and Mrs. Brown, that's who my mama work for. After school, my brother drop me off here."

"You go to school?"

Sally didn't have to wait for the puff of the lip to know she'd asked another dumb question. But there hadn't been any coloreds at school today except for Lavania, and she was just kitchen help.

"'Course I do," the girl answered, her lips still puffy.

"Where?"

"Booker T." Her chest seemed to expand. "I'm in Mrs. Tucker's class."

"What grade?"

"Sixth."

"Me too." Sally smiled, then felt it fade as she thought of the scowling teacher, the tittering students, and what had happened before school even started.

"What's wrong wit' you?" The girl's angular face softened into circles—chin, cheeks, eyes. She grasped steel barbs, her brown hands fencing in Sally's pale ones.

"I don't like it," Sally continued.

The colored girl didn't seem to be breathing; she stood that still. "Why? What happened?"

Something about the way she stood there, strong and tall, hanging onto the fence, made Sally feel strong too. Yet should she tell this thing to a colored girl whose name she'd forgotten? She thought of her friends back in Texas. Kids, even colored ones, would keep a secret like this. And so would this girl, she'd bet on it. "I got lost," she admitted. "A bad man showed . . . chased me." Even thinking about the man showing his private area made Sally feel dirty. There were some things she couldn't tell anyone. "Then he tried to grab me, and I ran away. Then a col—a nice boy gave me a ride. But I was late, lost my supplies, and all the kids laughed at me."

Tears glistened in the girl's eyes like it had all happened to her and not Sally. She shook her head in the slowest, saddest way, her eyes magnets, drawing Sally closer and loosening more of the story from its lodging place in Sally's chest. "And the teacher was mean, and the kids were mean."

Sally didn't flinch when the girl put warm, smooth palms over her hands. Their noses touched, just for an instant, yet it felt comfortable, not awkward. There was a hint of lilac in the air and something spicy, like pepper, just different enough to send a twinge through Sally. She didn't even know this girl's name. Should she have trusted her?

"It'll get better. Lord knows, it will." The girl patted Sally on the arm, her words and her touch soothing away Sally's doubts.

"Ella! You git in here right now." A boy stood on the top step of the neighbor's back stoop, his finger crooked toward the two girls.

Sally leaned back, nearly losing her balance. *That's it! Ella's her name.*

"Ella! You hear me?"

A gasp slipped out of Sally. Even though azalea bushes dwarfed the boy's frame and he was using his hand as a sun shade, Sally immediately recognized her rescuer. But if he recognized Sally, there was no hint of it on his grumpy face.

Sally's mouth suddenly went dry. *What if he tells his mother on me? What if she tells Mrs. Brown? What if Mrs. Brown tells Mama? I'll be in worse trouble than ever.*

Ella seemed to be in no hurry to respond. She got down off the fence, her eyes still glued to Sally's face. "My brotha Willie. You got one?" She rolled her eyes and suddenly was transformed. No hint of the queenly young lady now—Ella looked more like a circus clown.

"Yep, but he's little."

"Lucky you." She turned and ran, braids flopping against a lacy white collar.

"Hey!" Sally yelled. "Can we play? Tomorrow?"

A ballerina couldn't have whirled faster. The braids set to spinning too, then settled down. "Don't yo' mama care? I know mine won't allow it." Her head turned so that Sally saw half of her oval face, which the sun lightened to milk chocolate. In a voice as whispery as the rustling leaves, Ella continued, "Unless she don't know."

"Darn right she won't allow it." The boy slouched against the back door, hands in his pocket, a toothpick in his mouth. Sally still couldn't see his eyes, but both the kindness and fear he'd shown this morning had evaporated from his tone. "Now git in this house."

It was easy to imagine what Ella's expression was, judging from the hands on her hips. Probably those pouty lips again, a heavy-browed scowl. "You gonna make me?" Ella's voice boomed even though she faced away from Sally.

"If I sure 'nuf need to."

"I wouldn't do that if I was you." Syrupy words dripped with sarcasm. Ella reminded Sally of Mama, getting her body language and tone just right. *"You got to handle men like china,"* Mama always said, *"even though they're just everyday dishes."*

Her brother yanked the toothpick out of his mouth and waved it toward Ella.

"'Cause if you tattle on me for playin' with her," Ella continued in that drippy voice, "I'll just have to tell Mama 'bout those cigarettes I seen in your truck."

Sally thought Willie's eyes would bulge out. "Why you messin' in there fo'?"

Ella whirled, gathering her skirt as if it were a train of the finest silk. She waved what should have been a gloved hand toward Sally. "Bye. Don't let them fools at yo' school bother you." She winked, then threw back her head in laughter.

His sister's words seemed to stun Willie into silence but not politeness. He turned his back, yanked open the door, popped inside, and let the door slam in Ella's face.

Before she entered the house, Ella ducked her head to her chest and curtsied so low, her braids flopped over her head and grazed the concrete step. She mouthed "bye," and then disappeared.

The sun had also disappeared, and fall's warning chill sent a knife of cold through Sally. She clung to the fence, wanting some of the warmth and light that radiated from her new friend, whose name she vowed never to forget again. *Ella. Ella. Ella.*

Chapter 18

SOUTHERN TREES BEAR STRANGE FRUIT

Black bodies swinging in the Southern breeze,
strange fruit hangin' from the poplar trees.
—Billie Holiday, "Strange Fruit"

"Can I go outside now?"

"What are you doin' back there? I can't see a thing past that shed."

Sally jumped up from the table, took her dishes to the sink, and tried to see into the Browns' back yard even though she knew from experience that a big pine tree blocked her view. For a week, thanks to the weather, and Ella's mother, she hadn't gotten so much as a glimpse of Ella. But today was Thursday, Mrs. Brown's bridge day, Ella's mother's market day. Thursday would be seeing-Ella day, if Mama cooperated.

"Playin' school," she lied.

"By yourself?"

Sally could feel Mama's eyes on her. "Uh-huh." Mama usually spotted lies a mile coming, but since that first day of school, either Mama was getting worse at catching them or Sally was getting better at lying. Just in case, Sally kept her eyes on the sink and away from Mama.

"Guess that can't hurt anything," Mama shrugged. "But you be in here by dinner." With shuffling steps, she headed toward the hall.

Sally clanked her dishes into the sink and hurried outside, already thinking about the game Ella and she would play. "One, two, three—" Two months of counting, and Sally had the steps down pat. It was forty giant steps to Ella.

The ground squished, in spite of a thick carpet of Bermuda grass, as it gave in to Sally's shoes. For days it had rained, sheets of water at times so intense, Sally hadn't even been able to see the playhouse from the back door. But the sun shone bright now, and so did Sally's hope. Ella had smoothed out the tightness that had gripped Sally ever since this move—a mean teacher, classmates who still stared at her like she was from outer space, and the thing with Mama.

A time or two, when she'd come home, Mama'd been alone in her room, kneeling by the bed, her face buried in her pillow. She'd started, as if she'd heard Sally, then jumped up and bustled into the kitchen to fix a snack, pretending nothing was wrong. But the tears in her eyes didn't lie. Yes, something was definitely wrong with Mama, and it added to the burden of this move.

Sally was panting now—*thirty-nine, forty!* She clanged into the chain-link fence like it was home base in a tag game.

"Now, hop to it." Ella towered over her sandbox, bossing some pretend subjects. Then her attention turned to Sally, and the stern dictator became a gracious queen. "Hey dere." She darted a look behind her, then pointed to a place where the fence barbs were slightly bent. "Hurry. It's clear."

Nodding, Sally scrambled to the passage Ella designated for princesses from foreign lands . . . or in Sally's case, Texas.

Somehow they'd played like this for weeks, managing to avoid discovery and sheltering their friendship in Ella's make-believe kingdom. Sometimes they talked about serious things, like why Ella hated the *n* word. Sometimes they didn't talk at all. At times, a grumbling Willie had acted as their sentry. He'd never even smiled at her since that first day they'd met. But at least he hadn't told on them. Not yet, anyway.

Holding onto the trunk of a big oak for support, Sally climbed over the fence and with a soft thud landed in the Browns' yard.

Her back to Sally, Ella crawled out of the sandbox and gathered cones from under a pine tree.

"Hey!"

"How you doin'?" Ella stood tall and flashed a smile at Sally.

"Okay, I guess."

"School ain't betta yet?"

Sally shook her head.

"It will be. Don't you worry 'bout it. Some things take time."

All the tightness flowed from Sally. That was the thing about Ella. She talked like a grown-up, one who was very, very wise, yet played like a twelve-year-old.

"You be a servant," Ella commanded.

"I don't want to."

"You be one today, I'll be one next time."

That was another thing about Ella. She had manners, gentility—things that Mama said all good Southern girls needed. But underneath all those "Yes, ma'ams," "No, ma'ams," "Thank you, ma'ams," was a will of steel.

"Here." Ella bellowed out orders now. "Get us some mud."

Sally picked up the bucket and headed for the faucet, then turned to face her friend. "Can't we build a pyramid today? I'm tired of castles."

"Don't want no part of that." Ella shook her head so hard, her braids slapped against her cheeks. "Egyptians had slaves. And I ain't havin' any slaves."

"But aren't servants the same as slaves?"

"Servants can quit if they want to," Ella harrumphed, "plus they get paid." She folded her arms like that was the end of it.

Sally nodded as water splashed into the bucket. She didn't care what they built, what they called the people they bossed around. She'd never had a friend who'd play make-believe like Ella, so if Ella wanted her way, Sally would happily give in.

The girls hunched together on a splintered board propped across the sandbox. Sally used a Dixie cup to scoop up damp sand. With smooth motions, she packed it down with her fist and then overturned it onto Ella's growing castle.

"Harder, now. Do it right." When Ella used her haughty voice, like she did now, Sally sure felt like a slave. Still, she scooped, packed, and dumped out damp sand, over and over and over.

When the cup tore and sand spilled into her lap, Sally swept it off into the sandbox. Her hands flew to her hips. "I don't wanna be the servant."

Ella folded her arms across her chest, wide eyes becoming slits. Then she exploded into laughter. "Girl! I wondered how long you'd go for it."

Her giggles were contagious—Sally doubled over and laughed away the lonely days in school, Mama's tears . . . the face of Rufus.

Under the girls' busy hands, the castle grew.

"What yo' Daddy do?" Ella broke the satisfactory silence. The voice was regular Ella now—creamy, like the café au lait Mama sometimes let Sally sip.

"He teaches at the college."

"Wish I could go there when I grow up."

"Why can't you?"

"They don't let in coloreds." With her finger, Ella dug a hole in the sand, deeper, deeper, down to the really wet stuff.

Sally stared at the well of water, which swirled to match Ella's twisting and turning finger. Of course she'd known, deep down, that colored folks couldn't go to college. She'd walked with Daddy along the campus sidewalks, had seen all the shiny white faces hustling to their classes. But until now it hadn't bothered her that there were no black faces. Until her best friend—her only friend—said she wanted to go.

It was hard to resist running a hand across those kinky braids, trying to smooth away the hurt. But Sally wasn't sure about touching Ella's hair. What if she had lice? Daddy said a lot of coloreds did. Probably worms and other stuff too.

Still, Sally wanted to do something. "Aren't there colleges for you people?" she asked. Instantly Sally knew she'd said the wrong thing. The smoke in Ella's eyes, the pooch of the bottom lip, was that easy to see.

With flat palms, Ella molded a turret atop the castle. "Sho' dere is," she finally said. "And if I get a scholarship, I'll be goin' to one of them. It's called Tuskegee."

Even though they kept scooping and smoothing, like they'd been doing for the past hour or so, the quiet that now settled around them made Sally squirm. "What does *your* daddy do?" she asked, as much to push away the silence as anything else.

"Fixes cars."

"There's lots of cars that need fixin'." Using some twigs, Sally tried to reinforce the sagging wall of their creation. "With your mama working, y'all will have enough money, won't you?"

Ella shrugged her shoulders. "Ain't neva enuf. Willie's hankering to take off fo' New Orleans 'stead of helpin' Daddy. Wants to be a 'no-count musician,' play 'dem 'devil blues.' Least that's what Daddy says."

"What's 'devil blues'?"

Ella's eyes got big. "You ain't never heard da blues?" She hopped out of the sandbox, slapping sand off her legs. "Come on!" She pointed to the house.

"But—"

"The Browns done gone to the farm." Ella ran toward the back door.

Sally waffled, then hurried after Ella.

They streaked up a stone path that was lined with scarlet azaleas. Sally tried her best to keep up, but Ella moved like a cat, her muscles taut, her stride gigantic.

When the back door creaked in response to Ella's tug, a chill ran down Sally's spine. They shouldn't be in here, should they?

It was like Ella could read Sally's mind. "Momma visitin' with the Parkers' maid after she go to the store. Much as they talk, we can stay in here till Christmas. All we gotta worry 'bout is Willie. And I kin bribe him good."

Even though Sally giggled, the chill spread to her arms and legs. Her parents wouldn't like this; in fact, she'd be whipped if they caught her.

The Browns' house had an open floor plan, like Sally's, with a bar separating the kitchen from the breakfast nook. But that was the only similarity between the two houses. Once before, Sally had seen a place like this—on a dog-eared page of one of Mama's *Good Housekeeping* magazines. Of course they couldn't afford it, Mama had reminded Sally as she flipped through pages. But Mama liked to dream.

Tile gleamed with such perfect whiteness, Sally could see her reflection, down to the cowlick on her forehead. A cream-colored, L-shaped couch, accentuated with throw pillows, curved around two walls. Blocky coffee tables supported ceramic ashtrays and tall, thin flower vases. It was all perfect, too perfect, making Sally tiptoe and hold her breath. She darted a look out a plate-glass window that gave a perfect view of the sandbox and their castle. Except for the swish and hum of two ceiling fans, the room seemed to be daring them to break the perfect silence.

"Hey!" Ella pointed to Sally's feet. "We gotta take 'em off."

Sally fumbled to untie her sneakers.

Ella turned the slick floor into an ice rink as she slid on sock-clad feet toward one of the tables, which Sally now saw was a cabinet. Humming low, Ella hurried to a knapsack near the door, dug out some record albums, then, hugging the albums to her chest, darted back toward Sally. "They're my brotha's," she whispered, as if the furniture might tattle on her. "We be playin' them while everybody gone."

"Where *is* your brother?"

Ella rolled her eyes. "Prob'ly down by the bayou. Wit' that crazy horn of his."

"Isn't he scared?"

"Of what?" Ella, eyes blazing like coals, stepped toward the front window, which, through gauzy drapes, gave a view of a thick stand of trees. "Ain't no one 'cept a few dumb fishermen gonna set foot in them swamps. Some people say they's haunted."

Sally's earlier chill returned full force. "Haunted? Wha-what do you mean?"

"Girl, you don't know nothin'!" Ella huffed. She padded back to the console, still hugging the records. "First it was the Unda'ground Railroad. Then voodoo types did black magic down there." Her voice got quiet. "Last off, the Klan moved in. Supposedly hung a man on dem cypress limbs." Her eyes got round as marbles. "When the moon full, they say dem branches drip blood."

Sally moved to the front window, peeked out, and pointed. "Over there?"

Ella nodded.

Something about the way the sun shone across the trees, coloring their leaves Easter grass green, shored up Sally. "I don't believe any of it. I'd go back there alone for a nickel. Any time."

"I'll bet you don't. Not after you hear this." Ella edged one of the records out of its jacket. Then she turned a couple of knobs, set the record on a turntable, lifted the record arm from its holder, and placed it on the spinning disc.

At first there was static and a scratching sound as steel traveled across grooved plastic. Then deep minor chords poured from the speakers, along with a crackling sound.

Her eyes closed, Ella set to swaying like a reed rustling in the wind.

Sally eased her body onto the sectional, the sounds pulling her back, back, to the pews in the Waco Baptist church. Back, back, before the Sunday service started, when the organist, her back arched, her arms stiff, her fingers flat on the ivory keys, warmed up the huge instrument, coaxing out chords that pulled at Sally's heart, yet comforted her. Back, back . . .

The console vibrated with low humming sounds that seemed ready to shake the Browns' house loose from its foundations.

"Southern trees bear strange fruit," a woman moaned.

Tears filled Sally's eyes. Something bad was happening to that lady! Sally wanted someone, anyone, to stop the record, but she was paralyzed by the words, by the sounds.

"Blood on the leaves, blood on the root."

Ella kept swaying, her eyes closed, a whistling sound escaping from between her teeth.

Maybe the bayou was haunted. Maybe this house was too. Sally struggled to get off the couch, but her feet had become one with the cold white tile.

The voice moaned on and on, dark words of death and blood and despair. Everything in Sally agreed with the music, yet she wanted to break away. Nothing could be as awful as this poor woman claimed. Could it?

The record made a screeching sound, like fingernails across slate. Sally covered her face with her hands. As if it knew it had broken her, the music stopped. She glanced at Ella, wanting, needing an explanation.

"Billie Holiday. Tellin' 'bout a lynching. Tellin' you how it is down here." There was no anger in Ella's eyes, only a sadness that took over her face.

Sally flew toward Ella and threw her arms around her friend. "I'm sorry. For . . . for everything." She sobbed, desperate to show what was in her heart. She was sorry about the college. The hangings. She was sorry for the times Daddy said "nigger," sorry for the times she'd hurt Ella and didn't even know why. But right now, she thought she was beginning to understand.

"Oh, girl." Ella ruffled Sally's hair. "You sure got ya some stringy hair."

Sally thought her heart would burst from the sudden change. The music was over. And Ella had forgiven her! She shook her head until hair slapped her ears.

Ella howled like Sally's Texan aunt who loved bathroom jokes, knock-knock jokes—any joke at all. Then she grabbed Sally and pulled her toward the cabinet. With a flip of a lever, another record plopped onto the spinning wheel. "Listen to this!"

Crazy parade music began marching through the cold, quiet, immaculate house and into the den. Sally didn't know anything about this kind of music, with first one instrument—it sounded like a birdcall—taking control, and then another. A series of *boom, booms*, then a trill so high, it hurt Sally's ears. In the background, what sounded like a horn, giving orders to the others, but not in a bossy way.

Almost before Sally realized what had happened, Ella twirled her around, around, pulled her close, shoved her back. They were like the music, one leading, one following, yet both keeping a part of themselves. Ella jumped forward, shaking her foot. Sally stepped forward, but shook her head instead of her foot. Ella arched backward and spun like a top. Sally tried, but she could not move with the frenzy of her friend.

"It's jazz," Ella hollered, over the music.

They bumped into tables and the sofa, yet time seemed to stand still as the music blared on. And there were no words to compete with the energy released by the touch of that tiny little needle against the spinning disc.

"Christella Grace!"

The door slammed shut.

Ella froze; so did Sally. But not the music, which kept on playing, mocking the girls, now playing just for the furniture. Sally didn't have to look toward those wide plantation front doors to know that for the two of them, the fun was over. And it pained her something bad.

"Look'a here at me, girl."

The voice commanded Sally to obey.

It was a colored woman, one hand perched on a powerful hip. The other arm cradled a bag stuffed full of groceries. Muscles rippled under a flower print dress stretched tight over her body. Her hair was shiny, like Ella's, but in tight curls instead of kinky ones. "What in the world ya think ya doin'?" Her bosom trembled, her jaw locked.

"Momma . . ."

"They'd have my job if they saw this. I ain't taught ya to act like this on white folks' property."

"But they gone, Momma."

Ella's mother stalked toward the two of them, eyes blazing. "Ain't make a hill of beans' difference. What's right is right, and this ain't right."

"I'm sorry, Momma. I won't do it again," Ella mumbled, her head bowed.

"Darn right you won't do it again. Won't have no chance to."

"No, Momma. Don't say that," Ella cried.

Sally hung her head too, wanting to cry. She'd made a bad impression on her best friend's mother.

When the front door creaked open this time, Sally heard it.

With a whistle and a shuffle, a shiny horn in his hand, Willie sashayed inside, then nearly tripped himself from stopping so fast.

Mrs. Ward shoved past Ella, making her way to a new target of her wrath. "How dare you?" she screamed at Willie.

Sally felt sure if she hadn't been there, Mrs. Ward would've slapped him.

"Look at you. Jest carryin' on 'round this white neighborhood like a nigga fool."

Sally tried not to stare at Ella's mother. How could she call him the very word Ella said they hated? Sally glanced behind her. Should she slip toward the back door, dash home? Or should she intervene on Ella's behalf?

". . . one of you don't get me fired, the other will."

"But Momma, I wasn't—"

"You and that horn, runnin' behind the devil hisself!" She pointed to the record player. "And you, gal, turn that thang off!"

"Yes'm, yes'm." Ella dashed to the cabinet. The record screeched, then fell silent.

"Ma'am—" Sally trembled all over—her voice too. Should she call her ma'am? Or Mrs. Ward? She tried to start over, wanting to make things nice. "Uh, ma'am."

With a whirl, Mrs. Ward faced her, but she looked at some spot behind Sally, as if Sally weren't there.

"It's all my fault. I asked to hear it, and Ella was just—"

For the first time Mrs. Ward focused on Sally. "Ain't no white gal gwine do the explainin' for any chile of mine."

Sally swallowed down the rest of her lies, her face burning from the rebuke. She'd known it had been wrong to come here.

"Now git on home."

"But Momma!" Ella protested.

In two steps, Mrs. Ward stood before her daughter. When she slapped her cheek hard, Ella didn't make a sound. She didn't even turn her head.

Sally's hand flew to her cheek like she'd been the one slapped. Unless she'd killed someone, her mother wouldn't ever slap her in front of a stranger. And that's what she was to Ella's mother—a stranger. Or maybe even something worse.

Ella's reaction—or lack of it—seemed to change things. Mrs. Ward tugged at her dress, which had hitched up enough to display where the white fasteners of her garter belt met gray nylons. Her face slack and tired-looking, she pointed at Sally and then the back door. "You go on home, gal." The anger seemed to have drained off, like receding floodwaters.

"Momma, can I least walk her to the fence?"

Thick eyebrows met in the middle of Mrs. Ward's forehead, and Sally thought the anger would gather strength again and result in another slap. She was wrong. Broad shoulders shrugged.

When Ella grabbed Sally's hand, the two padded to their shoes and whisked them, laces flopping, off the floor. They hurried, barefoot, out of the house.

Near the sandbox Ella paused, her arm still linked with Sally's. "She ain't gonna let me play with you no more." There was a hint of fire in Ella's eyes even though her mouth was pouty. "But I got an idea."

"What?"

"The bayou. Ain't no one gonna see us dere."

A shiver cut through Sally. "The bayou? We can't go there. You said it's haunted."

"That's why it gwine work. Only fishermen down there, and dey won't tell."

Sally shook her head. "I don't even know how to get there." *And I'm scared.*

All the fire had returned to Ella. "But I do. Willie showed me."

Something thrashed around in thick briar bushes, then leapt to the branch of an oak.

Ella gasped.

"It's just a squirrel, Ella." Sally didn't add that she'd jumped too, until she'd spotted the bushy tail, the beady eyes.

"No. Look!"

Even though she squinted, Sally couldn't see anything more than the green leaves, the brown bark of an oak tree.

"That hollowed-out place, Sally! A squirrel's nest. Don't you see it?"

Oh! Sally nodded, her spirits beginning to soar as they had when that jazz music eased the memory of the sad woman singing about strange fruit. With Ella's strength, maybe she could do this. She wanted—no—needed Ella's friendship. With Ella, down bayou way would be safe.

Ella's spirits must have soared too, the way she hopped, then spun around. "We'll leave notes in that hallowed-out place. Coded notes. 'School's out,' means get down bayou way."

The warmth started in Sally's toes, spread through her middle section, and fired her imagination. "'Looks like rain,' means stay away."

"Yeah! And if we havin' meetings, seems like we're a club."

"And we gotta have a name."

Sally and Ella leaned against the oak. Their oak, with their secret cubbyhole, its huge branches hanging into both yards. Even though the chain-link fence and a mean mama stood between them, this tree made them closer than ever.

"How about the Boxcar Children?"

Ella shook her head. "That was your club. This gotta be our club."

Finally Sally nodded, giving in to the authority in Ella's clear eyes. This was her friend, the one person, other than Willie, who knew about . . . that man. "Okay. Shake on it?"

When Ella offered a sweaty palm, Sally clung to it like it was a lifeline.

"Christella Grace! You git in here."

"Think on a name. When it's right, we'll know it." Ella whirled and ran inside.

Sally put on her shoes, then staggered toward the fence, wondering if she'd only imagined everything that had happened in the Browns' house. A part of her wanted to stay asleep to see how it ended, but a part of her feared what would happen next.

"Sally Day Flowers, you get in here!"

Her name sounded so ugly, with Mama bellowing it loud enough to set off the neighborhood dogs. In spite of trembling legs and hands, Sally managed to climb over the fence, lies taking shape even as she kept moving. It hadn't been a dream. And Mama, standing on the back porch with hands on her hips, wasn't a figment of her imagination, either.

Chapter 19

THE SWAMP SISTERS

Do come along. Do let us go. Jesus sittin' on the waterside.
—Negro spiritual, "Jesus on the Waterside"

How long has this gone on?" Till Mama spoke up, there hadn't been a word since the prayer, just glances between her and Daddy. Even Robert had felt the tension, balking at being put in his high chair, then slamming his cup against the metal tray.

Her appetite gone, Sally stared at a plate of greasy pork chops, a grainy crater of grits. Gone too was the chance to be Ella's friend. If only there was a way to avoid trouble. She cut a look at Mama. Should she tell the truth, be evasive, or somehow try to do both?

"Sally, your mother asked you a question."

It was easy to nod, with that look on Daddy's face. And she'd better answer fast, because he looked ready to explode. "Since the first day of school." She wasn't counting the first day she saw Ella.

"Did you ever think you might mention it to us?" With a napkin, Mama fanned her face. "According to Millie, half the neighborhood's seen y'all back there, thick as thieves. For the life of me, I can't fathom what you'd see in a little colored girl."

"She's my friend."

"Sally, I've tried to get you to have your classmates over. You don't want anything to do with them." The more Mama talked, the more high-pitched her voice became. "You didn't even tell me about that Girl Scout meeting. I had to find out from a neighbor."

"Because I didn't want to do it, and you'd make me."

"Sally!" Mama's chair scraped when she jumped to her feet and grabbed another napkin off the counter. "I'm just trying to help you." She dabbed at her eyes.

"You listen here," Daddy spat out, thanks to Mama's tears, "if I ever catch you playing with that little coon again, I'll blister you."

The shiny hardness in Daddy's eyes hit Sally full in the face. She longed to spit a nasty answer at him for calling Ella a name. At the same time, she wanted to crawl into his arms and put her thumb in her mouth—something she hadn't done for ages. She reached for Daddy's arm, yearning for him to see that she was full of hate and love, all at once. "Why?" she managed to say. "Why is it so bad to have a colored friend?"

Daddy jerked his arm away from Sally, his face shutting off her question as well. "Go change your brother's diaper," he managed.

"But Daddy—" She had to try to show him, had to get through.

He slammed his fist against the table, rattling the plates.

The whole time Sally was undoing Robert's high chair strap and trying to shush him, she thought of Ella and how unfair the whole thing was. Yet there was something else under the unfairness, something mean and hard. It had been in Ella's mother's eyes. It was in Daddy's eyes. And even though it had been a thousand times worse in Rufus's eyes, it was the same hard hate.

Sally carried Robert into the hall, then crouched near the door. "Itsy, witsy spider," she whispered, hoping to keep Robert quiet so she could hear what her parents were saying.

"More! More!"

In spite of everything, Sally couldn't help but smile at her brother. It was so easy to get Robert to do what she wanted. She wished her parents were the same way.

"She's gonna hear it at school, anyway." Eavesdropping wasn't hard, the way Daddy's voice boomed toward her and Robert.

"But where do we start?"

They had the same problem as she did in knowing what to tell! She shifted a wiggly Robert about and inched closer to the door. But what was their problem?

"We've got to tell her about the fruity jig wandering around playin' his fool music. For safety's sake, if nothing else."

"But I don't want to scare her." There was a pleading tone in Mother's voice.

"She'll find out anyway."

"Oh, I don't know, Don."

"If the parents are talking, the kids are talking. And from what I've seen, these folks are yapping day in and day out."

The talk perplexed Sally. Were they talking about Willie? And why was he "fruity"?

Forks scraped against plates. The faucet gushed water. Dishes clanked together. Messing up Sally's hearing. She leaned closer to the door.

". . . it shouldn't be legal. I mean, this is the U.S. of A. If a maid brings her kids over, what business is it of some nosy neighbors?"

There was a thud and another scrape of a chair. Then Mama began sobbing.

It hurt Sally to hear this. She patted Robert's head, wishing it was Mama's.

"I . . . wish . . . we hadn't moved here," Mama cried.

Sally nodded so hard, she almost lost her balance, but righted herself when she thought about Ella. *Then we wouldn't have met.*

"That's right. Blame me for finding a way to feed our faces!"

"Don, I didn't mean that!"

Both her parents were shouting now, making Robert restless. Sally too.

"How is it my fault that some fools are scared of a few—?"

Sally grimaced. She knew Ella hated that word. And now *she* hated that word.

"It's *not* your fault, honey. It's just . . ."

"Half these folks have maids. Always have, always will. One little incident—for which they have no proof at all, from what I hear—lathers 'em up but good."

"A little incident? Some colored boy coming on to a young girl?"

Sally's arms went numb, and not just from the weight of Robert. That couldn't be Willie. Could it be Rufus? Just as quickly, she dismissed that thought. Even with that dirty, greasy skin, he didn't look black.

"More! More!" Robert wiggled so suddenly, Sally nearly dropped him. "Now, Fally! Now!" With his chubby fist, he drummed her arm.

"Sally Flowers!"

Daddy's voice boomed Sally into action. She hustled Robert to the bathroom.

"You get him changed right now. Or else."

◆ ◆ ◆

Sally ripped up the note and stuffed it into her pocket, being careful to trail Ella twenty or thirty yards, just as Ella had told her to do. That way, if anybody was watching, it wouldn't look like they were together.

All traces of civilization were gone now. The path meandered through scrub brush and live oaks that towered over Sally, making her remember Ella's bayou tales. Had the Klan really been here? Were they here now? To stay calm, she focused on puffs of dust that sprang about Ella's ankles in response to the pit-pat of her sneakers. That and the flash of white sash, the whipping skirt, as Ella zigzagged deeper into the woods.

The path turned muddy, hinting that water lay ahead. As further evidence, live oaks and brush gave way to gums, willows, and a few scraggly bearded cypresses.

A stench rose to greet her now—a dying fish and a hard-boiled egg smell that turned Sally's stomach. Was that smell the bayou? Cicadas hummed a greeting or a warning, Sally wasn't sure which. When the sharp cry of a kingfisher cut through a sloshing sound, Sally shivered. Should she really follow through with this? Break another rule by leaving the neighborhood, much less leaving the neighborhood with a colored girl?

A glance at black hair tamed into braids, the strong, straight back of her best friend, convinced Sally she should follow through. And that the lie, telling Mama she was walking to the store to get some candy, had been necessary. Besides, Nancy Drew lied in her books, even to her father. And her father was a lawyer.

"What—" The hammering of Sally's heart almost drowned out the cicadas and the calls of strange birds. She lurched forward, then fell onto mucky earth.

"You okay?"

Sally nodded, her friend's face blurry through her tears.

"It's jes' an old cypress root." Ella came into sharp focus now, a smile about her eyes and mouth.

Sally's lip quivered, but she took care of it by rubbing her knee and wiping mud off her legs. It hurt, but she didn't want Ella to think that she was a baby.

"Come on." Ella put a finger to her lip, as if someone were listening. "It's jes' around this curve."

How often did Ella come here? And why wasn't she afraid of this place? Sally ducked to avoid silvery gray moss, which hung from branches like witches' hair.

Something growled, low and slow, yet loud, making the hair on Sally's arms stand up. This place had to be haunted. "Wha—what's that?"

"A bullfrog. Sound like a chain saw, don't it?"

Sally nodded, even though she'd never heard a chain saw.

All of the strange creatures of this even stranger land joined voices, a chorus of clicks and moans and cries. Warning her, yet luring her closer.

"Look!"

The bayou creatures fell silent as the water lay black before them. Knobby cypress heads jutted out of the water, as if they were wading. What Sally guessed was algae drifted on the surface like tangles of green hair. The only sign of life was a weathered boat, mired along a distant bank in a sea of lime green plants. A rotten-looking rope trailed uselessly into the water. In spite of all the green, things seemed to be dying. Sally shivered. Why had she agreed to this?

"Over here!" Ella hissed.

When Sally stepped closer, a flash of white caught her eye. It was a bird, long stalks supporting a streamlined white body. A crown of feathers clung to a head so small, it made the creature look comical.

"What's that?" Sally tried to whisper, but she startled the bird into a rustle of wings and a loud squawk. With a whoosh, it disappeared into a thick grove of cypress.

"An egret."

"And that?" Sally pointed to the impossibly green plants on which the boat seemed to float.

"Duckweed."

Sally tiptoed forward until the toes of her sneakers grazed the water, which was not really black but tea-colored. "How do you know all this stuff?"

It seemed like a curtain fell over Ella's face. Her lips got tight, her forehead creased with lines.

Sally longed to pull away whatever it was that was separating her from her best friend. Even though they stood only inches apart, Sally felt their differences as much as she had that first day, when she'd been surprised by a colored girl on the other side of the fence.

The bayou creatures came alive again. The egret rippled the water as it tiptoed closer. A bullfrog croaked, another answered; this time, Sally didn't jump. The waters rippled, and dark heads surfaced, then popped back undercover. Strangely, Sally began to feel at home as she picked up a rhythm in the creatures' cries. Maybe this *could* be their secret place.

Ella knelt on the marshy land, cupped her hand, and dipped it into the bayou. Water streamed off her fingers, leaving a palm full of gray-black slush.

"When yo' people whipped us, my ancestors came down here, put this mud on dere bloody backs. When they would rather die free than be slaves, dese swamps hid them till they worked dere way north." Her eyes misted over, Ella talked in low tones. "All of us know 'bout dese waters." She told Sally about evil men, both black and white, who brought her people in chains to this country, about the plantations, about the Underground Railroad.

The swamp was still, even the wind pausing to hear Ella.

As Ella talked, Sally wished she were black so she could get rid of the burden of her white skin. "How could they do that?" she asked.

Somehow the sun found its way through all the cypress and oak and pine. Ella squinted, then shielded her face with a flattened palm. "Ignorance. Hate. All the usual things been goin' on since Adam and Eve."

Ella's words and the feelings in Sally's heart practically pushed Sally to her feet. She pumped her fist toward the sky. "I'll never be like that!" she declared to the birds and reptiles and amphibians and plants. She said it again, wishing that her parents and her teacher and all the kids at her school could hear.

For an instant, Ella's face got hard again. Then she wiped off the mud, grabbed Sally's hand, and pulled her along a footpath that she said some slaves from long ago had trampled into the marshy land at water's edge.

"Come on!" She pointed toward a thicket of trees. "You get a stick." Ella yanked off her socks and shoes and motioned for Sally to do the same. "I'll grab dat rope." Every trace of sadness had left her face. "We're sailin' to Africa."

"In that?" Sally made a face at the boat.

"It's a pirogue. If it worked for dem Cajuns, it'll work for us."

Sally sloshed into the water, mud oozing between her toes. "I've got a better idea. With this mud, those twigs, that moss, we can build the best castle ever."

Ella shook her head and stomped her foot, sending something slithery into the murky water. "Next time."

Next time. Like a club! Sally nodded, then grabbed a stick. "Hey, Ella? How 'bout Swamp Sisters?"

First Ella's eyes got wide, then they narrowed.

Sometimes, like now, Sally couldn't tell what Ella was thinking. "'Cause neither of us has a sister." Sally didn't like these silent times, so she hurried the words out. "And we're kinda like sisters, and . . ."

Ella didn't seem to hear. With careful steps, she waded into the bayou and, using flattened palms as oars, created a current that slowly drew the boat toward them. "I'll think on it." Even though her back was to Sally, her voice boomed across the water. "Swamp Sistas," she repeated. "It just might work."

At that moment, Sally believed they could sail to Africa, just on the strength of their friendship. She tapped Ella on the shoulder, loving the feel of sun-kissed brown skin. "So it's not really haunted, is it?"

Ella shook her head.

"And the bad men? What about them? Do they still come here?"

When Ella frowned, the magical boat became a peeling, splintered *pirogue* rather than a majestic schooner; the waters, just dirty brown bayou rather than rolling blue sea. "Dey still come here sometimes. So I guess you could say dis place is good . . . and bad."

◆

Sally paused, her lips dry, her voice faltering. Only those closest to her— Sam, Suzi, and Ed—had heard this part of her story. And none of them had heard the rest of it, the part hovering at the edge of her consciousness, threatening to seep out. She picked up the mug of coffee, which Ruby had refilled, and let the roasted bean smell soothe her.

"How long did the Swamp Sisters last? I mean, did they . . ." Shamika fanned her mouth, as if it were on fire. "Listen to me! Not makin' a lick of sense."

Her face impassive, Ruby rose from the sofa, stirred at smoldering embers, and brought the fire back to life. She'd sat down after bringing more coffee and hadn't budged during the last part of the story, yet it didn't seem to affect her the way it had Shamika.

"One more month." Sally pushed up the sleeves of a turtleneck sweater and wiped her brow. Couldn't she stop now? Didn't Shamika seem to be healing well enough on her own without any more of this?

When somebody rang the doorbell, Sally and Shamika jumped, but not Ruby. She nodded, as if she were expecting a visitor, and walked to the entryway.

Sally heard the click, click click. Then the squeaking of the door.

"Detective Price."

"Ma'am."

Ruby came into the room, the detective close behind. "Please, have a seat." What looked like an attempt at a smile became a lopsided grimace. "Can I get you anything? Water? Coffee?"

"No, ma'am, but thank you." With a nod, he acknowledged Sally, then gave his attention to Shamika. "Hate to interrupt you, ma'am. This'll just take a minute." He handed Shamika an envelope. "I wanted to deliver this in person. We've just arrested Jay Davis and charged him with aggravated assault and rape. And the DA wants to add hate crime to the laundry list here."

Sally busied herself picking cuticles as if that would work out the shocks buzzing down her arms. One of her students had charged another of her students with violent crimes. Of course they weren't technically her students, now that she'd been suspended. But it still pained her that it had come down to this. How had hate so twisted Jay's young mind? Could she somehow have prevented it?

"Why all the sudden?" Ruby asked.

Sally couldn't tell if Ruby was glad or not—the fog still clouded her face.

"Well, ma'am, another witness has come forward who places him at the scene."

"This Jay character?"

The detective nodded.

Sally expected a jubilant cry, at least a couple of snorts, but it was not to be. Shamika rubbed her hands together and stared into the fire.

"What about the other ones?" Ruby asked.

"Ma'am, we're still working on that."

Her arms folded, Ruby eyed the letter like it was poison. "And what's in that?"

When the detective nodded, not a hair on his head moved out of place. "Standard operating procedure, ma'am. It just explains what you're to do if the accused or any representative thereof tries to contact you."

"Thank you, sir." As soon as Ruby stood, Detective Price did the same. They faced off, bottled-up emotions stored inside powerful, silent bodies. Then Ruby ushered the detective out of the house.

Shamika, face buried in her hands, looked as if she'd just received an ominous medical report. With her head bent so low, a row of neat black stitches leapt from the part line of her hair. Her skin seemed to have lost its mocha glow; her interest in Sally's story also seemed to have faded. And Sally was relieved.

"Mrs. Stevens, we can't thank you enough for standing by us in all of this." Ruby stood at the threshold between the entryway and the den. "For listening. Tutoring."

Sally tried not to stare. Ruby hadn't cried since this whole ordeal had started, but Sally was sure tears brightened the bold brown eyes now. Everything else about Ruby seemed to soften—she slumped forward, her shoulders rounded, the skin slack about her neck.

"You don't have to thank me. Teaching's my life." Sally longed to say more, longed to release the truths that were pushing harder, begging to get out. When she'd been called to her profession, Sally had taken seriously God's admonition to hold teachers more accountable. But somewhere along the way, she now realized, she'd wandered far and wide, into brambles of subterfuge and lies that ended with a suppressed secret, a false résumé. Shouldn't a Christian be able to stop lying? Shouldn't a Christian forgive and forget the past and move on?

Questions flew at Sally, questions for which she had no answers. She longed to pour out her soul to Ruby, for something told her Ruby would not only understand, but relate to her dilemma. But she couldn't do it. What would that say about her relationship with Sam? With Suzi? With Ed?

Sally picked up a heavy briefcase and did her best to cover a heavy heart. But it was so hard to hide, so hard to pretend. And for the first time ever, Sally wasn't sure if she could continue all the subterfuge.

Chapter 20

A NEAR MISS

Sweep it clean. Ain't going to tarry here.

—Negro spiritual, "Ain't Going to Tarry Here"

"Hey, Dr. Stevens."

Sam assumed the cyclist pulling up beside him was female, based on the high-pitched voice, the hooded pink parka. He rolled his bike into a rack next to the redbricked math building, wound a lock around the front wheel, then glanced up. Yep. Definitely a girl.

"Won't be doin' this much more if we get that storm." The girl dismounted and rolled her bike next to Sam's. She gabbed on, smacking gum double-time.

Sam nodded. "Four to six inches. Definitely not bike-riding weather."

She looked familiar, with her bright smile, her eyes heavily lined with whatever kind of makeup girls used these days. His own Suzi put on quite a bit more than he would've liked. But that was something he'd always left to Sally.

They strolled past bundled-up students, the girl bobbing, smacking, and gabbing in a way that wore Sam out. Had he ever had that much energy? And it still made him nervous that he had no idea who she was.

". . . that paper—about as bad as the one you assigned."

"Ah, when was that?" Sam pointed at his head and rolled his eyes.

"Last fall. Remember, I had your wife over at MCC, then transferred. She told me to take your class, said you'd be a pushover." She blew a bubble, then popped it.

Her giggle grated on Sam, and the fact that his wife had said such a thing.

199

Of course, if he were Sally, he'd just smile and smooth it over with, "Of course. How could I forget?" But he couldn't lie like that. Sally always said it was just a little white lie, but wasn't a little white lie still a lie?

The girl stopped short, a tumble of hair falling out of her hood. "You tell Mrs. Stevens we're all behind her." Her breath came out in glazed puffs. "We can't believe what's happened." Angry gray eyes met his own. "And don't you worry, they'll hear from us."

An electric shock shot down Sam's spine. What had Sally gotten into now? And not a word to him about much of anything for over two weeks. Not the tutoring, not her job . . . He reached into his pocket and fiddled with keys, cold steel biting into his fingers. This was awkward. He *and* his wife would look like fools if he admitted to this girl he had no idea what she was talking about. But wasn't it worse to cut her off with a nod? "Uh-huh," Sam managed. He knew he sounded inane, but it was the best he could do. Anyway, five steps up the ramp, and he was in the math building.

Striding forward, he opened the door for both himself and the girl. Warm air hit him full force, and so did the knowledge that he was safe here with his numbers. Logical numbers. Reliable numbers. Numbers didn't lie.

"Hey, thanks, Dr. Stevens." A bubble gum smell tickled his nostrils.

Sam nodded, trying to keep from sneezing.

"And you tell her I'll write a letter, get a petition going, whatever it takes." Her eyes burned with a passion not unlike what Sam had seen back during his college days, when the issues were Vietnam and Equal Rights.

Suddenly the comforting heat trapped him, like he was in a locked steam room. He paused mid-step, sweat pouring from his brow, planning to rip off his jacket as soon as she bobbed her way down the hall.

"Dr. Stevens, are . . . are you all right?"

He could hear her gum smacking, smacking. But he wasn't seeing her. No, what he was seeing was the smiling, lying eyes of his wife. And for just a moment, he was sick of being married to her.

"Dr. Stevens?"

Sam managed a nod.

A mittened hand touched his arm. "Hey, don't you worry a bit. We won't just stand by and let them fire her."

◆ ◆ ◆

Sally reluctantly stepped out of the warm car. For over two weeks she'd choked down her secret during more than a few family meals, more than a few late-night Sam-Sal chats, till she wanted to puke. But she'd do more than puke if Sam found out she'd been suspended. She'd downright croak.

An early November sky hung heavy with what the weatherman predicted would be the season's first snow. As if to prove him right, needles of ice pricked her face, and the north wind blasted her with a deep-freeze chill. Sally locked her car and jabbed the keys, and her hands, into her coat pockets.

Ruby opened the door and ushered Sally into a warm hug, the smell of freshly baked cookies . . . Sally was home.

"Make yourself at home in there," Ruby said, an echo of Sally's own thoughts. "I'll bring in a little something."

The den's blinds had been raised, revealing a pattering of sleet and snow across the back yard. At the onset, a storm could feel cozy, like old house shoes. But as it intensified, it could imprison, piles of white covering the driveway, the streets, pushing against the very foundation of homes in an effort to entrap and smother. Sally ripped off her coat, laid it on the couch, and shoved up her sweater sleeves. She was trapped enough, without this weather.

"Hi, Sally!" Shamika seemed to glide across the room, then spun, arched her back, and melted into the chair.

The movements weren't lost on Sally. "Did you take ballet?"

Shamika nodded. "Till the money ran out. And it got too time-consuming. We had to make some choices." Her voice trailed off. "Now I have a choice to make too."

Before Sally could chew on Shamika's comment, Ruby set down refreshments on one of the occasional tables.

Nodding thanks, Sally cupped a steaming mug of cocoa to her face and inhaled deeply. It was so rich, brought back so many memories . . . sledding with the kids on snow days when school was canceled—*good* things about the Midwest winter.

Ruby glanced at her niece. Then, loudly humming a gospel chorus, she left the room. It seemed contrived, and set off a warning gong in Sally. *What choice?*

Sure enough, Shamika set down her nearly full mug. "I . . . I need to talk to you about something." The fire seemed to capture her attention. "But first could you tell me what happened with you and Ella?"

◆ ◆ ◆

Even though she used old rags they'd found in the pirogue to wipe mud off her shoes, the bayou left its mark all over Sally, especially her clothes, which had taken on its rotten-egg odor. And stringy sphagnum moss stuck to her hands. But somehow Ella, who'd run on ahead, managed to keep the white in that dress. Sally rubbed her hands against the bark of their oak. She'd have to clean up before dinner.

As usual, Sally watched Ella disappear into the Browns' house. Hurrying, she ran around the block and entered the side gate of her own yard. She tripped across the patio toward the door . . . which was . . . open. Sally gulped. There stood Mama. And Daddy.

"You're early," Sally said weakly to Daddy, sweat trickling down her back. Had they seen Ella? She hoped, she prayed, the answer was no.

"You're late." With sure strides, Daddy stepped onto the patio and grabbed Sally by the arm, then yanked her inside.

"Those shoes! And your new socks!" Wringing her hands, Mama set down Robert, who shot out of the room like he was on fire.

Daddy loomed over Sally, his face inscrutable, his arms folded like an accordion.

"It's past dinnertime. We've worried about you. How could you do this?" Her hands still flopping about, Mama eyed first Sally, then Daddy.

Sally pretended to focus on getting her laces, stiff with dried mud, untied, but her mind whirled. It would be stupid to lie about the bayou. But Ella? Her mind worked so hard, it seemed to buzz. If they'd seen Ella, Sally would have already heard about it. No, she already would've *felt* it. She'd stick with the bayou, the boat . . . The story grew inside Sally until her legs trembled. *It's like the crick in Texas, Daddy. You know, the crawdads and tadpoles and . . .*

One look at Daddy, and Sally's shakiness multiplied. His eyes bulged; there was meanness about his mouth. Barefoot now, she stepped back until her shoulder blades hit the sliding glass door.

"Where've you been?" Daddy spoke softly, like a growl born deep in a watchdog's chest, warning of barks and bites to come. "And don't lie."

Sally hesitated. This was the problem with lying. How far back did she go? How much did they know? She couldn't decide what to say.

Daddy grabbed her arm and jerked her forward until she slammed against the table.

Sally whimpered and rubbed the sore place. Would Daddy blister her? Or would the shove be enough to get his anger out?

"Stop it. Now!" Mother was a flash of pink as she flew toward Sally and Daddy.

From somewhere in the back of the house came a wail, then sobs.

"You've upset Robert!" Mama, headed toward the hall, hurling the words at Daddy over her shoulder. "Now don't touch her again!" She flew out of the room, then back, Robert in her arms. "It's okay, honey." Her voice got lower, shakier. "Mommy's here," she kept saying, as if Robert had to be convinced.

None of Mama's words seemed to affect Daddy. He loomed over Sally, his fists clenched, his shirt hanging like kite tails over his trousers. "Do I need the belt?" he asked.

Sally shook her head from side to side, her back against the table. She considered running, but that would make things worse. She braced for the pain, the humiliation of being hit. There was no way out if she wanted to keep her and Ella's secret.

Fiddling with his belt, Daddy stepped closer.

With a wince, Sally crouched, then straightened. She wanted to fly, like an egret, to the Swamp Sisters' hideout. Or sail away. To Africa or China, anywhere but here.

The leather belt creaked as Daddy pulled it out of the belt loops of his pants.

Sally crumpled onto the floor, her resolve to keep the secret melting in the face of the slashes that surely were coming. "I didn't mean to." She begged with her heart, her eyes, for him to stop. "Daddy, don't. Daddy. Daddy!"

Almost before she knew it, Sally was sprawled across the makeshift table formed by Daddy's thighs. "Please, Daddy. Don't!"

The leather stung her back like a swarm of wasps had struck.

She screamed. Another slash. Mother screamed. Robert screamed.

The belt slashed her again. This time, Sally bit her lip, determined not to cry. It made Daddy madder when she cried. She held her breath and clenched every muscle that she had. A blackness came over her. Right now she wished someone would beat Daddy with the belt.

"What do you think you're doing, lying to me?"

Something hard—the buckle—bit into her back. She screamed, then bit her lip. The blackness grew into a desire to kill Daddy, if only she could. Or at least kick him with her legs, beat him with her fists.

"If I have to, I'll beat it out of you." The belt again found its target.

"Don, quit!"

"Da-Da! Fally! No, Da-Da."

The whirling belt created its own dark wind, then bit into Sally again.

Robert's cry pierced Sally like the first slap had. She had to stop this before Robert got involved, before Robert got his first taste of this.

"Stay outta this, both of you!" Daddy waved his arms, letting go of his hold on Sally. "A man's gotta do what he's gotta do!"

"No! I won't let you!" Mother screamed.

Sally jumped to her feet, tears flowing unchecked now, but not just for herself. She'd gotten them all involved with her secret, and she had to stop this before they were all hurt. "Daddy, I'll tell. Just stop!" Her voice broke into sobs.

"There, there." Mama was at her side now, cooing like a dove, but it didn't really help things. Only Sally, and her story, could stop Daddy.

The belt fell in a coil to the floor.

Like a snake. Several times since their first visit, she and Ella had seen snakes down bayou way. Their bodies, patterns of copper and beige diamonds, coiled just like that belt as they camouflaged themselves at the base of tree trunks. "Leave 'em be," Ella had said. "Just don't never take your eyes off 'em." Daddy, and the belt, were like that. Sally didn't dare take her eyes off them.

Daddy's face had lost some of its redness; his eyes once again hazel. But his jaw was stony, his eyes unblinking. He watched Sally. And waited.

Sally had a choice. Everyone depended on it. Ella. Mama. Robert. Sally glanced about the room. Everything waited, not just her family. The pilgrim and Indian cutouts she and Robert had made, their funny buckled hats and headdresses colored Burnt Orange and Indian Red and Goldenrod, held their breaths from their place on the table. The sofa whose rips were covered by an afghan sat frozen. And the television, usually blaring with the news or one of Mama's afternoon programs, remained silent. Waiting. Everything waited.

Daddy made a motion toward the belt.

"Please, no, please, Daddy, I won't lie anymore. Please, please, please."

Using his hand to straighten his back, Daddy stood up, his face tired. He stepped away from the belt, giving Sally just the help she needed to make the decision. If Daddy knew about Ella, he wouldn't have stopped now. He would've already used the *n* word—the word Ella hated. Daddy had solved the mystery of which parts of the story to tell.

"I . . . I just got tired of being fenced in," Sally stammered. *Tell the truth. Don't lie to him. Just don't tell it all.* "Then I heard a . . . kid talkin' about the bayou."

Mama's hands flew to her face. "You've been in that filthy swamp?"

"Ann, hold on." Something like a memory flitted across Daddy's face.

Smile. Wave your hands. Sally did both things, hoping to remind Daddy of cricks, of fishing poles. Of Tom Sawyer. Daddy loved Tom Sawyer. "It's got an old boat and a tree whose branches droop down. If you scoot up the trunk—I hold on tight, Mama, don't worry—then stretch out, you can hang over the water. And there's herons and frogs and . . ." Sally caught herself before she mentioned the snakes that she'd seen and the gators that she hadn't seen but that Ella claimed were in there. For weeks, Sally had longed to see a gator "big as a boat." But of course it would never do to tell Mama that part.

Sally paused to take a breath, then cut a glance at Daddy.

It was a miracle. The skin about his eyes, his jaw, had smoothed out. A smile played with the corner of his mouth. "Sounds like the old fishin' hole back in Hillsboro, crawdads bigger than a puppy."

Sally smiled, glad he'd reminded her. "Is that where you tried to teach the chickens to swim?" Daddy's blackness was fading, yet Sally had to keep on talking, keep on smiling, or it might come back. She wasn't safe yet.

When Daddy laughed, Mama laughed. When Mama laughed, Robert laughed. When they all laughed, Sally let out the last bit of darkness with her own laugh. She was safe. Ella was safe. The secret that mattered was safe.

By the time Daddy finished talking about the fishing hole, the whole room had returned to normal. Robert gurgled a nursery rhyme. Daddy turned on the television, settled into his chair, and buried himself in the paper. Mama bustled about the kitchen, humming a medley of her favorite songs, keeping the pots and pans company. The fact that her voice was shrill and tears streamed down her face didn't seem to bother her.

Nature celebrated too. A breeze streamed through the sliding door's vertical blinds, and they clicked and thudded against the glass. Cape jasmine perfumed the air like a fancy lady getting ready for a big party.

As she set the table, Sally glanced toward the Browns' but, in spite of squinting, couldn't see a thing through swaying pines. It didn't matter—Sally had somehow managed to tame Daddy and still keep the Swamp Sisters a secret. But Sally had felt the damp darkness involved with such a secret, and it chilled her to the bone.

◆ ◆ ◆

"They're here!"

With quick strokes, Sally brushed her teeth, then wiped off her mouth.

Because of last night's "problem," Sally suspected, Mama said she had to walk to school with the Johnson boys, who lived down the block. They were okay, as boys went. And just in case Rufus came around again, they might be enough to scare him away. After all, they were boys and bad men didn't bother boys.

Sally hurried into Robert's room and planted a kiss on a cheek reddened and wrinkled from the imprint of a pillowcase.

"Now, Sally!" Impatience laced Mama's voice.

Sally's shoes made squeaky sounds as she ran to the entryway.

"Daddy and I talked." Mama leaned against the door frame, her arms folded.

A talk could mean problems. The pancakes Sally'd eaten stuck in her gullet. She looked out the window, eager to escape. "I thought those boys were here."

"Well, they are. Almost." Little lines creased Mama's forehead and the skin under her eyes. Her hair, usually combed into a smooth bun, clumped about her face like moss. Sally wanted to bury herself in Mama's apron and tickle her until she laughed. Was last night's problem aging Mama?

"Now, you listen to me, Sally." There was gloom in Mama's voice. Sally glanced out the window, just in time to see Donnie, the older Johnson boy, shove his little brother. Even though they looked as goofy as ever, Sally longed to push past Mama and join them. Anything to avoid this talk.

"Your father and I agreed you could go to that . . . that bayou. But you'd better be careful, Sally. Mrs. Collins told me there was a gator back there that ate a dog."

Sally opened her mouth, wanting to laugh at whatever that silly old woman who ran around outside in her nightgown might say. But the look on Mama's face made her keep quiet.

"But you're not to set foot out of this house, this yard, unless you ask me."

Nodding, Sally gave Mama the briefest of hugs and hurried out. So Daddy had prevailed, just like always. If Mama had gotten her way, Sally wouldn't be going to the bayou. But now there was hope. No matter how bad school was today, the Swamp Sisters might have a meeting down bayou way. And that would make everything else okay.

Chapter 21

THE DAY THAT
CHANGED EVERYTHING

Nobody knows de trouble I see. Nobody knows but Jesus.

—Negro spiritual, "Nobody Knows"

It was an ordinary recess, until teachers fanned out across the playground, waving their arms, beckoning the students to return to the building.

Sally jumped off a swing and staggered dizzily to Mrs. Reynolds, whose grim mask communicated the fact that something was wrong.

"It's the president." Several teachers had tears in their eyes, their voices whispery.

". . . Dallas."

Students buzzed about their teachers.

"Shush, all of y'all." Mrs. Reynolds took charge. "My class, line up!"

Sally and her classmates fell into formation and followed their teacher into the building and down the hall, which was quiet. Too quiet. Mrs. Reynolds opened the class door and flipped on the light. "Sit down and pack up," she commanded as she stuffed her satchel.

During a bomb drill, Mrs. Reynolds had barked orders like this. It had filled Sally with uneasiness then; now she was about to burst with it.

"Bus riders, carpoolers, when the bell rings, line up out there." Mrs. Reynolds pointed to the hall. "The rest of you, stay put till I dismiss you. Go straight home. Do not—I repeat—do not stop anywhere. Go straight home."

"What is it?" a girl asked the boy in front of her.

"Mrs. Dooley told Mrs. Pierce that President Kennedy's been—"

When the ruler slammed against the teacher's desk, Sally, and half the class, jumped. "Not another word." Mrs. Reynolds's eyes narrowed to pinpricks behind her glasses. "Do I have to send you to Mr. Jones?"

Sally swallowed hard. She'd never been sent to the principal's office, but his paddle was common knowledge. And she'd had enough spanking to last for quite a while.

Again the classroom fell silent, thanks to the suggestion of the paddle.

With jerky motions, Mrs. Reynolds cleared off her desk.

The front of the school became a whirlwind—cars clotting the circular drive, children collapsing into the arms of parents. Sally knew now that something terrible had happened, something that scared even the teachers, the parents. She longed to crank open the windows, run down the hall—do anything to get home.

A plane buzzed overhead, then another. Sally trembled. Of course! It was nuclear war! The Commies had attacked; the Air Force was scrambling to retaliate. Snippets of sentences started to make sense. President. War. Death . . . They'd have to go to a fallout shelter—wasn't it at that Baptist church that they were going to visit when they settled in? Mama was probably getting their things together right this instant. Mama. Daddy. Robert. Ella. Were they all right? Could Negroes go to the shelter too?

It seemed to take forever for Mrs. Reynolds to dismiss them. When she did, Sally was the first person out of the classroom. She joined what seemed like an army, thumping on the pavement, dashing across the street.

No one said a word as bands of students hurried home. The unusual silence made Sally's heart beat faster. Could whatever happened be *worse* than a war?

A car pulled close, the engine humming. Praying it wasn't a dark truck, Sally tried to catch up with the other students. The louder the engine, the faster Sally's heart raced. *God, no! Don't let it be him.*

Out of her peripheral vision, she glimpsed a blue blur and dared to look. It was Mrs. Johnson. She was safe! Tension came out, in puffs of breath.

"Have you seen my boys?" Mrs. Johnson gripped the steering wheel with both hands, her face pale, her eyes without their usual shadow and mascara.

Unable to talk for the fist of fear about her throat, Sally shook her head.

Mrs. Johnson rolled up the window. She must have floored the pedal, the way the car lurched forward.

The whole world must be ending for Mrs. Johnson to lose her easy smile, what Mama called her bred-to-the-bone manners. Sally broke into a run, passing houses and children after barely a glance. She turned on Idell, her heart in her throat as she paused to look both ways. Where were all the preschoolers playing Red Rover and tag? Even the big collie that herded Sally from its side of the white picket fence was strangely quiet.

It was enough to make Sally run again.

A blur of red, then a bigger blur of blue, got closer. As Sally kept running, running, she saw that the red blur was Mama, with a little blur of brown in her arms. And Daddy was the blue blur. Sally threw out her arms, longing to embrace them all. Her family never looked so good.

"Mama . . ." Her sides heaved as Sally tried to get out the words she'd dammed inside. "What . . . happened?" She groped for Daddy, breath, words, spurting out. "Are . . . we . . . gonna die?"

Daddy swooped up Sally and crushed her to his chest. Normally, she'd wiggle around and beg to be let down, but not today. With the world ending, she needed Daddy's strong arms.

"No, silly. Of course not."

Sally arched her back so she could see Daddy's face. "But . . . what happened?"

"The president's dead." Daddy didn't change either his tone or his expression, but what he'd said was enough to set Mama sobbing.

"I just can't . . . who . . . ?" Mama wept so hard it was difficult to understand her. Still holding Robert, she moved into the huddle that was Sally and Daddy.

Sally reached across and patted Mama on the back, puzzled by her emotions. She was sorry about the president, yet relieved it wasn't something worse. But maybe the president's death would make things worse. "Is there gonna be a war?" she asked, her voice quavering.

"Of course not," Daddy insisted, but the lines on his forehead argued with his words.

Sally squirmed out of his grasp and slid down his legs. Daddy's arms had strengthened her. Why was Mama crying? Why had they closed school? "Why . . . are you home, Daddy?" she managed to ask.

"They've shut down the college."

Mother's wailing began anew. "Who could do it?" she cried. "Who could hate him that much?"

"There, there." Daddy took Robert from Mama, then tried to pull her close. But she jerked away and ran, sobbing, up the walkway and into their house.

The prickles started again. Why was Mama acting like this? Sally tugged at her father's sleeve. "What—" Sally tried to start over. "Why—" The questions tangled in her throat.

Daddy nudged Sally toward the front door. "Someone shot him. In Dallas." He caught Sally's arm as she started into the house, then leaned close to her, as if he were telling a secret. "You know how she feels about Jackie."

Sally nodded, beginning to understand. On what Daddy called their shoe-string budget, Mama tried to dress like Jackie, talk like Jackie. From the library, she'd checked out *Learning French* so she could become "continental," like Jackie.

"She's actin' near as silly as those colored folks about this," Daddy whispered.

Sally jerked out of his grasp. What did that mean? And did it involve Ella?

"I thought we'd go for some ice cream or something," Daddy continued, not seeming to notice Sally's uneasiness. "Help her get over this."

Robert raced into the den, Mother close behind. "Ice cweam! Ice cweam!"

"You too, son." With a swoop, Daddy had Robert again. "Whaddya say, Sally?"

They had money for ice cream? On a school day? Sally stared out the back window, wishing she could see past the trees and into the Browns' back yard. Something awful had happened, making life worse for coloreds. Was Ella going to be okay? Sally shook her head, slowly, slowly, begging her mind to work faster, faster . . .

"Sally?"

An emergency meeting of the Swamp Sisters. Her best smile plastered on tight, now that she had the idea, Sally squeezed Daddy's hand. "Can I stay home, Daddy? I want to make Mama a card."

Touches of gold softened Daddy's eyes. "That's real sweet, Sally. She'll love it."

As if she didn't hear them, Mama plumped cushions and rearranged knick-knacks on the coffee table. Tears trailed down her cheeks, though she'd quit sobbing.

Still cradling Robert, Daddy moved into the den and managed to corner the nervous bundle that was Mama. "Come on." His voice had a tenderness Sally rarely heard.

A sob caught in Mama's throat. "Where to?"

"Gonna get you some ice cream."

"How could you think of ice cream at a time like this?" Mama asked, pushing away from Daddy. "The president dead, that little girl . . ." She paused to stare at

Robert, who was bobbing up and down, saying, "ice cweam, ice cweam!" Then a clown's smile took over her face, as if she was forcing herself to be happy, just for her son. "Yes, let's!" Mama said, her voice shrill.

"Here, Annie, hold Bobby. I'll just grab my billfold."

Sally followed Daddy down the hall, then beelined toward her room.

"Aren't you going?" Mama called out.

Sally paused. She had to be careful, or Daddy would make her go, just to keep the smile on Mama's face. "Huh-uh," she called, her voice cheery. She hurried into her bedroom, wanting to shut out the pretend cheeriness, wanting them to leave so she could get serious. Get to Ella.

Mama poked her head into Sally's room. "Why not?"

Daddy, billfold in hand, edged close to Mama and Robert, then put his hand on Mama's shoulder. "She's stayin' here. Got a little project." He winked at Sally.

"No! Not with what happened to that little girl . . ."

What weren't they telling her now? "What little girl?" Sally asked.

Mama sagged into Daddy, burying her head in his shirt. "Tell her." When he hesitated, Mother tapped her foot on the floor. "We've put it off long enough."

"The Groves' daughter didn't come home from school yesterday," Daddy finally said.

Didn't come home? Had she run away? Sally rubbed her arms. "Who is she? Where . . . What . . ."

"Lives the next street over. She's in third or fourth grade, I think."

"It's fourth," Mama insisted.

"You mean someone . . . kidnapped her?"

Daddy shrugged. "Either that or she's wandered back in those bayous."

With a wrench, Mama pulled herself out of Daddy's arms. "I told y'all that wasn't a good place to play."

"Now, Ann, we're not gonna get into it right now. We both know it's not the bayou that's the issue here."

A chill ran up Sally's spine. "What do you mean?"

"Seems a colored boy's been hangin' around, up to no good."

Every muscle in Sally went rigid. She'd forgotten the eavesdropped conversation; now every fiber of her body twitched to life. "A colored boy?" she asked, making her face a question mark and being very careful to speak slowly, as if the idea were foreign to her. "What does he look like?"

"Teenager, kinda tutti-frutti looking. Rumor has it he hangs out bayou way."

An image of Willie bouncing up and down, coins clinking in his pockets, slender fingers gripping his horn, grabbed Sally's mind. It couldn't be. Could it?

Mama stepped close to Sally, her eyes narrowed. When it came to protecting her children, Mama could be as good at questioning as Daddy. "Why, Sally?" she asked. "Have you seen him?"

Just in case they were talking about Willie, Sally had to protect him. Had to. He was Ella's brother. And he'd saved *her*. Sally shook her head.

"If you're holding something back . . . ," Mama said.

"She'll get blistered."

Daddy's look scared Sally. It scared Robert too. The gurgling sound that would soon change to sobs started deep in Robert's throat. Now she really had to do something, or no telling what would happen.

Making sure not to blink, Sally smiled at Daddy. "I've got . . . a big test." She made her eyes big so Daddy would remember about the card she was making for Mama. "Y'all have fun." She hoped her voice sounded normal.

"Are you sure you don't want to go with us?" The edge had left Daddy's face, and his voice. He draped his arm over Mama's shoulder.

Every muscle in Sally tightened, including the ones that put a smile on her face. Everything would be okay—actually, it wouldn't. Not until she talked to Ella.

"Don't set foot out of here." Daddy's footsteps muffled his words—Sally could barely hear them. She hurried to her desk, intent on making a note. But it wasn't going to be addressed to Mama.

Chapter 22

BABYLON'S FALLING

Babylon's falling, to rise no more.
Oh, Babylon's falling, falling, falling . . .
—Negro spiritual, "Babylon's Falling"

E-e-, *E-e. T-t-t-t.* Even on a day like today, the bayou creatures didn't startle Sally. Herons, egrets, frogs, and cicadas said hello. She knew their habits, knew their sounds. It was when they got quiet that she worried.

She reached the fork in the road, then broke into a run. Her heart rushed her on as she streaked past oaks and sweet gums. Faster! Faster! Somehow the president's death made the news about the little girl seem worse. She prayed Ella would check their tree, like she did most days. Get the note she'd left. Everything—including Willie's future—might depend on it.

At water's edge, she fell to her knees. Her sides heaved. "God, please!" she gasped. "Let her find it. Don't let anything happen to Willie. God . . ." Sally jerked up her head. Rubbed prickly arms. What had quieted the swamp creatures? Were they praying, in their own silent way? The water was a sheet of glass, the trees motionless.

A limb cracked.

"There you are." It was a man's voice. Then a cackle.

Sally tripped and fell, then crawled, her elbows, her fists, sinking into mud and rotting leaves. *He'd found her.* She choked down grit and spit. *I've got to get out of here!*

"Where are you?" That crazy singsong voice, the crackles, the scuffs, sent a silent scream through Sally. He was getting closer. She had to get up and run. But there was nowhere to go. It was too late for anything, too late to—

An eerie cry cut through the quiet, followed by a flutter of wings. The egret had deserted her.

Don't You desert me, God. Please, God! As she scrambled, she prayed, her words chasing after each other. An occasional stick stabbed her hand. Images of his face pierced her chest.

"Did you think you could hide from ole Rufus?"

Her prayer had failed. Sally gagged, not only from the mud on her lips but from the sound of his voice. Hoping to disappear, like God seemed to have done, she drew her legs, her arms, so close together, she smelled her own sweat. Her own fear. God could come back. He could do anything! "Can He will He . . ." Something like a prayer streamed from her mouth.

◆

Ain't no time for clumsy fingers. Ella rubbed her knuckles, forcing calm into them, and got the note from the hollowed-out place in the tree. *SCHOOL'S OUT NOWWW!* The capitals, exclamation point, set her fingers to shaking. *They done killed the president, but look like something else is going on. Momma say Babylon fallin', whatever that means.* Now Sally had left the strangest note. Something was wrong!

Ella crept to the Browns' side gate and eased up the fence bolt, then passed through and set it back into place. Shading her eyes and squinting hard, she looked down the road, expecting to see the usual white kids tearing about in their yards, after sittin' all day in dem fancy classrooms. Yet nobody stirred. Even the wind was nappin'. Ella wadded the note in her pocket and headed to the bayou. Mama was right. Babylon and some other kind of thing was falling fast. She had to find Sally.

◆

"Little girl, little girl. Been waitin' a long time for you."

No, God! Daddy! Mama! He'd gotten closer, the smell of his breath, his sweat, hanging in the air. She burrowed into the mud; waiting, dreading. She squeezed her eyes closed, then opened them wide.

A very black bug, with fuzzy legs and little knobbed antenna and big bug eyes, crawled right by Sally, slowly, slowly, as if it was going for an afternoon stroll. *Use those funny legs, little bug. Get away, away . . .* She couldn't quit staring at the bug, couldn't—

"You think I wouldn't find you? You and your nigger friend think nobody watchin' you? Ole Rufus finds all of you." Every thud of the man's shoes made Sally wince. Any second now . . . Again, she squeezed her eyes shut.

A sandpapery hand grabbed her and jerked. She flopped over like a hooked fish.

"Looky!"

Something ripped. Sally's eyes flew open.

A lopsided grin on his face, Rufus held up a frayed swatch of Sally's shirt. "Looky! I got me another souvenir!" Somehow he wheezed and laughed at the same time.

Sally's muscles burned as she again tightened into a ball. *God! Please! Take me away if You can't get rid of him!* "Please, God!" The words came out in a whimper.

"Make another noise, and I'll cut you up. Just like I did her." A muddy black shoe came down on her chest, pinning her in place. Cackling all the while, he pulled out a billfold and stuck the shirt swatch inside, then jammed the billfold back in a pants pocket.

Is that all he wanted? A piece of my shirt? Relief flooded Sally. Maybe he'd let her go. Heaves welled up in her throat. Then he grabbed her again.

◆ ◆ ◆

Usually Ella prided herself on keeping her nice white shoes clean. Not today. She sloshed down the path, thoughts pounding into her skull with every step. *What's wrong? Where's Sally? Where's dem birds?*

Roll on, roll on, roll on. Faster, faster! It was those scraggly bearded trees, older than Momma and Big Momma combined, rustling like they never had before. A wind comin' outta nowhere, tellin' her with every needle and leaf to get on bayou way. Ella worked her legs like no one's business. She had to get to Sally.

◆ ◆ ◆

"Look at me, you little brat!" Rufus slapped Sally, then yanked and tugged her arms, her legs, until she was spread-eagled. He loomed over her, his face contorted into a smile that showed those crooked mossy teeth that had haunted

Sally's memory. Brown spittle pooled about his lips and chin. A filthy plaid shirt and torn jeans hung off a whiplike body. "Do you like Daddy Rufus?"

As she tried to sit up, Sally shook her head so hard, stringy hair flapped against her cheeks.

He grabbed her shoulders. Shoved her down. "You better be nice," he ordered, pinning Sally on her back as if she were a butterfly about to be mounted and displayed. Helpless, only a flutter left in its wings.

If he'll just go away, I'll say anything. She nodded, yet the motion made her choke and retch.

With his free hand, Rufus fiddled with his pants, making an awful moaning and groaning sound all the while. The belt slid to the ground, the buckle clinking against a rock.

No! Not the private parts! Again Sally retched.

Cursing, he knelt next to her, his hands constricting her throat. "Look at me."

I have to do it. She managed to look briefly into his crazy hateful eyes. Desperate, her gaze flew to the tree limbs. Could they help her? Could they, would they? She opened her mouth to scream, but nothing came out.

"No, little girl. Down here." Rufus grabbed her chin and forced Sally to look.

"God. Mama. Daddy." The whispering helped Sally look where the man wanted her to look.

"There, there. That's a good girl."

He patted her on the head, and Sally thought he meant to smile, but his lips curled into a sneer. "Look at me. Up here now."

Sally shivered as she looked into the white-blue wells of craziness. *So cold. Winter's coming . . .* Suddenly sleepy, she closed her eyes.

◆ ◆ ◆

"There, there. That's a good girl."

Someone's here! Ella froze, then hurried behind the safety of a cypress tree.

It was a man, his back to her, leaning over something with legs . . . and dirty shoes.

Ella's mouth dropped open. *What that white man be doin'? Wha*—she bit her lip hard and tasted blood. Dirty shoes. Muddy shoes. Sally's shoes. *That man be abusin' my friend, right on our ground? Sacred ground, Momma done call it. Sacred. But nothin' sacred 'bout what he doin'.* Knowing what lay ahead set up a coldness in Ella that kept her limbs quiet, her eyes unblinking. *Toe, heel. Toe, heel. Around the bend, so slow. Quit, heart! He'll hear! No man gonna do this to my friend. Huh-uh.* Ella's eyes traveled wild about the bayou. She had to find something.

◆

The breeze goose-pimpled Sally's bottom. So, so cold. She had to get away, like the swamp friends had. Sail away to Africa. She squeezed her eyes shut, but it was no use. She wasn't moving. She wasn't even in a boat.

Grunts came from deep within the man. "That's a good girl. Not like the other one. She was a bad little girl, so I had . . . to . . . stop . . . her." As he panted, faster, faster, pain ripped into Sally like an explosion. The sky went black, except for flashing lights. Blinking and winking lights. But it was daytime, not a time for stars. And it was white-hot, like the sun, this thrust of horror. Sally opened her mouth, but once again, she could not make a sound.

◆

Sweet Jesus, please, help me. Ella crouched down, trees hiding her, she hoped. Pine needles pricked her, but she couldn't bother with that. It was hard to keep from hollerin' with those awful noises coming from the heap by the water. She ordered her eyes to look left, right, left—there! *God done answered, like I knew He would.* Ella tiptoed strong. *God done help me. God gwine see this thing through.*

◆

Sally couldn't seem to open her eyes, as if sleep had glued them shut. Where was she? Her fingers massaged gumbo mud. The bayou! What's that smell? She sniffed, then turned her head. It always smelled down here. Dead bloated fish floating on the water, their eyes pecked out by gulls. Thick mud, oozing with plants and all sorts of crawly creatures. She blinked. Today there was something else. Something sickly sweet, like cough medicine. Something—the smell grabbed Sally and shook her, made her remember what was happening to her. That man. He was gonna kill her. Or had he already? She struggled, then settled back into the mud.

◆

On the third heave, Ella pried the rock from its settling place against a tree trunk. It made her gag, the way her grunts sounded like the man's, but thank the Lord Jesus, he didn't notice nothing except Sally, who lay there white and pale. She'd never seen nothin' so white and pale. *She ain't dead, is she, Lord?* It set her knees to knocking even as she lifted up the rock and thudded forward.

She gritted her teeth good, then rushed at him, her legs, her feet, her arms on fire, somehow the Lord Jesus liftin' that rock over her head. Every muscle in her body begged to be released, so Ella gave them their way. She smashed the stone with everything she had right on top of that greasy white man's head.

◆

The stars whirled, faster and faster. Why was Ella sailing in circles? Hadn't she said the Big Dipper would guide them? Sally tried to move, but the blanket Ella had put on her felt so, so heavy.

"You gotta wake up. Can't you hear me? Sally!"

Sally groaned. Why would Ella think she was deaf? She struggled to get up.

"Sally!"

Ella shook Sally and slapped at her cheeks.

The next thing that hit Sally was the smell. Sweat. Rotten fish. The man. She retched, then tried to turn on her side.

"We gotta get him offa you." Ella was on both knees, sobbing now, her arms pulling at the man's shirt.

Sally moaned again. God had rescued her, after all. But why hadn't He come before the man . . . did those horrible things? She half-sat up. There was a cut in Rufus's head, a big cut—long as a finger. Oozing sticky red—blood!

"Sally!" Ella pulled at Sally's sleeve. "I done that to a white man." Her face was one big set of ovals—her mouth—her eyes—her cheeks. "Whatta they gwine do to me?"

Had the man hurt Ella too? Sally rubbed her eyes, hoping to make them focus. "Wha—what happened?"

"*What happened?*" Ella, on all fours now, tugged at the man. Harder, harder she pulled, her brow beaded with sweat. He didn't budge. "He done raped you." Her eyes wild, she let go of the man, grabbed Sally's arm, and yanked it until they were only inches apart. "You gotta help me or they'll lynch me fo' sure. Ain't got a prayer, my word 'gainst a white man's, even his."

It still made no sense, but Sally nodded. More than anything, she wanted to help Ella. She tried to prop herself up by her elbows, but they sank into the mud.

"Look here!" Ella snarled, her sweaty face right in Sally's. Mud blotched her nice white dress. "When I say three, I'm a roll him ovah. You push up with ya knees."

It would kill her to look at him—*No!* She wouldn't! Sally turned her head. "I can't . . . touch him."

Ella grabbed Sally by both shoulders and shook her. "You touching him now. I am too. And they gon' kill me if ya don't help. Now!"

The look on Ella's face made Sally shiver. She nodded.

"One." Ella took a huge breath. "Two."

Sally squirmed, then tried to roll out from under the man. She had to get him off of her. Had to.

"Three!"

The man rolled off Sally and landed facedown at water's edge. A moan came from him, then a whistling sound that shook his bony shoulders.

"Sally!" This moan came from Ella, who staggered past, then knelt by the bank. "They gon' kill me." She scooped up water and splashed it onto her face, her arms, as if that would wash away everything that had happened.

"No, they won't." Sally got up, though pain flooded her body. Ella had saved her. Sally didn't know who was after Ella, but now it was Sally's turn to do the saving. She patted Ella's tangle of braids and tried to smooth the fear off her brow.

"I'll hafta leave." Fear stayed on Ella—in fact, it seemed to get worse. "Gon' get Willie to take me outta here."

Sally patted Ella again. "They'll arrest him." She pointed toward Rufus.

The words seemed to hit Ella full force. Her mouth arced and sparks flew from her eyes. She stomped her foot and shoved Sally backward.

Rufus groaned when Sally stepped on his hand.

"Stupid white girl!" Ella snarled. "You don't get nothin'! They gwine kill me and Willie. We ain't gittin' outta Ouachita Parish alive!"

The man groaned again and turned his head to the side, giving Sally a glimpse of the scar on his face. Why hadn't she seen it when he was on her? She looked again, shuddered. Even with his eyes closed, he looked like a devil. Was he a devil? Was he—

This time, the man's groan seemed to rouse his arms, his legs, to action. With broken, stained nails, he clawed at the ground, then rose. Clawed. Rose.

Clawing . . . clawing . . . *just like he did to me*. Every muscle, every bone in Sally's body sang, the notes coursing through her veins, sending power, now that she'd told them what to do.

"Sally . . ."

Pretending not to hear Ella, she stepped over the man.

"What you doin', Sally? You gotta tell me!" Ella's shriek ricocheted off cypress knees and hollow stumps.

Sally picked up the rock, groaning, staggering from the weight of it, but not even flinching when she saw the streak of blood on the smooth gray surface. She would help Ella. So help her . . .

"God in heaven!" Ella screamed now, her mouth heaving along with her chest. "Holy Jesus! Sweet Jesus, gonna take me home!"

The buzzing in Sally's ears muffled Ella's words, but she heard them anyway, walked to the beat of them, let them empower her arms, her legs, her hands, her fingers. She stared past Rufus, stared at the moss hanging from an old cypress. It was a witch tree, and he was a devil man. With both hands, she held the rock over the devil man's head and smashed it down as hard as she could. The body leapt up to meet her once, but Sally fought back. He wasn't going to do this to anyone else. She hit him again, again, again, until his eyes rolled back into his head and his body went still. Stone still.

An egret landed on a rotten stump, judging Sally with beady, unblinking eyes. Hugging her aching arms to her chest, Sally began to cry. Devil man or not, she'd just murdered him.

Ella moved close and stroked Sally's face, as if she could wipe away all that had happened. "We gotta git him outta here, then git outta here ourselves."

Sally nodded, over and over. *Ella's the boss. Ella knows best. She took care of me. Yes.* Then she glanced at the man. "But what are we gonna do?" she whispered.

Ella smoothed out her forehead and folded her arms, as if they were solving a mystery back in the sandbox and not figuring out how to get rid of a real live dead man. "We gon' bury him."

"Wh-where?"

"Out dere."

An early fog so blanketed the water, Sally could barely see the pirogue. Were they sailing off with . . . him? Even though she told them not to, her eyes sneaked looks at him. And he stared back, like he knew everything about her. Even dead, he knew her. Sally shivered. This place *was* haunted.

"Now!" When Ella shrieked, so did the egret. It flapped away, alighting on the prow of the pirogue.

The bird knows all our secrets too. Sally glanced at Ella, wondering why she wasn't worried. "Is he sailing with us?"

Ella took hold of Sally's arm and shook it. "Listen to me."

With more flaps, the bird swooshed across the bayou with an earsplitting cry. Sally watched it, begging, praying, to fly with it.

"Look at me. Now! We gon' get him out dere so them gators can finish him off."

Sally nodded, over and over.

"You grab his feet."

As if she were hypnotized, Sally obeyed.

Once they got him in the water, it was easier to pull him. Barely conscious of the water lapping her calves, Sally sloshed forward, her feet sinking into the muddy bottom.

"You stay here."

A look at Rufus's head made Sally gag. She couldn't do it, not alone.

"Now, Sally!" Ella's voice was a hiss. "You just hold him. I gotta get the rocks."

I'm goin' to Africa, me and Thee. Jesus, Savior, pilot me.

Sally closed her eyes. Was that Ella singing, or an angel? She ignored the nibbles at her toes—*just my little fish friends*—and tried to sing along. "I'm going . . . Jesus . . ."

Grunts punctuated Ella's efforts as she sloshed in and out of the water, carting rocks back and forth, dumping them on the body.

"Now." Again Ella shook Sally's arm. "Sally, let go! Sally . . . Sally!"

Sally let loose of a bloody plaid sleeve. Even though she tried to keep her eyes shut, the sun managed to pry open her lids and shine light on her, just enough to see the body floating. She was floating too. Weightless now. She could float away . . . float away . . .

With a sucking sound, the body began to sink.

Ella spun into action again. She splashed water on Sally's face and arms, then rubbed off dirt and muck and blood. Rubbed so hard, Sally thought she might rub away skin. Then Ella cleaned herself the same way.

No matter how hard she tried to avoid it, Sally's gaze remained fixed on the spot where the man had gone under. Was he really dead, or would he rise up?

"Come on! Come on!" Ella grabbed Sally's hand and led her toward the shore. The water parted, as if to help them out. Sweet waters. Helping. When they reached the shore, Ella let go of Sally, then plopped down on the bank, ropy strands of moss plastered to her dark legs.

Sally stared at her thighs, at her shirt. She remembered more about how the man grabbed her, the things he had done . . .

"Sit!" Ella patted the ground right next to her.

Sally obeyed. It was important to do everything Ella said. Plus when Ella talked, Sally didn't have to remember. She had to mind. Had to mind. Had to . . .

Her brow wrinkled, Ella now worked at cleaning her legs, using pine needles and her hands. Then she set to work cleaning Sally's legs. They seemed to stay that way forever, yet the sun didn't move but stood still, stuck in the tops of the cypress grove right at the bend.

"Lord Jesus, I done it," Ella kept muttering. "You gotta help me now."

Sally scooted closer to her friend and wrapped her arms around trembling shoulders. "What's wrong?" Rufus hadn't hurt her too, had he?

Ella jerked away. "We done killed a man. And we gotta clean up this mess and get outta here." Smoothing down her dress, she jumped to her feet, then clawed into the mud. "Where'd I put it?" she asked as she darted about the bayou bank. "Where'd—" She bent over, dug in the mud, then stood up, Rufus's billfold in her hand. "Here." She thrust it at Sally.

"No!" Sally protested, shrinking back.

"Open it."

Sally took it gingerly, as if it were a snake. She turned her head and held it as far away from her as she could. "Wh—why? Why do I have to open it?"

"We gotta find out 'bout him."

Her hands shaking, Sally opened the billfold and stared at the State of Georgia driver's license of Rufus E. Beauregard. In the picture, his hair was neatly combed, the scar on his face barely visible. But he had the same watery eyes, the same mean mouth. The same mouth that had tried to inhale her face.

Gagging, Sally dropped the wallet. Patches of fabric fluttered onto the mud. Tiny pink flowers on a red background. Purple and gold plaid. Plain old white—*my shirt!* Sally snatched up that last swatch, her muddy fingernails leaving brown half-moons on the cotton, and flung it into the water.

The bayou came to life. Turtles stuck out glistening heads. A snake, his body a graceful curve, held his head high as he skimmed across the water surface. All of the bayou creatures, in on her secret. All of the creatures, mocking her.

The piece of Sally's shirt floated, just for an instant, then got yanked to the deep. A ripple went through Sally as well. It felt good to get rid of even the smallest reminder of that awful, horrible man. She leaned over to get the billfold, ready to throw away another thing of his, ready—

"No!" The mud made a sucking sound as Ella slogged forward and plucked the billfold off the shore. Muttering all the while, she picked up the remaining swatches, smoothed them off, and stuck them back in the billfold. "You can't do that!" she huffed. "It's evidence. We might need it."

Sally slumped over, rubbing at eyes irritated by dried bayou grit. Why had he saved all the pieces of cloth?

A blur of white and brown, Ella dashed about the bank, rubbing the ground with more boughs of pine needles. She lugged another stone to the vacant spot under the old cypress. She thudded to the pier, examining a splintered board, searching for something.

Somehow Ella drained away all of Sally's energy. Her spine, her shoulders, fell.

A jerk, then a slap. Sally's head bobbed up. Not him again! Not—she sighed. It was Ella.

"You messin' up all my work. Now get up."

Why had Ella done that? Tears stung Sally's eyes. Her whole body ached.

As if Ella understood, she rubbed Sally's back, then helped her to her feet. "We gotta get home." She stepped close to Sally, hoarseness weakening her voice. "But first we gotta promise we ain't never gonna tell no one 'bout this."

So it had happened. Why did she keep thinking it was a bad dream? Sally moaned, scaring the egret. As it flapped away, she heaved, sick to her stomach, then lurched forward and threw up. She straightened and swallowed hard. *Maybe that'll get rid of him.* But a horrible taste remained lodged deep inside her.

Ella wiped Sally's mouth with the back of her hand, then threw her arms around Sally. The musky smell of Ella's skin encircled Sally, pushing away the other smells. She breathed deep, longing to stay like this forever, Ella holding her tight.

"It gon' be okay." Ella again patted her back. "Jesus a carry us."

Through the glaze of tears, Sally found Ella's eyes. "Why did He let it happen?"

Ella looked at the bayou, as if the water, the creatures, would answer. But they had hushed again. Not even a croak cut into the whiteout of sound.

"I don't know." Ella's eyes had kidnapped the sun's golden cast. "But we can't let it get out. As God's our witness."

The chiseled profile of her best friend, so sure, so calm, convinced Sally. She had no choice. She had to do it. Her lips set in a tight line, and she nodded.

With a splinter of wood, Ella pricked her index finger. A perfect red droplet clung to the whorl that Ella held up for Sally to see.

"You do it."

"N-n-o," Sally protested, stepping backward, toward the path that led home.

"We have to. Blood sisters. Blood oath."

Sally hesitated. Did they really have to finish up this horrible thing with more blood?

The sun caught Ella full in the face. She squinted and grimaced at the same time. "We can't never tell nobody, Sally. They kill me fo' sho'. Maybe throw you in jail. Then ain't neither one of us goin' to college."

Sally took the wood splinter from Ella. She didn't blink when she poked herself. One crimson drop, then another, slipped down her finger.

The girls clasped hands. Not just Swamp Sisters now. Blood Sisters.

It surprised Sally that Ella's palm, slick with sweat, trembled. It surprised her even more that hers was strong and steady.

Ella tucked the billfold into her pocket. "I'll keep this. If da police catch anybody, I wan' it to be me."

It all came back to Sally: why she'd left the note, what the police thought about Willie. She had to tell Ella. Now.

She grabbed Ella's arm, leaving a red smear near the elbow. "That's why I left you the "emergency" note! The police think Willie snatched that girl."

Ella's eyes became saucers. "Wh-what girl?"

"Some fourth grader didn't make it home from school." The words hung in the heavy bayou air. "They think something bad happened to her. And they think Willie did it."

Now it was Ella who stepped backward. When she stumbled over a cypress root, Sally steadied her.

"Your folks have to get him out of here. And fast!" Sally took charge now, energized by the fear in Ella's face. Without another word, she yanked the billfold from Ella's hand and ran toward home.

◆

Shamika couldn't quit staring at her teacher. And she thought she'd had it rough when James pulled her into his lap and tried to mess with her while Momma been at work. She kept thinking of what this white woman had told her, looking for the trapdoor, the false front. "How'd you know what Ella saw? What Ella heard?" she blurted out.

The cuticle-picking took on a life of its own. "We talked; exchanged letters," Mrs. Stevens mumbled, her head bowed. "Somehow I knew it, anyway. It had become a part of me. We were blood. Blood sisters." Shamika had to lean forward to hear. "I think what happened to me had become a part of her."

And did that help? Shamika wanted to ask, but she didn't dare. What had happened to her in that parking lot was going to stay in that parking lot. "What happened next?" she asked, forcing her own story into the dungeon of her mind.

Chapter 23

THE AFTERMATH

De little baby gone home, de little baby gone home
De little baby gone along, for to climb up Jacob's ladder.
—Negro spiritual, "The Baby Gone Home"

Oh, God. Let them still be gone. Please, God." Over and over, Sally repeated the words. She half-walked, half-staggered down the street, past ordinary-looking houses. Alone felt good now—no one to notice the ripped sleeve, the bleeding elbow, the bits of dried mud on her arms and legs, the touches and smells of that man. Sally blinked as she walked. *Why does it all look the same when everything about me is different?*

They have to be gone. Desperate for things to get back to normal, she made her way up the sidewalk, ticking off the things Ella had told her to do. Hide the billfold. As she walked, thoughts crept in uninvited. *What if they're home?* Take a bath. *What will I tell them?* Get rid of the shirt, the panties. *What will they do to me?* Run a load of wash.

The door creaked when Sally opened it, sending a chill up her spine. Her breath caught as she waited for Mama's voice, Robert's cry. But nothing happened. The couch stared at a blank television screen. The newspaper, neatly folded, lay in Daddy's chair. The antique clock ticked, ticked, ticked from its spot on the bookcase, then got quiet, just for an instant. Three thirty, it chimed, in the same musical way it had for as long as she could remember, slender black hands assuredly pointing to the three and the six. Everything in Sally's life had changed in an hour and a half, yet that clock kept ticking like nothing had happened. She stared at the glassed-in Roman numerals until they got fuzzy. When she blinked and looked again, the clock face had been taken over by the dead-eyed stare of Rufus. *You'll never get away with it*, the clock seemed to say as it ticked, ticked, ticked.

She would get away with it, keep it hidden. She had to. For Ella's sake. For her sake. She flew to her room. Threw open a drawer. Tucked the wallet under some pajamas. As she worked, she strained to hear Robert's shriek, Mama's laugh. Nothing yet, but they were bound to be back any minute.

Next on the list was cleaning up. She tried to ignore the bathroom's sparkling countertop and sink. She was so dirty; they were so clean. She stripped off her clothes, then took a long look at the girl in the mirror. There was a scrape under her right eye. Moss and twigs had created a bird's nest in her hair.

The longer Sally looked in the mirror, the more she hated that girl. How dare she let him do those awful things? Her groin throbbed with pain. There was a stinging too, like when she'd had a bladder infection. Mama hadn't let her use bubble bath then; should she bathe now?

The rotten-fish stench of the bayou, the odor of the man, the smell of her own sweat made the decision easy. She hurried to the tub and cranked the faucet full force. When steam rose from the pink porcelain, she gingerly climbed in. The clean, clear water sought and found new centers of pain. Grimacing, Sally grabbed some soap, dug her nails into the firm white bar, then scoured her body until it smarted. But no matter how hard she scrubbed, she couldn't get him off of her. Somehow, he'd become part of her, and Sally didn't know what she could do to get rid of him.

◆

Mama had never allowed the television to be on during dinner. But tonight it was a member of their family, Mama staring at it, Daddy watching it as he shoveled in food. And Sally wanted to thank the new family member for distracting her parents and keeping the focus away from the fact that she hadn't eaten a single bite.

"See it, Sally?" Daddy pointed to yet another replay of the president's head getting blown off. Sally managed a nod, wondering how much more death and ugliness she could choke down in one day.

The black convertible, showing off the president and his wife to wildly clapping Texans, peeled away, becoming a blur.

"There!" Daddy pointed to the screen. "See her huddling over him!"

Sally saw nothing except Rufus's face. Felt nothing, except his hands, groping, grabbing. She tried to focus on the headline news, but no matter what the television showed, Sally saw the bayou. And wondered how long her mind would replay what happened today.

When her family had clattered in from the store, their faces brightened by ice cream and chattering neighbors, only Mama noticed the cut, the bruises. It shocked Sally, not just how easily Mama accepted her story, but how easily she lied. "I was climbing that big old oak tree," she'd said. "You know, the one with the rough bark?" By the time she'd rambled through the next part, Mama had been captured by another film clip of Jackie. And to Sally's relief, Daddy had forgotten all about Mama's homemade card.

The program cut to a commercial. Mama took Robert to potty. Daddy went outside. Sally wandered into her room, drawn back to the mirror. The ugliness of Rufus was all over her, reflected for anyone to see. Yet for some reason, her parents were blind to it. Frightened by the mirror, and the empty room, she rushed back to the den.

"This is Mack Ward, reporting for KNOE news." The newscaster's usual smile had disappeared. He gripped a podium and stared right at Sally. "The police have released this school photo of nine-year-old Susan Groves."

It can't be! Blood pounded into Sally's ears, making it hard to hear. She leaned closer.

". . . four feet two, approximately eighty pounds, blue eyes, blond hair, a birthmark on her left hand. She was last seen yesterday, wearing a pink-flowered dress and carrying a lunch pail, between the time of three and three thirty in the afternoon, on Old Sterling Highway . . ."

Sally quit listening. Pink flowers. One of the swatches in the wallet. She sank back into the couch, perfect little flowers doing a crazy dance across her line of vision. Shivering, she rubbed her eyes. So he'd killed that little girl. Each piece of cloth represented a dead little girl. If not for Ella, she would've been his next victim.

The newsman's stare reached into the den and locked on Sally, as if he knew what was hidden in her drawer. Could he also see the dirty things she was hiding inside?

Another picture flashed onto the screen.

"This young Negro, approximately five ten, a hundred and fifty pounds, was seen driving a white pickup in the vicinity of Sterling Highway at the time of the abduction. If any viewer has information concerning Susan or the suspect, please call the Ouachita Parish Sheriff's Department at . . ."

Sally sat up straight. It wasn't the black numbers flashed on the screen, or the newsman's face, or the little girl's dress, that gripped her attention. It was the face of a younger, happier Willie Lee Ward.

◆ ◆ ◆

"Come on, now. Jes' take a sip." As seemed to be her habit, Ruby had wandered in sometime during the story. With a handkerchief Ruby provided, Sally dabbed at tears, then picked up the cup of cocoa Ruby'd given her—it seemed like a lifetime ago. She'd had to stop several times to get ahold of herself, but she'd somehow managed to tell her story. She drank deep, then tried not to grimace. Stone-cold. She was cold too. Her own story had chilled her, right to her core.

Ruby's hand pressed against Sally's as she took away the cup. "Here. Lemme warm it up." She seemed to understand what telling the story had done to her.

"It's okay, Ruby. Really. I'm done." They might both be done with her, when they learned what had happened next.

Ruby faced Shamika, who now sat on the hearth, her body a knot, her head cushioned on her knees. "You need anything, baby?" Ruby asked. "Baby?"

One touch from her aunt was all it took. Shamika convulsed with great sobs.

"Baby?" With groans and moans, Ruby eased herself onto red bricks, doing her best to cradle Shamika's head in her lap.

Sally's face flamed. She'd gone too far; she'd do anything to take back her story. Her eyes closed. *Lord, why did You insist on this? Or was it me insisting? Lord? Lord!*

Shamika jerked about, fighting off Ruby's ministrations. "Oh, Auntie! Auntie! What have I done?" Sobs morphed into ravings.

Sally went numb. Should she go? Was this the place for an outsider? As quietly as she could, she gathered her things and tiptoed toward the door.

"No! Mrs. Stevens! Come back!" Shamika jumped to her feet.

The rawness of Shamika's voice made Sally's heart flip-flop. Dredging up those memories had been a mistake. She'd been so sure that Shamika would see how she'd survived, even thrived. Yet had she really thrived all these years? Or just managed to survive by covering that body in lies, which, now that they'd surfaced, might ooze around her, like that bayou mud, and muck up her life?

"I can't keep it in anymore, not after hearin' what you been through." Shamika pulled Sally back toward the fire, close enough that Sally felt the heat. "Keepin' Ella's secret. Doin' what was right." She let go of Sally's hand and with clenched fists rubbed her forehead. "Oh, Lord, Lord! Why did You let me do this?" Her knees buckled.

Ruby jumped to her feet, caught her niece, and held her close.

"You know, don't you, Auntie?" Shamika's whisper was paper thin.

Ruby just bowed her head.

Lord, what has *she done?* Despite shaky legs, Sally tucked away her own feelings and slipped back into the rocker that surely by now bore the imprint of her body. She had to stay professional. Calm. She tried not to stare at Shamika, who was raking her face with her fingernails.

"I lied."

What? Sally searched Shamika's face, searched her memory. What was happening?

"Baby, you better be careful." It came out of Ruby like a rumble of thunder.

Shamika pulled from Ruby. "No, Auntie. I'm gonna do this." Calmness captured Shamika's voice and reined it in. "Weren't those boys that raped me."

The one attacker that had cloned into three. Shamika's selective memory. No, it hadn't added up, and all Sally could do now was stare and stare and stare. So Shamika had lied, like Sally had. But why?

"It was some crazy black man." Bitterness tinged Shamika's voice with a metallic ring. "And I'm turnin' myself in." She fumbled in her pocket and pulled out her cell phone.

Ruby grabbed Shamika and shook her till the phone clunked out of her niece's hands and onto the rug. "I ain't gonna let you do this."

A tortured look took hold of Shamika. "Don't you see? I got to."

"I'm not gonna listen to this. You hear?" Still gripping Shamika, Ruby averted her gaze from her niece, as if that could stop her from hearing. From knowing.

With a wrench of her arms, Shamika jerked away. "Why? It's true. Some black dude put his filthy hands all over me, spewing out crazy stuff, 'bout white horses and dragons. Twistin' Revelations into devil-ations. Some lunatic done raped me."

Blood gushed to Sally's temples, her wrists. So a black man had done this, not those boys? Detective Price's statements, her emotions, Shamika's earlier answers, made a dust devil of her mind. "So Rex, Hugh, Jay weren't there that night?" she asked, when she was able to speak. "I thought—"

"Oh, he was there, all right." Bitterness soured Shamika's features. "That Jay character came up when the other man had . . . finished with me." She stalked to the fireplace, looking ready to spit. "I begged him to call the cops, begged him to help me. He just gave me that ugly smile of his, said I'd gotten what I deserved."

"Baby!" Meaty arms tried to envelop Shamika, but her niece would have no part of it.

"I'm going to confess," Shamika said, then clamped her mouth lockjaw tight.

"No, you ain't!" Ruby grabbed Shamika's shoulders, steered her past the fire, then pushed her into the creaking rocker. "Ain't riskin' you catching a case over this. I'm gittin' you outta here." Now Ruby had the bitter voice. "Takin' you down South to yo' godmother's."

"New Orleans?"

"That's the last place they'll look for a couple of . . ." Ruby's head drooped, as if convicted by her thoughts.

Television images flashed across Sally's mind. Not New Orleans. The city of death and rot and brutality and . . . rape? Besides, this wasn't legal. She had to stop this.

"But what we goin' do down there?" Shamika asked, before Sally could speak.

"Roll up our sleeves. Take our mind off this. Maybe help some folks with some real problems." The plan seemed to energize Ruby, who tugged on her niece's arm. "Get up! We got packin' to do. Gotta call the boss. Stop the mail." Still talking to herself, she bustled toward the hall.

Shamika struggled to her feet, meeting Sally in the space between the rockers.

Sally's resolve to intervene melted with one look at Shamika. She loved this girl. Yet an innocent, albeit unsavory, boy was in jail because of her lie. Her mind raced forward, backward, desperately searching for a solution that would help everyone. What if she called that detective, hinted around? No. She'd lied quite enough.

She stepped close and put her hand on Shamika's sleeve. "I'll let y'all handle it." She tried to keep the quaver out of her voice. "At least for now."

"Thanks, Sally." It was Ruby, answering for her niece, sounding like she was in a tunnel far, far away. Footsteps clattered against the wood floor, then stopped.

Shamika leaned toward Sally. "I had to tell you the truth, after all you went through."

Sally's eyes darted toward the crackling fire, to the picture window . . .

everywhere but Shamika's face. If she had really been so heroic, why did she feel there was so much left unsaid? Images niggled from the locked-away place of her mind. Ella's tearstained face, pages from old letters . . .

"I gotta git. You take care, Mrs. Stevens."

Something about the way Shamika shuffled away, her head bowed, stabbed at Sally. Hadn't she watched another black girl walk away, her heart broken? Something else stabbed at Sally—the truth. She'd been lying and denying, and not just about the rape.

Sally picked up her things, whispered a good-bye, and headed out. It was time to unlock her padlocked past. Fifty-three-year-old legs struggled to keep up with fluctuating emotions. Her present, her future depended on finding the box that held those letters and the truth, not the whitewashed story she'd just told. And maybe those letters would lead to Ella, the friend Sally wanted, needed, to see more than ever.

Chapter 24

HEADING SOUTH

De blind man stood on de road and cried, O, my Lord, save-a-me.
—Negro spiritual, "De Blind Man"

S*he moves pretty fast for a big woman.* Detective Price slumped over, hoping the spot he'd picked away from the streetlight ensured his cover. The way that teacher's hauling buns, she was unlikely to glance at this unmarked car, wasn't she? He wouldn't bet money against Sally Stevens, wouldn't even be surprised if she knew the truth about Shamika. He'd seen plenty of gray matter at work behind that blond hair, that flashy smile, those dimples. And she didn't even have access to the piece of paper he held in his hand, the paper that he'd memorized as he sat on the surveillance ordered by the chief.

> Illinois State Police, Division of Forensic Services,
> Microscopy Section
> Pubic hair combings from said complainant Shamika
> Williams:
> Findings positive for hairs present foreign to victim. Race
> of origin consistent with African-American. DNA negative
> for Jay Davis.

DNA negative. All the rest, a good defense attorney could reduce to mumbo jumbo, but not the DNA sample, which would give that slimeball Davis a "Get Out of Jail Free" card. In no time, he'd be performing his neo-Nazi act again. But at least as far as the evidence proclaimed, no rape.

Price balled up the report and then played catch with the damning evidence. He'd suspected the truth long before it hummed across the fax line and was laid in his in-box downtown. Even without the DNA report, Davis's attorney would hint at a promiscuous, party-girl life to make the jury cast baleful eyes—and doubts—Shamika's way. Oh, sure, a judge would overrule, but the seed would be planted with the jury. As if that should matter. The same gut in turmoil right now—probably because of those greasy fries and butt-expanding burger he'd called dinner—told Price that Shamika was all the good things her character witnesses claimed. But that still left a million-dollar question: Why had she lied?

Mrs. Stevens started up her old clunker. Price straightened a bit against the seat, the balled-up report plopping onto the floorboard. It didn't matter what Shamika knew, what Shamika did. He needed to take that report to the tempest that was their chief, then wait to be sucked under by the tidal wave of anger that would surge from the press, the black community, the chief himself. As if he'd manufactured this report, just to cause more headaches.

He glanced at the house, which was quiet and dark. His cop's sixth sense told him something was about to happen behind the American dream Ruby had managed to acquire. Truth be told, nothing they did would surprise him. What *did* surprise him were his own feelings. He wanted the best for that stalk of a girl with the fiery eyes, that brick of a woman whom the system hadn't yet crumbled. He was a cyclone himself, twisting first toward them, then against them, sucking up debris as he vacillated.

With tight lips, Price radioed central, logged a line in his notebook, started the car. He was going home. Going to sleep on it. For now, their secret was safe.

◆

Even from her bedroom, Sally knew Sam, not Ed, had come in from his faculty get-together. The controlled click-shut of the door. The thud of shoes into the rack. The slow padding down the hall. She had just enough time to set down the book she wasn't really reading, cut the light, and slip under the quilt's protective cover. Protection from talking to Sam. Facing what she needed to face. She'd do it tomorrow. She just had to think awhile. Get a good night's sleep.

She continued to track Sam's nocturnal routine as he entered their room. Clothes whooshed into a hamper. Bristles swished across teeth. Mouthwash was gargled, then spit out. Then the clicks of flossing. The faucet gushed. Sheets rustled. The bed creaked. Sally feigned slumber. She wasn't going to tell him now.

"Sally?"

Sam's breath tickled her hair . . . still she feigned slumber.

He pressed into her, all male. All awake.

She ground her teeth together, then rolled to face him.

He kissed her shoulders, neck, moaning like an animal, like . . . Rufus.

The image slithered out of Sally's mind and under the sheet, coming to a slimy rest right between her and Sam. And she couldn't stand the way it crawled onto her. "Sam, stop it!" She jerked to a sitting position, her breath coming in heaves.

When Sam drew away, the bed groaned, as if it had seen and heard too much. With one click, the floor lamp blinded her, the hundred-watt bulb seeking out every lie hidden in the crevices of her gray matter. Seeking. Ready to destroy. She blinked, then looked at her husband.

"What is it now?" His eyes were hard pebbles, the usual curve of his mouth gone.

"Nothing." Sally tried to smile, but the way he stared at her, unblinking, like one of those slithery bayou creatures, cut off her effort at pleasantries. For one of the few times in a long history, Sally feared Sam was looking behind the facade she'd spent a lifetime perfecting.

"Don't tell me it's nothing. It's something, and I'm tired of trying to figure it out. If you want a happy ending to this whole thing"—his wave encompassed their bed, her dresser, even the ceiling and the door—"you're going to have to get real with me."

She threw a glance at her husband. How dare he talk to her like that, just because she wasn't in the mood to have sex? And look at her with such . . . animosity was the only word she could think of. *No. A better word would be hate.* She didn't have to pretend she was aggravated. "What are you talking about?"

"Don't lie to me." Sam's voice dripped with a whole passel of emotions now. "Any more than you already have."

How had he found out? And which lie? Sally worked to make her eyes big. "What do you mean?"

"It's all over town, Sally. Your job, those students . . . I didn't want to bring it up like this, but . . ." He threw his hands up in the air. "Anyway, there it is."

So they all know what I am. And he's in on it. Tears burned Sally's eyes and a bit of Sam's hate took hold of her. He had been getting intimate with her, even though he knew there was something they needed to discuss. Underneath, her sweet husband, Sam, was an animal, just like—she jumped up, grabbed her robe, and stormed into her study. For several minutes, she huddled against the familiar weave of her Bauhaus chair. But the dark closed in on her, as did the lies. Why was she blaming him for her actions? She clicked on the light, not wanting to be alone with herself. There was a box—*the* box—in the middle of the floor, a Post-it note, in Sam's block print, stuck on top. *Here's what you were looking for. Hope it has what you need.*

Sally eyed the box as if it were booby trapped, but no matter what the danger, she had to open it and expose the truth. She'd lost control—of her past, her present—and if she didn't act fast, the future might be impacted as well. And not just her future with Sam. Her children, colleagues, friends—everyone. She slid the box close to her and pulled off the lid. The musty smell of old paper tickled her nose and sent a chill through her. She swished her hand into the pile of letters as if she were the master of ceremonies drawing a name out of the hat for the door prize. For just an instant, she hesitated. Did she really want to know? Did she really have the stamina to go through with this? Sally clenched her teeth. No, she didn't. But God would give it to her.

April 3, 1964

Dear Sally:

It's been too long since we talked. I hope you got my other letter—Camille said she stuck it in our tree. Congratulations on making the yearbook staff! Doesn't surprise me a bit. We got a journalism club, too, but you can't be in it till you're in eighth grade.

Ella

P.S. Ain't heard a word from Down Under.
P.P.S. I got saved when I was ten years old and baptized on Easter Sunday.

Sally rechecked the date. Why hadn't she bothered to put these letters in order? Down Under? What godmother? As she read and reread the letter, snippets of words brought back a flood of memories. Some rushed up like rip-tides, others barely touched at the shore delineating past from present. The Browns had hired Camille, Ella's godmother, when they fired Ella's mother. "Down Under" had been the code for the prison down in New Orleans where they'd put Willie. Sally buried her face in the letter, hoping the faded lines had managed to preserve the half-spicy, half-flowery scent that was Ella. But there was nothing except decay. Dust. Death.

Again reaching into the grab bag of recollections, Sally pulled out a surprise. She didn't have to look for a signature to know her own pubescent scrawl, the loops full of self-importance. But why were *her* letters in here? Why didn't Ella have them?

With her palm, she flattened the single crinkled page. No date. No signature.

> Ella, I can't do it. You can't, either. How would we explain the fact that we left him in there for a month? A neighbor told Mama something pecked out his eyes and bit off his fingers and toes and private parts. Ella, don't you see? We just can't!

That first friend. That dear friend. Sally eyed her computer, hoping that she could befriend technology as she befriended everyone else. First thing tomorrow, she had to find Ella.

The door banged open. There was Ed, still starry-eyed from some high school event. "What are you doing up, Mom?"

Sally's heart pounded. When had Ed come in? She put her hand over the letter. Smiling eyes traveled to the box, then to her lap. "Some old boyfriend, huh?"

Sally, back on familiar turf, matched his grin. "Of course not. You know your daddy's the only man I've ever loved." She managed to maintain eye contact with her son while stuffing the letter back in the box. "Hey, how was the match?"

"Oh, fine. You should've seen the dude at number one. He had hops that . . ."

Sally fidgeted through a discourse she normally would've paid money to hear. When Ed finally ran out of things to say, she hurried in with the first thing that popped into her mind. "Where'd you go after tennis?" She had to do something to keep him talking. To keep him from looking too closely, either at the stack of letters or into her eyes.

Ed drummed a frenetic tune on his pants. "Uh, nowhere, Mom," he managed. "Just hung around the tennis center."

Which closed three hours ago, you little . . . Something sagged deep inside of Sally, yet confirmed what she needed to do. She managed to kiss her son and tell him good night even though he was lying to her, even though she wanted to tear first his hair out, then hers. She of all people could recognize lies, even good ones. And this was not a good one. No, he needed years and years of practice like she'd had. *Lord! My son's lying to me. And why am I surprised, Lord? Why am I surprised?* She'd lied to all of them for years. Lies of omission, lies of commission, white ones, black ones, big ones, little ones. Ed was only modeling the behavior she'd demonstrated, over and over.

"Love you, Mom. Love you, Mom," Ed kept saying, yet she didn't answer. There was a wall between them, a wall *her* lies had erected, a wall *his* lies were mortaring in place.

Ed left the room. His bedroom door clicked shut.

"Uh-huh, son," Sally said, to the empty room.

Ed's door opened. Tennis shoes squeaked on the hall floor as he reentered the study, his face gray. It wasn't until he whirled, squeaked back to his room, and slammed his door that Sally realized she hadn't finished off their pet phrase. "I love you more," she whispered. But Ed couldn't hear. Not with that wall between them.

◆

March 30, 1970

You asked me about plans after graduation. I'm headin' to New Orleans. Gonna make a home down there for Willie, if and when he gets out of prison. Don't know if I'll be a doctor now, but I sure do plan to be a nurse.

I heard you telling the girls on the drill team about some Christian school in Texas. You'll do fine there. You always do.

Ella Ward

P.S. Here's all your letters. I won't have room for them in New Orleans.
P.P.S. Happy birthday.

"No, God. I never helped them, never told. How could I have been so blind?" The betrayal, another swirling memory, slammed into Sally's conscience and almost brought her to her knees. With frenzied jerks, she flipped through the pages, more for confirmation of what she already knew than out of any need to refresh the Technicolor images in her mind. She read and wept, then read and wept some more. Then she set aside the stack of unread letters and reached for the phone. *They have to be there.* Her nails clicked against plastic buttons. *They couldn't have gotten away so fast. Could they? Answer me, Ruby! Shamika!*

"Mrs. Stevens? What's going on?"

"Shamika!"

"Yes, ma'am?"

"I need to talk to your aunt!" Sally winced. *Quieter, Sally!* She couldn't risk Sam, or Ed, hearing. Not now. Of course, they'd hear, all right. There'd be the publicity of the MCC hearing, discussions around Ed's locker . . . "At least *my* mother didn't have to forge her vitae." They'd sneer and poke Ed in the ribs. Sally cringed. And how seriously did the church enforce accountability? Surely she'd have to resign from her mentoring, her teaching. "I want to go down South with y'all," she continued, a steely tone infusing whispery words.

"What? Wh-why?"

"Just put her on, please."

Cradling the phone to her ear, Sally fished in a drawer and found a rubber band. By binding up the letters, maybe she'd ease the constriction around her heart. She had to do something, anything to keep busy. *Oh, God. If it's not meant to be, Lord, stop me now.*

"What in the world you doin'? It's nearly the middle of the night!"

Sally cringed. How hard would Ruby make this? "I need to go with y'all. To N'Awlins."

The line went silent except for what sounded like the drone of a dishwasher.

"I have to set something straight," Sally continued.

"What you think we gon' do down South wit' a white woman?"

"Same thing I'm gonna do with two black women."

The laugh that Sally loved rolled across the phone line, and she joined in. But it didn't reach her secret place. She'd reserved that for the letters she planned to read on a midnight ride back home. The letters that laid out, in Ella's mix of Black Southern and Queen's English, the trip Ella had already taken and the trip Sally had yet to take. And she wasn't just talking New Orleans here.

⋅ ◆ ⋅

"Come on, now!" Sally's love-hate relationship with technology continued as she chastised the computer. She'd done this a few times, usually with Ed's help. Once they'd even Googled her own name, then roared to see the results from 10Ks she'd jogged in years ago. But never had she been so pressed for time. And never had everything depended on the whims of a computerized search engine.

E-l-l-a W-a-r-d. The words materialized on the screen, responding to cramped fingers. *Ella Ward Genealogy. Ella Ward, D.O. Obituary: Joan Ella Ward. Virginia Board of Education . . .* Sally scanned the first page of one million, three hundred thousand hits, hit "Back," typed in Ella Ward, New Orleans. Names, names, and more names, three hundred thousand of them, crowded around her, the unseen faces condemning her from their place in cyberspace. *You'll never find her,* they whispered in computerese Sally managed to understand. *It's too late. Too late.*

Tears welled up, yet words from her past battled a temptation to quit. *"You're a Flowers,"* Daddy had said, time and time again. *"And we don't give up."* Sally took a deep breath, her keys clicking on the keyboard for a third time. *C-h-r-i-s-t-e-l-l-a W-a-r-d.* She closed her eyes, said a prayer, and pressed "Enter."

Unsung Heroes of New Orleans—Day Three, Katrina Diary

Due largely to the valiant efforts of Christella Ward, R.N., and Reginald Powers, M.D., over sixty patients were safely evacuated from Old Baptist Hospital. "They loaded me on a food cart, we clunked down two sets of stairs," reported Iona Jones, 72, "and they shuttled me right onto a rescue boat."

Awaiting them, a lifeline in swirling water, was perhaps the most surprising . . .

There was more, but Sally quit reading, her heart soaring, her fingers flying now over a user-friendly keyboard. Ella was still down there! It was going to work! She searched again, typed in some words, more words, and hit "Enter." *Mapquest directions, Old Baptist Hospital New Orleans.* Sally scanned the page, then hit "Print." Words on the screen blurred; in their place was the image of a girl, her face regal as one of the women on Daddy's old coins, staring, staring; waiting, waiting.

⋅ ◆ ⋅

"You've reached the Flowers'." It was her brother's sure, strong voice. "We can't come to the phone. Please leave a message."

Sally hesitated, wanting to hang up. But Robert had caller ID and was just crazy enough to call her back at a quarter to twelve. A ringing phone would rouse Ed, if not Sam. "Robert," she started, her voice hoarse, "I'm coming South. And I might need your help. Call ya later, Bro-Bro." With a sigh, Sally hung up the phone. She'd never used Robert like this, but his military connections might help pave a few rough patches on this road. And Sally was all but certain he'd help her. After all, he was her baby brother.

Just one more call. Then you're good to go. The third time Sally dug through her briefcase, she found the card. Bent, a bit torn about the edges, but still legible. She punched in what she hoped was her last phone call of the night.

"You've reached the voice mail of Detective Price. Sorry I missed your call."

"Yeah, right," Sally whispered.

"Please leave a message at the beep."

The buzzing seemed to last forever; Sally fidgeted all the while. Why had she called this know-it-all? Why hadn't she let the idea fizzle out, like a spent sparkler? It was too late; surely *he* had caller ID. "Detective, I hate to bother you." Her mind rushed ahead even as she spoke. "But I just realized I'd seen Jay hanging around here about the time . . ." The words died on her lips. Lying again. What she couldn't do. Like a desperate sailor, she tried another tack. "Something happened down in Monroe, Louisiana, where I grew up. And . . ." The words caught in her throat as she peeked out the window, knowing Ruby'd be here any minute. Knowing she could no longer manipulate things like this. Her heart heavy, she hung up the phone and got a paper and pen.

Words usually flowed from Sally like blood from a wound, but now a tourniquet had been applied. Only after staring at the second hand on her watch did she manage to scratch down anything at all.

Sam: I'm heading out with Shamika and her aunt. I could never explain all of this to you. My prayer is that you'll understand and somehow find it in you to forgive me for everything. I guess that's two prayers. I'll be in touch.

Love, Your Sally

She itched to write more, but where would she ever stop? She hurried into the bedroom and set the note on Sam's dresser, where he'd find it in the morning. Tiptoeing about, she quickly dressed, then gathered her things like an army reserve called to emergency duty. Staring at her husband's curled-up body, she battled the urge to collapse back in bed, move into his arms, tell him all the things that she should've told him years ago. But she couldn't. She just couldn't.

Praying she hadn't forgotten anything, she moved into the hall, set her bags by the stairs, then stepped into Ed's room. "I love you the most," she whispered to a rising-and-falling mound of quilts. Again she pondered what her latest decision would do to the family she loved most. Thinking of love, she thought of Mama. Mary. But Mama was on a tour bus somewhere on the East Coast, and Mary was probably tripping up Croagh Patrick like a gazelle, this time with Paul and her girls. *What a strange world this is,* she couldn't help but think as she left Ed's room.

Somehow she got downstairs with her bags, then shot up silent thanks that Sam could be engaged in a crucial battle of Marriage War III, then sleep like Rip Van Winkle, that Ed's snores were rattling his bedroom door. Her mind full of spoken and unspoken words, the lines of tattered old notes, she waited in the entryway. When the twin moonbeams of Ruby's headlights signaled, she slipped into the night.

Chapter 25

IN KATRINA'S WAKE

O Never you mind what Satan say,
goin' home in the chariot in the morning.

—Negro spiritual, "Going Home"

Ineed Thee every hour, most precious Lord." Ruby clutched the wheel, her words atonal, as if she were at the end of a tedious choir practice and only had enough energy to eke out the last few notes.

It was the oddest feeling, hurtling south, nothing between them and the harsh elements of the cold Midwestern night except the steel and chrome of Ruby's car. Sally listened to Ruby sing, her mind tumbling backward thanks to the pile of letters in her lap.

Shamika leaned against the passenger window, shivering in spite of a wool coat and hat. Occasionally she glanced back at Sally. Like a swathed bedouin, her eyes had to be counted on to gauge her emotions. Those eyes fired questions at Sally. *What's in that heap of pages? Can I take a look?* But Sally wasn't ready. First she wanted to read every word.

By Springfield, she'd organized everything chronologically, her and Ella's letters mixed together. Not every sheet was dated, making it a bit tricky, but the subject matter was clear enough. Maybe too clear. Sally picked up the first sheet.

Reflections from taillights and garish billboards danced across the page, making it tricky to see. She switched on a map light mounted in the car's ceiling and squinted to catch every faded word.

December 3, 1963

Dear SS:

　You told me to wait at least a month, but I couldn't. Did they fire your mother because of Willie? Speaking of Willie, have you heard yet?

　I hate school. I hate everything. Days, I can't get settled, thinking about how there's more than that fence between us now. Nights, I can't sleep, because something's scratching on my bedroom window. Do you think it's his ghost? I asked Mama if I could sleep in their room and she just shook her head and looked at me funny. And now we're supposed to act all cheery, hanging up lights and decorating the tree.

　Could we meet somewhere? I don't even know where you live.

　Your best friend forever, Sally

　P.S. Your godmother is pretty. She pretended like she didn't notice me, just stood there and swept the back steps, but she gave a little nod when I got the note out. P.P.S. I just watched the news. They found his body!

◆　◆　◆

Dear SS:

　They've been to our house more times than I can count on one hand. Same men smelling of cop even though they don't wear uniforms. Asking the same questions. Momma gives them the same answers. I guess it's official now. Willie's been charged with the murder of both Rufus and the little girl.

　We trying to go on, but it's hard. Daddy working himself to death on those stupid ole cars, Momma's taking

in laundry since the Browns done let her go. But Daddy
says we'll get by. And I know we will.

   If they catch Willie, he'll go to the pen and Daddy
says the Dixie Mafia'll make alligator bait out of him.
Sally, we got to tell the truth. I'd do it myself, but you've
got the billfold, and I can't do nothin' unless you do.
They'd never believe a colored girl.

   Ella

   P.S. Please write back soon.

◆ ◆ ◆

SS:

   A pack of bloodhounds done ~~tore~~ sniffed him out. He
on the way to prison, and Daddy says he'll only come out
in a pine box with some of his parts missing, like Rufus
when the gators got through with him. Can't you see,
Sally? He's done for. You still got that billfold? ~~Maybe we
should~~—We gotta show it to somebody.

◆ ◆ ◆

   Sally dug in the box until her fingers found worn leather. It was still in there;
she'd checked last night. The swatches of cloth had rotted, the driver's license
picture had faded, but the name was still legible.

   Rufus E. Beauregard. It was imprinted in her mind now, the name of the man
who, his heart blackened by hate, his body crazed by things that she could never
comprehend, had changed their lives. Why hadn't she acquiesced to the pleas of
at least a dozen letters, their writing a jumble of slashes and crossed-out words,
begging her, imploring her, to come forward, for Willie's sake? For Ella's sake?
For her sake? Sally bit her lip but didn't even wince at the iron-sharp taste of
blood. *Whatever made me think she'll join me in this way-too-late confession? I'll be
lucky if she doesn't murder me on the spot.*

• ◆ •

When the night lights of St. Louis splashed the letters with neon, Sally was time-traveling in the 1960s and had to blink several times before she could see.

A curve and a rise, and the arch loomed before them, a postmodern wonder that gazed down haughtily at the mighty Mississippi. *You're just a river. And I am in charge here*, it seemed to say. But Katrina had proven how little control they all had when the watery deep and the wild winds decided to take over.

As they crested the bridge, the Mississippi remained silent, a willing pipeline for the tugboats and barges that, even now, moved like funereal pyres down sluggish waters. Sally fought the urge to drift away too. It would be so easy to let the road rhythms lull her into a state of mindlessness, for the chill to numb her mind and her body to the past, the present, perhaps the future. But she had a job to do. She couldn't stop now. She groped through her purse, found her glasses, and put them on.

SS:

How do you like my stationery? It was a present from my Sunday school teacher. My parents asked her to "counsel" me. At first I was mad, but now I'm glad. I didn't tell her about what happened, not in so many words, but she seemed to understand. She showed me the Scripture about Jesus, the children, and the millstones around the bad men's necks. Do you reckon he's in hell? I may get baptized, along with some girls in my Sunday school class. Have you done it?

Talk to you soon. Sally

P.S. My teacher recommended me for coeditor of the high school newspaper.

Nothing about Willie. Sally skimmed it again, but the words she wanted to see, prayed to see, weren't there. Nausea gripped her, and it wasn't because she'd missed two meals. Why hadn't she said anything? Words like *I'm sorry, Ella. I'll think about it, Ella. Do you really think we should tell, Ella?*

Persistent as the widow before the unjust judge, Ella had filled pages and paragraphs and lines with the family's hardships. *He's on a chain gang, Sally. They done misused him, Sally. They done beat him to a pulp, Sally. Sally. Sally. Sally!*

"Mrs. Stevens? Sally!"

How had Ella found them? A letter or two fluttered to the floorboard as Sally snorted out of a half-conscious state. "Wha-what?"

"I asked, are those her letters?"

Just a dream. Not Ella. Not yet, anyway. The questions in Shamika's eyes all but blinded Sally. Blood pounded in her temples with the realization of what she was about to do. "Here." She handed Shamika some of the first letters. It might change their relationship forever, but if Sally wanted to come to grips with what she'd done, she had to start revealing it. Now.

Snail-like traffic, another glimpse of the Mississippi from chalky bluffs and another mammoth bridge, and bleary-eyed Sally said hello to Tennessee. Ruby bore south, her eyes catching Sally's on occasional forays via the rear-view mirror. From Shamika's seat came nothing but a rustle of papers, sighs, and snorts.

Dawn caught them south of Elvis's old home, making it easier for Sally to read. She rubbed her eyes every now and then, barely able to comprehend the fact that she was streaking nearer to the Mason-Dixon line and hurtling away from the family she'd lied to for so many years, the family who didn't really know the woman they called wife and Mom.

◆

"See you, Dad." Ed's wide eyes and slack jaw—most likely the result of reading his mother's cryptic note—had disappeared. He stepped into the breakfast room, looking like a pack mule with his tennis bag, backpack, and a handful of CDs.

Trying to smile, Sam kissed his son. When Ed left, Sam dropped the pretense. How could things have boiled over in one night? Of course things had simmered on low for years. Yet for the first time—at least that Sam knew of—Sally's lies had affected much more than their sex life. And it steamed him. She'd always put their children, their friends, first. Now she—and as a result, their world—had gone mad, with her rushing off to New Orleans because of something in a dusty old box. And what had he just done to contribute to the insanity? He'd also lied—to their son, no less—borrowing heavily from his wife's well-honed techniques. "Oh, just a mercy trip, son," he had said as Ed read the note over his shoulder. "All those hurricane victims got to her. You know how your mother is. And with Uncle Rob down there . . ."

Sam stalked to the coffeepot and slopped coffee into his cup, not bothering to clean up a dribble. He picked up the newspaper, hoping his box scores could reestablish order. As he flipped to Section C, an article in the "Local" section caught his eye.

An estimated crowd of two hundred, quoting everyone from Jesus to Martin Luther King, gathered outside the administrative offices of Midwest Community College to protest the suspension of Sally Stevens, a humanities instructor.

When it became apparent that the sign-wavers had no plans to disperse, Doris DelRio, college spokesperson, hastily scheduled a news conference.

"Following an October 27 meeting, Mrs. Stevens was placed on unpaid administrative leave. Per our collective bargaining agreement with the union and state policy, we have no comment on personnel issues," DelRio read from a prepared statement.

"We can't let them do this. She always stood by us, and now it's our turn." Emily Messenger, 21, a Normal resident and a "born-again believer," said the campus Christian organizations planned to continue the protest for "as long as it takes."

However, some students disagreed with the sign-waving majority. "She should've left her propaganda at home and stuck to the syllabus," said Marshall Clinton, a Fairview resident currently enrolled in a section of humanities that Stevens taught until recently. "That's how this all came about. She slipped religion into the classroom."

Others share his opinion, including three of Stevens's former students who have sued the university, claiming Stevens violated their rights. Neither the three students nor their attorney, James Pierce, were available for comment. In a rather bizarre twist, one of Stevens's students is currently being held pending trial for sexual assault.

An unidentified source claimed the suspension involves a variety of allegations against Stevens, including falsification of personnel documents. Stevens could not be reached for comment. Dotty Jones, *Pantagraph* staff reporter

The phone rang.

Sam tossed aside the paper. Dare he answer it? With sure strides, he reached the desk. *You bet.* Sally's subterfuges weren't going to change the way he lived his life. "Hello."

"Dad?" Suzi shrieked into the phone.

"Yes, Suzi."

"I got the strangest message on my cell. What's going on with Mom?"

Sam swallowed. This was the problem with lying. What would it do to his youngest if he switched tactics and told the truth to his eldest? "You know your mama, Suzi," he began, his words coiling about his throat and pulling tight. "The New Orleans tragedy just finally got to her. She had to get down there and make a difference." After they hung up, he thought about that box he should've opened but didn't. If he'd gone through it, as his heart had urged him to do, perhaps he'd have found that his statement about "the New Orleans tragedy" wasn't totally a lie.

The beeping got louder and louder. Detective Price pulled out of a dream about Ruby and her niece—what was her name?—the women who were invading his nights now as well as his days.

With a yawn, he kicked off already-tousled covers and managed to turn off his alarm without tripping over mounds of dirty laundry. Being single and forty had some advantages, but having a tidy house wasn't one of them.

Itchy eyes stared at the numerical reality. Nine o'clock. And he was supposed to be at the office by nine thirty. Shuffling to the bathroom, he continued to be assailed by that teacher's drawly phone message and the conflicting snippets of story he'd pulled, harder than old taffy, from that strange girl—it came to him with a flash. Shamika. Her name was Shamika.

He got in the shower, soon discovering that steam and suds couldn't wash away that nutty teacher's words, his confusion over Shamika's statements, *or* his hangover. Something was wrong; a cop's intuition told him it went way back.

To something that happened in that hick town down—where had she said it was? Water streamed onto his neck, his shoulders. Monroe, Louisiana, she'd said, somehow making Louisiana a six-syllable word. Price set mushy soap in a chrome dish. It was ridiculous, the last thing he needed with his workload. And what did it have to do with the pending case? No matter; his mind was made up. *I'm dialing up one of them good ole boys down South. And they'd better dish up some of that hospitality that's reputed to ooze out of their pores.*

◆

At a rest stop in Arkansas, Ruby finally agreed to let Sally take the wheel.

Rolling hills sprang about their car. An occasional hawk swooped down to patrol the swath of highway that cut through its territory. But Sally was more interested in the young woman an arm's stretch away, the young woman who had said next to nothing for two hundred miles, the young woman who'd just sighed and unfolded another letter as Ruby snored from the back seat. What was Shamika reading now? The first betrayal? The last? What was she thinking as the truth unfolded in front of her eyes? And what would it do to Shamika when she learned Sally was as racist as all the rest? Oh, maybe not like Jay, Rex, and Hugh, their hate tattooed all over them, but even more dangerous, disguised under a facade of friendship and empathy?

Somewhere in Mississippi, Shamika drifted off and joined her aunt in a slumber that had to be induced by both road rhythms and mind-numbing exhaustion. At first Sally had been glad Shamika's baleful stares had stopped. But since they'd transitioned into Southern lowlands, Sally wished she had company of a human sort.

Pines and live oaks lined the highway as if, after thirty-five years, they were welcoming her home. But it wasn't the trees that dominated the scenery. Huge vines had roped about everything, weaving a tapestry over the native flora, deceiving everyone with their verdant beauty. "Kudzu," an attendant at a filling station had told her. "Brought it in from some foreign place," he'd said, his laugh bitter. "Supposed to stop erosion." Kudzu had taken root in the fertile Southern soil, had spread noxious green tentacles, and if unchecked, would smother everything.

Choked, strangled . . . she knew the feeling. She'd been like those trees, presenting an attractive front that hid stagnant yet poisonous memories. But now they were strangling her. The pressure rose within Sally, and she stifled an urge to make a U-turn in the median and head back north. *No! For your family's sake, you have to do it. For Ella's sake.* She tightened her grip on the steering wheel. *And your own.*

The Presence whispered, oh, so softly, but the message was clear. *For Me, Sally. Because it is right. And I am who I am.*

Sally reached for the radio and turned it on.

"Peace, perfect peace, in this dark world of sin? The blood of Jesus whispers peace within."

Sally hummed along with the chorus in her quavering soprano voice. When she saw a turnoff for Monroe, the comforting words died in her throat as she barreled on south toward New Orleans. "I'll be back," she whispered to the big green sign. "You can count on it."

◆

If she tries to jive her way outta this one, I'll scream. And Shamika nearly did, as her teacher kept bangin' a blasted iced tea spoon against her glass. The only other sound in the joint was a droning dishwasher and chattering diners. Nothin' at their table. Shamika hated the thick cloud of silence that had fogged up Auntie's car, had traveled south with them, and hung over them right now. Yet if she let the silence condense into words, she was afraid she'd shower hate over the woman she'd learned to tolerate. *Git along with.* Without wanting to, she again looked at those Barbie doll eyes. *Nope. Not jes' fond of. Yep. Admit it. The white woman you grown to love.*

"How's your fish?" Mrs. Stevens finally asked

Speaking of fish . . . Shamika fixed her dead-eye stare on Sally. "A little hard to swallow."

A jab from Auntie pushed Shamika against a sharp edge of the Formica table. If she didn't watch it, old school Auntie was liable to backhand her. *'Course Auntie ain't read those letters yet.*

Mrs. Stevens plunked down the spoon, then slid down in the booth like a child expectin' a whupping. And the tremble in her lipsticked lips kept Shamika from thunderin' down insults on her blond head.

Auntie's cell rang, for the third time since they'd stopped in Jackson for food.

"Hey." Auntie dug through her purse and found a pen. "I-10? Hold on. You're breaking up." She groaned as she got up from the booth, like her back hurt, pushed past customers waiting for a table to open up, and went outside, probably gettin' directions from G-Ma. Her ole godmother didn't hear too good ten years ago. She bound to be strugglin' now.

"You gals need anything else?" The waitress's dark brows practically hollered that all her corn-colored hair was 'bout twenty shades too light. And wit' that horseshoe belt buckle and a tractor load of eye shadow, she look like the Jackson rodeo queen. Of 1955.

"We need lots of things, but nothin' you got." Shamika hurled pent-up anger at another blond. Another white woman. But not the right one.

Ms. Rodeo Queen went as white as her caked-on blush allowed. "Uppity nigger," she muttered. Her shoes squeaking, she trotted to a nearby table. "Well, hello, y'all! Can I get y'all some coffee? It's a beautiful day, ain't it?"

And I thought it was bad up north. 'Course I started it.

Mrs. Stevens picked up the spoon again, then banged it against her plate like she was playin' the bongos. "I'm sorry," she whispered.

Her words parted the silent skies. "You outta be. What you people don't get is that kind"—she pointed to the waitress—"is easier to take than the other kind."

"What other kind?" Her teacher flinched, then drew back, as if expectin' a backhand. Course that fool lip trembled.

"Kind that act all friendly, then kick you where the sun don't shine when you ain't lookin'." Now Shamika flinched. Auntie'd have a cow if she heard this kinda talk. *No, she'd have a slap—aimed right at my face.*

Mrs. Stevens rustled around, like she was struggling to collect her thoughts. "It's really not how it seems," she finally got out. She wrung those white hands like she was washing them. "I really couldn't believe it myself until I saw every word. In black and white. And I—I didn't know what I was doing," she whined, as if that were the honky storyline and she was sticking to it.

Shamika leaned across the table until their faces were only inches apart. "But she was your friend. How could you have done it?"

"Please try to understand. It was a long time ago." Her teacher reached across the table, her hand opening and closing widemouth-bass style. "And I was just a little girl."

Shamika tossed down her napkin. She'd been waiting for that one. "Oh, no, you weren't," she said, hitting the highest note she could. "Not that last time." She dug in her purse for some money, threw it on the table. As her teacher stared at a lumpy piece of half-eaten chicken fried steak, she got up, clicked out of the main dining room, out the front door, and met Auntie by the car. No, Mrs. Stevens had been practically a grown-up woman that last time.

Chapter 26

A FINAL BETRAYAL

Now ain't them hard trials? Great tribulations?

—Negro spiritual, "Hard Trials"

Monroe, Louisiana, 1969

Here she comes. Miss Jenny Bowman, Neville High's Most Likely to Succeed. Most Popular. Most Everything. *And she's gonna talk to me?* Sally shut her locker and made her smile big.

A frown darkened the face half the boys in school mooned over.

"Hey, Jenny." Sally practically curtsied.

Jenny thrust a paper at Sally. "This stinks. Of all times for the coons to mess with us."

Sally scanned the high school hall, hoping none of the black students were around to hear Jenny's comment. "What do you mean?" she finally asked.

"Haven't you heard?"

Sally shook her head.

"It's not enough that they got in here. Now they're gonna dance with us too."

The single white sheet fluttered to the floor, escaping the mutterings of Jenny.

"I said, doesn't that stink?" Jenny thrust out her hip, her tone demanding an answer. And Jenny always got what Jenny wanted.

Sally nodded, the tightness in her throat not allowing any other response. Since this integration nightmare started, she'd been paralyzed every time she set foot in school. *What if Ella acts like she knows me? And what'll my new friends think if they see us talking?*

With the toe of her shiny loafer, Jenny tapped the paper, signaling for Sally to pick it up. Of course Sally complied.

May 1969

> Attention: Bengal Belle parents. Effective immediately, three members of the former Carroll Bulldog drill team will be added to our squad. Please inform your daughters that we expect full cooperation with this mandate, which has been approved by . . .

Struggling to hold the paper still, Sally skimmed the list of important names. Important titles. Important white men in the community. Starting three years ago, with the enrollment of one black student, integration had managed to climb up the majestic steps of Neville High and slip inside. But now, things had escalated, National Guardsmen all over the South stomping the message of change on sidewalks in front of all-white schools. *Tromp, tromp, they will come. We can't stop them. They will come.* Helmets hid pale, unwilling faces, enforcing the new laws most of them did not support. Yet changes marched on. And they were starting to affect Sally and the life she'd built, one friend at a time.

Jenny glanced up and down the hall, then rolled up her skirt waistband until her hem teased her thighs. "Why can't they just go back to their own school?"

Because their school got shut to them, stupid. She pictured Ella walking into Neville High that first day, taller, slender now, more striking than ever, her hair pulled into an elegant twist. Ella, with more character than anyone she knew. Smart and strong and brave and loyal. The friend who'd kept her secret, at great cost. That day, a still, small voice had whispered to Sally that racism was wrong, and Sally had almost clattered across the foyer and into Ella's arms. Instead, she listened to other voices, those of her parents, her Sunday school teachers, railing about Negroes staying in their place, about the Bible's command not to mix with "foreigners." And Sally had chosen to listen to loud voices instead of the still, small One.

Sally looked into cool blue eyes, still seeing brown ones. "Would it really be so bad to dance with them?" she asked Jenny, her voice squeaky.

"So bad?" Jenny jabbed her finger into Sally's chest. "It'll be worse than you can imagine." Forgetting that she was the drill team captain and a class favorite, she wiped her nose with the back of her hand. "Do *you* want to stand by one of them? Touch that black skin? Smell that skunk breath?"

Sally's spirits sank. There was no way to keep her new friends and rekindle her relationship with Ella, which was now reduced to a rare note. Still, they had killed a man together, had vowed to be best friends forever, a promise sealed with blood. They—

"Come on, Sally! Now!"

When Sally opened her locker, books cascaded onto the buffed floor. By the time she got the ones she needed, Jenny—and a gathering entourage—was halfway down the hall.

◆ ◆ ◆

"We oughta boycott like *they* do."

The bathroom buzzed with the news. All of it about blacks. None of it good.

"Daddy's lookin' into a lawsuit, or maybe that private school. This whole thing's illegal, you know."

Murmurs rose from half a dozen girls changing for drill team practice and mingled with the scent of baby powder, hair spray, and musk oil to give Sally a splitting headache. She focused on undressing, giving great attention to her shirt buttons, the hook and eye on her skirt, desperate to stay out of integration talk.

"Did you see the letter?" Brenda asked as she slipped on a T-shirt.

Her good friend got a tiny nod. As Sally continued to change into practice clothes, she prayed for a way to keep out of this.

A cluster of teammates stared at Sally, whose face burned as if she'd been caught wearing raggedy underwear. How many hours had she practiced dance steps so she could call these girls teammates? And what about Mama's scrimping to buy Sally knee-high white go-go boots, symbol of the storied Bengal Belles? She'd rather amputate the legs that looked so sleek in the boots than risk it all by being sympathetic to Negroes. If her teammates knew a black girl—and not just any black girl, but one walking these very halls—had once been her best friend, what would they do? Shun her, at the very least. Maybe get her kicked off the team.

The stares continued, forcing a smirk on Sally's face. "Who wants to talk about jigaboos?" She hoped her frown looked convincing. "They make me sick."

"No kidding."

More girls banged into the locker room, the attention deflected from Sally.

"Anything's possible, with Johnson in the White House."

"There outta be a law against them."

"But the law's for them."

"Not the real law."

"You mean . . . ?"

"You betcha. White sheets and all."

Sally bent over, tying and untying her tennies. How could educated, "nice" girls even *mention* the Klan? For nearly a year, she'd practically lived with her teammates, as often as they practiced. She knew who had a rich daddy, who'd slept with the quarterback, who wore a D cup. But right now they seemed like total strangers.

"Time for the circus."

"More like the zoo."

The grumbling continued as they made their way to the auditorium stage. Sally walked stiffly, every muscle taut as a hanging noose. What would these girls do when they saw the black girls? What would she do?

The planked floor creaked as the girls went to their usual assembling point, midway between the velvet curtains and the podium from which Miss Pamela, their sponsor, would bark commands.

A gasp escaped Sally's throat.

Huddled like lost children at far stage right, near a set of steps that led down to the auditorium seats, were three girls, their foreheads pearly with sweat. All three seemed obsessed with staring at rows and rows of empty wooden seats.

"Well, looky there!" Tess, drill team cocaptain, didn't bother to lower her voice.

"Those coons sure stink. Don't they?" She poked Sally in the ribs. "*Don't they?*"

Sally opened her mouth to agree, but nothing came out. There stood Ella, the tallest and prettiest of the three black girls. But her elegant twist had been replaced with a frizzy Afro, somehow making her look hard. A buzzing began in Sally's ears and drowned out the catcalls and hisses. She and Ella locked eyes.

There was so much for Sally to read in Ella's face. A tremble about the mouth—she was scared. Arched eyebrows—she was curious. An intangible glow that gave her an otherworldly appearance—she was still good and kind and all the things Sally loved. Or was she? Didn't that Afro signify protest? Violence?

A battle raged in Sally. Desperate to fit in, she longed to add to the wall erected by the nasty retorts, the icy glares. Yet another part of her longed to take a battering ram to the wall, then fling her arms about her Swamp Sister, tell her she'd missed her, tell her she was sorry she hadn't answered her latest letters.

"Just look at them!" Jenny hissed, her hard, bright eyes capturing Sally's and refusing to let go. "Aren't they ugly?"

As if hypnotized, Sally nodded, even though her spirit told her to disagree. But how could she disagree with the girl who'd promised to invite her to a sorority dance? The girl who lived on Pargoud Boulevard, a fancy little T-bird in her circular drive? The girl who drove about in that car, gold hair glinting in the sun, surveying the town she owned? The girl who'd blackball her from everything that was anything, everybody that was anybody, if she even spoke with a Negro, much less claimed a Negro as her friend?

With a toss of thick blond hair, Jenny broke the spell. "Hey, c'mon, you guys. Ignore the sideshow and get in line."

Sally sighed, yet she still couldn't move. Nobody did.

"I said line up. Now." The stomp of Jenny's petite foot sent girls shuffling to the line.

"I'm sick of this."

"You? I've got ten hours of homework I need to be doing."

Girls continued to line up, spitting out complaints. Things were returning to normal, now that talk had turned to school.

"All right, y'all. What smells?"

Sally's mouth became cottony. Of course things weren't normal. She was stupid to think this issue would just blow up and go away.

Barbs and racial slurs ricocheted off the stage floor and onto the three girls, dulling shiny faces until they were as lackluster as the worn hardwood.

A door at stage left banged open. "Girls? Girls!" Miss Pamela, looking important with a clipboard and papers, hurried onto the stage. She set down her things, then bent over and fiddled with the record player that Jenny had set up and plugged in near the podium.

As if they sensed the presence of their leader, the usual stragglers dribbled out of the locker room, muttering things Sally didn't hear. But she knew what they were saying.

Usually a glare from Miss Pamela, a former Neville Beauty, killed even a giggle from "her girls." Strangely, she let them mutter awhile while she fluffed her hair and fiddled with the papers.

"Girls . . ." When she finally spoke, her usual sugary drawl was gone, replaced by a piercing squeak. "We have some new, uh, gals joining our squad." Forgetting the rule about wearing street shoes on the stage floor, she tapped close in her high heels to the still-forming dance line. "Listen up, now. When I call your name, come over here, uh, gals."

The three black girls, eyes round as full moons, turned and faced the squad. "Christella Ward?"

Somehow Ella moved forward without making a sound. Black gym shorts emphasized her graceful legs. Gold crosses dangled from her ear lobes. Her skin was like velvet, a startling contrast to the wiry Afro.

"What kind of name is that?"

"That jigaboo thinks she's somebody."

Miss Pamela clacked toward Ella. "Should we call you Chris, dear?"

"No, ma'am." Pools of brown blazed. "I'd prefer to be called Ella."

Miss Pamela cleared her throat. "Well, now," she said. "We'll see about that."

All the noise seemed to have been sucked from the stage except for the rustle of Miss Pamela's papers. Sally wanted to hide. What would happen now?

When their names were called, the other two black girls, quaking like aspens, moved closer to Ella.

"Come on . . . Chris." Miss Pamela stopped a good ten feet away from the trio, then fanned her hand, waving them forward. "You come over here, dear. Come on, now."

Ella stood motionless, her frown hardening into stone.

Miss Pamela's jaw tightened. "You listen to me, gal, do what I say. Or else—"

"Or else what?" The auditorium walls seemed to shake, as if they might collapse from the pressure of this change. "What're you going to do to me now? You ruined our school. Ruined our community. Bussed me to a part of town I'd never set foot in for years. Since . . ." Ella clapped her mouth shut.

Since you and I killed a man. Sally longed to say the words that would really give them all something to buzz about; longed to say something, do something, to help Ella. Instead, she just stood there, picking her nails.

Miss Pamela drew up to her full height of five foot two and strutted toward Ella. "Rest assured that I"—a polished fingertip aimed at Ella's chest—"did nothing to any of your kind." Her eyes blazed the flinty gray of an angry sea. "But what I *will* do is make this squad the best it can be. With or without your help."

Her words seemed to deflate Ella. She nodded.

Sally rubbed her hands against her shorts. Perhaps it would be all right.

It was all as usual now, Miss Pamela in control. "Ella, over here, dear," she said, in a compromise that shocked Sally. She said some more things, but Sally couldn't hear, not with Ella stepping closer. Next to her. A dark cloud engulfed Sally. She longed to run for the bathroom, to claim food poisoning or the flu. Anything to get out of here.

"Sally. Take off your shoes and stand up straight. Sally? You too, Ella. Back to back, now."

Now Sally prayed for the creaky floor to split open and swallow her. Ella, her Swamp Sister, her partner in crime, her once best friend, stood inches away. But who was she now? And how could Sally acknowledge her, with all her new friends watching?

"Am I not making myself clear?" The pointy toe tapped, louder than ever.

They bent over and untied their shoes, Ella's breath ruffling Sally's hair. Her spicy scent, both comforting and foreign, washed over Sally. Sally held her ground, not taking a step toward Ella. And Ella held her ground too.

"We're gonna get this kick line straight and get on with it. Hear me?" Grimacing, Miss Pamela shoved the two girls back to back. Her flat palm a measuring stick, she leveled it across first, a bushy Afro, then a blond shag.

"My goodness. Aren't you a tall thing, Ella?"

"She's one tall . . ."

"Wait'll my daddy hears 'bout this!"

Voices rustled, Ella's new status as line center setting off a wildfire of gossip.

"That's quite enough. Get in line, girls." Somehow Sally knew that Miss Pamela was moving the other two colored girls into position, but she couldn't hear anything but the mutters all around her.

There was a blur as Ella wedged into the line right next to Sally.

Sally cringed. How could God set Ella right next to her in the line? Just what did He expect her to do with this colored girl who used to be her best friend but now looked like a stranger, with that bushy Afro, those long, thin legs?

"Get ready! Step ball change, then five straight kicks when the music starts." Her decisions about the lineup over, Miss Pamela bent down and set the needle on the record player. "Watch me!" She took her position, right in front, like she always did. Girls groaned, like they always did. Yet everything had changed for Sally. And she wasn't sure she could kick and strut like nothing had happened. Not with Ella just a breath away.

Ella's black fingers touched Sally's white skin for the first time in six years.

This time Sally's cringe shook her whole body. How could she be expected to do this? Everything was different now!

"Sally . . ."

It was a whisper, soft as a breeze through live oaks, but Sally heard. Sally was sure eighteen white girls heard too. And their parents. The whole white town had crowded into the space made cloying by the things girls used to prettify themselves—Charlie and Shalimar and Chanel No. 5, fighting to overpower cheaper, stronger waves of bubble gum and hair spray and cherry-flavored lip gloss. The whole town waited. And Sally couldn't let them down. Not when her whole reputation depended on it.

"I can't, Ella. I just can't." The words slid so fast from the corner of Sally's mouth, she wondered if they'd really come out. But they had. And she knew by the droop of those brown eyes, the sag of that firm chin, that Ella had heard.

◆

"Thanks to Katrina, this is WWOZ in exile, givin' you some local blues from our sister station in Baton Rouge."

"Well, it rained five days and the skies turned dark as night . . ."

Sally stared out the window. *After what I've read, just what I need; more blues.* As they neared the Crescent City, the landscape gave Sally no cause for cheer. Trees had snapped in half like used matchsticks. Some, their tops gone, had blackened as though a raging forest fire had swept through the canopy of pines and live and scrub oaks, incinerating their leaves. Bleak as Sally's soul, now that she grasped the enormity of what she'd done to Ella. Miles and miles of a ghostly forest, their midlines smudged with a charcoal-like substance, their trunks streaked with chalky white. White and black. Always white and black.

But evidence of Katrina's manhandling didn't stop with the coastal flora. The Big One had mocked those attempting to escape, sucking up cars and trucks and motorcycles into a boiling cauldron of sea and river water and human excrement and toxic chemicals and then dumping them in great piles about the ditches, ramps, and medians of the freeway, to corrode and deteriorate into a powdery mess. Would it do the same to her as she tried to escape the consequences of her past?

"We stepped way back for that one, bringing you Jimmy Witherspoon and 'Backwater Blues.' Hang on, now. I'll be comin' at y'all with Trombone Shorty and his brother James."

Again music oozed from the speaker, music that normally soothed Sally's spirits, warmed cold bones. Today, it was nothing short of irritating. The last thing she wanted was a reminder of what priceless treasures had been lost down here, what nightmarish truths had been found. She itched to reach over the seat and turn off the radio, but she didn't dare. Ole Ruby might backhand her.

Sally's cell phone rang. She fiddled with her seat belt, her jeans so tight, it was difficult to get the thing out of her pocket. With grunts and groans, finally she managed. It was . . . She couldn't flip the phone open fast enough. "Bobby!"

"Sally! Where are you?"

"Hold on." Sally leaned forward. "Hey, Ruby! What did that last sign say?"

"Something 'bout the airport."

"We're somewhere around—"

"I heard her, Sally. Now listen to me."

Robert's tone pulled a giggle from dry lips; it felt good to have someone else in charge. So good, she longed to weep. "Aren't you the bossy one today?" Giggles and sniffs mixed together.

"Somebody needs to boss you. Do you have any idea what you're doing?"

Not a clue. Sally's lips tightened, but she forced steel into her tone. "Yes, Robert. I do."

"That's debatable." There was a pause, like the connection had been lost. Sally stared at the phone, willing Robert to speak again. *Dear baby brother . . .*

"Sally, listen to me. You've caught a break. I think the checkpoints are down."

"Checkpoints?"

"Yeah. You've driven into a war zone with nothing but a camouflaged canteen."

Sure, everything was torn up, just like they'd been showing nonstop on CNN. But she hadn't seen anything dangerous. It had been well over two months since Katrina swept through here. So far, they'd been okay.

"Here's the deal," Robert finally managed. "You're with the SPCA."

"The what?"

"Humane Society. The Illinois Pet League. Something. Anything." Robert spit out the words. "You're down here to rescue animals. Got it?"

"Ten four."

"Yeah, SPCA. Yeah," Robert repeated, in a way that made Sally think he was making it up as he went. "They've all heard of that. And—"

Such a high note was trumpeted on the radio's easy-listening jazz, Sally covered her ears. "What?" she asked.

"I said make a sign, put it on your dash."

Sally nodded, the lie already incorporated into her biography. Ruby and Shamika and she ran a kennel, one of those upscale ones with a swimming pool, a masseuse . . .

"Sally? Sally!"

"Yeah, Bobby."

"If that doesn't work, tell them this." Robert spouted military jargon.

"Hold on." Sally dug through her purse and found an old deposit slip. Robert repeated the information.

Sally wrote Robert's name, rank, and cell phone number.

"Got it?"

"Yep."

"Hold on a minute, sis."

Pen still in hand, the phone at her ear, her mind racing ahead, Sally tapped Shamika's shoulder. "Hey, you've got some paper in that notebook, don't you?"

Grumbling, Shamika nodded, then shoved a folder toward Sally. Still cradling the phone, Sally pulled out a sheet and started on the poster that would get her to Ella. If all went well, that is.

"And . . . sis?" Sally managed to hear Robert's voice over acronyms, curse words, and enough static to launch a rocket.

"Yeah?"

"Where are you goin'?"

The force in Robert's voice was enough to make Sally stop working on the sign. Part of her longed to tell the truth to her brother, but the last thing she needed was Robert storming the hospital where Ella worked. Besides, she wasn't *really* lying. She didn't *know* that Ella would be there. "I'm not sure." She ignored stabs of guilt by focusing on the S, the P, the C, the A that she was printing. *Focus, girl. You've got work to do.*

"What are you looking for, Sally?" Robert asked.

She had to be careful here. "It's not what. It's who."

"Who is 'who'?" In the background, what sounded like a shortwave radio sputtered and hissed. "Look, sis, this isn't the time to play games."

Sally hesitated. She might need his help tracking down Ella. Wouldn't it be easier to just go ahead, pour it out now, rather than later? "Christella Ward. An old friend."

"Hmm. Okay."

"She was before your time." Sally breathed easy. She'd worked it out, even told the truth. And she'd told Robert just enough to keep him satisfied but not enough for him to interfere with her plan.

"Call me when you're done and I'll come get you."

"I will," she lied, her vow to be truthful pushed so far back, it didn't even try to bother her.

"And Sally? Be careful. I love you."

Chapter 27

THE AWFUL TRUTH

Oh, sinner man, you'd better pray. For it look-a like judgment day.
—Negro spiritual, "Oh, Sinner, You'd Better Get Ready"

No matter what you say, ain't dumpin' you out like dirty dishwater." Ruby used the rearview mirror to glare at Sally. "Huh-uh. Not in this town." Shamika just harrumphed.

"My brother's meeting me." Sally leaned over the seat. "He'll probably be there waiting." Digging into her purse, she found the map she'd downloaded. A twinge ran through her, but she shoved it away. She hadn't lied to Ruby, just rearranged logistics a bit. Tough words for tough times. When she got through this, she could work on her little problem.

Mention of Robert seemed to quiet Ruby and Shamika. Either that, or the looming monstrosity to the west—the Superdome, a defiled temple to the great athletes, the scene of post-Katrina looting, rapes, and all the other ills man had wrought upon man.

"Is that it?" Shamika whispered.

Sally nodded. Even though garbage had been shuttled off, the howls of the injured, the stench of the dying found a way to infiltrate the car. With a lump in her throat, Sally turned, just in time to see—"Hey, Ruby! That's our exit!"

Ruby hit the brakes and swerved onto the ramp. The car screeched to a stop not ten feet in front of a barricade. A National Guardsman, his arms folded, his well-padded rear end leaning against one of five sawhorses, hid his eyes behind mirrored shades.

With a snap, Sally's seat belt was off.

Ruby jostled about in the front seat. "What in heaven's name—"

"I'll be right back," Sally said as she jumped out of the car. Sign in hand, she jogged toward the man. "Hi, officer. We're with the federal SPCA. Sergeant Powers has asked us to respond to an emergency a block from the hospital." She beamed with the knowledge that she hadn't really lied, just mispronounced Robert's name so as to deflect any fallout from her brother.

Nothing about the officer's expression changed. When he pulled an earplug out of his ear, twangy country music filtered toward Sally.

"So we'll just pull onto the shoulder." Sally slathered a thicker-than-usual drawl onto her words. "Y'all won't even have to move this little barricade."

With a shrug, the man stuck his earplug back in, then turned his head.

Relieved that her little ruse had worked and she hadn't had to use Robert's name, Sally climbed back into the car and dug out her instructions. "Just pull around that barricade, and it's a couple more blocks," she told Ruby.

If this street was any indication, Katrina had picked up the city, chewed it up, and vomited it out. Piles of twisted metal, splintered boards, and soggy boxes lined the streets like demons cheering on a parade route to hell. Sally gulped. How could this be God's plan? Massive oak trees had withstood the onslaught yet paid a heavy price, their once-proud branches strewn and suffering in pools of stagnant water. Animals had fared even worse. Bloated carcasses of squirrels, birds, what looked like a cat, made a graveyard of medians and ditches.

As they drove on, the stench of a dozen slaughterhouses, a hundred town dumps, roiled into one sickening wave that managed to seep into the car even though the windows were rolled up. It wasn't just the refuse of Katrina dogging Sally. It was the stench of her own behavior, creeping in, now that she was down South. She closed eyes heavy with remorse. "Lord, forgive me. Let me find her. After all these years, help me."

One more turn, and the hospital complex sprawled before them. Except for the telltale waterline across a redbrick classical facade, the main wing put up a good pretense that nothing untoward had happened behind those walls that were supposed to heal and comfort, those halls that were supposed to be hallowed and safe. As Sally knew personally, a facade often hid ugly things. And she was going to dig past it and find Ella.

Ruby pulled to the curb, the car idling heavily, as if it too were struggling to catch its breath in the dense humidity and fetid air. "Who you think you gonna find here? Ain't nothin' but bad memories."

"Hey's it's a big complex. You know how city hospitals are. She's bound to be here somewhere." Sally fought off a niggling fear that no living thing other than patrolmen could be found within a one-mile radius. "Besides, Bobby'll arrive any minute." There it was again. That lying.

Shamika's cell phone rang. She snapped it open. "No, G-Ma. We're fine. We're on our way." She glanced at Ruby, then returned to her call. "Now."

Somehow Ruby managed to twist her large frame around and embrace Sally, not content to let the seat be a barrier between them. "You keep in touch." She pointed at Shamika's cell. "That's why we got these blasted things."

"Pray for me," Sally whispered into Ruby's ear.

"What you think I been doin' for the last couple of weeks?" Fire flashed into Ruby's eyes, along with a smile that tugged at Sally's heart. In spite of all she'd done wrong, God had gifted her with a real friend. And considering what she might face when she got back to Normal, a real friend was going to come in mighty handy. She got out, heading to what looked like the main hospital wing after waving a halfhearted good-bye to the back of Ruby's car.

Her arms aching from holding her bag, the straps of her backpack cutting into her shoulder blades, Sally plodded about the hospital grounds. Crushed bricks, insulation, and Sheetrock had been heaped into great mounds that towered over her and seemed to mock her plan. *Nothing's left. You're too late . . .*

Something skittered from the closest mound.

A scream was born in Sally's throat.

It was a rat, sleek and fat as a pampered pet, not two feet in front of her.

"Get!" she hissed.

The rodent held its ground, tail twitching, its boldness unnatural.

Sally stomped her foot. The rat sauntered back into its nest.

Sweat poured off Sally, a reaction to the sweltering sun, the rat, and the silence that pushed in on all sides. No honking horns. No squawking gulls drifting in on an air current. No doctors, nurses, patients. Had this been a mistake?

Her steps quickened to match the pounding in her chest. The first entrance was padlocked; so was the next. Clutching her bag, Sally circled the hospital, stepped about crushed bottles, and approached the rear entrance.

"He warned us!" A man sprawled on a top stair near double doors, eyes red and wild. Filthy shirtsleeves had been shoved up, revealing festering sores.

Rufus? Adrenaline surged into Sally, tensing her arms and legs. *No. It's just some homeless man. Not Rufus.* Still, nobody was around to help her, just in case he was a sicko. She stepped back.

"His name is Legion, and there are many of him." Spewing spit and phlegm from between broken teeth, the man grabbed a bag from a pile near his feet. He clawed at brown paper, shoving it away from the neck of a bottle. "And he has sent me to tell you that your lies have caught up with you. Behold, it is the day of wrath." He cackled, choked, and coughed the deep, thick cough of a smoker, drank deep, then coughed again.

Lies? Legion? The words slammed into Sally. Even though she claimed to be saved—she *was* saved, the Holy Spirit assured her of that—her lying was as filthy in God's sight as this man's clothes. Sure, she'd given her life to Jesus, back when she was thirteen, but how about her *lies?* She'd never given *them* to Jesus.

"Get away from me, you with unclean lips!" His voice quavering, he waved the bottle like a flag.

Sally tried not to gag as the smell of booze and urine assailed her. Stepping back, a quivering finger pointed toward the doors. "Where is everybody?"

The man's cackle sent a chill up Sally's spine. "In hell," he answered.

"No." She made sure to not blink, her eyes locked on the tortured face. "I'm looking for a nurse who works here. Her name's Ella."

The man's eyes got wide. For a moment a smile wreathed the gaping holes where teeth should've been. "El-la," he said, in a singsong voice. "El-la." He jumped from his perch, his voice crescendoing to the brink of insanity. "Voice of an angel, but a demon. You're all demons!" Scrambling legs flew at Sally. Grimy hands clawed at her bag, her backpack . . .

The man, the hospital doors, the steps, blurred into a smear of browns and grays and beiges. Sally fell onto the pavement, her blow softened by the backpack and satchel. When she clambered to her feet, her vision had returned, but the old drunk had vanished. There stood Rufus, spittle about his mouth, his eyes narrow and mean, his arms coiled to pound submission into her . . .

A low growl escaped from Sally's lips. "You're not getting away with it this time!" She grabbed his shoulders and shook him.

The bottle shattered as it hit the sidewalk. "You demon, get off of me!" he screeched. "Off!"

Shards crunched under Sally's feet. Was this living nightmare the price for her lying? A pounding started about her temples. Louder, louder . . .

"You little—" Profanities tumbled out, mixed with sobs. The man shook as if in the throes of a seizure, then got on his hands and knees and crawled toward the shattered remains of the bottle. As Sally stared, he licked at the pavement, then clawed it, as if his best friend had died. And perhaps it had.

Sally hugged her arms, ducked her head to her chest. She couldn't take another second of this. Everything was shaking, even the ground. Why was the ground shaking? And the noise? "Dear God," she cried, her fingers coursing through her hair. "Help me!"

Now the skies screamed. Wind whipped her blouse, a boiling wind, full of hate and anger—it was another hurricane, coming, coming . . .

"Sally!" A voice from above boomed over the storm. "I'm coming down!"

Was it God? A demon? Her past, moving in? Or was she imagining this loudspeaker-style voice, her mind surrendering to insanity?

The landscape became a whir of dust and litter and earsplitting sound. Every muscle in Sally's body tensed. She expected to be struck down at any minute.

"Sally!"

That voice . . . Her hands over her ears now, Sally dared to lift her head. She blinked. The man had vanished, nothing on the steps except a wadded-up sack. There was Robert, waving from the cockpit of a battleship-gray helicopter, which hovered not forty feet above her head.

◆ ◆ ◆

When Sally stopped crying, Robert handed her a set of earplugs. "I found your old friend," he yelled, over beeps and static and a nearly deafening roar. "She's up in Thibodeaux."

"You mean . . . she's okay?" Her heart, which had begun to slow down, beat harder. At least one prayer had been answered She struggled to put on the plugs, desperate to stop the ringing of her ears.

"She's okay. But how about you?" The luminous glow of gauges, dials, and circuit breakers reflected in Robert's aviator shades. He shifted his lean frame about on the lambskin-covered seat.

Leaning over, Sally peered out the window. "Where . . . where is he?"

Robert shook his head. "That old wino? They've hung around here for years. Even before I'd landed, he'd scuttled back into his hole." He thrummed his fingers on a control panel. "Katrina brought 'em all out, the hingeless, the homeless. They figure it's their turn to dish out some of the crap they think they've taken for years."

Sally stared at her brother. "But he wasn't . . . Rufus?"

Now it was Robert's turn to stare, and from the looks of it, he suspected Sally's mental state. "Who's Rufus?"

Sally swallowed once or twice. How could she tell Robert when she hadn't told Sam and her kids? Yet Robert deserved something—not only because he'd gotten her out of a terrible jam, but because he was her brother. "Oh, Robert," Sally started, wanting to do this, but not sure how. "I've—I've lied to everyone, most of all myself. And it's caught up with me. I ran down here, trying to make things better, but I think I've made things worse." She buried her head in her hands. "I should've told Sam, the kids . . ."

While manning the controls, Robert still managed to pat Sally's knee. "It's all right, sis. I talked to them. They know you're with me. Just settle back and try to relax. And we'll call Mama . . ."

"When she gets back from her trip," they both said at the same time. She grabbed Robert's hand and squeezed it hard before letting go. Family felt good right about now.

The helicopter, which had been careening through the air in a way that re-minded Sally of beaters in a mixing bowl filled with lumpy batter, smoothed out and clipped across the sky. Again Sally looked down. *It's even worse from up here.* Upturned cars. Limbless trees. Rubbish piles of American Dreams. Blown into a maelstrom and hurled back, almost fiendishly, as a grim reminder of who was in control here. The same God who was in control of her nasty little mess.

The city of New Orleans, inspiration for songs, films, books, music, the convergent point of a proud genetic pool of French and Indian and English and Spanish peoples, had been reduced to a city of rubble, as if a giant had stomped through in a fit of rage and crushed wood and paper and metal and plastic and all the strange fruit of mankind's pitiful attempt to civilize the land. Sally could only stare at a live shot of what she'd seen on CNN for months. What would it be like to have her home opened to the elements—books, furniture, paintings, underwear, drawers and drawers of nothing and everything, strewn about for everyone to see? Her home reduced to such con-fetti, she couldn't distinguish it from her neighbor's, except perhaps for a pink cloth fluttering from a limb, which, upon closer examination, was her baby's favorite dress?

Robert patted Sally again. "I'm just glad I found you. I thank God for that."

"I'm . . . so sorry, Robert," Sally blubbered. She'd imposed on him, put him in an awkward spot . . .

"I'm sorry too."

"What are you sorry for?" she asked, between sniffles.

"For not keeping better tabs on y'all. Guess it took a storm to get us together."

His smile took Sally back to fort-building days in the sandbox, endless hide-and-seek games in the front yard. "How did you find me?" she asked.

"The State police. Radar. Prayer. And it didn't hurt that y'all had Illinois plates," he continued, his voice soft now. "Of course, this place is swarming with all kinds of people from all kinds of places. And not all of 'em good." He flipped a toggle switch. "This is 624 Delta Delta, requesting . . ."

Sally studied lines etched into Robert's face, the stubble of whiskers, the loose-fitting fatigues, all suggesting a life on the edge. What had Katrina done to this brother she'd always loved, in spite of the yawning stretch of interstate between them? And was he angry at her for adding another item to what must be a colossal to-do list? She longed to reach out and touch him, to break through the horrors that he'd seen, smelled, heard, and tucked behind those aviator sunglasses.

Robert did it for her when he grabbed her hand. "Sally, it's okay. I understand. At least I'm trying to." He cleared his throat, then pointed toward what used to be a modest neighborhood, judging from the shotgun style homes, the flattened chain-link fences, the plethora of old cars and spare tires. "See those holes in the roofs?"

She nodded halfheartedly, glad that he'd changed the subject. Yet she barely glanced down, her eyes, her heart, her mind full of the images. Where would it stop? How would it ever be made whole?

"That's where we found 'em. Clinging to the last remaining beam, the—"

Empathy made her look. "You mean people had to cut their way out?"

"It was either that or drown." His voice flattened. "Some of them did drown. When we found the bodies, we tied them to a light pole, a bridge girder." He wiped his brow. "It seemed like a good idea at the time. You know, at least give the families something to bury. But when the waters receded, they were just hanging there, the breeze doing the strangest things with their limbs, their hair, their clothes."

"Strange fruit," Sally whispered, again thinking of the song Ella had played for her so long ago. Had anything changed? She shuddered at the answer her heart gave.

Robert pulled off his sunglasses, exposing puffy, red-rimmed eyes. "What are you talking about?"

She didn't answer. She couldn't. Instead she studied his face. "You're not sleeping, are you?"

With a sweep of his hand, Robert acknowledged the city where he'd met his wife, had his kids. His home. "Who can sleep with this going on?"

Disagreeing, Sally closed her eyes. She longed to drift away, to pretend none of this had happened. But there were those images. Rufus. Ella. Assailing her almost constantly, after years of playing hide-and-seek. But she was going to rid herself of all of them. One way or the other . . .

"624 Delta Delta, four miles seven hundred feet inbound."

Sally bolted to an upright position. "Wha-what are we doing, Robert?"

"We're circling over Thibodeaux, about to pay a visit to your friend Ella," he said. "And I personally want to shake her hand." Urgency cut into Robert's voice as he barked directions at some unknown controller. Rotors whirred toward a black X on a landing pad adjacent to a glass-and-brick building.

If there had been any armrests, Sally would've clawed them with what was left of her fingernails. Instead she clung to Robert's arm, which was shifting and pushing and—

"Hey, stop!" He shoved away her hand. "Do you want us to die?"

To prove the point, the ungainly whirligig bucked like an angry bull determined to shed its rider. The target point disappeared, Sally's wide-eyed view now a blur of black and gray. A cloud of what smelled like kerosene and something else, something metallic, encapsulated the cockpit. Sally tried to swallow down a steely taste.

Metal and fiberglass creaked, groaned, then plunked onto the ground. Sally's head jerked back and slammed into the headrest. She bit hard on her tongue, then tasted blood.

Robert continued his acronym-loaded aviation speak, but a calm tone had smoothed out the tension in his voice.

A glance out the window told Sally they'd made it. Unfortunately, their landing did not assuage the questions that gnawed at her. What would Ella do? What would she say? Did Ella need to purge decades of guilt, of lies too? Or had Katrina washed away her desire to do much of anything else, except cling to what remained of her life?

Robert fiddled furiously with dials and levers. The helicopter groaned and sputtered, then went silent. "You first." He leaned across his sister and twisted a black handle on the door. "Hop on out, sis. And duck your head."

Her knees wobbly and creaky, Sally made her way out of the helicopter.

The blades rotated, slowly now, their earlier roar reduced to a whipping sound, like shirts snapping on a clothesline.

A lean black man, dressed in pastel blue scrub top and pants, walked out of what looked to be the emergency room entrance of a medical complex. He strode toward Sally, his eyes inscrutable under thick brows. "You're Sally?" he asked. "Thanks to your brother's call, we were expecting you."

All Sally could do was nod.

"I'm William," he said, hands on hips. "You probably remember me as Willie."

Chapter 28

A REUNION

My sin's forgiven and my soul set free. And I heard from heaven today.
—Negro spiritual, "I Heard from Heaven Today"

With a curt nod, Willie motioned for Sally and Robert to follow him. Fear followed Sally as she walked through swinging double doors, fear and something else. In spite of the ammonia and citrus scent that seemed to be infused in the hospital walls, something rotten, something iron-sharp, managed to seep through. It was death, spreading its now-familiar stench over this sterile place, an ominous reminder of the city Sally'd just left. And revenge, its odor steely and hard. She wanted to collapse on this floor, beg Willie to forgive her. But did he even know the truth? She tiptoed, as if the floor might collapse and let a yawning void swallow her up. Before she could do anything else, she had to get to Ella. Resolve picked up her pace.

"This way," Willie said, his voice loud but flat. He pushed open a door.

Was she facing judgment or forgiveness on the other side of the threshold? Sally held her breath, then took mincing steps into the room.

There was Ella, thin and angular, a female version of Willie, with dark eyes that, from the pain etched into them, had seen too much to sparkle and dance anymore. Yet the years had been a friend to her in subtle ways, refusing to mark the creamy brown skin with wrinkles or scars. Her hair, pulled into a twist on the side of that still perfectly chiseled face, gleamed like onyx. Memories flooded Sally. She longed to run to her friend, to beg forgiveness. Instead, speechless, she clung to Robert, who'd apparently sensed her need and curved his arm around her shoulders.

"Ms. Ward." After a series of brother hugs, Robert pried Sally's fingers off his arm and stepped toward Ella, his voice booming praise. "I'm so blessed to meet you. Thank you for what you've done."

It was like the cheap miniblinds in the sparsely decorated room had been yanked up, light flooding the room as Ella smiled. "We did what we had to do." The sweep of her arm encompassed Willie. "But it's my brother you should thank."

"Is this . . ." Robert, a decorated colonel who'd served two tours in the Gulf War and emergency landed two F-15s, lost his voice amid a series of stutters and rasps.

Willie ducked his head but could not hide a sheepish expression.

Now Ella's eyes sparkled. "Willie Lee Lafitte, they call him. He's my bro."

"Did you really commandeer a Wildlife and Fisheries canoe?"

Pacing and shrugging, Willie grinned too. "Shoot, man. It weren't nothing."

"You ran a regular water taxi service, from what I heard."

Sally's head flopped back and forth, trying to keep up. Robert knew Ella? Willie?

"Tried to bring 'em in high and dry. Well fed too, courtesy of Wal-Mart."

"Did you really—"

"I didn't have to. They'd already used a two-by-four to bust out the doors."

Ella and Willie and Robert chatted with an intimacy that only those who have gone through a tragedy can share. It was impossible for Sally to understand a thing, except that all three of them deserved medals. And she deserved to be hung. Her heart thumped painfully as she edged toward the door. Maybe she'd just wait out in the copter. Or had Robert locked the darn thing?

"So what brings y'all here?"

Ella's words froze Sally. How could she explain this inane idea to burst onto the aftermath of a colossal battle with nature and culture and history and try to right some wrong she had perpetrated decades ago?

Silence blanketed the small lounge.

As if he sensed the tension, Robert clapped a hand on Willie's shoulder. "Why don't you show me around?"

"Sure thing." Willie pointed to a Coke machine. "You want something?"

Robert shrugged. "Maybe some coffee."

"Trust me." As Willie shook his head, a diamond stud sparkled in his ear. "You don't want any." The two men laughed and left the room.

The door clicked shut.

Sally inched toward Ella, who now sat on the couch, kneading her hands. She didn't know where to start, but she had to. She'd come all this way. "I . . ." Sally spluttered, then went silent. It wouldn't work. Her plan was a joke.

"You what?" Catlike, Ella sprang up and stormed to the window. Graceful hands, devoid of rings or polish, lay flat against the pane of glass. "What do you have to say to me that couldn't wait a few more decades?"

Sally nodded. It had been stupid to think "I'm sorry" would suffice. She turned to leave, but a saying of Daddy's swooped in again, just in time. "*A Flowers never gives up.*" She edged toward Ella, letting Daddy's words wash over her. "Please forgive me. Please, dear friend." She made no excuses, told no lies. She had to do this right, the way she should have years ago.

If Ella had intended to laugh, she failed. Something akin to a snort came out. "'Dear friend'? This from the one who condemned my brother to living hell?"

Sally extended a trembling hand. "Please, Ella. I know that now. I have no excuse for what I did." She stepped closer, praying that God would open up a place in Ella that her words, her expressions, had failed to reach.

As if Sally had leprosy, Ella jerked away. "Thanks to you, they caged him like an animal for twenty years."

"I know. I . . ."

With a whirl, Ella was inches from Sally's face. "You know? You don't know nothin'! Didn't know nothin' then. Don't know nothin' now."

She didn't blame Ella, not at all. But she dug deeper, thanks to the Spirit. For she *was* nothing. But He was something. *Father God, help me do the right thing,* she prayed. *For You, Father. Not for me. Not even for Ella. Help me, Father God.*

"You hear me?" Sally's silence seemed to incite Ella to even more anger. "You don't know nothin'!" Ella's voice slammed into Sally, and she half-expected a fist to follow.

"No, Ella." Inexplicably, a calm began to move in, giving Sally the next words to say. "I do know a few things. I know that I wronged not just you and your brother, but my family. Myself. What I did set up a chain reaction of lies that has stained my relationships, my credibility, my life."

Sally touched Ella's shoulder. This time, Ella didn't move.

"With God's help, I want to start over, admitting what I did, first to you, then to Willie, then to the police."

Ella jerked out of Sally's grip, her eyes hard as flint. "You think I'm goin' along with your little whitewash?"

Sally drew up to her full height. For one of the first times since this started, she was sure about what to say, what to do, and how to do it. "I've got to confess. I don't know if you're in with me on this or not. But it doesn't matter."

Ella's hands grazed Sally's wrist when she waved them about. "What—what exactly are you talking about?"

"I'm going to Monroe. It's about time to set the record straight."

In a flash, Ella was in Sally's face, her eyes boiling like whitecapped waves, her fists knotted and inches away. "What right do you have sashaying in here, opening up a can of worms when the fish have starved to death and are floatin' belly-up?"

It was as if a window had been smashed, exposing the room to a sweltering heat. Sally broke out in a sweat. But she wasn't stopping. No, she was finishing this. "Even rotten fish deserve a proper burial," she said.

The two women locked eyes. In that look, Sally saw a mixture of hurt and love. And this time, Ella was the one to look away.

"But we killed a man," Ella whispered, as she again looked out the window.

"Yes, we did." Sally grasped a hand that was as slick as her own. "A man who raped me and might have raped you too. And then killed both of us and dumped us in the bayou."

"Where we put *him*." A great tear slid down Ella's cheek.

"Look at me, Ella," Sally said.

When the two locked eyes this time, years sloughed away. Sally wore a pinafore, the one Mama had made for her to wear the first day of sixth grade. Ella had on that white lace dress that looked like it had been bleached and starched and pressed until it could stand up on its own. And Ella no longer had a stylish twist but wore that thick, dark hair in pigtails, each sectioned carefully, then tied with white bows.

"In spite of everything I've done wrong, that's one thing I did right. Plus we did it together." Sally's voice broke, but she kept going, determined to finish what she'd started. Mama again. "And if I remember, you threw the first stone at him."

A single sob tore out of Ella's throat. Tears coursed her face, leaving smudges about her eyes that made them look bruised. "I can't go along with it, Sally. It's been too long. We've—Willie and me—been through too much."

Sally tensed up. "Willie . . . did you tell him the truth?"

Ella bowed her head, revealing hints of silver along her hairline. "Had to tell him. Mighta been the only thing kept him alive in there."

A tentative hand grazed that fine, clear forehead. "Of course you had to."

Sally edged closer. "How is he, really?" she murmured, infusing love in her voice.

Ella walked to the window, her back to Sally. "Transformed," she said.

"I'm—I'm so sorry." Again the years pressed in. First Willie had endured the horrors of prison. Now Katrina had wrecked whatever life he'd managed to put together. Sally had nothing to say to make up for it all. Nothing to say except that she was sorry, over and over. And pray.

There was a touch on her arm. A spicy scent moved in to overpower the antiseptic hospital smell. Sally looked into eyes that, though still bright with tears, were suddenly shiny. Hopeful. She put her hand over Ella's, still praying.

"It's not like you think. Not at all." Motioning for Sally to join her, Ella stepped toward the couch, sat down, and patted the cushion next to her.

Sally complied, longing to pull Ella close, to inhale the scent Sally remembered to this day. How had she ever betrayed this friend who'd saved her life? Before they crept in and ruined things, Sally slammed the door on bitterness and regret, scooting closer until her shoulder grazed Ella's. It felt so good, so right. And she had no one but God to thank.

"When he got out of the pen, he got back on the stuff. You know, he'd started usin' in Mon-roe. Mama and Daddy had a reason to be worried sick 'bout him."

For a moment, Sally heard the mournful minor key that a curly headed boy pulled from a gleaming horn, its notes mirroring the sadness in sleepy eyes until they were nothing but glints of light in a dark face. "Did he ever get to play his music?"

Ella nodded. "Sweet Willie and his horn. Inseparable except for da bottle perched on a music stand, a bag of white powder stashed in his case."

"I'm so sorry," Sally whispered, for what seemed like the tenth time.

"We surfed the waves of rehab, then relapse, for more years than I can count. When Katrina hit, Ole Willie was hangin' ten on drugs. Anything and everything he could find. I didn't have any choice but to take him to the hospital with me."

"Old Baptist?"

Ella nodded. "It was hell on earth." She leaned back and let the couch envelop her. "Blood and vomit. Screams and curses. Over it all, like an awful mushroom cloud, death." As if she were trying to get rid of the sights and sounds and smells, Ella fanned herself and shook her head. "And all Willie cared about was getting another fix."

"Right on, sister. I got me a two-by-four." It was Willie; he and Robert had managed to enter the room without Sally having seen or heard them. "Threatened to smack baby sister with it if she didn't give me the pharmacy key." A fog shrouded Willie's face. "All dem folks beggin' me to get dem some water, get dem outta there. I didn't care about nothin' or nobody. Just gettin' the next fix."

His pause made Sally uncomfortable. It was partly her fault, wasn't it?

"But then you had a little meeting with God," Ella encouraged.

Willie shook his head. "God had a meeting with me. And I wouldn't call it little."

"More like road to Damascus."

"I tore through the halls, pounding past rooms full of dead, of dying, up the stairs, down the stairs." Willie raved as if the demons of his addiction had followed him into *this* hospital. "It was on the first floor that it happened."

"What?" Sally asked, the heat pushing in again until she could barely stand it.

"A light hit me like it been beamed down by an invisible fist. I squeezed my eyes shut, but that didn't do no good." Seeming to see it, Willie clawed at his face. "Then there was a voice." He shivered. "'No more, Willie Lee. No more! *No more!*' The Voice ruled the wind, the rain, even the tree limbs banging against the windows. Over and over, He tell me the same thing."

"God," Sally whispered.

Willie nodded. "I collapsed, that two-by-four plunking down on the floor in front of me. 'What, Lord?' I asked Him. 'What do You want from me?'"

"The next words God whispered, but they chilled my bones. 'Save them,' He said." Hoarseness took over Willie's voice. "'Save them.'" Willie locked eyes with his sister, then Sally. "'How, Lord?' I pleaded." He shook his head, as if he still couldn't believe it all. "There I was, groveling in 'dat hall fillin' with water filthy as the sewer. Groveling in a *life* filthy as the sewer." He took a deep breath, as if he needed strength to go on.

"And that's when you got the boat," Robert encouraged.

The words seemed to bolster Willie. "Something crashed against the walls. The floor shook." Willie paused, just for a moment. "'No, Lord!' I begged. 'Please, forgive me. Help me!'" While talking, Willie made his way to the couch, then sat between Sally and his sister. "I'll never forget what He said next."

"What?" Sally asked, her heart about to burst.

"'I am the Lord. And I will provide.'"

"He really said that?" Robert took Willie's cue and wedged next to Sally on the couch, which was now stuffed with sweating bodies. And about to burst with emotion.

Lines creased Willie's forehead. "He didn't say it. He yelled it. Drowned out them patients' cries. That wind. Drowned out my doubts too. Left 'em scattered on that flooded hospital floor."

From the window, beaming sun rays illuminated Willie's face. "I died, too, the old Willie. I got up, slogged through the muck, and shoved into the storm." He looked questioningly at Ella. When she nodded, he continued. "Not twenty yards from the front steps, there was a boat rocking back and forth. Just a small one—nothing like what ole Noah got—its three horsepowers chugging away."

"He saved sixty-three people." Ella's voice rang out, a church bell pealing good news. "Shuttled them back and forth, back and forth. To higher ground."

Robert nodded. "And picked up provisions for them here and there."

"Mainly there," Willie added. "I guess prison taught me a thing or two."

Sally felt her eyes get round. "That's why they called you Willie Lee Lafitte?"

Willie nodded. "Kinda a good pirate, if there is such a thing."

"It wasn't just that," Robert countered. "He did it in style, like a tugboat captain, weaving in and out of Katrina-made coves."

"That's 'cause God was at the helm. I hadn't been in a pirogue like that since I was a young-un down bayou way."

"Me neither," Ella added. Willie smiled.

Silence filled the room as guilt roiled up in Sally, strangling her. Threatening to kill her. Her shoulders shook from the strain, as did her chest. "I . . . so . . . sorry." The pain of it all made her collapse onto Robert's shoulder. "It's all . . . my fault."

"Dere, dere, now." Willie's words massaged away pain. Guilt. "Lawd, you was just a young 'un. You and my baby sis."

As decades of apologies flowed from Sally, a miraculous thing begin to happen, encouraged, no doubt, by the pats and murmurings of three very different voices. Joy freed the memories that had coiled about her mind, her heart. Letting her breathe. Not easy yet, but free. *Lord, Lord, free.*

When Robert finally quit patting Sally's head and jingled what sounded like a pocketful of coins, nervous giggles took the place of sighs and sobs. "If you don't mind, I'd like to hear the end of this before I have to head outta here."

"Sure, man." Willie stood up and stretched his legs, like he had a cramp.

"How did y'all manage to get those folks up here?" Robert asked.

"After commandeering the boat, copters were easy."

"Pilot Willie Lee Lafitte, eh?"

"One of dem old dudes had been in the Great War. Can you get a load of that? Slumped in that seat, half dead from diabetic shock, tellin' me which button to push, which stick to pull. Had the craziest grin on his face, I figured we all gone mad. Then some of you guys took ovah."

Ella nodded. "You should've seen these skies. Copters buzzing and hovering like hungry mosquitoes."

"They needed us here, so we just stayed on," Willie said.

"Was your home . . ."

"The lower Ninth Ward? Hah!" Sarcasm made Ella's voice raspy. "I figured, being a soldier and all, you'd have gotten to know the place."

The pressure from the last few months seemed to press in on Robert. He slumped forward, his hands cradling his head. "Does anyone know that city?"

"Touché," Ella replied. "I thought I knew her. Yet when those waters boiled over our little piece of her and pulled it out to the Gulf, I realized I knew nothing, had nothing. None of us do, really."

"Except the Lord." With an evangelist's persuasive voice, Willie boomed a rebuttal. "We got Him, and that's all we need."

Robert's cell phone interrupted a peace that had washed the room with light and forgiveness. He pulled it out of his pocket and answered it.

"PT25F. Ten four." Before Sally's eyes, her brother morphed into an efficient Air Force Reserve officer. He leapt from the couch, smoothed down his pants, pulled out a memo pad and pen, and scratched down notes, all the while spitting out acronyms and numbers. Still talking, he started for the hall, motioning for Sally to follow. He talked a bit longer, then shut his phone and stuck it and the pad and pen in a pocket. "Gotta go, sis." Regret filled bloodshot eyes as he pulled Sally into a hug. "It can't be helped."

Sally nodded, wanting to stay enveloped in the cloud of sweat and oil and hint of lime that was her brother. But he had a job to do. And so did she. And if Robert couldn't take her, she could take herself.

"But I'm not leaving until you tell me what you're doing. The truth this time, Sis." He glanced at his watch, then at Sally. "And I'm already three minutes late, so start talking."

"First I'm calling Sam, checking in. Then I'm renting a car." She tried to smile at Robert in spite of the pit in her stomach.

"I don't think you'll have any trouble, this far from the Big Easy." Duty called Robert to gently disengage himself from Sally. "But use my name if you have to."

Sally nodded. "If I don't get stopped or sidetracked, I'll be in Monroe by tomorrow."

◆ ◆ ◆

Sally wiped sweaty palms on wrinkled trouser legs. Twenty-four hours ago, she'd kissed Robert good-bye, then rented a car. She'd cruised north until a five-car pileup all but shut down I-20. Then she'd veered off the freeway just outside of Vicksburg, where months ago, Katrina had fizzled, gasping winds headed east. Last night, Sally had managed to wangle a cot in a water closet of a motel room. And she'd been grateful for it.

A mile marker announced that Monroe loomed near. Sally rolled up her window, hoping to stop the wind's assault. It was no use; the heat had flattened her shag. And makeup had run down her neck like rivulets headed seaward.

The rearview mirror brought Sally back to the reality of Katrina; concerns about her appearance evaporated. What complaints could she have, when the freeway was packed with people fleeing more recent nightmares, all wrought by the mother of all hurricanes? Families still camped out on the road, makeshift tents fashioned out of burlap bags and dingy sheets.

This morning, Sally had waited an hour to buy ten gallons of gas—no bargain, at six fifty a gallon. And she'd heard stories that made her little drama pale in comparison: a mother, blown off a battered roof in front of her three children. A granddaughter, managing to drag her eighty-year-old granny onto the roof, clinging to battered shingles, her arms a vise about ancient skin and bone; later, battling wind and rain to reenter a flooded tomb of a house, wading through oily sludge infested with wriggling snakes, desperate to find the insulin needed to fight Granny's old enemy, diabetes . . . only to hear her grandmother's death rattle in a rescue boat.

The heroism of her fellow northbound travelers revved up Sally in a way that manifested itself by an insistent drumming upon the steering wheel. "I can do this," she exulted, to a stand of pines and live oaks and the omnipresent kudzu. When they silently glared at her, her words died in her throat. What did she face at the Ouachita Parish Sheriff's Department? Would they put her in jail? Would there be a way to break her chain of lying without implicating Ella? And then the question that kept creeping in, no matter how Sally tried to push it away. Why hadn't Sam called her back? Had she lied one time too many? Would he do something drastic and leave her? Sally swallowed hard, then gripped the steering wheel. She had to leave that up to God. And no matter what else she did, she vowed not to lie.

Chapter 29

A SURPRISE CONFESSION

When the storm of life is ragin', stand by me.
—Charles A. Tindley, "Stand by Me"

She didn't remember Monroe being hot and humid in early November. But then she'd been young, didn't have menopause wreaking havoc with her body, and had been preoccupied with much more important things. Like getting raped. Betraying friends. Bad Southern memories crept in, pushing out lazy front porch talks, good cooking, warm breezes. Sally took the Civic Center exit, found the courthouse, pulled into the parking lot and turned off the ignition, then used her last tissue to mop up her face. More than just the weather, memories and hot flashes were making her sweat. Could she really go through with this?

A jewel of a building fronted the glistening Ouachita River. Talented craftsmen had erected arches and columns; a Southern adaptation of the classical architecture that epitomized the "frozen music" Sally loved to discuss. Today the aesthetics were wasted on Sally's pounding skull, her queasy stomach. Someone in this building could ruin her future. Her family. And all the aesthetics in the world couldn't do a thing to stop it. Sally bowed her head, her fists clenched. "God, help me," she prayed. "Stand by me." She got out of the car, wincing at the finality of the slamming door.

Sweat continued to pour as she made her way up a set of stairs and into the building.

"This way, ma'am." A burly officer pointed her to a conveyor belt, grumbling when he had to remind her to set her purse in a bucket. Wincing as if her guilt would somehow set off an alarm, she minced her way across and under the metal detector, then waited for her purse to plop out into the holding area. "Where do I go to report a crime?" she asked the guard.

He didn't say a word, just pointed to another series of steps, then settled hefty haunches in a metal folding chair and pulled out a handheld computer game. *Bored, huh? Well, I'll change that.*

Sally took a deep breath. Seven steps in this next step of her life. Dream-like, she glided up steps one, two, three, four, inanely counting each one. Blood whooshed in her ears. She resisted the urge to pinch herself.

A glassed-in registration area came into view. Cell-like. Jail-like.

Battling an urge to wheel about and flee the premises, Sally gripped the stair rail, then took steps five, six—her shoe turned on the seventh step. She lurched forward, her arms waving as she tried to regain her balance.

Still tottering, she approached a counter. She smoothed down her shirt, adjusted her sleeves. "Spirit, take over," she whispered. "Say what I need to say. Do what I need to do."

A calm infused every cell of her body, readying her for whatever lay ahead. Determined knuckles rapped on the sliding glass window.

Two women, their fingers flying across keyboards, did not look up. Sally knocked harder.

One of the women, her eyes shielded by thick lenses, granted Sally a glance, then returned to her pecking.

"I need to report a crime," Sally said, her hand poised to rap again on the window. She took a deep breath. "Let me correct that. I need to confess a crime."

Both women stopped typing, their mouths opening to counterbalance the arch of their eyebrows. One picked up a telephone. "I'll call a deputy." Her voice was so muted behind the glass, Sally supposed it was bulletproof. The woman made the call, then resumed her work, occasionally darting glances at Sally.

Double doors flew open. Sally studied the man coming her way like she was the one gathering evidence. Tall, dark-haired, with a doughy baby face. Was he old enough to do this? Sally suppressed a laugh, then wondered if she'd finally cracked under all the pressure.

The man met her gaze. "Good afternoon, ma'am. I'm Deputy Nelson. How can I help you?"

Pretend he's one of your students. She looked him in the eye. "My name's Sally Flowers Stevens." Her calm tone straightened her spine. "Forty-two years ago, I murdered a man and threw his body into Bayou DiSiard."

The deputy's face paled to the color of putty. Without turning his back on Sally, he edged to the reception area and shoved open the sliding glass. "Call the sheriff," he told the clerk, whose glasses had slipped granny-style to the tip of her nose. "Now. You"—he pointed at Sally—"sit over there. And wait."

His high-pitched voice drew a tight smile from Sally. She'd waited decades to do this. What was another few minutes?

◆

Why the sheriff's office would have *People* and *Star* magazines strewn about a nicked-up lobby end table puzzled Sally. More appropriate would be *Field and Stream* or *Detective Story*. Or perhaps a copy of the Bible, for those burdened with guilt. *Like me.* For the fourth time, Sally flipped past articles about Britney and Kate, barely glancing at the latest buzz. She'd been here nearly an hour and had endured the amblings-through of at least a dozen staff members, who gaped at her like she was an endangered species on loan to the zoo. She'd worked in an office before, so she knew what it was like. If some frumpy middle-aged woman had just confessed to a murder, she would've been the first to set down a stack of mind-numbing paperwork and check her out.

On her fifth flip-through of the magazine, Deputy Nelson burst back into the room. "This way, ma'am." He motioned for Sally to follow. "The sheriff's ready for you."

He led her into an elevator, which lurched and coughed before spitting them out on the third floor.

Judging by the framed portraits lining the long hall, Ouachita Parish had had a storied history of sheriffs. Big men. Proud men. White men. One by one, they stared at Sally, convicting her with somber gazes.

By the time they reached the end of the hall, Sally's heart beat so rapidly she wondered if she might faint. She bowed her head, praying for strength. Wisdom. Most of all, for God's will.

"Ma'am? Are you all right?"

About the time Sally nodded, a door opened. There stood a fierce-looking man, with grizzled eyebrows and deep-set dark eyes. He was a study of browns and blacks: clipped chestnut hair, a smooth tan sport coat, shiny ebony wingtips. If his dress were any indication, he'd be a real stickler for order. Protocol. Just what she didn't need.

"I'm Roger Hamilton," he said, his voice Southern cultured, the vowels drawn out long and low. He offered a hand, which was as warm as his voice. With a half-bow, he gestured Sally through a rather austere reception area and into what looked to be his private office.

Blinking, Sally moved forward, then leaned against the door frame in disbelief. She'd stepped into an art museum, not a sheriff's office. What looked like an antique gilt wood settee lined the long wall. A painting from Ellis Wilson's Caribbean period hung over a pair of French provincial chairs. Seeing the work of one of her favorite artists piqued Sally's interest and curiosity and almost made her forget her troubles. A black sheriff who collected art? Maybe she—and her past—were in the right hands.

"Why don't you have a seat—do you prefer Mrs. or Ms.?"

Sally eased onto a leather sofa. "Uh, Mrs. I've been married now for twenty-six . . ." A nervous giggle slipped out. "Oh, my husband would kill me. It's actually twenty-seven years."

Hamilton sat on the sofa next to Sally, eschewing a more modern office desk and chair on the other side of the room. One hand hovered over a speaker phone set on an occasional table. "Would you like some coffee, Mrs. Stevens?"

Sally shook her head. She'd chugged down four cups this morning in the motel lobby; if she had any more, her bladder would burst. Not to mention her nerves, which had frazzled into mere threads.

"Or water?"

Again Sally shook her head. It was time for the sheriff to quit acting as if his office was an antebellum drawing room with a butler bringing in afternoon tea. She needed to tell her story, find out what price she had to pay, and get on with fixing the rest of her life. If that was even possible.

With careful precision, Hamilton smoothed down perfectly creased cuffed pants. "What is it that's brought you down here?" he asked Sally.

"Back in 1963, I . . ." *Down here?* Sally did a double take. Had she told Deputy Nelson she was from the North? She gulped once or twice, trying to get back on track. She didn't think so, but who could remember, after all that she'd seen, all she'd heard? And what difference did it make where she lived, anyway?

The sheriff's eyes bored into hers, a misleading stillness that reminded Sally of a crouched lion, its twitching tail the only clue that it was poised to attack.

Sally closed her eyes. She just needed to tell the story. This man would take it all in, then decide what to do with her. She dug through her purse, past a notepad, a glasses case. On the third fishing expedition, she pulled out Rufus's wallet, slick with age. She flipped it open and handed it over. "On November 22, 1963, I murdered this man."

"How do you recall the date?"

Images of the handsome president, the beautiful first lady, a black Cadillac convertible, took control. When Rufus struggled to get his turn, Sally responded by visualizing Ella. Willie. She had to do this. "Kennedy's assassination."

Other than his brows scrunching up, the man barely moved. "Go on." He said it so softly, Sally wondered if she'd imagined it.

She crossed and uncrossed her legs. "See, we moved here that summer. One day, when I went down by the bayou, this man—Rufus—followed."

"Had you had previous acquaintance with the victim?"

"No . . . Yes." Sweat trickled down Sally's arms. The lies begged to take control; she struggled to fend them off. She only wished she could do the same to the awful image of Rufus, leering from his perch in that truck. "I was walking to school. It was the first day. I got lost. He exposed himself to me." Now that the words were out, Sally felt like she could breathe. "So if that counts, I had previous acquaintance with him."

The sheriff nodded. "Go on."

Sally licked her lips. *Here's where it gets tricky. Don't lie, but don't implicate Ella, either.* "I didn't see him for weeks. Then one day—a really hot day, if I remember right . . ." A warning bell went off. *You're doing it again. Taking a bit of truth, watering it down with descriptors until it's fiction.* "I went down to the bayou."

"By yourself?"

I did go down by myself. When Sally nodded, shaggy strands of hair flopped over her eyes. "It was kind of a getaway. I was upset over the president's death. And it was hard, being new at school."

The sheriff grunted in a noncommittal way. "What happened next?"

"No sooner had I got there than he came up behind me."

"Rufus?"

"'You're not getting away this time,' he said." Sally studied the wall of framed certificates and diplomas, which confirmed that the man sitting here was no fool. "In a flash, he was on me." The words flowed out now, fueled by the images that she couldn't seem to erase. When she'd finished, she folded her hands into her lap and studied shredded cuticles. She'd done her best. An odd kind of peace had settled in.

Stifling a yawn, the sheriff unfolded his legs. "An interesting story, Mrs. Stevens," he said, crossing his legs again.

Sally bit her lip. She needed to be careful here, very careful.

"However, there's a couple of things I'm not quite clear on." His voice was a monotone, as if they were discussing the sweltering Louisiana heat. "Tell me, how did you, a mere girl, manage to get Mr. Beauregard off you, find a rock big enough to be a deadly weapon, and smash it onto his head with enough force to kill him?"

Sally went numb all over. *God, forgive me, but I can't do it.* She had to tell the truth and implicate Ella or lie and keep her out of it. Otherwise, he wouldn't buy her story. Her heart clanked like an anchor against the side of a ship in a sea of silence. She had to do something, or the silence would sink her.

"I know it's hard to believe, but for some reason—I'd call it a downright miracle—he rolled off of me." She strafed her thighs with her fingernails. "That's when I did it—got the rock, I mean." Her eyebrows arched, she studied the sheriff's face. Nothing. Did the man even *blink?* Sally did, several times. "I know it's hard to believe—"

"Sho' nuff is, girl," came from the sheriff's reception area.

Sally jumped to her feet. How had they gotten here? What—

Ella and Willie, elbows jostling, burst into the inner office.

"Excuse me, ma'am. You can't go in there. You can't . . ." The office erupted with the thud of heels and shouts. Hands on holsters, Deputy Nelson and several other uniformed men shoved past Ella and Willie Lee.

There was a whir of brown as the sheriff flew toward the group. His silk tie didn't move, so securely was it held in place by an American flag tie tack. "Now, gentlemen, let's don't overreact," he said. "I told Ms. Taylor we were expecting them."

The officers' hands continued to hover about their belts. "But they should have waited—"

"Well, now they're in here, as we all can see. And I'm quite capable of handling them." A deft smoothing took care of one wrinkle in his trousers. "Thank you, gentlemen. You can go now."

It took a second stare by their boss to shake the men out of what looked like a hypnotic state. Footsteps finally echoed down the hall.

"Willie Ward, I presume." Sheriff Hamilton turned to Willie, nodding as if he were greeting a foreign ambassador. "AKA Willie Lee Lafitte."

Willie's mouth dropped open. "How did you know—"

"The newspaper pictures, Willie boy." The sheriff tapped his forehead.

"Once I see it, I've got it." He managed a serene smile. "Plus your sister's phone call didn't hurt."

Sally gasped. "You called?"

"Sure did." Ella's voice rang with a surety absent yesterday at the hospital. "I did some thinking about what you said."

In spite of all she'd done, Ella had listened to her? And called this sheriff, who knew *exactly* what she was doing all the time. What a sneak! Sally just sat there shaking her head. Nothing would surprise her now. Nothing.

Willie took his sister's hand and tucked it in his own.

"God worked good through what happened," Ella continued. "He allowed it all. But He won't allow me to hold this grudge. He won't allow us to keep this secret one more day."

"But I wronged both of you. Terribly. I . . ." Tears of joy, of regret, of thankfulness, mingled with the apologies Sally kept trying to offer.

"Lord, Lord, you were just a child." Ella pulled away from her brother and stepped toward Sally.

"We both were." Sally stumbled across the huge office, focusing on the perfectly sculpted face, the warm smile . . .

Ella threw her arms about Sally, pulling her into the friendship she craved. The friendship she'd once had.

"How could you do this for me?" Sally sobbed.

"Because we were both in on it. Swamp Sisters, remember?"

The reality of where they were and what they were supposed to be doing faded. They talked of Sally's kids, of Ella's career, of what had been, of what might have been. Sally wobbled to her seat, pulled out her billfold, and hurried back to Ella, fearing she'd disappear. "Look!" With a flip, her pride and joys were revealed. "Here's Suzi."

"Girl, she's so pretty!"

"And this is Ed."

"Look at those dimples. Just like yours!"

Sally's smile dimmed. Now wasn't the time to explain that they'd adopted her babies. She'd save it for another day. *But I will tell it, Lord. Oh, Lord, yes.*

The two talked and cried, cried and talked. Time seemed to lose its hold on both of them. After what seemed in one way like a second, in another way, like hours, the sheriff cleared his throat. "Ah, ladies . . ."

Ella was the first to jump up. "Heavenly days! We kept you waiting here . . ."

The sheriff waved the comment away. "Not at all. It's been my pleasure." He gave Willie a courtly nod. "Nice to meet a hero. However"—he strode to his desk and picked up a notepad and pen—"a few matters need to be cleared up."

Sally hurried forward. It was time to finish this. "It was my idea," she said.

In a flash, Ella was at her side. "We're coming clean. The truth, Sally."

Truth. It was as if God opened a portal from the past and let Sally take a peek at her lifelong descent into the pit of prevarication. *"Not me, Mama."* Sally had lisped, two front teeth missing. *"I'll come right back, Daddy. I promise."* Sally winced. There were the dimples and wide eyes of a first grader. *"No. I came straight home."* She was a teenager now, gum smacking in perfect harmony with lies pouring out of lips made shiny by cherry-flavored lip gloss. *"It was wonderful. It's no problem. I really mean it."* Now she was talking to Sam . . . to her children. Yes, she had lied, over and over again, even to her babies. Sally tried not to scream. Big lies, little lies, all kind of lies. She'd wasted half of her life lying.

". . . are you all right?"

The voices stopped, but Sally had to blink to erase the thousand images of little Sally, teenaged Sally, married Sally . . . lying through every stage. With that doggone smile on her face.

"Sally. Over here." Skilled nurse's hands guided Sally to the couch, then pushed her head to her lap. "Deep breaths, now." Her tone was all business too.

"I can tell you what you need to know, Sheriff." Somehow Ella managed to talk and massage Sally's neck at the same time. "It was the day Kennedy was shot. We had to sneak off to play together. They didn't want us to meet."

The sheriff's face became quizzical. "Who?"

"Everyone." Ella's snort shook the couch. "Blacks, whites, good, bad; all of 'em."

Those formidable eyebrows scrunched together and met in the middle of the sheriff's forehead. "Go on," he said.

Ella cleared her throat. "Sally—Mrs. Stevens got there first." Ella cast a sidelong glance at Sally. "Well, I take that back. I guess the man got there first."

"Do you know that for a fact?"

Ella shook her head.

"What happened next?"

"When I got there, he was on top of her."

"Had he penetrated her?"

Ella winced.

"As far as you could tell?"

"Yes," she finally said.

"And then?"

"I picked up a rock and hit him over the head with it."

Sally nodded, grabbed Ella's hand, and squeezed it. "Then she sorta fell apart," Sally said. With her friend holding her up like this, she could finish. And finish strong. She scooted to the edge of her seat. "Ella started screaming, 'They're gonna kill me,' and I screamed, 'No, they won't.'"

All that blood, the gray-flecked brain matter, clouded her mind, like a dust storm that blew in out of nowhere. Sally leaned against Ella. A squeeze from the softest hand got Sally back on track. "I picked up that bloody rock," she continued, "and slammed it on his head. Over and over and over until he went limp."

"Then we dragged him into the water."

Back and forth, like a well-rehearsed duet, the two women testified until the truth—the whole truth—had been told.

Occasionally Sheriff Hamilton asked a question, then jotted down some notes.

"I stashed his billfold in my bottom drawer. Even though Ella later begged me to turn it in, I . . . wouldn't." Sally, her voice nearly spent, sank into the cushions. She wanted to curl up and disappear, so heavily did the burdens of missed opportunities weigh her down. A sob cut through her, but no tears came. She was past crying.

Again, the soft hand touched Sally's shoulder. It felt no different than it had thirty-six years ago, when Ella and she had stood by each other in that dance line, their skin supple and elastic. But this time, Sally wanted the touch. This time, Sally needed the touch.

"It's all right, dear friend." All these years, and Ella seemed to understand.

Dry heaves wrenched out of Sally. After all that she had done, Ella called her a friend. Her eyes closed again. *Thank You, God. Oh, my Lord, my God . . .*

"I could'a come forward too." The hand continued its healing touch. "Don't take this all on yourself."

"Well, you both have come forward now. And it presents some, ah, dilemmas."

Sally bolted upright, more at the tone of the sheriff's voice than his words. They weren't out of this yet. Would they have to serve time, after all these years?

"I need to get the wallet." Hamilton extended long, gracefully tapered fingers. "And have you sign some documents."

The two women complied.

"And there may be something else." The sheriff flashed a hundred-watt smile at Sally, then Ella.

"Like what?" Ella's voice boomed sudden doubt, tinged with anger.

"But . . . but . . ." Sally could only stare at the man who was holding their lives in the palm of his well-manicured hand. What was his agenda in all of this?

Ella's hands flew to her hips. "What do you plan to do with us?" she asked, her voice edged with steel.

"Ms. Ward, Mrs. Stevens, please." When the sheriff stood, he became the subject in his own perfect still life—backdropped by the Ellis Wilson painting, the massive mahogany desk, and the wall full of accolades and declarations of his achievements in a world that, thirty years ago, would have killed him for trying to attain his current status. "I need to make a few phone calls, talk to a few people." Moving noiselessly, he was at their side, an imposing figure at point-blank range. Dark eyes flickered in response to the sun pouring in the office window. "Please be reassured that I'm on your side."

Sally grimaced, knowing a liar when she heard one. He was a politician, on his own side.

When the sheriff offered his hand to first Ella, then Sally, they rose from the couch and let him steer them out of the office. Willie followed close behind.

The way Hamilton strode down the hall, his shoulders pushed back, the folder tucked under his arm, Sally, Ella, and Willie became part of his entourage. It was not a bad thing to be swept up into a powerful presence. He was going to take care of them, wasn't he?

They marched into another office, where it seemed the air was at least ten degrees cooler than in the sheriff's office. Keyboards stopped clicking; uniformed men paused in mid-stride. Sally could visualize the questions behind the raised eyebrows, the dazed expressions.

"Ms. Taylor, would you please show these former esteemed citizens of Monroe into the lounge." In spite of the "please," it was an order, not a request.

"But—but—"

"If they're hungry, send someone out for some food."

"But—"

"If they want to go for a little spin, take them. Ditto if they want to shop."

Ms. Taylor nodded.

"Thank you so very much." Having paralyzed a dozen people, the sheriff strolled toward his office, then turned to the frazzled-looking Ms. Taylor. "Have Records pull up the files on the murder of Rufus Beauregard; the arrested adult, Willie Lee Ward. Key in '63, '64."

The woman blanched, as if he'd asked her to go to the moon. "Microfilm, microfiche—"

"Everything."

"And when might you need this?" she huffed.

"Yesterday." The doors and the secretaries, especially Ms. Taylor, seemed to shudder as the sheriff banged his way back toward his art museum/office, removing his formidable presence from the room.

Chapter 30

BEHIND THE SCENES

We've come a long way, Lord, a mighty long way.
—Negro spiritual, "We've Come a Long Way"

H ey." Sam did his best to keep his voice light, carefree, like Sally always did. Or like Sally used to do, until their world went crazy.

"Dad? My roommate gave me your message. "

"Suzi, uh, something's come up. Mom needs us."

"Did she get sick down there? Did someone—"

Sam cringed. The last thing he wanted to do was alarm Suzi. But if he didn't stress the seriousness of this, how would he convince her to take the next flight south? Might as well get some practice with Suzi. Next he had to call Ed's school. Even though he'd never been good, like Sally, at multitasking, he shuffled papers into folders, scratched out a memo as he explained this thing to Suzi. A glance at his Timex told him if he got a move on, he and Ed could be headed south in an hour.

◆ ◆ ◆

Hand in hand, Ella and Sally tripped down the path that, over forty years ago, had been the secret playground of the Swamp Sisters. It was like a dream, except Sally wasn't sure whether it was a bad dream or a good dream. She stubbed her foot on a tree root, keeled forward, and might have fallen except for Ella's steadying hand. Ella again, helping her. There for her.

The deputy, impassive behind mirrored sunglasses, her hefty body looking even heftier in belted police-issue pants and shirt, tromped through the brush-entangled trail. Like she and Ella used to do, until that November day.

The stabbing in Sally's chest got worse when they maneuvered around the final curve. Years fell away like the petals on a fading magnolia. She was eleven again.

Hello, the stilts whooped.

Come, come, the trees rustled.

Frogs popped out of murky waters, their eyes bulbous and unblinking.

Its body skimming the surface, grace disguising the poison in its fangs, a snake swam to greet them.

You're home, they all sang, the music roaring in Sally's ears. She longed to kneel right here on the path and sink her hands into the Louisiana gumbo, which was rich and black and smelled of peat and oil and . . . life. It smelled of life.

When the three women rounded a bend, the bayou came into view, its dark waters catching glints of the few rays of noontime sun that had managed to break through the canopy of trees.

Sally stepped closer, the marshy land sucking her in as though she were its next meal. Closer, closer, she stepped even though her mind screamed for her to stop before it was too late.

There he was, all bone and sinew, perched on a fallen log. A faded baseball cap hid all but the mean mouth.

She wouldn't let him do it this time. A rumble began in Sally's throat. "N-no . . ."

Ella tightened her grip on Sally's sleeve. "It . . . is . . . not . . . *him*." Her mouth had opened wide, but the words were coming out like the slow speed on an old phonograph.

"No!" Sally screamed. She shoved Ella away and, breath coming in heaves, she plowed toward Rufus. Somehow he'd resurfaced—meaner, uglier, ready to rape another little girl. Sally ground her teeth together. She'd stop him this time.

With a thud, she ran into a wall that smelled of . . . powder and starch and—

"It's all right, now, ma'am."

Where—where am I? The bayou scene had tilted upside down.

"You're safe now, ma'am. No one's gonna hurt you."

The deputy's voice righted the topsy-turvy world, but it was Ella's touch that brought Sally around. She blinked, then raised her head. Rufus had disappeared. In his place was an old fisherman as gnarled and wrinkled as the cypress roots that curled under his feet. A cigarette dangled from his mouth, and he studied the bayou with what Sally could only believe was a feigned disinterest in the hysterical woman not ten yards away.

"You're okay," Ella reiterated.

Sally nodded, though her heart told her Ella was only partially right. Years ago, she'd given her life to Jesus. This trip had convinced her to give her lies to Jesus. But one more load had to be placed on the shoulders of the One who had saved the world: her rape. It was the only way she could be whole again and free to love her Sam as he deserved to be loved.

Ella's hug started the tears flowing again, tears of relief and joy. She and Ella were safe here. And with God's help, perhaps Rufus could be buried forever.

"Away we'll sail on a silver boat . . ." Ella started the chorus, and Sally soon joined in. Even though the pirogue had probably rotted out long ago, Sally imagined them paddling a make-believe boat, their cupped palms for oars. Singing and laughing, no Rufus or racism or rape to cloud their perfect day.

"With the cockleshells and silver bells all in a row." Ella led, both in song and footsteps, as she had years ago. They strolled along the bank, years ebbing away, conversation flowing in, enriched by the nutrients of time and trials and forgiveness. Sally didn't care that cockles and burrs stuck to her socks and mud clogged the heels of her shoes. She was with Ella, after thirty-six years. And they had come home.

◆

This grand old school hasn't changed, at least on the outside. And that's a good thing. As she climbed out of the patrol car, Sally darted a look at the deputy who stared straight ahead, her fists on the steering wheel. *But Ouachita Parish law enforcement sure has. Women and a black sheriff . . . Maybe there's changes inside Neville's walls too.*

Feeling wobbly, Sally edged close to Ella. They veered around the circular memorial garden that welcomed visitors to the old high school. Were she and Ella visitors or proud alumni? Sally wasn't sure.

The American and state flags whipped in the wind, an incongruous mixture of whites, reds, golds, blues, and some rather unrealistic-looking pelicans. She glanced twice at her friend, whose scowl could've been due to the bright sun in their faces or her discomfort at returning here. As if she understood

Sally's worry, Ella linked arms with her old friend, and they climbed the front steps. The two of them stood before massive doors, the same ones that had tried to keep black students out so many years ago. Sally's knees continued to shake as she managed to pull the doors open. Together they stepped into the foyer, right next to the glass display cases where she'd first determined to shun Ella.

A chill cut through Sally as they clacked down the ghostly quiet hall. Had things changed here? Or were African-American students still treated like a black fungus that would rush in and contaminate lily-white sons and daughters? She cut a look at Ella. How did it feel for Ella to return to the school that she'd been forced to attend? Could it ever, truly, be her school?

The bell rang. Doors flung open. Students clattered into the hall. Black students. White students. Everything in between. They surged toward the older women like a cleansing tide, their chatter bouncing off the lockers and hurting Sally's ears.

It started as a nudge. Then Sally put her arm around Ella and rested her head on a shoulder that had borne quite a few of the world's pains.

Ella giggled. Perhaps Sally's hair had tickled her nose. Or perhaps she was remembering that day, over thirty years ago, when even touching a black girl's shoulder seemed as bad as handling poison.

Their giggles escalated into laughter so raucous, so uncontrolled, that kids stared. And when the two of them linked arms and did an impromptu high kick routine, middle-aged torsos wiggling and jiggling, the whole hall howled. Black kids. White kids. And everyone in between. As Sally held tight and tried to match kicks with the tallest dancer of the first squad of integrated Bengal Belles, she hoped, she prayed, if only for this magical moment, that Neville High was Ella's school too.

◆

Ms. Taylor pounded her keyboard as if that would exorcise the morning's strange occurrences. "He asked that y'all just go on back."

Ella nodded, then forged a path for herself and Sally through the door, down the hall, and into the sheriff's reception area. Sally mopped her brow, wondering what the next step in this whole confession process would be.

"Just make yourselves at home," came a voice from the inner sanctum.

In a sheriff's office? Sally paced about the room, too nervous to flip through a pile of *Architectural Digest* magazines, but Ella plopped down and pulled out her cell phone. "Gonna call my mother. We're stayin' with her tonight."

"Oh, no. I couldn't—"

"You can, and you will." She punctuated her words with a snap-open of her phone. "Momma?" Ella practically yelled. Either Momma was deaf or nap-time drowsy. "No. No. We're here, Momma. Me and . . . a friend." Ella glanced at Sally, then, talking much more softly, slipped out the door and clicked it shut. Though Sally strained to hear, nothing seeped past solid oak but the lilt of Ella's voice. The windowed door revealed Ella's sweet-tea smile. No doubt Momma was getting an edited version of the day's events.

Sally couldn't help but think of the first—and last—time she'd met Ella's mother. As she had back then, over at the Browns' home, Sally felt like a wanderer in a foreign land. Most likely novelist Thomas Wolfe had been right when he'd said *you can't go home again*.

A dial tone buzzed through the background elevator music of Ella's voice. A click. Then a creak and a plop. Someone—the sheriff—sitting down?

"Macon County Sheriff's Department."

Sally eased her exhausted body into a leather chair but put her ears on high alert. It sounded like someone from Georgia was on the speakerphone with the sheriff.

"Records, please." Hamilton sounded hoarse, but perhaps it was the creaking, the rustling of what sounded like paper.

"Jes' a minute, suh."

Sally picked up a magazine, just so she'd look preoccupied and not overtly eavesdropping in case someone walked in.

"Johnson here."

"Well, good mornin'. What're you ole boys up to over there in Jo-Jah?"

Sally sat up straight. The person in that office sounded like a . . . hick.

"Nothin' much. Who's this?"

"Al. Over in *Mon*-roe. Loos-ana. Wash-tah Parish."

Al? In spite of his phony accent, that *was* the sheriff's voice. Sally smoothed down the glossy magazine cover. Something strange was going on.

"Well, now, y'all got y'all's hands full with that marble-mouthed mayor down there in N'Awlins, don't y'all?"

"Ain't that the truth?" It sounded like Sheriff Hamilton slapped his thigh.

"And that gov'ner of y'all's . . . 'bout what you'd expect from a *woman*."

Sally lurched forward, the magazine rustling about in her lap. She'd sure pegged the sheriff as a cultured sort, with that tailor-made suit, expensive art-work, even these fancy magazines. And maybe he was. Maybe a strange little game was being played.

For the next few minutes, the two men jawed like big-butt bigots, ripping FEMA officials, the already mentioned politicians, then a U.S. senator. Sally kept darting glances toward the hall. Ella really needed to hear all this. Or did she?

A raspy laugh set off more off-color jokes. Then the sheriff cleared his throat, which set the speaker box to squawking. "Speaking of piles of crap," he said, when the static died out, "I got a long-buried one I need you to drag outta the grave for me."

"Cold case?"

"Naw. One of those that's reared up and bitten where the sun don't shine."

Cackles hurt Sally's ears. What in the world was going on here?

"You're talkin' exoneration?"

"Uh-huh. It might get me off the hook for a little overtime problem. You know . . ."

"Well, sure," the man guffawed. "Ain't much goin' on around here today. I'm waitin' for Homer to get the boat gassed up. Crappie are bitin'."

"If it ain't too much trouble, I'd sure 'ppreciate it." Tapping joined the squeaks and shuffles coming from Hamilton's office. "You know the routine—last known associates, pending charges—what?" Still using that uneducated twang, the sheriff shared Rufus's statistics, having to spell Beauregard three times.

"Will do," the Georgia good ole boy purred after he finally got the name. "I'll get right back with you—what'd you say your name was?"

"Al. Here's my cell number. Just call me direct."

"Al" and his new redneck best friend yakked a bit longer. Then Sally heard a dial tone. She flipped open the magazine and did her best to act interested in an article about a postmodern tree house in Hilo, Hawaii. But then the speaker blipped again, the sheriff apparently making another call.

"Yeah." Irritation laced a male voice.

"Hamilton here."

"Believe me, I know your voice by now." A sigh set off static. "What's so important you got me out of bed before noon?"

"Late night news keepin' you in bed, or a certain blond?"

"That's classified." A smoker's hack—and the tacky comment—made Sally cringe.

"Now, Tom . . ." The cultured voice was back, with a drawl thick as molasses stored in the fridge. "I'm doin' you a favor. After all, I owe you one."

"You owe me two or three."

"That's right. That's right."

Sally fanned herself with the magazine. It was that old black affirmation, placating away. How *could* the sheriff do this?

"So what's going on?"

A sigh made its way to the outer office. "Maybe it was a bad idea. It's probably nothing. Just an old murder . . . an exoneration of Willie Lee Lafitte . . ."

"The Katrina hero?" Such excitement entered Tom's voice, Sally could picture him leaping from his bed—or his couch—and racing about, probably grabbing his pants off the floor.

"That's right." The tapping began in earnest. "Seems his sister and her white friend committed a murder back when they weren't supposed to even be talkin' to each other." Like he was leaning on a porch rail, dangling a gossipy tidbit, the sheriff's voice had gotten temptingly quiet. "Course I ain't callin' it a murder, Lawd, no!" He stifled a laugh to gush more Southern colloquialisms. "Look like self-defense to me. But you know the DA . . ."

"Do I ever." Thoughts of the DA, or a need for a cigarette, set off another hack.

"Anyway, those ladies—quite photogenic, I might add—want to confess."

"Where?"

"Here."

"There?" the man screeched.

"I'll let you know the details later. Probably on the courthouse steps. Or in the DA's office."

A howl came across the speaker. "You mean your future office?"

They cackled as if they'd overdosed on laughing gas. Then a dial tone sounded—again.

The magazine became a sunshade for Sally's face.

"Ah, Mrs. Stevens." The cultured voice had returned. Sheriff Hamilton strode into the outer office, brushing at his lapels as if he'd walked near a construction zone and gotten bits of mortar and dust blown on him. And it was fitting, because his image had become a bit clouded, at least to Sally.

She darted a glance toward Ella, who was smiling now, and cupping her phone near her ear. This man seemed too together to allow someone to eavesdrop on his conversation. No, he'd intentionally had her listen in on those good ole boy tête-à-têtes. A free primer for the female pumps. Sally didn't really like this exercise, and she didn't think Ella would either, but they didn't have any choice but to play Hamilton's game.

"Your secretary said you wanted to see me—us." Sally faked a yawn and fanned herself with the magazine, though her heart roared like a Harley.

"Yes." The sheriff pulled a leather memo pad and a gold pen from his breast pocket and flipped it open. "There's a press conference in the morning. I'd like you ladies to be here at ten o'clock sharp. We'll walk down together." Dark eyes drilled into hers. "After I prep y'all."

◆

"Momma's fine with it. In fact, she can't wait." The two women headed toward Sally's car, Willie having taken Ella's.

I'll just bet. Sally grimaced at yet another hurdle. But this one, too, was long overdue.

Her cell phone rang. She pulled it out, and, recognizing Shamika's number, flipped open her phone. "Hey, girl!"

"Where are you?"

"Actually, I'm headed to Ella's."

"Y'all have made up?"

"Yeah. She's right here with me."

"She is? She *is*?"

"Uh-huh. And we're going through with it."

"She's gonna confess too?"

"We already have. And tomorrow we're announcing it to the world—" a twinge ran through Sally. Would she ever be able to break this habit? "Let me correct that," she added. "Actually, it's just a little press conference here in Monroe."

This pause was so long, Sally wondered if the connection had been lost.

"I'm—I'm sorry, Sally. For everything I said."

Sally softened to envision the big brown eyes, the trembling chin. "Oh, it's me who's sorry, dear girl. And I'll explain it later. We have lots of catching up to do."

◆

Price glanced twice at his caller ID. It was Shamika, all right.

"Uh, Mr.—Detective Price?"

"Yes."

"There's something I need to tell you. It's about my case."

Well, well. "Where are you, Sham—Ms. Williams?"

"In New Orleans. About to head up to Monroe."

He'd known they'd left, but New Orleans? "Well, I'll be . . . You're headed to Monroe?"

"Well, yeah. See, it's only about five hours from here, and—"

"Why Monroe?"

"Tomorrow, Mrs. Stevens and an old friend of hers are gonna confess—"

He was having trouble hearing her. "Confess? Confess to what?"

"A murder. And I need to confess to something too."

"What are you talking about?" He tensed to catch every drawly syllable. What had happened to her voice? She was sounding like that teacher.

"I lied to you."

Well, well, well. Like a jigsaw, evidence pieces were interlocking nicely. "You really need to come down to the station for this. When will you be back?"

"I don't know. But . . . until then . . . I'm really, really sorry."

"Well—what—" The sugar in her tone threw him off; he couldn't believe what he'd heard. Those pouty lips apologizing?

"Anyway, Auntie's hollerin' at me."

That I can believe.

"Detective Price?"

"Uh-huh."

"Thanks for everything."

There was a click. Price just stood there, staring at the receiver, shocked at what he'd heard. Shocked at what he was considering. The buzzing of his clothes dryer jolted him back to the present. He'd better get his rear in gear. He made his way to his computer chair, stepping over an Everest-sized pile of dirty laundry. His jaw tight, he clicked on Mapquest and weather.com and a couple of other sites. When was the last time he'd done something impulsive?

Images of his first, then his second wife flashed before him, and he shoved them away. Personal life aside, he'd been commended, both officially and unofficially, for being dependable. Sensible. Rational. And now he was going to take a personal day, hop in the car, and venture down South for the first time in his life, to some hick place called Monroe, Louisiana, ostensibly to reinterview

301

a complainant. But what really drove him to do this was something he could not explain. He printed out directions and hurried to get his Dopp kit. Something was going on here that was bigger than him, better than him. And he wanted to be a part of it.

Chapter 31

A Day for Truth

No frowns to defile, a big endless smile. Peace and contentment for me.
—Negro spiritual, "Peace in the Valley"

I t's gwine be okay." Ella's pat on the back encouraged Sally as they waited for Sheriff Hamilton to join them in the Annex Building foyer. This morning, Ella's mom had been just as reassuring after serving them a breakfast akin to a death row inmate's last meal. Sally groaned, not just from the thought of what the DA might do, but from a stomach made leaden by sausage and grits and fried eggs and biscuits. For the last hour, the sheriff had primed them and prepped them until Sally felt like one of his well-trained staff members. Showtime had come, and she'd better be ready to perform.

Smoothing back perfectly groomed hair, Hamilton trotted down the steps and nodded at her and Ella. "All right, ladies. Come along." They huddled on each side of him, iron filings drawn to a magnetic presence; not just his blocky build, but his sure, quiet smile and strongly set jaw. Sweat trickling down her back, Sally struggled to match his gigantic stride as they exited the building. Somehow in the blur of blue and white and green, Sally spotted her rental car in the parking lot, alongside all the official vehicles, and fought an urge to hop in it and drive north. Now that she'd confessed, would she be a fugitive if she left?

As if the sheriff understood, he tucked her hand so securely into his palm that his ring bit into Sally's knuckles. One, two, three . . . She willed herself to move forward.

The first *click* and *whirr* made Sally wince. She hadn't thought of this. Out of the corner of her eye, she spotted a photographer, kneeling near the bottom step of the courthouse. A camera rested on his denim-clad leg. What if her family saw this before she had a chance to tell them? But they wouldn't get Louisiana news up north, would they?

"Don't look at 'em," Ella whispered, sensing Sally's anxiety.

"How . . . how do I avoid it?" Sally's voice quavered.

The sheriff squeezed her hand as they reached the top step, where a podium awaited. He set a folder on the podium and looked out toward the river—and the crowd. "Find a friendly face out there." Somehow he managed to broadcast a smile and talk at the same time. "Don't take your eyes off of that face. Let it be your audience of one."

He sounds like Daddy. Sally was still searching for a friendly face when two men and a woman, all clad in dark suits, walked through a quickly amassing crowd and trudged up the steps.

"Henry. Jason. Ms. Stanley." Turning slightly so he faced the cameraman, the sheriff introduced Sally and Ella to Henry, the DA, and his assistants. They all shook hands and stood together.

A hot wind blew Sally's hair into her face, blurring her vision and scratching her eyes.

The sheriff nodded toward the cameraman—cameramen, Sally noted—and edged close to a microphone. Manicured hands rested on the podium. His gaze seemed to study the past, the present, and the future, dispelling any doubt that she was safe with this man in control.

"Forty-two years ago, two girls, one black, one white, broke through the racist wall that society had erected around them."

Cameras clicked wildly. "They did this to rid this city of a vulture. A vulture that raped, then murdered at least one little girl; maybe as many as a dozen more."

Find a friendly face. While brushing back a mess of tangles, Sally scanned gaping mouths, goggling eyes, searching for someone, anyone, who could help her get through this.

From the folder, the sheriff withdrew an enlarged photo of a face that Sally'd seen in one too many nightmares, an image that still made her shudder. "A vulture who left a bloody trail from here to Georgia." The sheriff paused to smile at both women. "It took the bravery of two heroines, whose hearts made up for the size of their little bodies . . ."

Her face burning, Sally averted her gaze from the sighing, murmuring people. She'd been a coward of the biggest order, and an innocent man had paid for her silence. On the verge of crying out, she remembered the sheriff's words: Find a friendly face. Desperate for rescue, she searched, searched, found . . . beautiful blue eyes, long brown hair pulled into a ponytail. Her eyes blurred, then focused again. It couldn't be . . . She tottered and might have fallen if the sheriff hadn't clamped down on her arm. It was Suzi. She blinked tears out of her eyes, then looked again. Ed. Sam.

The three people who meant more to her than anyone in the world gave Sally triple thumbs-ups. Speechless, standing only by the power of that immense forearm, she bowed her head and whispered a prayer.

"Without the help of our always proactive district attorney, the honorable . . ."

The sheriff's speech came to Sally in snatches, but she'd quit caring about what he was saying. Her family was here, and she could tell by the expressions on their faces that everything was going to be all right. She smiled at the cameramen, at the handsome young man standing by Suzi. She could smile at them all now, and would. She darted a glance to her left, to her right, then clenched the sheriff's suit sleeve. There was Shamika, her head on Ruby's shoulder. It had to be a dream. She bowed her head again, tears welling up. She didn't deserve any of this. But she'd take it. Lord, she'd take it.

". . . a new era, a new beginning for this catastrophe-plagued state that will spread justice and mercy to the far reaches of this great country. With brave women like Christella Ward and Sally Stevens, Louisiana will rise from the heaps of Katrina's debris to be a better place for our children, our grandchildren."

Applause roared in Sally's ears. Still she fixed her gaze on Sam, on Ed, on— was that young man's arm resting on Suzi's shoulder? Who was he, anyway? The wooziness returned full force; Sally fought it by focusing on the sheriff and his mesmerizing words.

"Ladies and gentlemen, I'm honored to shine the spotlight on District Attorney Henry Carter, one so reticent to speak, so willing to work tirelessly behind the front lines." The sheriff bowed as he stepped backward.

Scant applause ushered the short plump man with disproportionately large pink ears to the podium. "Thank you, thank you."

The microphone crackled, then let off an earsplitting squeal.

Cowering, Sally and Ella took a step back, toward the sheriff.

"There comes a time in the life of each individual when he must choose mercy and the spirit of justice rather than the letter of the law."

"Right on!" shouted one supporter, followed by a sudden silence, as if the person realized he might be one of the DA's few friends.

"Today is my chance to fall in step on the trail of justice blazed by our sheriff and these lovely ladies." The DA leaned forward, sweat beading on his forehead.

Sally shifted her weight from one foot to the other and stifled yet another desire to wipe away pools of sweat. Her eyes caught Sam, her Sam, and an ache started deep within her. She longed to crush herself into his cotton T-shirt, to feel his arms around her, to have him massage her shoulders, tell her that he'd forgiven her for everything. And could he? Would he? Could they light a fire, with some professional help, under the sputtering candle that her childhood trauma and age had dimmed? She swallowed hard. She had to, not only for Sam's sake, but for hers.

". . . for that reason, Sheriff Hamilton and I concur that, despite the dearth of corroborating evidence to support these women's stories—uh, testimony, we must stand as one before you in refusing to file charges." He glanced back at the sheriff, as if he needed affirmation, and received a slight nod.

"And to petition the governor of our great state to pardon Willie Lee Ward." Wiping his forehead, the DA gripped the podium with white-knuckled hands.

The clapping started, tentative at first, like the grumbling of a storm when it first blots the sun with cold steel clouds. It made a tinny sound in Sally's ears. Did the crowd realize she'd sent Willie to prison for twenty long years? That if she'd only come forward with her evidence, he might have lived a free life as a brilliant musician? She searched wildly for a friendly face. For Sam.

A figure darting through the crowd caught Sally's attention. Something about the strident yet stealthy steps, the crisp fatigues, caused Sally's breath to come in spurts. It couldn't be—tears streamed down now. It was Robert.

"And now, if there are any questions . . ." The DA stepped away from the podium and turned to Sally and Ella. His bulging eyes gave Sally the impression of a bulldog. "Could y'all . . . say something?" The bald spot on his head glistened. "Anything?" His breath smelled of garlic.

It took every bit of self-composure Sally possessed to keep from shaking her head and flinging herself down the stairs and into Sam's and Suzi's and Ed's and Robert's arms. She fought and conquered those impulses. "Not quite yet," she managed, her voice as wobbly as her legs.

"We'll talk about it and get back to you," Ella continued, the Swamp Sisters once again in sync.

As Ella and Sally took over the responsibility of holding each other up, the DA and the sheriff ended the press conference. The DA and his assistants hurried toward one of the cameramen; the sheriff stepped back to join her and Ella. "Good job, ladies. I applaud your courage." Both of them got what Sally thought was a photo-op pat on the back. He leaned close, a marvelous evergreen scent coming with him. "Now, y'all don't have to talk to any of 'em. Or you can talk to all of 'em."

Ella and Sally exchanged knowing glances. *Like you will.*

They both hugged the sheriff, then linked arms and descended the courthouse steps. Ella beelined for Willie, whose long arms had opened as if to receive the whole world. And hadn't she been his whole world? Hadn't—

"Thank you, Sheriff, for taking care of her."

"My pleasure."

Tears glazed Sally's eyes, but she didn't need the sheriff's arm anymore, the sheriff's reassuring voice. For another voice had risen out of the cluster of folks near the bottom step. It was the voice that had wooed her twenty-seven years ago, the voice that had soothed her when that blue baby had been wrapped in a blue blanket and carried away, the voice that had thrilled her when the adoption papers got approved, the voice that, in spite of all they'd been through, she wanted to hear until she closed her eyes to this earth and all its troubles.

One, two, three steps, and Sam's arms were around her, his lips on her forehead, in her hair. He delivered many messages with his touch, but the one Sally heard the loudest was *I forgive you.* "Mom! Dad! Come on!"

The giggles reminded Sally of times when ugly memories hadn't been able to spread stench over her and Sam's passion. There had been fire in their relationship. And there would be again. Reluctantly, she pulled away from Sam, not because she wanted to, but because their PDA was embarrassing her kids.

"Mom! Oh, Mom! Why didn't you tell us?" Suzi and Ed joined Sam, forming a tent around their mother, shielding her from the Louisiana sun and the curiosity seekers and perhaps a camera or two.

With trembling hands, Sally tousled the silky ponytail of her eldest, then the coarse mop of her baby, who looked a bit peaked. Biting back a barrage of Mom questions—how's school, don't you need a haircut, when's your next match, did you miss me—Sally basked in the glow from eyes that broadcast no condemnation. And where there was no condemnation, judgment was absent, and they could move forward.

Sally's sigh washed away a thousand questions. There was so much to do, now that things had calmed down a bit. She wanted them all to meet Ella and

Willie. And Shamika and Ruby, who'd been right over—"Just a minute, Sam, Ed, Suzi. There's someone I want y'all to meet. Someone . . ." Sally searched through a dwindling crowd. Things were getting things back to normal— Normal. Her home.

"Mrs. Stevens?"

Sally whirled at the familiar voice of the precious girl who'd been stained just like she had. Stained but on the road to healing, if Sally had any say in it.

Spiky heels and extensions added half a foot to Shamika's ladderlike physique. She flew into Sally's hug, settling her bony arms about Sally's shoulders. "I'm so proud of you." Her lips brushed Sally's cheek.

Guilt assailed Sally. If she'd shared her story sooner, could she have stopped Shamika's lies? "Don't be proud of me," she mumbled.

Shamika's jaw became a jutting shelf. "I am. You did what's right, you know. And I'm doing that too."

Sally couldn't handle another thing. "You mean you're going to . . ."

Shamika's smile freed up the closed-off parts of her angular face. "I already have." She gestured toward Ruby and . . . Sally did a double take. It was Detective Price, scratching at the nape of his neck like he had a heat rash.

"Never thought I'd see the day." Sally clasped the detective's hand. A warm hand. Smiling eyes. Had the Southern heat melted the detective, or had Someone, Something, warmed his heart?

Shamika edged in next to Detective Price. "He's gonna talk to his chief about it all. But whatever happens, I'm ready."

"You're not gonna wait forty-two years to come clean?"

Shamika covered Sally's hand with her own. "Huh-uh, thanks to you."

They hugged again, then Sally pulled out of Shamika's grasp. "Y'all have got to meet my husband, Sam. My precious kids." The sun mixed with glints of tears in Sally's eyes and dazzled her vision of the little group. Love, her desire to be forgiven, loosed her jaws and she yipped and yapped and hugged like family. And they were, now. They—

"Um, Mom . . ."

"Yeah, baby?" Sally pulled Suzi close, brushing back a strand of hair, staring at her face. Her mama detector buzzed, slowly at first, then louder. Louder. Something was wrong.

Suzi's cheeks flamed as she stared at the ground. "Mom, there's someone I want you to meet."

For the first time since she'd stood at the podium, Sally noticed the handsome young man. Who now had his arm wrapped around Suzi's waist. "Mom, this is Joseph Thomas, my boyfriend. He . . ."

The world tilted and spun and then reeled to a stop again, and somehow Sally managed to stand through it all. So this Joseph was the "friend" of the e-mails. The phone calls. Now a "boyfriend." Hadn't they just met? Her daughter . . . with a black boy?

"I e-mailed you to see if I could bring him home, but I never heard back. Then Dad called about . . . all this. And Joe . . ." Her face flushed an even brighter red, as if she saw through Sally's facade and knew her thoughts.

Years of proper breeding, of smiling no matter how she felt, took over. Sally offered a shaky hand. ". . . got you here, I assume," Sally finished for her daughter. "So nice to meet you, Joseph." But it wasn't nice. Not at all.

"You too, ma'am."

A little too quickly, Sally withdrew from the handshake. As she turned to speak to someone, anyone but this black boy, it hit her. Here she was, not only lying again, but picking up a brick and building a new wall of prejudice. Sure, the old Sally wanted to treat blacks as equals—on the surface, anyway—had wanted America to be *their* country too, wanted things to be nice and Christian. But the old Sally also felt Suzi was too good to be romantically involved with this seemingly very nice boy who had managed to zip her daughter across at least four states, her thinking based solely on the fact that he had dark skin.

She turned again, the smile gone, waited until Joe and Suzi finished a whispered conversation, then put a hand on Joe's shoulder. "Joseph, I—I'm—" Just in time, Sally swallowed down another lie. She had to do this. And it wasn't going to be easy. "I won't deny that this is a shock, Joseph." She worked hard to meet Joseph's clear-eyed gaze. "And as I'm sure Suzi's told you, we Stevenses are working through a couple of things. But I do appreciate this chance to get to know you." Her eyes sought out, and found, Suzi. "And I appreciate you getting her down here." When she took Joseph's hand this time, she gripped it with all the feeling she could muster.

She asked about Joseph's family, their trip, until Sam gently took hold of her shoulders and turned her to face Ella, who was trailed by camera-clicking reporters. Ella, gifting her with a smile so beautiful, it should be . . . on a coin.

Sally touched Ella's shoulder. "Could we all go out to lunch? I'd love for Willie and your mama to meet my Sam, my Suzi, my Ed. And . . . Joseph, Suzi's boyfriend."

Ella nodded. "Let's do this first, though." She tipped her regal head toward the entourage of reporters. "Get the hard stuff outta the way. Then the fun can begin."

"Ma'am, we'd like to get a shot of the two of you."

"Could you tell us how you met?"

"Who actually threw the first stone? Was it . . ."

As Ella addressed her subjects, Sally smiled, for the millionth time in her life. She smiled for all of them, the black, the white, the good, the bad. She smiled for what she did understand, didn't understand, and would never understand. She smiled for the things she had said, hadn't said, and, in the very near future, must say. And she prayed. Oh, how she prayed. And then she talked. And talked. And talked . . .

EPILOGUE

One year later

*H*ope it's not gonna be *"hairdresser."* Shamika glanced at her watch, then let the west wind push her into MCC's Career Placement Center. When she'd spoken to the counselor about changing her major, the woman spouted out a buncha nonsense 'bout a battery of tests. They'd tested her aptitude, her interest, her psyche—what seemed like a zillion tests, all biased toward WASPs, of course. Now she was here to have some WASP tell her what she was supposed to do with her life.

She stepped toward a reception desk, running her hand over a weave put in so tight, a hurricane couldn't mess it up. Too bad she couldn't tame her mood. "Good afternoon. I'm Shamika Williams." She used her business voice on a long hair who'd cleaned up his beard and wore a cheap suit. "I've got a two o'clock with Ms. Anderson."

He nodded. "She'll meet you in the conference room. Go through that door. It's the first room on your right."

Her high heels clicking on the tile, Shamika hurried down the hall. She needed to be outta here by three, at the latest, for her after-school shift at the Y. Thanks to Detective Price, who'd retired from the police force and had taken a new job as a probation officer, she'd worked out a plea agreement with the state attorney. They'd dropped charges of filing a false police report provided she logged fifty hours of community service. Just thinking of the rosy cheeks and wide grins of those kids put a groove in her get-up-and-go and shored up her mood. If she told the paper chasers how much she loved it, they might make her dig ditches or something.

The door was open, so she walked in.

"Hello, Ms. Williams. I'm Carol." A blond woman, her curly hair pulled back in a ponytail, jabbed a slender hand across the table as Shamika sat down.

"Hi. I'm Shamika." She shook the woman's hand, wishing she'd tone down that knuckle-aching grip, the "I'm sure I can help you" voice.

"Well, it's so nice to meet you—you're a sophomore, right?" Enthusiasm bounced that ponytail.

"Uh-huh. With the AP credits."

"I see." Carol showed horsy teeth when she smiled, which was about every other second. "And you're intent on a pre-law major?" The brow furrowed as she flipped through a folder.

What? You think I can't do it? "Yes," Shamika lied, unwilling to share her doubts with Ms. Perky, who was what—a year older than she was? She'd send Sally an e-mail, set up a coffee date. Talk this over with someone who mattered.

The chair scraped as Shamika scooted back. She made a point of looking at her watch, then shot a glance at Carol. "I really need to go. Just give me that—"

"Oh, no no no no no." Carol tsk tsk-ed with her pink tongue. "We don't allow files to be removed from the premises without a placement discussion."

Shamika fought the urge to snap like a turtle. Where did this woman think she was, Harvard? This was a podunk community college in a podunk town . . .

"But this really won't take long," Carol continued, batting thick eyelashes. "You see, unlike some students, whose scores are all over the place, your profile is quite easy to interpret."

Curiosity ate away at Shamika's resentment. She'd always thought of herself as complex. "It is?" she asked, not disguising her surprise like she usually did when she talked to white people.

Carol handed Shamika the booklet with all the little circles she'd spent hours filling in with a number 2 lead pencil. "Clear as a bell." The grin took over a pie-shaped face. "You were born to be a teacher. Not a doubt in my mind."

Shamika's jaw dropped. A teacher? She didn't have the patience to teach a baby Einstein, much less the brats in today's schools. And where was this white girl coming from, telling her what she was supposed to do with herself?

"If you'll look at . . ." Carol droned on, but Shamika was listening to another voice, a still, soft one, from God's Word, talking about teachers being held to higher standards. She looked at Carol but saw other faces, black and white, including the face of Sally, with her big blue eyes and multicolored, shaggy hair. Overwhelmed, she gripped her handbag. Now she saw not Sally, but Mrs. Channell, her old English teacher, the one who'd introduced her to Shakespeare. The cool old lady who must be a hundred by now. She blinked again, surprised at what she saw now: a roomful of squirmy, sweaty, bossy, mouthy kids . . . the students she'd one day teach.

"Well, all right, then." Shamika didn't have to fake enthusiasm, didn't have to fake respect as she moved around to sit by Carol to study the results. Maybe this woman knew what she was talking about. And even if she didn't, God did.

◆ ◆ ◆

Chicago Police Department. Records. Price grabbed a padded envelope out of his mailbox and headed back into his house. Just as he dug his nails into the thick mailing tape, his cell rang. He set down what he assumed were the files surrounding the death of Shamika's father and snapped his phone out of his pocket.

Area code 504. It was Willie, probably calling to give recaps on Sheriff Hamilton's mercurial rise through Louisiana politics, on the bog-down of rebuilding in New Orleans, on his twelve-step progress. The usual things they chewed on. Sometimes Willie talked Price through his TV dinner and a couple of drinks and eased him right into bedtime. He'd never had a friend like this, certainly never a black ex-con. Yep, that trip down South had been good in more ways than one.

"Yo, brother." Price hurried into his living room, eased into his recliner, and pulled up the footrest lever. Even though a gloomy November wind seeped through the cracks around his outdated casement windows, his laid-out body relaxed like he was sunning on a tropical beach.

"Have you heard the latest on Hamilton?"

"Huh-uh." He hated to tell Willie that Midwesterners didn't give two cents for the news about some small-town Southern politician, even if he was rising from the sludge of Louisiana politics faster than swamp gas.

"Got hisself appointed to a civil rights committee up in Washington. Yeah, dat brother's on the way up, and I ain't whistlin' Dixie. But dat ain't why—"

Roars of laughter and some twangy strains of Cajun music garbled Willie's last words.

"What's goin' on down there?" Price managed, when the noise eased off. "Sounds like a party."

"Ain't nothin' goin' on down here. 'Cept fishin' and crabbin' and relaxin' out here on the deck."

Price stared out the window at the steely gray day and shivered. "Sounds like a party to me." His mind's image of Willie in cutoffs and a T-shirt muted his enthusiasm over the call. Why did some guys get all the breaks?

"Ain't no party. Just Bobby and some of his pretty flyboys over for a spell."

Price chuckled. Robert Flowers had treated them like they were Air Force brass down in Monroe. And for a religious man, that Bobby kicked up his heels pretty high. Yep, he'd made two friends on that two-day blitz of a trip. More than he'd made in fifteen years down at the precinct. "Bound to be a party, with you two."

"Actually, it's a bid'ness meeting. And dat's why we're callin'."

"Business?" Price jerked up the lever on his La-Z-Boy and sat upright, feet planted firmly on his dusty floor. He could never quit being a cop, not if people always bugged him like this. And he'd thought Willie and Bobby were real friends.

"The Feds makin' a little dough available down here for small businessmen, and we're aimin' to get in on it."

"And you want to know if it's legal?" *Call a lawyer*, he almost said, jumping to his feet and pacing about the den.

"Hey, what's eatin' you, Price? We know it's legal. What we don't know is if a good ole boy from up North wants in."

"Wants in what?"

"Willie Lee Lafitte's Swamp Boat Tours and Fishin' bidness."

Laughter and static buzzed into Price's ear, and he held out the phone and stared at it, then cupped it over his ear like he was on undercover and it was his only connection to base. "I don't know nothin' about boats."

More laughter, and a tinny sound that told Price he was on a speakerphone. "You don't have to," somebody called out.

"You cut plenty of bait in your day. I guess that's enough."

Static again made Price cringe. He put the phone to his other ear and rubbed the sore one.

"Hey, Pricey?" It was Bobby now, inordinately loud. "Are you in or not?"

"Hey, what are y'all on down there?" he asked, stalling. Could he really dive into something like this?

"Nothin'. Just makin' the most of opportunities. We figure Willie can handle the day-to-day. My part? All the army brass swamping the area, actin' like they're helping with cleanup, need a little R & R, Southern style. I'll have 'em lined up like privates outside boot camp latrines."

"And what'll I do?" he yelled, then resisted an urge to slap his cheek. *Don't be so eager, Price. You're a cop.*

"You'll be our Northern connection. Set up some tours or somethin' for pasty ole boys who need a little Southern comfort. And not the kind outta a bottle."

Again, guffaws made him pull the phone away from his ears. And think.

First the new parole job. Now this. Price didn't know what was going on, if this God they all kept talking about was somehow behind this. But for the first time in his life, he was relinquishing skepticism and disbelief for the possibility of something exciting. Something . . . risky. Something—he'd use the word *passionate*, but that reminded him of his second wife.

They chatted a bit more. Then Price checked his watch and started the long, slow process of ending a telephone call with a Southerner. He had an hour till his meeting with Shamika, and he needed to go over that file. If her story matched the evidence, he figured he'd put a burr in some Windy City cop's behind. Or maybe some handcuffs on hands greasy from taking a bribe.

As he said good-bye and pocketed his phone, he realized that in spite of these new opportunities, a part of him would always be a cop. But he'd do it on his terms now . . . or maybe God's terms. Yeah. He'd have to ask Bobby about that, next time they talked. Which, if they were gonna be business partners, would be pretty soon.

◆

Beep. Beep. Beep. A year of five-day-a-week, twelve-hour shifts. And I can't grab a cup of liquid lead without them breathin' down my neck. Ella turned off her squawking pager and yanked a cup off the top of a foot-high Styrofoam tower. This coffee was as thick and nasty-lookin' as that floodwater that swirled closer, closer, in her nightmares. Her stomach churning, Ella plodded over to the couch, the site of last year's drama. Oh, she'd crested those waves of cameras snapping, Willie and Sally and her beaming. She sipped coffee, then grimaced. Willie moving out had been bittersweet. For more years than she wanted to count, she'd poured whatever energies remained after her job, her church, into Willie. Thank God he was clean. But it was hard to open the door of a sterile apartment here in Thibodeaux and see nothin' but empty rooms, blank walls, a rented bed. Katrina had blown away her every possession. Mama's old Bible. The last of Daddy's tools. And in an odd way, Katrina had carried off Willie too.

Ella swallowed hard, not just to get the coffee down, but to hold in a sob. Then she raised her chin, straightened up her back. She'd insist on some time off. Get up there to Normal. At least that'd shut up her crazy friend. But she'd never liked traveling alone. Not that she'd ever traveled much.

She tried to drink more coffee, but it just wouldn't go down. Sighs accompanied her to the sink. She dumped out the coffee, dumped the cup in the trash. Turned on her pager. She was a nurse, after all. And things still hadn't settled in after that witch of a storm. Maybe they never would settle in. Maybe—

"Miss Ward?"

It couldn't be . . . Wasn't he in Baton Rouge, with the big boys? She leaned against the counter, not caring that water spots were dampening the front of her uniform, then whirled about, thanks to what that voice had done to her heart.

"I didn't mean to startle you." The same voice that had soothed death rattles from gasping throats, that had calmly yet firmly requested clamps and scalpels and trocars, spoke to her now. "They paged you, but for some reason, it didn't go through."

Because I turned it off, she bit back. Why was Dr. Powers here in Thibodeaux? Her legs refused to move. Probably a state inspection. Or did he think he'd talk her into goin' back to work in that nightmare-inciting place?

"Come sit down." The doctor guided Ella to the couch, and it was then that she felt the tremble in his arm.

"I really need to get back." Now *her* lip trembled for some fool reason.

From out of nowhere a hand found hers. "You need to get back. And I need you back."

Anger sizzled from her scalp to the feet inside her clogs. Every hospital in this state needed licensed nurses. Unlicensed ones, in some of the desperate places. And what made him think she'd just pick up and move because the great Dr. Powers wanted her down there?

"I'm quite content here in Thibodeaux." Guilt made her tug on her lip with her snag tooth. Lying didn't come easy to her like it did to Sally—like it *used* to come to Sally.

"Are you?" He moved closer to her, a rolled-up shirtsleeve brushing her shoulder. Setting it on fire.

She nodded and turned her head. He didn't need to see the loneliness in her eyes. Or the dad-blasted tears.

"Christella. Baby . . ."

A sob caught in her throat; she quickly disguised it as a hiccup. No one had sweet-talked to her like that since . . . Daddy. And he'd been dead and buried for years. The huskiness in Dr. Powers's—Reginald's—voice sparked every neuron, every proton, every electron in her body.

A surgeon's fingers found her chin and turned it to face eyes heavy with compassion. Concern. She'd seen it when he'd talked to the families of the deceased. The patients facing a death sentence.

"I need you." His voice quivered more than it had on that awful night. "Not as a nurse, Ella. As a woman. To have and to hold, from this day forward."

Confusion and doubt made her scoot away from him. "But . . . but . . . we haven't courted, we haven't . . ."

"I've known you for eleven years. Seen the good of you. The bad of you. The ugly of you." He chuckled in that low, deep way that caressed her heart. "Not that there's much of any of that." He slid so close, a prescription pad couldn't have been wedged between them, then wrapped his arms around her. Smooth lips found hers.

Yearning such as she'd never known, never allowed herself to know, made her moan out loud. She pulled away, shocked at what she was doing, right here in the break room.

"I—I need to think about it," she gasped, even though she didn't really mean it. That sassy girl she'd once been had dreamed of becoming a doctor; never a doctor's wife. But God had *His* dreams for her, didn't He? And God had timed it perfectly, what with Willie not needing her, what with loneliness hollowing her out till she was an empty shell. No, she didn't need to think about it at all.

"And it's just possible that a slot will open up for a part-time instructor—"

Sam leaned across the arm of his chair and squeezed her hand. *You're exaggerating,* he said in Sam-Sal.

Sally glanced at Dr. Evans, who thankfully was busy scribbling notes and didn't seem to notice their little marital text-messaging. "I mean, I could teach literature or humanities or—"

Sam squeezed her hand even harder.

Sally focused on the counselor's perfectly cut bob to keep from yanking her hand out of Sam's. By squeezing twice, in classic Sam-Sal, he'd told her to shut up, and she really didn't know why—yes, she did. Midwestern would never let her set foot on their campus again, at least not in a teaching capacity. She sighed. Breaking her lying habit was about to break her.

Their therapist adjusted cool black spectacles that made her look smart and cute. Then she tucked a loose dark strand behind her ear. "If that avenue remains . . . closed, do you foresee working on your novel and teaching that new couples' class—what is it called?"

"Marriage, Up Close and Personal," Sam chimed in, his hand back in his lap. "It's for people struggling with . . . intimacy in their marriage. And not just . . ."

"In their sex life." Sally couldn't help but smile at Sam's reticence to say the word "sex," even after all they'd been through. And of course cautious Sam had been reluctant to agree to coteach with Sally after the elders had refused to accept her resignation from leadership and teaching positions. But she'd talked him into it, and now he couldn't wait for Thursday nights, when half a dozen couples showed up at their house. Then there was the new neighborhood group, and cooking frenzies with Maureen, which had been expanded to include a Hispanic woman, and a black woman—

"Yes. Well, do you see those things advancing your career path? Your interests?"

Sally and Sam eyed each other, Sally seeing dollar signs in Sam's eyes. "They're advancing everything but our bank account." Sally studied her hands, then picked at a cuticle until Sam cleared his throat and tapped her hand, Sam-Sal for, "Stop it!"

"And with Ed attending ISU, with Suzi and Joseph's wedding next summer, money's a problem," Sally continued.

"We'll get by." Sam put his arm around Sally, comfort talk in any language. "We always have. And with God's help, we always will."

Dr. Evans closed the folder, then took off her glasses and laid them on her desk. "I think we're about done here." She rose, leaned forward, and shook both their hands. "Of course, if you need to . . . revisit any issues, just schedule an appointment. However, at this point I see no reason to continue our monthly sessions. I'm comfortable about releasing you to 'consult on an as-needed basis.'"

Arm in arm, they left the office, a cold wind shoving them to their car. Another monstrous winter had been predicted, baring icy teeth and puffing chilling winds. With the pressure of the wedding, the graduation, the occasionally frigid sex life, storms still threatened. But the guerilla attacks of lies and subter-fuge and denial had been flushed out. And truth and hope and dozens of other weapons in God's arsenal would help them prevail. Sally gave Sam a Sam-Sal squeeze. *We're gonna make it, honey. No matter what.*

Author's Note

In contrast to my first novel, *An Irishwoman's Tale*, which was inspired by a true story, *What the Bayou Saw* is primarily a fictional text. However, several key events in the novel draw from the oral narratives of specific Southern women.

Sheila Flanagan, assistant director of the Museum of Mobile, provided the inspiration for Ella. During the 1960s, Sheila, a resident of a section of Mobile called Toulminville, befriended her next-door neighbor, a little girl who happened to be white. When both sets of parents forbade the girls to play in each others' yards, the girls kept their friendship alive by sticking toys through a chain-link fence and engaging in parallel play. This image of two hands, one brown, one white, reaching through steel links, captured my heart and mind and prompted me to begin this novel.

It was pure joy to fictionalize my early years as the daughter of one of Baylor's dorm directors. I have such fond memories of living on a campus made fascinating by bears and beanie caps and the Noze Brotherhood.

The setting of Monroe, Louisiana, was chosen because I lived there during the 1960s and early 1970s and desired to incorporate personal experiences into the text. However, when I "moved" Ella from Mobile to Monroe, research showed that with very few exceptions, Monroe residents lived in separate neighborhoods, blacks entering white neighborhoods only as hired help. Thus, Ella's mother became the maid for the fictional Brown family, allowing Sally to meet both Ella and Willie.

I relied heavily on oral narratives of Crescent City residents and the fine text *The Great Deluge* by Douglas Brinkley to describe conditions in New Orleans pre- and post-Katrina. Willie and Dr. Powers were inspired by snippets from stories of dozens of hurricane heroes.

I endeavored to maintain historical accuracy with dates, with one exception. While it is true that federal mandates imposed desegregation orders in Monroe during 1969 and 1970 and at that time some black students enrolled in white schools, the Neville High School drill team squad did not add three black girls until the spring of 1971. To incorporate both Kennedy's assassination and de-segregation within Sally's story, the timeline was adjusted.

Sobering national statistics and heart-wrenching women's narratives led me to include Sally's sexual assault in this novel. The Rape, Abuse & Incest National Network (RAINN) reports that one in six American females becomes a victim of sexual assault in her lifetime. Every two minutes, somewhere in America, someone is sexually assaulted.

I chose to include the character of Rufus in *What the Bayou Saw* based on an incident that happened to me as I walked to school in fourth grade. For reasons I still do not understand, I never told my parents or any adult about that incident or another unrelated incident that occurred when I was in junior high.

Despite recent strides in education and reporting, individuals still may be reticent to report an attacker. If you or someone you know has experienced a sexual assault, please report the crime immediately to the local authorities and contact the RAINN hotline (1-800-656-HOPE) or visit the RAINN Web site, www.rainn.org.

Failure to bring the incident to closure by reporting the crime to the appropriate authorities may have a deleterious effect on the victim's recovery from a sexual assault. However, it is not uncommon for flashbacks, depression, lack of normal sexual libido, and other psychological symptoms to occur in all victims, even those who had successful prosecution of their cases. According to Dr. Barbara Bogorad, Psy.D., a wide range of life changes, particularly those of a physiological nature, such as onset of menopause, may cause flashbacks and delay emotional healing.

For several years, I collected oral narratives of both black and white women who grew up in northern Louisiana during the 1960s and black and white women with Southern ties who currently live in the Midwest. Freely acknowledging my own biases, I did my best to reflect the prejudices of both groups of women, enlisting the help of two black professionals in editing the novel.

Unfortunately, when I conducted interviews on a 2006 research trip down South, militant attitudes still surfaced in regard to race relations.

"When will they ever stop playing the race card?" a fifty-three-year-old white professional demanded of me.

"In some ways, they're worse than ever," explained a black man who taught in public schools during desegregation, "and nothing's gonna be solved till Jesus returns."

As Katrina so graphically displayed, racism still stains not just the South, but our entire nation. The "we/they" thinking that slips above the Mason-Dixon Line impedes dialogue and has continued to hamper social progress.

However, these shackles may be loosed from our thinking faster than many have supposed. As I began final edits on this book, America elected its first African-American president, a president whose residence in the White House evidences change thought impossible a short time ago.

It is my hope that through the issues addressed in *What the Bayou Saw*, victims of both sexual assault and racial prejudice will understand that they are not alone in their struggles. Through trust in His Son Jesus Christ, the Lord God promises that He will work for good in all things in the lives of those who love Him (Romans 8:28). *In all things*. Even a rape. Even bigotry.

I thank you for reading my book and pray God's blessings for each of you.

Artwork taken from a Christmas card designed by Jordan Qualls, an eleven-year-old New Orleans resident and the author's precious niece.

PERMISSIONS

BOOK DISCUSSION GROUP QUESTIONS

1. What character traits would you assign to Sally? Is she a woman you'd like to befriend?

2. How does the approaching Midwestern winter heighten Sally's angst about the conflict with her racist students?

3. Discuss both obvious and hidden prejudices that unfold in the first few chapters of the novel.

4. Compare and contrast racism in your community with the incidents in twenty-first-century Normal, Illinois, and the 1960s Deep South.

5. Does Shamika garner your sympathy? Ruby? Detective Price?

6. Do you feel the author did an effective job of portraying the novel's male characters? Can a female writer truly get "in the head" of Sam and Detective Price? In the same vein, can a white writer effectively capture the voice of African-American women?

7. Sally's awareness of her lying problem increases over the course of the story. Discuss the use of Sam, Ed, and Ella as vehicles to convict Sally of her sin.

8. Through the eyes of young Sally, we glimpse images of race relations in the South during the late 1950s through the early 1970s. Which images resonate with your own experiences? Which images are outside of your frame of reference?

9. What role does the Holy Spirit play in this novel?

10. Compare and contrast the novel's portrayal of the Colossians 3:18 admonition for wives to submit to their husbands with your own views.

11. As Sally glimpsed Ella through a chain-link fence, her view of black folk began to change. What personal incidents have transformed your mindset on sociopolitical issues?

12. Was the rape scene difficult to read? Should the portrayal "down bayou way" have been less graphic? Why or why not?

13. Though Ella has limited scenes in the novel, she plays the role of a heroic character. What Christian values does she exhibit?

14. Sweet Willie, the horn player, was chosen to represent the highs and lows in the life of a jazz musician. Discuss the ways that role was developed in the novel.

15. Despite (or perhaps because of) the gritty issues examined in this novel, the author chose happy endings for the book's characters. Do you agree or disagree with that choice?

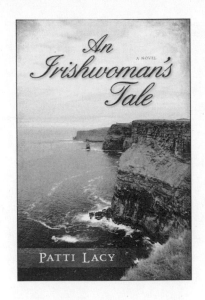

Read more about Sally and her friend Mary in Patti Lacy's first book, *An Irishwoman's Tale.*

PROLOGUE

G et 'er out of here." Moon-shaped faces stared at Mary across the round, oaken table, then guzzled tea. Stared. Guzzled. Cup after cup of the steaming stuff.

"Ye can't mean it," Mam screamed. "Not now. She's all o' a bloody five."

"The little eejit. Get 'er out."

A fist crashed to the table. Cups and saucers and cigarettes flew. Tea splattered onto the wall, onto the front of Killian's shirt.

"Ye swine." Mam was in Killian's face. "For the sake of St. Patrick, she's my flesh and blood."

"She's got to go."

Mam's screaming curse sent a chill up Mary's spine. "Ye lured me here, promised to take us in."

"She's got to go. Now."

"All right, she'll go." Mam's words slapped Mary in the face. "And you'll be cursed, all of ye."

Mam? No. Not you, Mam? Mary flung herself on the floor, legs and arms flailing. *Mam on their side?* Her heart broke in two, not by the others, but by her own mother.

Mam jerked her to a standing position, letting those horrid, horrid faces burn holes into her. Still, Mary stared at them, refusing to be the first to look away.

They glared back at her and sloshed watery tea all over themselves and the tabletop. Words floated overhead. *Harris, Chicago, America.* What did they all mean? She heard a slap and cowered, but the blow did not fall on her.

One of the sisters half-carried, half-dragged her to bed.

"Why, Mam, why?" Over and over Mary sobbed the same thing into her pillow. She knew the foul-smelling faces that loomed over the table didn't want her, but Mam? The black reality engulfed her, and her body convulsed with waves of despair.

CHAPTER 1

Run the straight race through God's good grace;
Lift up thine eyes and seek His face.
—John S. B. Monsell, "Fight the Good Fight with All Thy Might"

Terre Haute, Indiana, 1995

Mary Freeman had done all she could to make it special. The skillet was hot. Creamy yogurt waited to be dolloped onto nutty granola. Raspberry scones cooled on a wire rack. Steel-cut oats from County Kildare simmered on a back burner. She whirled about, trading a spoon for a spatula, determined to suit the palates of her husband, Paul, and her two teenage daughters, Claire and Chloe. Every morning, the four of them ate breakfast together in this big kitchen, with its copper pot rack and granite countertops. Then Paul would leave, heaving this tool or that box into the old farm truck, a quick hug to suffice for a day without him. The girls would leave too, armed with backpacks and racquets and changes of clothes. The house would be empty—except for her and Mother.

For now, Mary's world became Paul and the girls. She checked her watch, then stepped out to the garden and clipped purple asters off spindly stems. It pricked her to think of the approaching void, when she and Mother would coexist within the walls of this cavernous Victorian Painted Lady. Bustling back inside, she arranged the flowers and twigs of hypericum in a crystal vase, hoping to add the final touches to a memory she could cling to when the walls closed in.

She stepped back and surveyed her handiwork, plucking off a rogue leaf, then headed to the laundry room. Three more loads, which she could easily wedge in between mother's feeding, the upstairs cleaning—

"Get 'er out of here."

The voice bounced off the laundry room walls. Mary tried to ignore it, as she always did. Yet the thick Irish brogue assailed her, conjuring lifelike images.

Moon-shaped faces stared at Mary across the round oaken table, then guzzled tea. Stared. Guzzled.

"The little eejit. Get 'er out."

Mam screaming. Crashing. Cups and saucers flying. Tea splattering.

"Ye swine." Mam spat into Killian's face.

"She's got to go. Now."

"All right, she'll go. And ye be cursed, all of ye."

As quickly as the voices had come, they faded. And left Mary trembling, damp laundry chilling her hands.

Overhead, steps pounded across the planked floor. It was Claire, banging her fist against the balustrade as she had for the past ten years, then thundering downstairs.

Mary dropped the laundry and bustled back to the kitchen. "Breakfast's ready, honey." She cracked some eggs, beat them until they foamed, and poured them in the skillet. *If only the voices could be handled so efficiently.*

Claire whooshed into the kitchen, bringing life and light and the smell of green apples and hair mousse. "Morning, Mom." At five foot ten, Claire towered over everyone in the family but her daddy. Her younger sister, Chloe, dubbed her a red tornado, not just for her mane of hair but for her temper.

Cabinets banged and the refrigerator door creaked. "Where's the jelly?"

"Over there, dear." Mary slid her arm around Claire and managed to hug her.

Claire offered a cheek, then grabbed a bowl of granola, plucked a scone off the rack, and slid onto a bench seat. "Don't forget, I've got Key Club tonight. I'll just grab something after practice."

Mary nodded, then turned back to Paul's eggs, which were seconds away from being just the consistency he liked them. "Paul?" she called to the figure clattering about in the front room. "Your breakfast is—ooh! Quit it!"

A scratchy beard chafed the nape of Mary's neck, yet she didn't really want him to stop. If only she could hop with him into that rickety truck, patter about the barn with their goats and wooly-backed sheep, then meet for lunch under their sycamore tree . . .

"Mom? Where's my blue jacket?" Unnoticed, Chloe had crept down the stairs, gotten her cereal, and squeezed onto the bench.

"In the utility room. Pressed and ready."

"Thanks, Mom."

Mary smiled, both at the love in Claire's voice and at the way sunlight chose this moment to filter through the window and blush her daughters' cheeks.

This was the way she'd planned it. She backed out of Paul's grasp, dished eggs onto a plate, and beelined back toward the laundry room to finish what she'd started.

"Whoa, girls. Let's bless the food." Paul grabbed the sash of Mary's apron, pinched her tantalizingly close to her back pocket, then led her toward the table. "That means you too," he said, kissing her on her ear this time.

"Oh, Daddy." The girls' giggles and rolling eyes suggested they'd witnessed their father's middle-aged shenanigans. But there was pride in their tone—and love.

"I'll just get another load—"

"This comes first." Paul had always been lean, but years of farming had hardened spare muscles into steel. He pulled Mary onto the bench across from their girls, and they all joined hands. "Heavenly Father," he began, "thank You for this food. Watch over my girls today. Thank You for—"

"Where are ye?"

Mary blinked, then cut a glance at the girls and again bowed her head. Couldn't Mother give them five minutes of peace? Five minutes for the four of them? As Paul kept praying, she clenched her jaw, willing her mother back to sleep.

"Jesus, Mary, and Joseph! I swear—" Mother's screech shook the room.

"Why can't she just shut up?" Claire jumped to her feet, tossed her napkin down, and shook bangs out of her eyes. "She ruins everything."

Mary felt heat rising to her face. She wished she could blurt out exactly what she felt, like her daughters did. But what kind of example would that be? She struggled to get her thoughts together, to make the best of the time they had left. "Claire, she's your grandmother. And I'll not have you saying that about her."

"Why not?" Chloe dabbed at her lips, which managed to stay Hot Hot Pink or whatever the name of her latest lip gloss was. "It's true." As usual, Chloe never shouted. Yet the words cut into Mary as if she'd yelled louder than the woman in the next room. "Besides, she's not really our grandmother," Chloe added, the napkin now a wad by her plate.

Mary looked long and hard at her daughters, seeing her nose in Chloe, her eyes in Claire, and her resentment of Mother in both of them. Claire and Chloe felt free to spill their feelings all over this well-set table. She, with the Lord's help, had been able to keep hers bottled up. But pressure was building.

Paul smoothed out his napkin and laid it by now-cold eggs. "Of course she is. And we're gonna honor her like we did Gran. It's our way."

"Why?" Some of the sting had left Claire's voice.

"Because it's His way."

"I'll have yer head for this, I will!" Mother's tirade had risen to a feverish pitch.

A glint entered Chloe's eyes. "I'll have yours first."

Claire's spoon clattered to the table. "Just shut up, Chloe!"

The sisters glared at each other, faces red.

"Not another word, either of you!" With a jerk, Mary untied her apron and tossed it onto the island cluttered with the remains of what she'd so hoped would be a special breakfast. Soon they would leave, and she'd be alone with Anne Harris, the eighty-three-year-old who was and wasn't her mother.

"Get in here, girl."

A breeze tickled slatted blinds and carried the scent of Irish roses into the room, but the heady fragrance didn't still Mary's trembling hands or calm her thumping heart. She was still *girl*, not *daughter* or *dear*, words she'd waited a lifetime to hear. All the sacrifices they'd made for Mother—even moving into town when she couldn't manage out on the farm—didn't seem to matter. Mary flipped on the light switch in a vain attempt to brighten her thoughts. *But no matter what she calls me, Anne Harris is the only mother I've got now.* "I'm here, Mother." Somehow Mary managed to put a lilt in her voice.

"Girl?" The voice came from a huddle of quilts, only a stubborn jaw jutting above cotton and satin bedding.

"I'm Mary. Your daughter." Mary said it to herself as much as to the woman on the bed.

Mother's mouth twisted into a bitter smile. "You're not my daughter. Not really."

For just an instant, Mary longed to hurl some of Mother's bile back in her face, then stomp to the phone and reserve one of the "spacious suites" that the new assisted-living center was touting as the latest in "modern adult community." Let them clean her linens and change her diapers and puree her food and bathe her and listen to her. Most of all, let them listen to her.

"I'm off, honey!"

Mary whirled about. Paul stood at the threshold of Mother's room. She flew into his arms.

"What's this about?" He somehow managed to run one hand through her hair and pull her close with the other.

"N-nothing."

"It'll be okay," he assured her, nuzzling about her neck.

Mary breathed deeply of wood smoke and damp wool until her heart resumed its normal beat. It would be okay . . . wouldn't it? She willed Paul to forget about the calf with the gimpy leg, the trees that needed grafting, and stay home today. But she knew he couldn't. The farm was his lifeblood, and hers too. If not for Mother, she'd be out there by his side.

Too soon, Paul pulled away. After good-byes and air kisses, the girls pattered down the hall, right behind their daddy. The front door slammed, then clicked. She and Mother were locked in. Safe, but not necessarily sound.

Her heart heavy, Mary sunk to the plush carpet on her mother's floor. "Forgive me," she prayed. "I do love her, or at least I try to. And give me a friend, Lord. Someone to help me get through this loneliness."

She rose to see something akin to a smile softening her mother's withered face, the set jaw. That hint of a smile carried Mary through the diaper-changing, dressing, and resettling back into the old iron bed. She would be a daughter, regardless of what she was or wasn't called. "I'll be back with your breakfast, Mother," she announced as she hurried down the hall. The second breakfast shift was about to begin.

"*I'm the last of the Irish Rovers, bathed in a bed o' clover,*" she sang as she stirred the oatmeal, which was mushy, just like Mother liked it. Or used to, when Mother still expressed likes and dislikes. Still singing, Mary buttered toast, poured tea, squeezed juice, sliced fruit, and set it, along with the vase of asters, on a tray. "A good diet," the doctor had told Mary over a decade ago. "Plenty of love." Her hands gripped the tray a bit tighter, certain she'd succeeded at the first of his orders. But the second gave her cause to shake her head. *Lord, I've done my best. You know I've done my best.*

"Good morning." Mary smoothed back a shock of her mother's white hair. "Here's your breakfast."

Mother's mouth opened and closed like a baby sparrow's, yet there was no recognition in the filmy blue eyes.

Mary propped up her mother with pillows and pulled a stool near the side of the bed. She fed her a spoonful of oats, a smidgen of toast, prattling about anything she could think of, as emptiness edged in until she felt its cold fingers about her throat.

When the pale lips clamped shut and the papery thin eyelids closed, Mary dabbed crumbs off her mother's mouth, then carefully folded the napkin and set it down.

A blessed quiet filled the room. Mary stepped to the casement window and let the wind soothe away the tightness about her throat, her shoulders. A few brave rose blossoms remained amongst a tangle of stems and leaves in a futile gesture to stave off the approaching fall. Their scent permeated every corner of the room, from the mahogany wardrobe to the antique chest, transporting Mary to another place, another time . . . *'Tis the last rose of summer, lass, left bloomin' all alone. All her lovely companions, faded now and gone.*

For a moment, she was back on the cliffs, breathing deeply of salty spray, the smoke from a turf fire in her hair . . .

Mary jumped, then sighed. It was Mother, thrashing about in her sheets. She hurried to her side. *"Tura, lura, lura,"* she sang, stroking the wrinkled cheek.

Perhaps the eyes brightened for an instant. Then the bony limbs resumed their thrashing. "There, there," she kept saying, in between the gasps and grunts and heaves it took to get Mother into the rocker and in front of the television.

"You're the next contestant . . ."

The raucous laughter grated at Mary. They'd never wanted a television, never needed a television. Out on the farm, they'd survived just fine without it. She sighed as blue-haired grannies shrieked their way down the aisle. Yet the boob tube settled Mother as nothing else did, and for that, Mary was grateful.

"Come on down!"

Mary surged about the bedroom-bathroom suite, determined to let busyness still the nerves set on edge by the TV. She plumped cushions, straightened orthopedic shoes and slippers, and was washing out her mother's hosiery when the phone rang.

She let the answering machine get it. "Pick up, Mary." It was the voice of Sue, a family friend and the doctor who'd delivered her girls. "I need you."

Mary wrung out the stockings and hung them over a towel rack, hurried into the study, and picked up the phone. "Sue. What's going on?"

"Hey, Mary. Listen, could you sub today?"

Mary hesitated. Mother'd be okay by herself for as long as it took to play a couple of sets, or she could call Dora, who always wanted more hours. "Who's playing?"

"Mona and JoAnn and some new lady. She's pretty good, I hear."

Mary frowned. Two hours with Mona and JoAnn could last a lifetime, not to mention some stranger. "What's her name?"

"All I know is she's from the South. Listen, Mary, I don't have time for twenty questions. A patient's in the ER, and you're the only one I've gotten through to. It's just for a couple of hours. How about it?"

"Well, there's Mother . . ."

"Take my word for it, Mary. She's fine. Besides, she isn't going anywhere."

Mary bit her lip. It was true; Mother hadn't taken a step unassisted in five years. She'd call Dora. Besides, what else was there to do? The house had been scrubbed and oiled and waxed until it glistened. The garden had been winterized. Her summer clothes had been pressed and hung in garment bags. "No problem, Sue," Mary said. "I'll do it."

"You won't regret it, Mary. I promise."

For a moment, Mary stared at the phone. What did Sue mean by that? She'd been subbing for Sue on a regular basis since Sue opened her own clinic. And it helped Mary get in more practice, which she definitely could use to compete in the A League. But Sue's tone had hinted at something mysterious. Something hopeful. She picked up the phone and called Dora, the strange comment still ringing in her ears.

ABOUT THE AUTHOR

When Patti Lacy left the Louisiana swamps for college, she returned to Baylor University, where as a girl she'd lived in the boys' athletic dormitory. Her "big brothers" entertained her with magic tricks and wild tales that planted the love of stories in her heart.

Patti graduated from Baylor with an education degree that allowed her to continue the passion and tradition inspired by her school-teacher parents and husband.

The Lacys moved to the Midwest in 1995, where a red-haired Irishwoman befriended Patti and shared an amazing story of forgiveness and betrayal. By 2005, the Spirit's urgings culminated in a new career path: novelist. Kregel Publications released Patti's debut novel, *An Irishwoman's Tale*, in 2008.

What the Bayou Saw continues Patti's quest to explore secrets women keep and why they keep them.

The Lacys live in Normal, Illinois, and have two grown children and a dog named Laura. They attend Grace Church, where Patti facilitates Bible studies and the family supports Ministry & More, an organization offering the true Bread of Life to clients.

To contact Patti, visit her Web site at http://www.pattilacy.com.